Black Point

Black Point

Jerome T. Burke
HollyCourt Press
Elgin, Illinois

Printed in the United States of America. For information address HollyCourt Press, 1030 Summit Road, Suite 205, Elgin, Ill. 60120.

Library of Congress Cataloging-in-Publications Data

Burke, Jerome T.
Black Point
ISBN 0-9639096-0-6
CIP 93-80487

First Edition.

1

May 3rd, 1895...

Lora Lockerby arrived in Lake Geneva on the morning train. Walking down Broad Street, she sneezed only once, her head cold clearing in the bright spring sunshine. She smiled as she walked, remembering the flustered conductor calling after her as she hurried from the train.

"Young lady, I think the trainman wants you," the stiff matron who had been sitting behind her said in a loud voice. When she turned around, he had been dubiously holding up the handkerchief she'd forgotten and left on the coach seat. With a blushing laugh and a word of thanks, Lora reclaimed it and left the train.

She had just used the offending hankie once more and replaced it in her handbag when she glanced across the avenue and saw a tall, grey-headed figure standing on the steps of the old Dennison Hotel. That unmistakable head of hair belonged to Judge Seaver, and Lora, fearing recognition, moved along at a faster pace, not looking back.

Two days earlier she had discarded the idea of wearing a disguise up here. It had seemed silly back in Chicago—the stuff of a pulp novel—but now, seeing the judge only minutes after her arrival, she began to wish for one.

The Clair Cafe was ahead just across Main Street. She hurriedly crossed the intersection, dodging a carriage that swerved around her. The door of the Clair was open to the spring breezes and she stopped briefly in front of it as though to check her reflection. She saw that Broad Street looked empty except for a single wagon that slowly approached. If Judge Seaver had started down the street after her, he must have turned aside.

While looking in the glass door, she did take the opportunity to inspect her appearance. She pushed a loose lock of hair back in place and managed a small grin before the clock on the wall caught her attention. It read 11:10, giving her almost an hour before her appointment with Doctor Malcolm MacDougal. The lakefront was ahead and she walked toward it, this time at a leisurely pace. The site of the old Whiting Hotel was a busy place this morning. Last year the old resort had burned beyond repair, and today workmen were busy clearing away the last of the remains.

Lora spun around at the sound of lumber crashing, a cloud of dust rising up from the site. The rubble that had been the Whiting reminded her of the ghostly pictures she'd seen of the ruins of the Columbian Exposition buildings, where she'd once worked. The scene was just too melancholy and she turned back toward the lake.

The large, Y-shaped Lake Geneva dock had already been put in. As she stepped out onto it, a young worker called over to her to watch her step. "We're still working on her, ma'am. Some of the boards out at the end aren't in yet, and I won't guarantee that all the ones you're walking on have been nailed."

"Don't worry, I won't go out beyond the junction," she answered, taking off her hat and shaking out her auburn hair, relaxing as she leaned against one of the posts. Lora noticed that the workman had paused to study her before continuing down the pier.

He was probably about twenty, she guessed, only a few years younger than herself. Was it the dark dress she wore or perhaps something in her mood that caused him to address her so formally. "I wonder how old he thinks I am?" she said aloud. Turning her thoughts away from him, she leaned out over the edge of the dock, looking down into the clear water. She watched as a large bass moved out from the shadow of the dock, its black tail giving a lazy flick. *How often I waited as a young girl, fishing pole and hook ready, and never saw a fish even near his size,* she thought.

Two days earlier, back in Chicago, Lora had sent the telegram to Malcolm MacDougal. "Could you please see me," she'd asked, "concerning a matter …" The Western Union agent looked up, waiting for her to continue. "Concerning a matter of advice." The agent returned his attention to his key as she finished, dictating her name.

Doctor MacDougal responded to her at the offices of Collins,

2

Goodrich, Darrow and Vincent that very afternoon. Marilyn Price, the receptionist, brought the telegram over to Lora's desk, waiting as Lora opened and read it. "Friday would be a fine day to see you," he had replied. "Always my pleasure to have you visit, my dear. Looking forward to your arrival." He made no further inquiry, merely providing her with the time of the morning train out.

"Everything's fine, Marilyn, thank you. Just some news from a friend."

"If there's anything I can do, Lora, you just let me know." Marilyn moved back to her window.

Lora replaced the telegram in its envelope and walked down the hall to the door marked C. Darrow. Clarence had gone out of town for the week and Lora paused at the door, then closed it behind her.

She sat down on the couch, aware her forehead was damp. Last week she was on the verge of taking Marilyn aside and confiding in her—before she thought of Malcolm. Lora was sure that Marilyn, discreet as she was, already knew about or at least suspected her relationship with Clarence. She had to talk to someone. Malcolm was a good friend of her father, and her instincts told her he was someone she could trust. He had lost his wife two years ago. The couple was childless, and Lora had gotten the feeling he might just have seen in her the daughter they'd never had.

Her last visit with Malcolm had been almost nine months ago, on a beautiful Sunday in August. He'd come to visit their new, almost-completed home at Black Point. Lora, her father and the doctor had been sitting out on the veranda, whiling away the afternoon. She could smell the aroma of their pipes as the two of them, flanking her on the big porch swing, talked easily.

The conversation swung around to the Pullman strike, and to the federal troops President Cleveland had stationed around Chicago. Malcolm knew that Lora had been very active in the strike, first losing her job as a teacher at Pullman for her outspoken views, and later becoming directly involved with the union and with Eugene Debs during the strike and subsequent nationwide boycott.

"Your father's been filling me in over the summer, young lady, but I daresay I'd rather hear the exciting Pullman story from your own lips."

Lora had been enjoying listening to the two men gab about the lake, the homes going up, and which Chicagoans were rumored to be buying property on its shores. It was a welcome lull from the turmoil of the strike. She relaxed, letting her mind drift as she watched a couple of sailboats racing out on the lake, both of them heeled far over. The strike, with all its bitterness and violence, even to the sight of Bill Anslyn's murder in cold blood right in front of her, had seemed a blessed million miles away.

Malcolm's request snapped her out of her reverie. She told him about Eugene Debs, careful as always when she described this noble, complicated man. Malcolm listened, nodding and asking an occasional question. Like so many others, the doctor had taken a surprisingly keen interest in Debs. In fact, public curiosity about him seemed to be on the rise. She'd thought that Eugene, with his introverted nature, would have been forgotten after the strike and boycott. It had been on Debs' recommendation, Lora told the doctor, that she had been hired by Clarence Darrow, the attorney who would be representing Eugene and his co-defendants. She would work as a clerk in Darrow's office, concentrating on the upcoming trial.

Malcolm stood up, pulling his watch from his pocket as he stretched. "The time has flown, my friends, and as much as I hate to leave, I'd better start down to the pier. If I miss the *Commodore,* you might wind up with an overnight guest." They started down the walk toward the steps, Lora continuing her defense of Debs and the strikers—repeating her belief that they all would be exonerated in the upcoming trial.

"But how can you account for Debs' flouting of authority, my dear?" His question as they walked along was mild, even conversational.

"Authority!" she shot back. "Authority is whatever you can put over on the people. And that's *just* what we're challenging!"

"You see what I live with, Mal?" Paul put his arm on Malcolm's shoulder as they started down the steps of the bluff leading to the pier. Lora knew her father was trying to soften her tone. She was used to his doing so around his friends, but Malcolm wasn't having it.

"I'm sorry about your being furloughed or fired—whatever they termed it," the light burr in his voice carried over the water. "But what about life at Pullman? I've read so much about everything that's been done for the workers and their families. You obviously don't feel it's a model town anymore, do you, Lora?"

"I never did! And all those dull, antiseptic little bijous that pass for homes. Just *think* what they do to the people who live there." Even as she spoke last summer, she realized the words were Darrow's, not hers, though she completely endorsed them. In truth, Lora had never really questioned the status of the model town until a couple of summers before. But, working for Clarence Darrow, with her life now revolving around the Pullman strike, Lora sometimes bristled at the cavalier, joking references Clarence himself would toss off about the strikers, even Debs, and to the gaudy rhetoric they favored.

"Now don't go being so serious, my ally," he had told her. "If you're going to work with me through this trial—and eventually become a lawyer as well—you're going to have to learn to distinguish between mere words and the thought behind them. Besides, I wasn't poking any more fun at *their* rhetoric than I do at my own."

"Well, Lora," Malcolm said as they stood out on the pier, "you're living and competing in a very harsh arena, though you certainly seem like you can take care of yourself. It almost sounds like you're describing a war."

Malcolm spoke even as he doffed his hat and waved it at the passenger steamer which had just rounded Black Point. The captain had missed spotting them on the pier, and Pullman and Debs were forgotten by the three as they waved and called to the passing boat. Finally, a single passenger saw them and had gone up, tapping the captain's shoulder. He answered with a blast on his whistle while the squat *Commodore* started its wide turn back toward the pier.

"You write me during the year, my dear, if you find the time. I'll follow the Debs trial with great interest, as well as news about your fascinating employer, Mr. Darrow." Telling Paul he'd see him again before the end of the summer, he reached over and took Lora's hand in his before stepping aboard the *Commodore,* smiling gamely as he reached out with his other hand to steady his balance.

The shrill whistle of a nearby yacht brought Lora back to the present. She looked up and then away quickly as it eased in toward the dock, preparing to berth. She walked toward the shore. That boat, while she didn't recognize it, might well contain someone else she knew from up here and the last thing she wanted was to have to explain her presence in Lake Geneva so long before the season.

5

She headed back along Main Street toward Malcolm's home. She desperately needed someone to talk to, to confide in. *And Maybe,* she smiled as the thought came to her, *I'll even get something for this annoying cold.*

How much has happened in my life this past year, she mused, *how much I've changed since that conversation with Malcolm last August.*

During the train ride out she'd filled her time by scribbling on a legal pad, writing down the pluses and minuses of continuing to see Darrow. She needed to have something in hand as she talked to Malcolm, but after a couple of minutes she gave up the project and put the pad aside.

Oh, Clarence, my very married Clarence, she'd said to herself, wiping at the tears that ran freely down her cheeks as she turned and looked out the train window, shielding her face from the other passengers.

During the previous week, Clarence and Lora had again been working late. Clarence had gradually swung back into his old work habits he had let go in the depressing aftermath of the Debs trial. The two left work at eight o'clock and entering Henrici's, settled into a table at the rear of the restaurant. It was the third night in succession that they had dined together. Darrow seemed to Lora to be oblivious to anyone's observations as he casually took her arm crossing Randolph.

Lora ate heartily while Clarence moved his food around his plate, a cigarette working in one hand as usual. As they reminisced about Eugene Debs and the trial, Lora still felt bitter about Judge Woods having found Eugene in contempt of court and sentencing him to prison, especially after the mistrial that had all but established his innocence.

Clarence's own earlier rage at the outcome had dissipated, to Lora's surprise. It was becoming clear to her that with Clarence, the trials were themselves as important as what followed. His equanimity toward Judge Woods dismayed her, though she kept that to herself.

Clarence chuckled as he exhaled cigarette smoke. "Do you recall what the *Chicago Journal* said, my dear, on the morning after the trial's first day?"

"I do," she replied, pleased at the casual words of endearment he had begun dropping into his speech.

"Let me see if I can remember the exact phrasing. 'And *who,* an eye-witness observer of yesterday's courthouse proceedings might have wondered,' " Clarence paused and reached to take Lora's hand, 'was the winsome female assistant that Mr. Clarence Darrow was seen —' "

" '—was seen conferring with—so intently?' " Lora laughed, finishing the newspaper piece and returning the pressure of his hand.

"That's exactly what I mean, Lora. The repartee we have." He had taken up the theme of their last night's conversation. "The way you so often outsmart me, thinking faster than my stumbling, male mind can function. Unfair, using your intuition. But, you know, I enjoy no such bantering at home." Darrow had grown suddenly grave.

"Jessie's not like you. She doesn't have your restless buoyancy." He shook his head. "Good woman that she is, but…we never *have* had this sort of kinship." She withdrew her hand. *If this conversation is going to drift back to Jessie again,* she remembered their dinner last night and Clarence's ruminations about his floundering marriage. And Lora knew better than to level the slightest criticism of her own at Jessie.

"Lora." He was using the hesitations between his words just as he might before some jury, even as his melodious voice was working on her.

"I'll be in St. Louis tomorrow," he started.

"And you're going to Springfield afterward. Are you forgetting who made your reservations?" Lora heard the anxious, brittle tone that had crept into her speech. Clarence would be out of town for ten days, bad enough in itself, and now she was going to have to hear more about his wife tonight.

"Listen to me. On Wednesday I'll be arriving in Springfield. For a full week." At his pause, Lora glanced up.

"Meet me there. I'll have a room for you at the St. Nicholas. Think of it! The time we'll have: Abraham Lincoln's tomb and his law office, still intact. So many of the things we've talked about. So much for us to see. We can be away; alone together. It's what you've wanted yourself. Don't tell me it isn't." Darrow's speech had taken on a firmness.

"Don't say 'no' right now. At least let me believe you're coming. Here. This is for you. Don't be angry." His voice shifted again, suddenly softer, little more than a whisper. He passed an envelope across to her. She opened it and extracted the round-trip ticket to Springfield.

Lora set the ticket aside. "I'm not offended or anything like that," she said. "You misunderstand. I'm not afraid, at least not in the way you think."

And in spite of all her warnings to herself, she began pouring forth the story of her relationship with Karl Bitter almost three years before—how they had met and become lovers during the construction season of the Columbian Exposition. "So you see," she said at last, "it's time you learned that you're not sitting across from some virginal, modern Joan of Arc who assisted you during a trial."

"Joan of Arc really was a virgin?"

"Stop!" Lora was fighting back tears.

"A New York sculptor, hm' m? And he did the decorations for the Administration Building at the Fair." Clarence's tone was neutral, even admiring. His poise in the face of her emotional state was upsetting her more.

"I think I've heard of Karl Bitter."

"Then perhaps you've heard he's single as well."

"I love you, Lora, for your honesty and pluck. But when you're angry—like right now—you are irresistible. Tell me you'll spend the week with me. I want you even more."

Lora could feel her pulse pounding and her resolve beginning to weaken even in the face of her anger. "And then what? Oh, of course. You've told Jessie you're taking me to see Lincoln's tomb…for a week or so." Lora balled up her napkin and flung it across the table, then got to her feet and abruptly strode from the restaurant. Clarence started to rise but sat back down, grinding out his cigarette in the middle of his forgotten dinner.

"Tell me something, Doctor MacDougal, tell me something that will ease my saying goodbye to Clarence," she said out loud as she neared his house.

2

Jeremy had no sooner started up the long hill out of town, when he realized he'd waited too long to downshift the gears on his bike.

"Damn it," he muttered, getting off and surveying the damage as a car sped past him. He pulled at the chain. It had wedged itself between the rear derailleur and the frame and wouldn't budge. Taking a pliers from the saddlebag, he pulled, bracing his foot against the wheel. It was no use, he knew. The same thing had happened once before.

What he needed now were a screwdriver and hammer to knock the chain free. He looked at his hands, covered with grease from the chain.

Well, I'm not going to let this spoil my day. He remembered earlier seeing an old-fashioned service station back on the other side of town, the kind that would have real tools and not just gas, soda pop and milk.

The "town" was Williams Bay, Wisconsin, one of several on Lake Geneva. Jeremy was up here for the day to unwind after finishing a long two-week trial. It was one with too many witnesses to round up, too many objections, a too-shifty opponent and a cantankerous, short-fused judge, confident that his black robe hid his mediocrity. So, he decided, walking his bike toward the service station, he could live with a stuck bike chain.

And, he consoled himself, looking up at the sky, it had turned out to be a nice day after all. The sun had been in and out as he had driven the seventy miles from his apartment in Chicago. There'd been the threat of rain in the morning, but as he pedaled around the lake, the clouds had disappeared.

The fisherman he had stopped to talk with earlier saw him walking back. He reeled in his line and walked down the pier, wiping his hand across his plaid flannel shirt.

"Bad break," he sympathized, bending over and reaching into his tackle box. "But with that kind of luck you'd better think twice before you take up fishing."

"Take up fishing? No chance," Jeremy called back, giving his chain a light kick. "And miss all this fun?" As he wheeled the bike along he gazed across the road from the pier. He hadn't noticed as he was pedaling through the village earlier but now he realized that he was looking at the site of the old North Western Railroad depot.

The building had been torn down, he guessed, about fifteen years before and the tracks had been pulled out. The area was now a kind of nature preserve, with the prairie and young trees having reclaimed the old train yard.

He remembered that depot from the summers when he had grown up out here. It was an old wooden one, the traditional kind with a bay window. Standing next to it had been the old, rusting railway express cart, with its huge, flat metal wheels and long handle, a much too heavy cart for a skinny ten year old to push. He'd always felt good as the train pulled in at Williams Bay, the end of the line. The trip up signaled the start of his summer vacations.

He let the memories of childhood flood back over him as he walked the bike over to where he guessed the old depot had stood. Looking down at the prairie grass, he spotted a rusty spike and stooped over, picking it up.

Hefting it from one hand to the other, he recalled those let-down feelings as he stood at the depot on Labor Day, waiting for the train with his mother and sister. Their summer house would already be closed up and Dad headed back to the city, leaving before them, the family Buick loaded down with all the summer's belongings.

This was the same depot where in years past, long before *his* family began coming to the lake, the millionaires: the Marshall Fields, the Cranes, the Allertons, would arrive in their private coaches. They crossed the road to board their luxury yachts for the trips to their homes, often racing each other out across the bay. He let the spike fall to the ground as he walked out to the road again.

Jeremy reached the old garage and left his bike in front. The whine of a ratchet came through the doors, left open to catch the spring weather.

He stepped in by the bay and called out, "Can I borrow a screwdriver and hammer?"

"Help yourself," a heavy-set man wearing a Green Bay Packer hat looked up. "Right over there." He was matter of fact and friendly, pointing to a work table before going back to his ratcheting. In a few minutes Jeremy had freed the chain and started back on his trip, careful this time to downshift before the hill steepened.

Outside Williams Bay he picked up the main highway. Route 50 is four-laned with a grassy center. For cyclists, it also has a little paved shoulder outside the white line. This was the final leg of his trip. He'd started from the park in Lake Geneva and had circled the lake clockwise, going out on South Shore Drive.

Jeremy pumped harder, testing himself—still no stiffness after almost twenty miles. *Not bad for a thirty-seven year old lawyer on his first bike outing of the year.*

He saw the wooden sign marked "Elgin Club" and stopped, straddling his bike as he gazed down the blacktop road. He squinted into the sun, thinking about gliding down there, but that would mean a long uphill detour coming back. Besides, he could drive back in his car later to check out the old gray stucco house along the shore. *The old house...* Jeremy wondered how he would find it and if it would look the way he remembered it. He was musing as a car climbed the road and turned past him out onto the highway.

After his father's death his mother had lost interest in coming up here and had sold the house. High school years melted into college and summers were spent working and vacationing out east. Cape Cod had become more familiar than Lake Geneva. It had been years since he'd been back, until his divorce three years before, when Lake Geneva seemed a convenient place to take Amy and Danny on weekend visits. Coming up here with his kids had reawakened an old interest in the town and its history.

An idea began to form as he pushed the bike back to the side of the highway and got on once again, pedaling beside the old school house at the side of the road. After lunch and a beer at Popeye's, he'd go back to the library in the park. He had all the time in the world. And he could really begin some research he'd started halfheartedly a couple of times before, an anthology of the old families of Lake Geneva.

11

After a few more minutes of pedaling he came to the top of the long hill which led down into the town of Lake Geneva. He stopped on the crest and took off his sunglasses, wiping his face on the sleeve of his sweatshirt. In the distance on the other side of town, he could see the spire of the Catholic Church. Across the street from the church was the spot, covered now by condominiums, where the old, red-brick insane asylum had stood. "Oak—something," it had been called.

He remembered when he was about eleven or twelve riding into town with Artie, the caretaker at the Elgin Club. After leaving the hardware store, they had headed out of town. Jeremy hadn't the slightest idea where they were going as Artie turned down the dilapidated driveway, the overgrown branches forcing him to pull his arms in from the pick-up truck's window. They rolled to a stop, and he found himself looking up at the gothic horror in front of them. "They're supposed to tear her down this fall," Artie said.

The old building was surrounded by a rusted, half-missing wire fence. "Absolutely No Trespassing!" the sign inside the fence warned. It had been pitched forward and left ignored.

"We won't go in. The college kids have wrecked her. Half the floors are out."

Looking up, he knew he wasn't going any closer than where he stood. He'd heard people talking about the "crazy house" or simply the "place" for as long as he could remember. It lived up to its reputation for horror, at least to an adolescent with a lively imagination.

Driving back to the Elgin Club, Artie gave him a quick history of the asylum, complete with stories about people who had been put in there, never to emerge, as well as legends about the screams and the peals of laughter coming from there at night. The haunting, crimson tower stayed in his nightmares all that summer and for long afterward. He wasn't sorry, he remembered, to hear that the building had been torn down.

Standing on the top of the hill, Jeremy could feel the tensions of the recent trial draining away from him. Next week, he decided, he would bring his kids up here. If the weather stayed good, they'd rent a boat and go fishing; if not, they could just take in a couple of movies.

He reached the bottom of the hill, letting the bike slow as he crested a last rise and then relaxed, enjoying the spring air as he started down the incline which led into town, the lake front park and the end of the trip.

The road, as it approached town from the hill narrowed. It had been curbed on both sides to channel rain water.

In the town itself, Edna French, seventy-seven years old and today feeling every year, had just finished her shopping. She was simply going to have to do something, she concluded, as she started her car, about living so far out of town. Her driving was getting worse, she knew. A horn blared at her as she backed out. Maybe one more year would be the most she could go on. Sometimes it seemed to her the big Lincoln Town Car was leading her. Maybe, she thought, if she got one of those little Japanese cars she'd have a better chance of controlling it. She was simply going to have to talk to her husband, Tom, about their moving closer to town. Edna was driving on Main Street, past the library and the lakefront park, unaware her car had started drifting over the centerline.

The bakery truck had descended the hill some distance behind Jeremy. The driver was running behind this morning. All his customers were laying in big stocks. They expected the weekenders would be up in force, brought out by the first nice weather. Hard rock music was blaring in his earphones and he tapped his big school ring on the steering wheel in time to it as the truck picked up speed on the downgrade. He followed the turn of the road as it narrowed.

Then he saw the oncoming car. It was over the centerline, coming straight for him. He instinctively turned the wheel to the right as the car passed him, only then catching sight of the bicyclist ahead. He couldn't swerve back in time. Just as he jammed his foot on the brake pedal, the truck hit the bike.

Jeremy felt the jolt as the truck slammed into him and he was pitched forward like he'd been shot from a gun. For a split second, he feared the bike would go down under the wheels of the truck, but he managed to keep it from tipping as he heard the screech of brakes.

For just a brief moment, Jeremy even thought he'd righted the bike and cheated death or serious injury, even at the crazy speed he was careening, and he likely might have if its front wheel hadn't hit the curb. As the wheel hit, he experienced what every cyclist most fears—he flew head first over the handlebar.

He felt suspended in the air. The huge, old double-trunked tree at the side of the roadway seemed to rush toward him. He managed to get one hand out in front of himself before he hit the ground at the base of the tree. The impact to his head was so intense, he was beyond feeling the pain.

The growing blackness surrounded him, followed by a sensation that he was spinning out in a widening circle—the same sensation he'd gotten from the laughing gas at the dentist's office when he'd had a wisdom tooth pulled.

Edna righted her car, aware that once again it had almost gotten away from her. She glanced around nervously in her mirror, looking to see if anyone had noticed her. She thought she had heard brakes but the truck had already passed by her. She had never seen the cyclist. Edna turned her attention to the road ahead of her, climbing the hill, thankful that once more she had escaped an accident. Looking back in her mirror, she decided that she absolutely could not keep driving to town.

The truck driver swore as he struck the bike. For a moment, he too thought the cyclist might make it until he saw the bike hit the curb and the rider fly over the handlebar.

"It isn't fair, goddamn it! It wasn't my fault! It was that car that cut across in front of him, and what was that goddamn bicycle doing on this narrow road anyway?" He looked in his mirror. There were cars descending the hill behind. Cars were also coming out of town toward him. They could look after that guy. Not thinking beyond his panic, he gunned the engine, careening the truck down a side street.

3

The terrible, relentless dream finally faded and Jeremy groaned as his eyes fluttered open. His first thought, *Oh, God, please don't let me be paralyzed,* flashed past. Lying face down, he smelled the damp grass beneath him as he warily pulled himself to his knees. A shiver escaped him at the memory of that endless black tunnel he'd been falling through. He was surprised at how clearly he could remember everything—from cycling around the lake and down the hill—right up to the point of impact. At least there was no amnesia. He tried taking a breath, feeling the stab of pain from his chest as he did. Standing up, Jeremy leaned against a little tree for support, checking his legs for any obvious breaks before taking a few tentative steps. A searing ache rose from his ankle. Reaching down and running his fingers inside the already loose desert boot, he felt the ankle and foot. No bone stuck out or felt broken to his touch but he was going to need an x-ray. Maybe, he hoped, it was only a sprain, but my God, had *any* part of him survived that spill without some hurt?

There was no doubt in his mind he'd have to get himself to some hospital and fast. The nearest one he could recall was up in Elkhorn, fifteen or so miles away. Could he drive, he wondered? Later on he would try, very often, to place just *when* that indescribable, eerie feeling first began to descend over him. Perhaps it was when he had looked around for his bicycle and found it gone. "How about that?" he said aloud. "I get hit from behind by some bastard who doesn't even bother to stick around, and when I come to, someone's stolen my bike."

Glancing around, he saw he was still in the park, although everything looked somehow...*different.* Two men dressed in work clothes were advancing toward him. The taller, younger man walked slightly ahead of his short, stocky companion who wore an old battered derby. It had the look of a "goofy" hat you'd expect to see on a college kid, not someone this guy's age. As they covered the distance between them, he suddenly remembered people like this one approaching, those who'd worn odd hats for effect. Mainly he'd tried to avoid them.

The taller one spoke first. "You all right, fella?" He came up and stood next to Jeremy, ready to support him. Jeremy couldn't place the accent: Dutch, maybe?

"I'm OK." There was a stammer in his voice when he answered. "Did you see that son-of-a-bitch who hit me?"

Both men stepped back at his words. Finally the shorter one spoke, without any accent, but in a slow, measured cadence. "We saw no one. Judd," he indicated his companion, "and I were walking along the shore path and we saw you. You've been lying there a long time." Jeremy noticed that as he talked the men had moved closer, close enough to have sniffed his breath. *They think I'm some drunk, sleeping it off in the park.* Their eyes shifted to his hand, still grease-stained from the stuck bike chain.

"We thought you were sleeping," Judd contributed, "but look at your head." Jeremy put his hand to his head, feeling the blood that had caked there and run down his cheek as well. He leaned back against the tree for support. His head began to reel and he was afraid he was going to be sick.

Gradually the nausea began to pass and glancing down he saw that his sunglasses lay on the ground just a few feet away. The pain in his ribs was agonizing as he reached to pick them up. Both workmen had seen them at the same time. Their eyes were glued to him as he slid the glasses into his pocket. *Oh great,* he thought for a moment as the wooziness flooded back over him, *am I going to be rolled now, too, and for a pair of sunglasses?* No one else was in the park. He slid his watch off, putting it in his pocket, hoping they hadn't noticed. He turned his back toward them, wary, but they seemed unthreatening, more curious than anything.

God! How long have I been unconscious? He glanced over at the road. *That's what's wrong,* he told himself. *It's not there.* He was in the park, but the road was gone, or at least it looked very different. It was no more than a rutted, dirt path that ran along the lakefront park. An old-fashioned, horsedrawn wagon approached. The driver glanced over at the trio then returned his gaze to the road ahead.

Jeremy half-walked, half-stumbled, down to the lake, the two work-men following anxiously. There was a seawall there he couldn't remember, but kneeling, he leaned over and plunged his hands into the icy water. He cupped his hands, bringing some up, washing the blood off his face as best he could. No more than two or three small piers were in out on Geneva Bay. *It's only a weekday in early May, true enough, but there's something damn strange. On the other side of the lake where I biked earlier, both at Fontana and Williams Bay, most of the piers were already in.* He didn't expect there'd be many boats, but all he could see were two old wooden rowboats, one bobbing at a post in the water and another pulled up on shore.

"Can you help me get to town?" he asked, suddenly wanting company. The two nodded and fell into step with him, studying him as he hobbled painfully along the path. His already jumbled thoughts were suddenly jarred by a sound both familiar and strange at the same time. There was a gentle *chug-a-chug* sound. Out at the mouth of the bay was an authentic, old-fashioned yacht, sitting low in the water. A high funnel in the center was giving off clouds of black smoke. Jeremy remembered the sound. It was an honest-to-goodness steam engine. Someone had gone to a lot of trouble to restore that old yacht.

The Riviera, that landmark chalet, was nowhere in sight, not to men-tion the rest of the buildings—Popeye's, or even the incongruous white high rise across the street.

A young couple, walking arm in arm, approached from the opposite direction. They were wearing old-fashioned costumes. The woman had on a long dress with puffed sleeves, a vest, and on her head wore a high, plumed hat. They stopped to watch as the three men drew near. The cou-ple returned Jeremy's greeting and continued their walk. They had almost passed when he was suddenly struck by an idea. He called to them. "Excuse me folks, but I seem to have misplaced the Riviera," he chuckled. "Do you know where it is?"

"Riviera?" the man turned and replied. "I'm sorry. We're only here for the weekend. What is the Riviera?" he looked to his companion, but she shook her head, pulling close against him.

"The *Riviera,* that large pavilion that sits on the water. You'd *have* to have seen it." Jeremy heard the new, strained sound in his voice.

"Well, possibly it's that structure that burned. Everyone talks about it, but I thought they called it some hotel." The man was now warming to the conversation, more at ease with the trio than he'd been at first. He pointed back toward the open space. A group of workmen was gathered around the remains of a large building, clearing away debris.

"That old place, least what's left of her, was the Whiting." Judd had spoken. And just at that moment, Jeremy's watch beeped for the hour. Both the young couple and his comrades were startled, jumping back at the sound. Jeremy shrugged, fished it from his sweatshirt pocket and held it in his palm. The others moved in closer.

"What *is* that?" the girl asked, staring. She had overcome her earlier shyness.

"What *is* it? You're kidding. It's just one of those sport-alarm models. You know, a Timex." Jeremy scanned their faces.

The woman nudged her companion. "The numbers are changing," he said softly, never taking his eyes off the watch.

"It's the seconds," Jeremy was becoming annoyed. And his headache had returned in force.

"That certainly is an amazing timepiece you have. It must have cost you a good fortune," the young man said, stealing a glance at Jeremy's torn blue jeans and his face, with the remnants of dried blood. "We'd best be off. We hope you find that pavilion you're looking for." The two continued down the path, stopping to glance back over their shoulders.

"Can you beat that," Jeremy said to the two. "Now where in the devil do you suppose they come from? If it weren't for that ridiculous plumed hat she's wearing, I'd have bet they're Amish or something."

"I've lived up here in Lake Geneva all my life, stranger," the derby wearer spoke up, "and I've never heard of any Riviera. Isn't that what you called the place? So I'm thinkin', where the devil do *you* come from? Jeremy saw him again staring at his watch, and he pocketed it.

"He's broken loose from the asylum, Judd, you mark my words," Jeremy heard the man whisper. "I'm sure of it. Look," he pointed toward Jeremy. "See those clothes he's wearin'? It must be some kind of outfit they give those lunatics now. And the timepiece he had. You saw it. All his crazy talk…about his bicycle…he's gotten out of Oak Hill and that's a fact."

Jeremy was facing out toward the bay, but he heard enough to send a chill up his back. In his condition, he'd be no match for these two if they wanted to take him somewhere.

"I don't know," Judd was pondering. "I worked on the grounds at Oak Hill two years ago. Most of the folks were either real quiet, keepin' to themselves or they were locked away in the upper floors. Those were the ones that hollered all the time," his head shook slowly at the memory. "He don't seem like any of them." It *must* have been the same old asylum he'd known, Jeremy realized, the one he'd been musing about as he'd stood at the top of the hill before his accident.

"I still say we should take him back, Judd. I'll bet he's one of the rich ones. Don't forget most of them out there got money, or at least their families do. Even if he's gone and gotten himself all cut and dirty, he'll still bring a smart reward, and we'd be doin' the right thing, too."

Jeremy had to get away. He painfully raised himself up while they were talking and started to hobble off, putting distance between himself and them, damning his condition while he tried to catch his breath. Looking back over his shoulder, he saw the two behind him, keeping the same distance. He reached the road, now paved with cobblestones. The two seemed to be arguing, probably trying to decide what to do next. For the first time, Jeremy noticed others nearby. They were also staring at him. It wasn't his imagination.

If I can only catch my breath and maybe shake the pain in the damn ankle a little, I'll find my car and get out of this nightmare situation. Where the hell did I leave my car? He couldn't see it or any cars for that matter. The nausea had come back stronger than ever and he reached for support, holding onto an old-fashioned hitching post, feeling himself about to lose consciousness.

Judd's arms were around him, holding him up. "You take it easy, mister. None of us are going to hurt you. We're just going to take you into Doctor MacDougal's." Jeremy couldn't resist. Arms were supporting him, setting him down on the ground.

He was dimly conscious of a heavy-set, middle aged woman beside him as he was carried down a dark hallway. "Bring him in here. The doctor will be down in just a minute." He felt himself being laid on a table. Instinctively, he reached for the wallet in his back pocket. It was still there. He tried to thank Judd, but the woman in charge had shooed the men out of the room and down the hallway.

She looked down, appraising him. "My! You *do* look like you've suffered a nasty accident. No, now you lay back down," she commanded. "I'll bring you a glass of water."

Jeremy took the glass from her and gulped it until she had to warn him to slow down. She wiped his head with a cool cloth. "You just try to relax until the doctor gets here." With a last look at him, she stepped out of the room.

She herded the others toward the front door. "You all did your part. Now let the doctor look at the poor fellow." He couldn't hear what they asked her, but she said, "Yes, I saw it. Let the doctor decide what to do."

Ignoring her warning, he sat up. In contrast to the hallway, the room was light, with two windows that overlooked the park and lake. Still another carriage passed by outside and two small children chasing each other darted across the front lawn. They were wearing the same, dated clothes. The office had the familiar smell he remembered of doctors' offices from long ago. Like all patients in examining rooms, he began to look around closely at his surroundings. The desk, chairs and examining table were authentic antiques, although they seemed to have hardly been used.

On the far wall was another old classic, a glass cabinet. Inside it were jars of all different sizes, holding colored liquids and swabs. They seemed non-functional, probably venerable decorations. Except that one of the jars containing cotton swabs had its lid off, as if someone had forgotten to replace it. He stepped over to the case. The glass door was ajar and from inside came the smell of—alcohol? No, it was sweeter. Ether.

Jeremy looked out again over the park, noticing as he did a calendar hanging on the wall between the two windows. He blinked his eyes to try to clear the halo, then walked over to the calendar hanging on the wall between the two windows. It was an old-fashioned print of a horsedrawn sleigh. A bundled-up family was smiling as they passed a waving farmer.

He stared out the window again, but the calendar pulled his attention back. The date. The month was May all right, but the year was *1895!* He grabbed the heavy paper, flipping through the remaining months. It was no typo. They all said 1895. Sweating now, his confusion mounted. As though mocking him, a horse-drawn carriage clattered by, followed by a single rider. He looked at the lake, so familiar in its shape. The single, small yacht he'd seen before out in the bay had tied up at the large dock.

20

The lake was empty of any other boats.

He slumped back on the edge of the table. He had to *think,* to force his mind to work. He touched the ends of the table with both hands just to be sure it was real. The dizziness and headache had returned in full force, and he lay down.

The voice startled him. "I'm told you had an accident. Suppose we take a look at you." The doctor was standing directly in front of him. "Malcolm MacDougal," he extended his hand. Jeremy could tell he was being appraised even as he shook the doctor's hand. He was in his sixties and stood about five-ten or eleven.

Doctor MacDougal carefully put his hand to Jeremy's head where blood was caked and felt the swollen area. Next he checked his face and neck. "Let me have your wrist," he felt for his pulse. "And please take off," he paused, looking closely at Jeremy's hooded sweatshirt, "your shirt."

Jeremy raised the sweatshirt over his head, feeling his sunglasses inside the pocket as he did so. Pulling it off, he noticed the doctor studying his tee shirt. He glanced down. *"Oh, no,"* he groaned to himself. He'd forgotten about the shirt. It was an old one he'd grabbed from his dresser that morning, and there—printed across the chest in once-bright letters—were the words "Another Tequila Sunrise". Worse still, underneath the lettering was a silly, three-colored rising sun.

"Tee-kweela?" he asked. Jeremy corrected the pronunciation, quickly stripping off the shirt. "What does it mean?" the doctor turned as he spoke, taking a primitive stethoscope from his jacket pocket. A trace of a Scottish burr was in his voice.

"It's Mexican. Indian, I suppose, for a drink made out of cactus." Then, realizing he might be saying too much, Jeremy cut off his explanation. He had just made up his mind that he would say as little as possible, electing to play for time until he could find out exactly what was happening and where he was. He *had* been bothered of late by intense, troubling dreams...not quite nightmares but vivid dreams that seemed to go on and on, ones he couldn't bring to an end. If this was another of those hovering dreams, it was far and away the worst he'd ever had.

The doctor had him lie on his back and proceeded to examine him all over, checking carefully for any breaks. He felt cautiously around the ribs, stopping when he saw Jeremy wince. He had him turn on his stomach, repeating the exam. Finally he reached his ankle, by now swollen and painful. He looked it over, probing to see if it was broken. At last he had his patient sit up as he took the chair by the desk. "Will you please put your shirt on," he said, reaching into an inkwell as he scratched out some notes, stopping now and again to dip the pen.

"I can find no fractures, but that doesn't mean you didn't crack a rib. Also, your ankle is becoming badly swollen and you should stay off it for a few days. Those ribs will be giving you much pain as well.

"How did the accident happen?" He was facing Jeremy, his pen on the desk.

He told him he had been thrown. "At least," he allowed, "I believe I was thrown from a bicycle. When I came to, it was gone."

"Bicycles! Personally, I hate them. They're dangerous things, damn nuisances! I've treated many a person for injuries from them. I wouldna' ride one myself."

Jeremy provided his name and a few sparse details, but said he couldn't remember anything prior to the accident, only that he'd been thrown from the bike. There were, in fact, no gaps whatever in his memory. He simply didn't know *where* he was—or why—and thought it best to conceal as much as possible. It might be wise for now, he thought, to have a memory loss until he could sort out what happened. The doctor asked him several more questions, frowning now and then as he would scribble an additional note.

Doctor MacDougal stopped his note-taking, waiting a few moments as he seemed to be considering his next statement. "Do you know anything about Oak Hill? Does that name mean anything to you?" He studied Jeremy.

"No. I can't say that it does. Is that bad?"

"No. That's good," the doctor smiled. He jotted a further note. "Well, your loss of consciousness," he started, "indicates to me you've suffered a concussion. There is a swelling here," and he pointed on his own head to a spot above his right ear by way of demonstrating.

"This is really a bruise under your skull. That would account for your loss of memory. You have suffered what we term an episode of amnesia. Din'na worry," he burred, "Your memory will be returning in a day or so, but I'd like you to rest here. I want to make sure you're recovered."

Jeremy started to protest, but the doctor interrupted. "Please, the most important thing is that you rest. You'll soon be able to communicate with your friends or relatives. Perhaps you're staying on up here with someone as a guest, or…" his eyes moved inadvertently to Jeremy's soiled hands, "…or perhaps you're in the employ of someone. Don't worry about payment now. When you get your health back you can settle up.

"Besides, Lake Geneva is a small town and it's not often, except for the elderly, that I see a memory-loss case."

He had mentioned not to worry about money, but Jeremy was almost sure the doctor had seen his wallet in his back pocket, his now apparently useless wallet. And just at that moment, his watch beeped again for the hour. The doctor, startled, looked over. Jeremy fished it from his pocket and handed it over to him.

Malcolm examined it closely, watching the seconds flash by. He produced his own watch, a ponderous Waltham with Roman numerals, attached to a long chain. He held the two up. "Quite a difference," Jeremy said lamely. The doctor studied the digital watch for a few more seconds before handing it back.

"It's going to be interesting, my friend, talking to you when your memory returns." Rising up from his chair, he asked Jeremy to wait there. "You can wash up in the sink. I've already taken the liberty of having my housekeeper, Gertrude, prepare the guest room. When I was told you were hurt, I thought it best to have you stay at least overnight, but I can see you might need several days to get back your strength."

Jeremy hobbled to the sink, dropped in the stopper and proceeded to use a rough powdered soap to clean the grime from his hands. The grain in the soap was surprisingly effective. As Jeremy washed, the doctor rattled off some very familiar old Lake Geneva names, trying to jog his memory. They were the names of the most prestigious families, he remembered. *I ought to be flattered,* he told himself, *being thought of in such company.*

After he had washed up, Malcolm opened the door and led him down the dark hallway. He began to get another siege of nausea and had to lean against Malcolm, blinking to clear the cobwebs. He saw a young woman in the hallway, off to one side, but feeling faint, he slumped against the doctor's shoulder as they turned a corner.

Jeremy woke and looked around the room, blinking his eyes, unable to recall where he was. Memories of the previous day flooded back and he realized yesterday's events were no nightmare. And if what he had gone through had been some kind of near-death experience, there surely had not been the comforting, soft white light that the supermarket tabloids had described. Jeremy reached down and rubbed the old-fashioned night shirt he'd been given. The dinner tray Gertrude had brought him was on the table, untouched.

He gingerly touched the side of his head. It was still sore and swollen but at least it wasn't throbbing anymore. He got up, stretched and winced. The doctor was right. His ribs were sore, more so than yesterday, and he found it was hard to draw a breath. The view through the single window overlooked a yard and house next door. The window was open a crack and the warm spring air rolled in.

He was going to have to try to figure out what to do as he got up and paced about the room. First he'd piece together what had happened and try to find a way somehow to get himself back—to get out of this situation.

His growing panic was punctuated by a rap on the door. Gertrude appeared with a breakfast tray. She eyed his uneaten meal. "If you're going to get well...it's Jeremy isn't it? You'll have to start eating better than that."

"I'm afraid I was too sick last night, but that bacon, eggs and coffee—I'll make it up to you this morning." She hesitated, not catching his idiom at first.

"Oh, also the doctor wants you to stay in bed this morning. He'll be by to see you later." She left, closing the door.

Small children were playing in the yard next door. They must have been the same ones he had seen running around in front of the doctor's office. Their noisy play drew him back to his own children. Everything was now so far away from him. A feeling of claustrophobia overtook him; he was locked out of his own real life and didn't know how to reenter it.

He heard a knock and looked up to see Doctor MacDougal at the door. He had opened it a crack and was looking in. Another man stood behind him. The two entered as Jeremy moved over to the bed. Sitting on the side of the bed, he noticed that the other man was also about sixty, the same age he guessed Doctor MacDougal to be.

"This is Doctor Wilson, Jeremy. He is another physician in town. I talked to the doctor here about our meeting, my examination of you and my findings. He'd like to have a look at you himself."

Jeremy shook hands with Doctor Wilson, thankful he'd thought to put his watch in a dresser drawer. The doctor had him sit up, then stepped back, his hands folded across his chest. "So, you fell from a bicycle, hit your head and you remember nothing, correct?"

"Nothing before the accident."

"Has your memory of the accident begun to return at all?" Doctor Wilson regarded Jeremy through thick wire spectacles that magnified his eyes.

"No, it hasn't as yet," Jeremy answered.

The doctor measured his words. "Yet you're sure that this bicycle was taken from you. How about your money or paper. Do you remember if you had any with you?"

"I only know that when I awoke I had neither my bicycle nor my billfold."

"Do you feel that you were robbed? Perhaps we should call the constable. This may be a matter for the police." He was watching Jeremy for any reaction.

Malcolm interrupted. "Doctor, I don't think that's necessary at this point. He may well have wandered around the park, away from the scene of the accident. As far as a billfold goes, I believe it will turn up with his friends or his employer as soon as he locates them. I think the first order of importance is for Jeremy to get himself well."

"I agree," Doctor Wilson said. "You stay off that ankle for another day or so. Good day." He turned and began walking out of the room. Jeremy for a moment thought to ask a question about his amnesia, to draw out Doctor Wilson's perception of him. But he checked the impulse, watching as the the two doctors strode from the room.

4

A small knot of people was gathered in front of Malcolm's. Lora was so caught up in her thoughts that she hadn't noticed the crowd until she was directly across the street. One of the men who'd been at the front door was now heading across the street in her direction. Satisfied she didn't know him, she stepped forward. "Can you tell me what happened over there."

He regarded the slim, attractive young woman. "I didn't see it, ma'am," he said, tipping his battered hat. "Judd Stearns, he's inside. Judd found a man wanderin' in the park. He was pretty thumped up, full of blood…he said he'd been knocked off his bicycle. Funny thing though, ma'am, no one could find the bike. I think someone may have nabbed it from the poor fellow." He nodded his head in sympathy for the injured man's bad luck. "And did you happen to see his clothes?"

Lora shook her head. "I just got here. Why? What about his clothes?"

"They were real funny. And Judd said he had a strange timepiece he was wearin' on his wrist. When he saw he was bein' watched, he put it in his pocket, like he was hidin' it. Said it didn't look like anything he'd ever seen."

Lora glanced over at Malcolm's. She was only half listening as this fellow rambled on about the injured man's…timepiece? Was that even what he'd been talking about? At last she saw what she was waiting for. The men who'd carried the stretcher into the house appeared at the door, and saying goodbye to Gertrude, they moved off.

Lora gave her informant a quick smile, thanking him for his time and trouble. Taking his cue, he again tipped his hat, then left to catch up to the small knot of men walking toward the center of town. She looked up and down the empty street, suddenly realizing that the longer she stood alone outside, the more likely she was to be recognized. After a glance around, she crossed the street and climbed the stairs to Malcolm's house, rapping the knocker.

Once again the housekeeper answered the door. "Gertrude, I'm Lora Lockerby. Paul's daughter." She wasn't sure if Gertrude would remember her, but a smile of recognition began to cross the older woman's face. "I have an appointment with the doctor…I saw the commotion. I can see I came at a bad time."

"Miss Lockerby, how good to see you. Please, come on in. We've had some excitement, all right." She led Lora into the darkened hallway of the house.

"I saw the crowd from across the street. Some sort of a bicycle accident, I heard. Is that right?"

"Yes, the doctor is with him right now. He was knocked off some way and hit his head as nearly as I could learn. He was cut and bleeding, too. Here, dear." She guided Lora along the hall and into the living room. "I hear from the doctor that your father is going to be busy building that Observatory out at Williams Bay. Around here, that's all anyone talks about anymore."

"I could say the same. At home, the Observatory is just about all I ever hear of, too. Father will be in charge of all the electrical work out there."

"You just make yourself comfortable, Miss Lora. I've got to go and straighten up the back bedroom. I have a notion the doctor is going to want to keep," she pointed toward the hall and the closed examining room, "that fellow overnight, keep an eye on him. Here's the *Herald* and on the table you'll find a *Harper's.*" Gertrude moved off toward the rear of the house.

Lora settled down on the couch, her thoughts returning to Clarence. She realized she would soon be talking about him to another person, something she hadn't done before. A feeling of vague disloyalty came over her. She picked up the *Herald,* glancing at it. As if to mock any efforts at distancing herself from him up here, there was a picture of Clarence on the front page. His head was cocked to one side, listening to the questioner. Those same penetrating eyes that so unmasked her were looking out from the page. She stared at the picture a moment before reading the article about Clarence's handling of Debs' appeal.

The door at the end of the hallway opened. Lora stood and looked down toward it. In the darkness she could make out Malcolm supporting someone, the bicycle victim no doubt. The soft murmur of his distinct voice carried to her as he reassured the shaken man. Then Malcolm noticed her.

"Lora! What a surprise to see you. Why don't you step into my office and I'll be along shortly." The man glanced up, his eyes meeting Lora's, and then he seemed overcome by wooziness. He turned away, again leaning heavily on Malcolm. She waited as they passed, watching him and listening. His speech was quite different. She'd heard so many accents at Pullman, during the trial and working for Clarence. She tried to place his, but couldn't.

She took a chair opposite the one at Malcolm's desk. He returned after several minutes, bending down and kissing her cheek. "Every time you go away from here, young lady, I swear you get prettier on your return. Is that what the strike and that trial did for you?" He patted her shoulder affectionately as he sat down, filling her in briefly about the stranger and his mishap, or at least as much as he could piece together.

"Jeremy is the fellow's name. Thrown right from his bike. He's suffered a worrisome memory loss—doesn't know who or where he is. That watch of his..." Malcolm seemed lost in his thoughts. "You ought to have seen it."

That watch again, thought Lora, just as the doctor brightened and abruptly changed the subject. "How's that hardworking father of yours?" He continued without waiting for a response. "Do you know I've been helping him look for an assistant over at the Observatory, preferably someone from around here, but so far I haven't found anyone. Malcolm sat back in his chair, his hands crossed. It was her turn to talk, she knew.

Taking a deep breath, she plunged right in. Her experiences of the last couple of years, both at Pullman and working for Darrow, had given her a directness uncommon in women of her age and background. Besides, she reasoned, she'd come all this way for answers. She gambled that she'd picked the right person to seek out. Starting with telling him about her work, she moved slowly onto rockier territory, briefing him on the strike, the trial and her roles in both. "You remember Clarence Darrow?" Malcolm's look intensified at the nervous tone in her voice. She had brushed at a tear.

"Of course. His name is on every lip, even up here in remote Lake Geneva."

Lora went on. She felt her face begin to flush. "Well, the fact is, I more than worked for him. We've become—close. That's a big part of why I'm here. Oh, Doctor—he's married, but I'm so in love with him!" Lora heard the words rushing out unchecked. "I guess I thought we'd be marrying."

"I know he's not happy in his marriage—that he and his wife Jessie aren't well mated anymore—he told me so. But, I'm also becoming sure, finally, that he's not going to do anything about it. Maybe I'm only a person who brings their unhappiness into focus."

Malcolm shifted in his chair, stifling the start of a frown. "Do you know Jessie?" he asked quietly.

Lora shook her head. "What I told you I heard from Clarence."

Malcolm realized his question and his steady gaze had unnerved Lora. "I know how hard this is for you, my dear, but I want to listen and help."

"I'm here for your advice. I'd thought about canceling my trip to see you, but I had—I *have* to talk to someone." She sneezed again and pulled out her handkerchief to dab at her nose.

"Well, first things first." Malcolm walked over to his medicine cabinet and extracted a vial of powder which he shook onto a spoon. Drawing a glass of water, he handed both to Lora. "Take this powder. We'll deal with that cold of yours before anything else."

Lora took the powder, grimacing as she washed it down with the water. After she'd finished, she set the glass down, relaxing for the first time since she'd begun talking. "I even owe this cold to him," she smiled wryly, remembering Clarence's cold and her spirited nursing attempts at the office. Then she proceeded to set out for Malcolm her relationship with Darrow, even to telling him about Clarence's proposal that they meet in Springfield. Her intuition told her that the doctor would likely guess how close she came to accepting. She *did* keep to herself that the offer was still open.

As she talked, she noticed Malcolm had from time to time been dipping his pen into the inkwell and making marks on a sheet of paper. At first she thought he was taking notes and at one point she stretched, leaning forward for a closer look. Malcolm had only been doodling as he listened. A barely recognizable drawing of a sailboat occupied the paper. The name "Jeremy" had been written beside the boat.

29

"You're here, Lora, and you didn't go to the St. Nicholas Hotel." A melodic burr had softened his voice. He'd done a good job of drawing her out, nodding and listening as she spoke. "What do *you* think you want?"

"I've been thinking about getting away for awhile. Maybe if I leave…Clarence," Lora hesitated at saying his name. "Leave Chicago and the law office, I can straighten out my thoughts. With Eugene's trial over, things are a little quieter now. I've already told him I was thinking of taking a short trip. I may even spend the summer up here. I feel as though I've been short-changing father lately. I don't want to spell out for you, either, the stories I've had to tell when father's asked about work."

"What does your Mister Darrow have to say about all this?"

Lora thought a minute before answering. "I'm not sure. Our working together, our seeing each other after work has been a strain on Clarence as well. Maybe," she paused, "maybe he would just as soon I got away for awhile, too." As she spoke, Lora realized it was the first time she had even acknowledged to herself what must have been Clarence's same concerns about their future.

"Do it. Take some time off. Think things over," Malcolm said in his soft, Scot's voice. "Your friend is a powerful figure. He sounds like a very compelling one, too." Lora looked down, catching his meaning. He reached over for her hand. "Most of all. I know he's worthy or he wouldn't have earned your deepest feelings.

"I don't have to tell you the emotionally heavy cost of falling in love with a married man. The lord knows you've earned that wisdom yourself the hard way."

Lora, having once opened up, felt a need to talk about Darrow. She knew she couldn't possibly describe to Malcolm the powerful physical attraction that she and Clarence felt for each other, but she needed to leave him with a sense of the depth and goodness of their bond. She found herself telling him about the courtroom drama at Debs' trial, even detailing some of Clarence's lovable eccentricities.

Lora had been talking on when she looked over at the clock. "I've taken so much of your time already. I'd better get started if I'm to catch the afternoon train."

Malcolm stood, putting his arm on her shoulder. "You've come through so much in the past year, Lora. Sometimes love extracts a very costly toll, especially love for one who's not free. I can't tell you *what* to do, but I'm sure you'll do the right thing."

He walked her to the door, returning the squeeze she gave him. "Malcolm, thank you. I don't know who else I could have turned to. You'll never know how much it meant to have somebody listen to me. And I'll promise you this," Lora had just made up her mind. "I won't be…with him anymore…at least for now. I wouldn't be able to give him up if I were to." Smiling one last time, she stepped down the stairs, then turned and waved as she walked toward town.

Seeing her pretty, light smile and wave, no stranger could have guessed the nature of her conversation with the doctor. Lora was, even with all her problems, the daughter that he and his beloved Molly had wished and prayed for throughout their marriage. He was grateful that she had chosen to confide in him, but his heart ached for her and the difficulties she would be facing.

Malcolm returned to his office which suddenly seemed so empty, reflecting on what Paul's daughter had just told him. He sat for a few minutes, thinking. Then he opened his desk drawer, removing the strange, hooded shirt and the dark, wire-rimmed glasses the stranger had been wearing and studied them, perplexed.

Where had that man been coming from before his accident? Still pondering the items, he walked over to his bookcase and started to rummage through it, frowning at the accumulation of papers inside. He vowed he'd clean it out first chance. At last he found what he was looking for, a map of the Lake Geneva area. He wished he had invested in one of the newer ones which showed the latest homes and camps.

Malcolm spread open the map and taking a pencil, he traced the likeliest route his new patient might have traveled in arriving at the park and the site of his bicycle mishap. The stranger had told him that he thought he had been coming down the hill from the west. In the next few days he'd have time to make some discreet inquiries of the Sturges clan and maybe the Fairbanks and Leiters. Malcolm lit his pipe. It was that speech pattern of his, he thought, that and the way he conducted himself. The man was shaken up, no doubt, from the injury he'd gotten. Yet, despite the strange, shaggy clothes and his soiled hands, there was a kind of self-assurance about him you didn't see in a workman.

It's likely, he thought, *I'm making more out of his identity than I should. Didn't the Sturgesses have a reputation for inviting up eccentric guests? Maybe he was simply one more, and the clothes and glasses just represent some new, quaint fad.*

There was one more possibility, an unlikely one, but Malcolm had checked into it. He'd taken aside Judd, one of the men who'd carried in the stranger, and one he knew would keep a closed mouth, and asked him to go over to Oak Hill, the asylum for the insane, to see if they were missing anyone. He was sure his patient was no inmate of the place, but all the same, he had to get the facts.

For a passing moment, as he thought again about Lora, unsure about her future, and Jeremy, having lost his past, it seemed as if there were, in some obscure way, a connection between the two.

"What a far-fetched notion," he said out loud, sighing as he rolled up the map. He'd put in quite a tiring, curious morning for a country doctor.

5

The next several days found Jeremy's strength slowly returning. His head had stopped spinning and his vision was recovered, though he still couldn't shake the forlorn dreams that took place in what had been the present. After a day or two, he began to settle on a rough plan. He'd play for time while he tried to find the key to unlock whatever had dropped him into 1895 Lake Geneva, whether it was inside his head or not.

The brooding sense of loss kept stealing back to overtake him, along with a terrible awareness that he was marooned. He'd told Malcolm his memory was coming back in fits and starts and that he remembered he was from Indianapolis. It was a city he'd visited and he gambled that few people in Lake Geneva would ever have been there, eliminating hard questions. Jeremy also sketched out a vague picture of himself, telling the doctor he had been a kind of white-collar worker, a rarity in the 1890's. He was careful not to take the return of his memory much beyond that.

Malcolm had in turn opened up, explaining why he had asked him questions on that first day about Oak Hill. It was the sanitarium, the same red brick building Jeremy had been remembering as he'd looked down from the top of the hill just before the accident. Malcolm had made a discreet check, learning Jeremy hadn't fled or wandered off from there. Oak Hill was missing no patients. "I hope my investigation hasn't offended you, but at least we now know one place you *haven't* come from."

A small shudder went through Jeremy. "I'll try to keep behaving like I don't belong there," he said as he recalled the foreboding building.

Jeremy had also learned things about the doctor, about his generosity as well as the loneliness he'd felt since his wife's passing two years before.

Childless, they'd been married forty years at the time of her death, a death Malcolm still mourned. Had medicine been more advanced, he told Jeremy, he knew Molly could have been saved.

On waking up Friday morning, he peered out the window of the back bedroom at a dark, somber day. It was time he ventured outside to explore his surroundings. Malcolm hadn't placed any restraints on him. Gertrude had shown him the closet of the guest room, which contained wearing apparel of every description: work clothes, jackets, shoes and boots. Malcolm's guest room had sheltered family, passing visitors and patients, many of whom had left behind clothing articles on their departure.

He tried on some of the clothes. Amused but satisfied at his own appearance, he stopped at the door to the kitchen on his way out. Gertrude was standing over the sink, her back to him. As casually as possible, he asked her if she wanted anything from town.

She turned, studying his appearance for a moment, then smiled. "No, no thank you, Jeremy. I'm glad to see you're up and around. You look so much better." The clothes he'd picked, as near a workingman's as he could guess, had passed, apparently, Gertrude's inspection. "Don't go off too far—and remember your way back."

He walked along Main Street. Many of these very homes he saw had survived into the 1990s, Malcolm's own Georgian corner house included. Favoring his ribs and avoiding the temptation to take deep breaths, he could almost forget the pain. At the corner of Broad Street he started across, then stopped, letting a fast moving pair of horses drawing a heavy wagon trot past. He had always been indifferent to the busiest traffic, fearlessly dodging between cars along LaSalle Street. Horses were going to take some getting used to.

The site of the old Whiting Hotel was directly in front of him. It was the same building Judd and his friend, and the young couple had spoken of. The Whiting's very last remains were being loaded onto a wagon. Jeremy tried to call up a picture of the old resort from photos of early Lake Geneva. A vague impression of a large, gingerbread building with gables and verandas was the best he could manage.

He looked out over the wide municipal dock. A solitary workman was out at the end of its north arm, applying finishing touches for the new season. Jeremy was anxious for somebody to talk to and also to test how well he could adapt to conversation. Walking down the pier, he noticed a small, steam-powered craft at the mouth of Geneva Bay. It turned and headed toward town. The young workman was kneeling with his back to Jeremy as he hammered. As he approached, the man stood up, shaking his head.

"Isn't it always the way," he started, "no matter how many tools you bring out, you're going to forget the one you need." Jeremy smiled in agreement, noticing the worker hadn't done any double takes at his appearance as he stepped past, walking toward shore and his forgotten tool.

He tried to piece together his accident, something he'd had trouble doing back in his room. Taking a deep breath, he tested his ribs, wincing at the pain still there. He breathed in the familiar, welcome smell of the lake.

So I shot over the handlebar. That much I remember. And I hit the ground at the base of a tree. Then what? Then it became distinctly harder to recollect. He forced himself to remember—the blackout and with it the outward spinning—that sickening spiral that had contracted as it rushed faster, thrusting him toward its center until he'd fallen into the vortex. His head physically ached with the memory of the long, terrifying tunnel. He knew he had been deeply afraid in that shaft, more afraid than ever before. Of what, though? A fear—some fear that he could not escape from the tunnel. Was this his near death experience? He consciously squared his shoulders, at last facing the next question. Was it *in fact* death that he'd experienced? Was this the "other side," some entry into a different time sphere? Even as he forced these thoughts, he knew the answer. If everyone had experienced what he just had—or would have to experience—life itself would be nothing but paradoxes. No, whatever had happened to him, he was sure, was unique.

Was he going through some trauma-induced mental illness that didn't want to end? People like Malcolm, homespun Gertrude, the down-to-earth derby wearer who'd planned to reap a reward from returning him to Oak Hill, even the smell of the lake all confirmed that he was very much alive even if deranged.

The pier laborer, an extra long saw in one hand, was walking back out toward him. Jeremy felt a bump against the pier and turned. Two men were preparing to leave the little boat that had just docked. The older one was brawny and dressed in some kind of police uniform. Absorbed in his own thoughts, Jeremy had been only half paying attention to the boat, but as he watched he saw the older man was roughly pushing the younger ahead of him.

He looked more closely. The other, wearing a torn, soiled shirt was little more than a boy. A bright, fresh cut ran downward from his mouth. His dirty cheeks were streaked with tears. And his hands were tied behind his back.

As the two exited the boat, it bumped lightly once more against the pier. The big man was partly turned, talking to the boatman who was already starting to back away. Jeremy's eyes were on the boy. As he was shoved to the pier, he found himself suddenly free with the policeman's back to him. He wrenched away, then turned, hesitating a moment before starting his escape. The other, recovering and moving with surprising quickness for his size and age, put a foot out and tripped the lad.

His momentum pitched the youth forward and he landed hard on the boards, sprawling over the edge of the pier, his breath bursting out from him. For a second, Jeremy thought he would go clear off. The policeman quickly knelt over the boy. With his meaty hand, he reached for the knot at his wrist, giving it a cruel twist. At the same time he yanked at the lad, pulling him further out over the side.

"So that's all you wanted by breaking loose was to take a little swim, eh? I can help you." The voice was cold and flat. The boy was dragged even further out until only the hands that held him by his wrists and shirt kept him from dropping into the water.

The youth hadn't made a sound, even when he had hit the pier or when the knot on his wrists was twisted. But feeling himself suspended helplessly above the surface, he broke. Jeremy heard him whimper as he crabbed his feet and knees desperately against the boards, trying to get back.

"I think I'll give you that little swim. Who'd miss you, anyway?"

"I would," Jeremy said. "Get him back." The man swung around at the sound, still holding the lad.

"This is my prisoner, a bawling thief he is, and on his way to justice." He was studying Jeremy. "This is police business I'm about and it'll pay you to hold your tongue." His tone was harsh, his authority returning even as he continued to examine Jeremy.

"Drowning teenagers is police business? If he *is* on his way to justice, he'd best get there safely."

Jeremy felt a hand on his shoulder. Half turning, he saw it was the pier workman. During the exchange, the lad had managed to get to his feet, stepping back as far as he could get from the water's edge. With a final, glowering look at Jeremy, the husky lawman grabbed the youth by his wrists and shoved him forward.

All of Jeremy's resolve to be anonymous until he could piece things together had just been cast aside. Delayed nerves caused a tremble to run down him as he watched the two walk down the pier toward shore, the policeman moving with a distinct limp. The workman exhaled loudly. "I like what you just did, mister. I'd never a' said that, but you be careful around that one. He's mean and dangerous both."

"Who is he?"

"Don't know much about him. Lowery's his name. He's the constable out at Williams Bay. He hasn't been around very long." His eyes left Jeremy, briefly following the constable and his prisoner as the two left the dock and moved up Broad Street. "He's the reason I don't go to Williams Bay anymore." He turned his back, returning to work and ending the conversation. Jeremy walked down the pier, heading toward Malcolm's.

Back at the house, he tried putting the brutish constable and his own response to him out of his mind. Malcolm had told him in the morning to be ready at six for dinner in town. He eventually decided on a stiff fitting, dark suit he'd taken from the closet. Jeremy inspected himself in the mirror. Satisfied, he walked out to the living room.

"Now you look a little more like a townsman," Malcolm said. Jeremy's own clothes had been discreetly taken while he recuperated. The doctor had likely not wanted him attracting attention by wearing them into town.

The spring day had turned chilly and Jeremy was glad when they finally reached the Geneva House. "I may have some good news for you tonight, but let's have a drink first," said Malcolm as they entered the lobby. The hotel's summer business hadn't started in full. A small knot of men were congregated in the lobby as they stepped to the bar. It looked surprisingly like the restoration bars he had known that imitated the gay nineties period. "Two, Leo," the doctor called out, catching the portly bartender's attention.

"Evenin', Doc." He set the two foaming steins in front of them as Malcolm made introductions.

"Mr. Slater is visiting us from Indianapolis." Jeremy had provided himself with the new last name.

The three talked for a few minutes about the chilly weather before Leo moved off down the bar. Malcolm took a few long draughts of beer, losing himself in thought for a minute. He set down his stein, turning toward Jeremy.

"I've enjoyed your company this week. I haven't been able to say that to many people. This past winter has been long and lonely.

"You know," he began, signaling Leo to refill their steins. When he had, the doctor seemed to toy with his, moving it across the wet surface of the bar, brushing a bit of foam off the top of the rim. "I've missed Molly," he said, studying his stein. Jeremy found himself caught up in Malcolm's description of his late wife. It wasn't a tale of grief but of happy, loving memories.

As they spoke, Jeremy watched the other diners, now beginning to thin out. The roast beef was excellent and Jeremy was grateful for something that was familiar. There may have been restaurants where women dined, he thought, looking around, but he'd seen none here. Only a mixture of business and workingmen were present. Suddenly, in the far corner of the room, at a table with two others, he saw the constable he'd faced out on the pier. And his eyes had just met Jeremy's.

"I wanted to tell you about an opportunity," Malcolm was talking, "for me as well as you. We're growing up here, my friend. Oh, we've had our ups and downs in this town, I know, what with the Whiting burning down and all. Still, solid people with money have come here and are coming in greater numbers all the time. Why, do you know there are a dozen major estates that will be built on the lake this year alone and thirty or more smaller homes.

"I know some of these people don't like all the Chicago and Milwaukee folks coming here and buying the lake land but there's no stopping them. I say it's progress, and that's the direction this town should keep to." He signaled the waiter for coffee. "Of course, I'm not some merchant millionaire, but I think it's all for the best."

Jeremy nodded, spooning sugar into his coffee. From his own knowledge, the area's development at the turn-of-the-century had revolved around the very rich. The big sociological changes brought to the lake by the subdivisions would be far off—in the twenties and thirties, and they would move at the measured pace that set Lake Geneva's tone. He was thinking, delving into his own thoughts when Malcolm brought him back.

"So what I'm telling you is that we've been selected," he slowed his narrative for impact, "to receive the greatest telescope in the world! The lens is being built right now in Cambridge, Massachusetts, and it's going to be housed in a giant observatory six or seven miles away from here, over at Williams Bay." He described some details of the Observatory, how it would have the world's largest refracting telescope, enthusiastically predicting that it would unleash the secrets of the Martian canals. Its construction had just recently begun and was expected to take another two years.

He took a packet from his pocket and unfolded it on the table. It was an artist's depiction, startlingly large and accurate, Jeremy realized. "Quite impressed, aren't you," the doctor said, mistaking his friend's reaction, as the waiter filled their cups, deftly moving them out of Malcolm's way.

Jeremy remembered talking his own father into taking him to see this very same Observatory. The day they went inside was a Saturday, the only day the public was allowed on tours. He guessed he was about twelve at the time. The size of the telescope up close was awesome. He recalled the astronomer was the tour lecturer as well. That day's lecture was about space and time and the interrelation of the two. All too heavy for a twelve year old. The lecture had finished, but he remembered the astronomer briefly uprighting the huge telescope as he opened an aperture in the dome. Even those who had been drowsing came alert with the movement of the huge telescope and the roof.

He was looking down at an old friend. Many times he'd played golf on the adjacent course. The Observatory's main dome was so large it was possible to look up at each hole and align yourself with it. He remembered taking his own children later on the same visit. Had it only been two years ago that he and Danny had gone over there, and he had been able to see the Observatory again through his son's eyes? Jeremy saw an expanse of blue serge next to him. The policeman was standing alongside their table. "Quite a drawing you've got there, Doctor."

"What a coincidence," said Malcolm, moving his chair back. "We're talking about the Observatory and here is the very constable of Williams Bay. Jeremy, I'd like you to meet Officer Lowery."

"I've already met your friend this morning," he said, ignoring the hand Jeremy had started to put out.

"How's your leg, constable?" Malcolm asked. Lowery shifted his weight and Jeremy remembered watching him limp off the pier.

"It would feel better if this damn weather would change," he growled, looking back at his companions who were standing at the door, waiting for him. He repeated Jeremy's name slowly, committing it to memory. "You from around here?"

"No, I'm…from Indianapolis." Lowery noticed the answer came a beat too slow.

"Jeremy is staying with me awhile. We hope he'll decide to live hereabouts."

"Indianapolis," the constable repeated. He placed one of his large hands on Jeremy's shoulder in a clumsy parody of friendliness. "What part?"

"I've lived all around the town," he answered. The only way to get rid of the powerful hand on his shoulder was to stand. He pushed back the chair, feeling as he did a firmness in Lowery's hand as he started to get up—as though to say, "I can hold you down as long as I want." His hand relaxed finally as Jeremy stood up and walked off to the men's room.

When he came back, Malcolm had paid the bill and Lowery was gone. "Let's take a walk down by the lake. I haven't told you the heart of my news." They crossed the street, moving toward the public landing. A single excursion boat had moored at the dock, joining the rowboats.

The two walked slowly along the shore. "Warner and Swasey of Cleveland are in charge of the Observatory project," Malcolm resumed. "It will be operated entirely by electrical power, generated right on the site. The man they've chosen to handle the electrical construction is a Paul Lockerby. Does the name sound familiar to you at all?" Jeremy shook his head. "Well," he continued, "I shouldn't think it would. He's a builder from Chicago and one of the best in the business.

"He's also built several of the large houses up here. Last year he even put up a place of his own, down the lake on Black Point." Jeremy listened, wondering what any of this story could have to do with him.

Lockerby, Malcolm said, had begun specializing in the installation of electrical systems. Jeremy knew from reading the papers over the last few days that the big construction news items of 1895 were such electrical installations. From what he'd read, virtually every city, factory and even homeowner across the country was dying to have electrical power installed. "I met him like I've met so many of my friends—as a patient."

The doctor propped his foot up on one of the rowboats which had been pulled onto shore. "Do you see that big house over there?" He pointed midway across the bay. Jeremy gazed in the direction he pointed, barely able to see in the near-darkness. " 'Fair Oaks.' That's the name of that estate. The very place where I met Paul."

Lighting his pipe, he told the story. Three years before, he had been returning from the market when one of the laborers he knew rode up, cutting him off. He said a young worker had gotten a bad shock. It seemed he'd contacted a live wire.

He got his bag and followed the workman over. When he arrived, he found the youth, burned along his arm and shoulder, shivering and suffering the after-effects of electric shock. Malcolm checked him over and had him placed in a wagon for transport back to his home where he could observe him.

That, he said, was when he noticed the stocky, middle-aged man who had been limping around on a make-shift crutch. "Doctor," he called over, "take care of my man." It was then he learned that this was the same person who'd pulled the worker off the line, getting knocked back by the jolt himself and injuring his ankle.

Paul Lockerby rode back with him in the wagon. He brushed aside any questions about his ankle, wouldn't even let it be seen until his worker was checked over and put down for the night. Malcolm could barely get Lockerby's boot off, the ankle had become so swollen. When he saw it, he knew right away it was broken and would need setting. He gave him a shot before he attempted to manipulate the ankle, a very painful procedure. While waiting for the shot to take effect, Lockerby told Malcolm his story. He had lived in nearby Waterford before moving to Chicago and was a widower with a daughter.

Jeremy and Malcolm had left the dock and were walking along Main Street. The night had turned cold, and the wind had come up from the west, building a chop on the lake.

The setting of the ankle proved very difficult and lengthy. Lockerby was, he told Jeremy, one of the bravest and most stoic patients he'd ever had. Malcolm had to insist that he stay over, putting him up in his house along with his young laborer.

When the two reached Malcolm's home, he invited Jeremy into the living room. "Have a seat. I'm going to pour us each some brandy to take off the chill. You probably wonder why I'm going on so, but be patient. I'm just coming to *your* part of the story." He handed Jeremy the brandy, taking a sip himself and settling into a chair. Over that summer, he said, and for the next two years, he and Lockerby became good friends, Paul dropping by now and then to talk to Malcolm when he was in town.

"This last March," Malcolm said as he sipped, "Paul wrote me he'd be up. He said he'd been put in charge of the electrical work at the Observatory, but he would have a favor to ask. When he arrived, we talked about the Observatory. That's when he confided he was stretched for manpower. This job was by far the biggest single one he'd ever handled, but it came at a time when he was busy in Chicago.

"He asked me if I knew someone who could act as a bookkeeper over at his Observatory operation; someone he could trust to be a kind of assistant who could handle payroll, oversee the delivery and inventory of all the materials they would be receiving over the summer. Above all, he had to be someone the men could get along with.

"Jeremy, this is a small community, and no one came to mind. He told me I had a couple of months to find somebody, because his phase of the construction wouldn't start much before mid-May." Jeremy began to see where he fit in. "Also," he continued, "Paul told me that the University of Chicago people in charge wanted as many locals as possible out there to head off antagonism to the Observatory. I must tell you as well that there is some, by the way.

"I hadn't been able to come up with anyone satisfactory. Oh, I had some names, but they were all a little too slow," he tapped his head meaningfully, "or they had no leadership. Providence, it seems to this good Presbyterian, has delivered me someone to fill the needs—yourself."

Jeremy felt flattered and grateful, telling Malcolm so. And this might be a rare opportunity. He was going to have to support himself some way, and being at the Observatory might be the best place for him. Also, he'd begun to think that he'd be better off staying around a town like Lake

42

Geneva, an area that at least held some familiarity. The 1895 Chicago he'd read about wouldn't be the friendliest place.

"I know you can handle the job." Malcolm was speaking again. "You have a sophistication about you one doesn't see often, at least not in a small town. I daresay when your memory returns we might have a laugh at what a position you held—or still hold.

"In the meantime," he walked to the roll-top desk. "I have something here for you somewhere…and…ah yes, here it is." He pulled out a magazine and held it up. "Here's what I was looking for, *Harper's Weekly.* I've told you what I know about the Observatory and what Lockerby's responsibilities are. But you read this article and you'll have a good idea of what's involved."

Jeremy took the magazine. "And when do I start?"

The doctor slapped his forehead. "Merciful heavens! I've been talking all this time and never told you. You start tomorrow, so don't stay up too long reading. You can borrow any of the clothes you need from the closet. No," he held up his hand to stop Jeremy's protests. "You can send me something when you're on your feet. As for this old man, he's got to get some sleep. We'll be going out on the morning train."

When Jeremy reached his room, he took off the stiff collar and too-tight jacket and shoes. He lit a candle and lay down on the bed, letting his eyes adjust to the dim reading light. He flipped idly through the magazine, smiling at the ads. He found the marker at page 305. The article covered far more details than Malcolm had at the restaurant. As he read, his interest grew and he even began feeling a sense of involvement in the project, looking forward to being more than just a curiosity in town.

6

Saying goodbye to Gertrude was harder than Jeremy had expected. She'd been warm and kind to him, never showing the slightest curiosity about any strange mannerisms or unusual expressions he used. He was sorry to leave any safe harbor, and Gertrude had been one. She'd gotten up early to make breakfast, but Malcolm had cut off that idea.

"You say good-bye to Jeremy, but we've no time for breakfast here. We have to make the train."

"But it doesn't leave until 10:45," she protested.

"Gertrude, you know that every Saturday I've been taking breakfast at the Dennison for—how long now? Jeremy can eat with me as well, and we'll only be a block from the depot."

"I just didn't want to see this poor fellow poisoned at that Dennison, and on his first day at work as well. You're used to that food, if that's what they call it." She put her arms around Jeremy. "You know that the Doctor's going to miss you," she said, her voice lowered. "You've been great company for him, even though I think you mystify him at times. And I'll miss you, too. Come back and see us, and don't you get too close to that telescope thing. You can't tell what it will do," she called after him as they stepped out onto Main Street.

The weather was finally warming, and the spring day had brought out a parade of bicyclists, wagons and buggies streaming by, as well as an occasional horseman. They turned into Broad Street. "Don't listen to Gertrude about the Dennison. It's only half that bad, but it's also the regular Saturday meeting place." They hadn't gone a block before the doctor had greeted a dozen or more people. Malcolm had become talkative again, and Jeremy found himself gazing at the still-new sights. "I made

44

some time for us to have breakfast."

He started to describe the old hotel and its origins, stepping across a side street ahead of his companion. Jeremy glanced up to see the two wagons bearing down on them. With no time to call out, he dove, pitching Malcolm ahead and into the gutter, rolling over and pulling him along. The lethal wheels of the nearest wagon clattered by, inches from them.

Jeremy saw that the two wagons, still racing each other, had careened across Broad Street. Both were driven by boys no more than fourteen or fifteen. The driver of the nearest wagon looked back. At first he seemed about to rein up his horse. Then, thinking again, he put his head down and cracked the horse, following his friend who was disappearing around the corner.

The doctor had been thrown to the ground and had the wind knocked out of him. With his hands under him, Jeremy raised and lowered him several times, letting his breath come back. "Are you all right?" he asked. As the doctor's wind returned, he nodded, pushing Jeremy away as he stood up.

"Damn little rascals!" Malcolm exploded. "And to think I probably delivered them, too."

Jeremy sat his companion back down on the curbside. "Thank you, my friend," the doctor gripped his hand. "You saved my life. If I don't learn to talk less and pay more attention to traffic, I may never live to see next year."

"Listen, old boy," Jeremy responded with his arm around the doctor. He'd fallen fallen back into the slang he had been trying to shake. "With all you've done for me, I haven't begun to square accounts. Let's get you back to your office. You've taken a bad spill."

Malcolm stood up unsteadily and began to slap his hat against his pants. "I'm dusty as a bin, but it's important that you arrive out there today." With that, he set off briskly once more down Broad Street, leaving his younger companion to catch up.

As Malcolm climbed the wooden steps of the old hotel, Jeremy stopped to look up. It was three stories high and surrounded by a circular porch. Even given the small town hotel standards of 1895, it barely qualified as second-rate. Clearly, the Dennison had seen better days. The arm chairs on the porch were already filled by seniors enjoying the sunny day.

They called to Malcolm as he reached the top of the stairs. He greeted them, damning the young scamps who had nothing better to do than to go racing their wagons through the center of town.

He introduced Jeremy to the two nearest. "Where is Sam Wright?" he asked, as he reached to open the hotel's front door.

"Down at the pier again, Doc," the nearest one said. "We haven't seen much of Sam since he brought in that three-pounder."

"A three pound small mouth. That could change a man's habits, Jeremy," he said, as he walked inside. "But it won't help his rheumatism. I wager Sam will be in my office next week, half bent over."

The interior of the hotel was dark, coming in from the sunlight, and Jeremy pitched forward as his foot caught on the frayed carpet. "Watch your step," Malcolm cautioned too late. They entered the dining room. "This place is still a lively junction for all the townsfolk on Saturday morning. But the old order is passing," he led them to a table. "I can see it happening. This old inn will be lucky if it's still open ten years from now except as some sort of seedy rooming house."

He exchanged greetings with the other diners as he looked around. "See him," he pointed to an older, heavily jowled man scraping up gravy with a large biscuit. "That's Lou Paxton, the last postmaster. I guess we shouldn't let him hear us talking about the Observatory. All that fulsome praise for the project you read about in *Harper's* isn't for everybody around here."

"Why not?" Jeremy asked, his attention suddenly caught by the direct smile of a cute young waitress in a red-checked dress as she filled their coffee cups. He returned her smile as she leaned over more than she needed, placing a basket of rolls in front of them. He was pleasantly surprised. She had brought out the first sensual reaction he'd had since the accident. Maybe, he thought, he was recovering after all, albeit in some crazy, delusional time frame. He watched her cross the dining room and disappear into the kitchen.

Malcolm scooped preserves onto a roll. He continued talking. As he did he lapsed into the melodic burr he had when he was enthused about a subject. "As ye know, we're in an age of wonder: anesthetics, medicines, whatever," he gestured for emphasis. "Things that would have boggled the mind only thirty or forty years ago. Why, just look at the boys that were lost in the Civil War from injuries that we could easily heal today.

But if you were to ask most of the people around here, they would have an anti-" he paused, "anti-technical attitude, so you can see how many of them feel about the Observatory. There was even a rumor of how the sunlight coming in the telescope could start the trees on fire."

The waitress had returned to fill their coffee cups, brushing her hip against Jeremy as she turned. "In all cities, even Chicago or your own Indianapolis, there's a backwards element, but it's strongest in small towns like this one. Oh, they want doctors and such true enough, only they don't want their medicines or anything too fancy.

"And another thing, never forget the Observatory is going into Williams Bay. The boys in town here," and he looked around the dining room, "are just a little afraid of Lake Geneva town being eclipsed by its little brother down the lake. They read in the papers about noted professors coming to the Observatory to join the staff, and all of the articles are datelined from Williams Bay.

"Do you know, there's even talk that the University of Chicago may move its whole science school here. I'm telling you, in a few more years it could even change its name, and move up here. Can you imagine how the world famous University of Williams Bay would sound?"

"It does have a certain unlikely ring," Jeremy answered. Just then a tall, angular man approached their table. He was along in years but wore a crinkly smile on his well-lined face. He brushed his thinning hair across his forehead, making the most of it.

"You know, Malcolm," he said, bracing his hand on their table as he leaned forward. "I'm getting too old to do much more than just watch the scene as it goes by, but I've been noticing how our favorite little waitress, Leslie, has been 'surveying' your friend here. Sir, if you have any magic potion, I wish you'd spread some of it my way. I'd pay dearly to get a look, just one, like you've been getting from Leslie since you arrived."

"You see, Jeremy," Malcolm said with a chuckle. "I was just about to say what a high-toned judiciary we have in this town and look what happens. I'd like you to meet Justice Seaver, our town judge." Jeremy stood up and shook the judge's hand. Judge Seaver had an easy self-effacing manner and returned the handshake.

"Thank you for the compliment, your honor. I hadn't noticed her," he said.

"Your friend lies, too. I'd almost be willing to wager he's a lawyer,

Malcolm."

"You're close, Judge," the doctor answered. "Actually, I'm taking him to the Observatory this morning. He's starting work out there—for Paul Lockerby. Paul's doing the electrical work and Jeremy here will be his bookkeeper and assistant."

"Paul Lockerby...Paul Lockerby," the judge repeated. "Oh, of course, the builder I met last summer. With his daughter. Was her name Louise?" he asked. "Wasn't she the one involved with Debs? I never could understand how a charming thing like that could be...ah, oh well. You know, it's a coincidence, you're mentioning Paul Lockerby—these old eyes aren't what they used to be—nor is much else of mine, but I could have sworn I saw her walking down Broad Street, right past this very hotel a week or so ago."

Malcolm paused for a moment. "I doubt that, Judge. Lora's her name and...her father wrote me that she was going on a trip out east."

"Well, Jeremy, it's been a pleasure meeting you. It looks like Williams Bay's gain shall be little Leslie's loss." The sound of a shrill train whistle, pulling for a distant crossing interrupted. Malcolm tossed some coins on the table as they started away.

"You'd best watch that constable out there in Williams Bay." Judge Seaver called after them. "Lowery is his name. He seems to have a bone to pick with Observatory workers." He gave them a wave as they left the dining room.

48

7

They arrived at the depot just as the ten forty-five was pulling in. The train looked surprisingly familiar. The North Western had kept vintage rolling stock like this train on its branch lines longer than most railroads and as a child he had actually ridden on a train similar to the one that was squealing to a halt.

"How long do we have, Luther?" Malcolm called out as he stepped up to the ticket window. The agent was meticulously making out reports and putting things in order. A conductor had gotten off and was standing next to the window, chatting with Luther.

"I guess our train won't leave without you, Clyde."

"Doctor, you're the very man I want to see." The conductor brightened at seeing Malcolm. "They," he pointed toward the train, "got me picking up bags and loading 'em. Doc, you've *got* to give me a letter or I'm going to throw this back out again. Not one single porter on this whole damn branch, unless it's for a charter. And you know the luggage all these…" he hesitated, studying Jeremy, deciding he was safe. "…all these rich society folk are bringing up here."

"Stop at the office, Clyde, and I'll give you that note, for all the good it will do." Malcolm bought their tickets, a round trip to Williams Bay for himself and a single fare for Jeremy.

"I read in the 'People's' column in the *Herald* where you're selling steam yachts now, Luther. Are you really recording *all* the fares you take in here?" Malcolm allowed a chuckle at his joke as he moved away from the window.

"Not me at all, Doctor," Luther called through the barred window. "That's a summer resident who asked me to place the ad. He thought the locals would take advantage of him."

"See how you're helping to keep up those myths about us." Jeremy and Malcolm stepped aboard the waiting coach and settled down in facing caneback seats as the ten forty-five lurched away from the depot and chugged slowly out into the countryside.

The branch line roadbed was every bit as rough as Jeremy remembered, and the train's wheels pitched and squealed against the rails as it entered a long curve. In moments they were running along the shore of nearby Lake Como, a small, shallow body of water all but undiscovered. Outside, the greening branches of the trees brushed against the side of the car. Someone would soon have to be out trimming, even on this backwater, six mile stretch.

Malcolm had settled into reading his paper and Jeremy's thoughts roamed. For the past few days, he had been forcing himself to take things slowly. Now, thanks to the doctor, his health was coming back and he would at least be earning some money. He hoped the job would leave him some time to sort things out.

He had read up on all the magazines and local papers at the office, and he had dropped over to the little town library, poring over every copy of the *Chicago Tribune*. His disorientation was entirely one of time, not place. He reasoned he'd have a better chance of getting back—or waking up from his nightmare if he stayed put.

A sudden, fleeting vision of his children brought the gnawing feeling back into the pit of his stomach. He wondered momentarily if he wasn't really lost in time at all but just some very ordinary Joe from 1895—ordinary except for that mental derangement causing him to want to project himself into the future. A shiver coursed through him as he pictured the red brick insane asylum he had seen back in Lake Geneva.

He guessed that if a diagnosis of mental illness were made, he might very well wind up in a place like that for the rest of his life. No, he vowed, he'd find a way out somehow, find some way back. To reassure himself, he took out his wallet, making sure Malcolm couldn't see. He riffled through his credit cards and then slowed to study the photos of Amy and Danny for several minutes. He nonchalantly shrugged, stood up and walked down the aisle to the rear of the coach.

The vestibule was open and he watched the landscape roll by, listening as he did to the clatter from the rails. No one was paying any attention to him, including Malcolm who was still lost in his paper. He stepped down to the bottom rung of the stairway and tensed his muscles.

This train isn't moving more than ten miles an hour. I can jump down to the trackside—make my escape. Yes, to where? With a final glance down, he frowned and climbed the stairs, returning to his seat.

Malcolm had in fact been discreetly but very carefully studying his patient. He read the anxiety on Jeremy's face. He saw him go through his chunky, curious billfold, although he couldn't see, without being obvious, what occupied his attention. As the train bumped along, he reviewed their conversations, particularly the early ones. Jeremy's alien manner of speaking was intriguing, along with his worldly knowledge that continued to surface. Malcolm noted, too, that from time to time a genuine anguish crossed Jeremy's features, much as he tried to conceal it.

Malcolm was very touched at how hard Jeremy kept trying to overcome his strange speech pattern. He had succeeded for the most part as well, except for random expressions that escaped his lips before he could catch himself. Over the years the doctor had encountered many foreigners, and he prided himself on being able to sort out their origins. Indeed, he was only second generation in the country himself and his Scottish burr easily gave that away. He could not, however, place his guest's speech.

When Jeremy had gotten up and gone to the rear, Malcolm felt for a moment that he ought to follow. No, he decided, Jeremy would have to work things out for himself. He had developed a real fondness for this stranger who had been brought to his home just before Lora Lockerby's visit. He doubted very much the young man came from Indianapolis.

Malcolm wished that he was more familiar with amnesia and its effects. Should he contact a colleague, perhaps Doctor Curtis in Racine? And what about this morning? Hadn't Jeremy saved him from being run down by that wagon, and at great risk to himself? Jeremy's awareness, his reactions, were almost cat-quick. Judge Seaver, Malcolm was sure, had noticed *something* about him as well.

The train turned sharply to the left and then to the right, slowing as it approached the end of the line. The locomotive's whistle blew and Malcolm heard the engine hiss as they pulled into the depot. He put his paper down and tapped Jeremy lightly on the knee. "Time to see that Observatory."

As he alighted from the train, Jeremy glanced up and down the platform. It was virtually the same as he remembered from his childhood. Down the track freight cars were being unloaded alongside a shed. His eyes were drawn to the shore road that led up the hill and out of town— the same hill where just over a week ago he had thrown the chain on his bicycle.

Malcolm hailed a buggy. On the way up the hill, Jeremy was startled to see the garage at which he had repaired his bike chain. The building was almost unchanged except for the level of activity. Where last week's garage had been a sleepy, small town gasoline alley, this version was a bustling blacksmith's shop, resounding with loud laughter and the clang of metal.

"Are you sightseeing at the Observatory?" Their driver had glanced back at his passengers as they crested the hill. His eyes took in Jeremy's suitcase.

"My friend is going to be working there, so you'll be seeing him regularly, I'd guess." The driver was a heavy, middle-aged man with a weather-beaten face. By way of delayed introduction, he tipped his hat. Jeremy nodded in return, refraining from shaking hands. People, at least of the driver's social rank, he had noticed, did not shake hands.

"Name's Ross Hatcher. I live here in town now. Used to farm, but with all this work goin' on out at the Observatory and what with more summer folks arrivin' every year, it's better liveryin'. When I think how hard I worked out there..." Ross pointed toward some distant, unseen farm. "Anyways, you have a place to stay? Things're tight in this little town."

"Not yet. I haven't really hired on yet. You have any place in mind?"

Ross thought for a minute, then took another look at Jeremy. "There's a place ahead, but it's a pigsty. Then there's the dormitory, but I don't think you'd...like it."

Was Ross about to say that the dormitory would be too rough for me? Jeremy wondered.

"Wait a minute. I do know of a room down on Congress Street. Lady who owns it is a bit of a snoop, at least that's what I hear, but she keeps the place clean and she's one fine cook."

Malcolm cut in. "I have to go back on the five forty-five. Why don't you pick us up an hour before. We'll talk about her place then." Ross had drawn up into what would one day be the circular drive for the

Observatory.

Ross left the two off in front of the construction site. The excavation machines, huge steam powered devices with power shovels were still present even though all the foundations had been laid. Jeremy looked around at the machines and workmen, beginning to feel more at home as he listened to their shouts and the noise of the machines.

The two walked around to a side of the construction and crossed an open area. Jeremy realized it was where the golf course would one day be. "This is just a small part of the grounds. It's to be landscaped, probably for a commons," Malcolm explained.

"How about a golf course?" Jeremy couldn't resist asking.

"I suppose anything's possible, but a golf course seems incompatible with that scientific marvel over there." Malcolm pulled from his pocket the artist's drawing of the completed Observatory he had snipped from the *Herald.* He was studying the drawing, trying to place where they were in relation to it. "I don't know where you came up with the idea for a golf course, but you might just have something. There *is* to be a golf club on Lake Geneva starting up next year and with my Scottish ancestry, maybe I should give the game a try."

Malcolm's companion had started ahead of him down the path. "Isn't it about time I met my boss?" He called back as the doctor hurried to catch up, wondering how Jeremy seemed to know his direction. He followed, stepping over boards and bricks strewn about the ground. As they neared the half-completed power house, a man emerged from a construction shanty. He carried blueprints and had stopped to talk with a tall workman in denim overalls.

Jeremy felt Malcolm's unnecessary nudge. "That's Paul." The man was in his mid-fifties, stocky and broad shouldered with white hair and a ruddy, lined face. Paul Lockerby wasn't handsome, but he was friendly looking and seemed to exude confidence. Jeremy could easily picture him charging over and pulling his worker off the power line as Malcolm had described.

When Paul caught sight of the doctor, he strode over, offering his hand, then gave Jeremy's hand a firm grasp while Malcolm provided an introduction, which included a brief reference to Jeremy's bike accident and memory trouble. He explained to Paul how his friend and patient had saved him from the wheels of the delivery wagon only hours before.

"I've been waiting for you two to arrive. God only knows I could use your friend if he's anything like you describe." Paul walked them down the incline to the power house site.

"They're finally starting to give us some cooperation." He indicated the bricklayers working on the main building. Jeremy saw that the men had started to slow down in preparation for stopping work on Saturday afternoon.

"I've been pointing out that they aren't going to get very far on any Observatory if they don't have a generator or any place for it. So, our power station ought to be finished in a few weeks unless they stop construction again. And I'll tell you, Mal, I'm not about to have that happen."

Jeremy recalled from the *Harper's* article that a very large direct current generator would be installed in the power station and provide electricity for the entire Observatory and all machinery. "We'll be working out of here most of the summer," Paul said as he led them over to a small shanty nearby.

Jeremy noticed he had said "we" as though he were already hired. He instinctively liked Paul. The engineer was direct, exactly as Malcolm had described him.

He took them on a quick tour of the spartan office. There were two or three chairs, a few wooden work tables and electrical equipment lying on one of the work benches. In a corner there was also a small, working lathe.

"Over here," Paul called, showing Jeremy a pair of ledgers that were on a rolltop desk. "Can you keep books?" Jeremy sat down on the stool and opened the first. They were a mess, just as Malcolm had predicted. He turned a couple of pages at random, studying Paul's informal, disorganized entries. He decided to take a bold tack.

"I can straighten these out," he said, wagering that enough of his college accounting would come back.

"Well, the sooner the better. I've never kept my own books before and I've had to develop my own system, but you can see that I'm no bookkeeper."

Right you are, Jeremy said to himself. Just then the door swung open and two workmen came in carrying a large piece of machinery between them. "One of the transformer cores arrived, boss."

"Well, praise be. We've waited long enough. Set it down easy there on the workbench." He turned to Jeremy and grinned. "It arrived on your very train. Maybe that's a lucky omen." As Paul made introductions, Jeremy could tell the two workmen were sizing him up.

A few minutes later the three left the building and walked to the now-deserted construction site. Paul explained that there would be five to ten workmen at any given time at the power station. "That's in addition to you and me. You'll keep the books, including the payroll. Don't slip on that, my boy, whatever you do, or you'll have five or ten husky fellows ready to pitch you in the lake." Jeremy's time would be split between the work at the power station and the freight shed down at the depot. "You'll be in charge of checking our supplies. They're arriving every day now. You'll be the one to make sure we're not being shorted. And you have to be sure as well that what we've ordered arrives out here on time. Remember, I pay these men whether they have supplies to work with or not.

"You'll like the two fellows who'll work for you down at the freight shed. They're good boys—good workmen, both of them, but you'll have to do their thinking for them," he tapped his head. "And give them detailed directions for everything you ask them to do."

Ross Hatcher had pulled his wagon into the circular drive and was waiting. "Malcolm, hold that cab. My new assistant and I'll join you shortly." He took a watch from his pocket. "As usual, you're way ahead of time. I'm going to Chicago on your train, so you'll have to put up with me as far as Lake Geneva."

"Jeremy, I need to put put my trust in you and put you to work right away. I told you about some of the delays we've been having." Jeremy nodded. "I have to leave today for Cleveland. I'm off to see Warner and Swasey, the general contractors. I've got to make them see how vital it is to keep us even or a bit ahead of the overall work. I won't be back until Thursday or Friday. If I show you around here and at the depot, can I rely on you?"

"You can, Paul." Jeremy was grateful for the show of faith.

When they returned to the driveway, they boarded the waiting wagon. Jeremy fell silent while Paul and Malcolm brought each other up to date on their lives.

"How's that daughter of yours?" Malcolm asked.

"Oh, Lora's out in New York. She's gone out there with a friend from the World's Fair. You know, Mal, that whole strike thing last summer out at Pullman—then the trial afterward—I think Lora wore herself out. I'm hoping she'll be able to spend some time out here this summer."

Jeremy was watching the cottages as they rode, but he was listening closely. The two talked for a few minutes more about the strike at Pullman. Paul suddenly tapped Jeremy on the shoulder. "Listen, I didn't mean to exclude you from our conversation. I don't know if you've ever heard of Clarence Darrow?"

"Of course," Jeremy answered before realizing he had responded much too quickly for someone with amnesia. He couldn't be sure if Malcolm noticed or not. "I can't remember details, but I know I've heard the name. Isn't he a lawyer?"

"Right you are," Paul answered. "My daughter Lora has been working for him this past year. She's really an art teacher by profession and a damn good one," he added with obvious pride. "Oh, hell! I'll tell you about that story some other time.

"She's been working in Darrow's office ever since the strike." He turned back to the doctor. "And Mal, you wouldn't believe what hours she's put in for him. Anyway, I'm glad she's taken some time off to visit out east, and maybe think about her future—whether she'll stay with Darrow or go back teaching."

Ross circled the buggy at the depot. "I can wait here and take you over to Mrs. Ingalls' boarding house." Jeremy hesitated a moment, then nodded, frowning as he pictured the worthless money in his wallet.

Paul showed them to the freight shed and introduced Jeremy to Deke and Bill, leaving no doubt that Jeremy had been put in charge. "There's damn little capacity, either here or at the power station," Paul said. "It'll be up to you what you keep here and what you send up."

"I can handle it, Paul."

"I have to say I like your confidence. You're going to learn the job quickly."

The three men walked back alongside the tracks, reaching the platform just as the train pulled in. Paul reached into his pocket and pulled out a small pouch. "You'll need money for your room and some extra clothes. Here's a little advance." He'd turned and boarded the train before he could be thanked.

"You know to contact me if you have any problems." Malcolm had paused at the steps to the coach. "You'll be fine. I think we both did well today." He gave his shoulder a pat.

"All aboard," the conductor bellowed. The doctor entered the coach and Jeremy kept sight of the train until it rounded a curve and left his sight. The knot in his stomach tightened.

"Hey." He turned at the sound of Ross's voice. "Let's get you over to that room before someone else grabs it."

8

Jeremy quickly settled in at Mrs. Ingalls'. She had proven a tough bargainer. In fact, there had not *been* any bargaining. Her price was $3.00 a week for the furnished room, including breakfast and dinner, except Sundays. She looked to Jeremy to be in her early fifties, possibly younger, but her plumpness made it impossible to fix her age. At their first meeting she spoke on and on, telling him about the house, her late husband, and the rules: no hard liquor in the rooms and *no* women. And she shared a common trait with the other working class people of the era; her vocabulary was pitifully weak. Jeremy couldn't decide if it was the isolation of their lives, poor schooling or both. Her conversation was nothing but a repetition of all her previous statements. Jeremy learned he would be sharing the house with her son as well as another roomer, Ben Hazelwood, who worked at the Jewell boat yard in town.

Her son Earl was a big husky boy and "as gentle as a lamb," she had described him, but—she placed her pudgy hand to her head—indicating he was a little "teched." Earl worked as a stock boy in the grocery story. It was her description of Ben Hazelwood, however, that set off an alarm bell in Jeremy's brain. He was told *exactly* when Ben left, when he returned, that he drank some in town at "Charley's" but never at the house. She told him about Ben's mail. "He gets letters from St. Louis." *So*, thought Jeremy, *she's gone through Ben's belongings.*

He paid her for a week in advance and settled into his spartan room. It was small, with a bed, dresser and a chair in the corner. A single window overlooked Congress Street. Sitting down in the chair, he took out the wallet and once again looked at the pictures of Danny and Amy. His credit cards: American Express, Visa, Texaco and Shell Oil, as well as a number of equally useless business cards were still in place. He shuffled slowly through the cards and pictures again, looking at each one as though it were an old friend. Standing, he walked over to the far wall where Mrs. Ingalls had hung a print with a scene of the lakefront on the wall.

The frame would be too small to put anything behind. He looked in the closet. The wallet couldn't be left in any of his clothes, either. That would be the first place she'd look and the shelf in the closet was no better. Maybe he would just have to leave the wallet out at work, taking his chances that no one would find it.

On a hunch, he knelt on the floor and looked up. Sure enough, the mattress was sitting on wooden slats that lay on a frame. There would be enough room for the billfold between one of the slats and the mattress. And just to make sure he could tell if it was tampered with, he carefully aligned it with the slat.

Two days later, again sitting on the bed, he realized beyond any doubt someone *had* gotten into the wallet. The currency was there, but it had been rearranged. He checked through his driver's license, credit cards and business calling cards, his anger building. His Visa card was gone, and he couldn't be sure if any business cards were missing. At last he opened the compartment that held his children's photos. There was absolutely no mistaking that the photos had been taken out. A photo of Amy on her bike had been reinserted upside-down.

Mrs. Ingalls now possessed more information about him, much more, than he'd dared tell Malcolm. Jeremy's sense of entrapment rushed back. After his feelings had simmered down, he made up his mind. Putting everything back into his wallet, shoving it into his pocket, he stood up, checking himself in the mirror. His mustache was fairly well grown out and his borrowed clothes lent him an 1890's appearance. The reflection smiled back.

He went out to the living room to wait for dinner. Mrs. Ingalls was clattering about in the kitchen cooking supper. He picked up a copy of the *Herald*, only half reading it as Ben Hazelwood came in. This was the busy season at the boat yard, readying and launching the yachts. With no time for breakfast, he and Ben had previously only passed in the hallway, exchanging quick greetings as Ben ran off to work, rolls stuffed into his pocket and his face drawn. He slumped in the davenport opposite Jeremy. His face was fatigued and he looked much older than his thirty years (Mrs. Ingalls had supplied *that* fact as well).

"Tough day?"

Ben nodded, seeming too tired for words. "Sorry to be such bad company," he shook his head, launching into a narrative of his trying to get all of the excursion boats launched by Memorial Day. "But how are things at the Observatory?" he asked at last.

"Oh, real quiet, compared to your boat yard," Jeremy answered. Just then, Mrs. Ingalls entered, announcing supper was ready. Jeremy studied her face for any telltale traces that she'd been snooping. The problem, he realized, was that she *always* looked as though she had been snooping.

At the table, Jeremy greeted Earl, who had been quietly waiting in the dining room. He looked up and smiled as his mother flounced about, setting out the dinner. She glanced at the tired men, scolded her son to sit straight, asked Jeremy about the construction and Ben about the boat yard, all without missing a bite. "I been hearin' at the store about all the delays at the Observatory. You people still havin' trouble hittin' water?" Before he could answer, she'd gotten up, started clearing the dishes off the table and had disappeared into the kitchen.

Jeremy looked over at Earl, quietly finishing his dinner. He was shy and awkward and Jeremy decided some small talk might bring him out. "What's new at the store?" Earl shrugged, then surprised him with his response.

"Have you ever played golf, Jeremy?" Ben looked up, first at Earl and then at Jeremy. Feeling this might have something to do with the eavesdropping, he answered. "I've never really played the game," he said, measuring his response, "but I *have* swung some clubs. It seems like a lot of work and a lot of walking. How do you feel about it?"

Earl perked up at being talked to. "Oh, well, uh, it's fine I guess, but not for me," he mumbled in his bashfulness.

"Why did you ask me, Earl?" Jeremy pursued. "Do I look like a golfer?"

"No, but I thought you might have heard something . At work they say they're fixin' to put in a golf course next to the Observatory after they're done buildin' it." Jeremy was touched. Like himself, Earl was only trying to make conversation, a chore which couldn't have come easily to him. Mrs. Ingalls reappeared bearing a huge apple pie. One thing he had to say for the woman, she could bake up a storm. Earl was sent out to bring in a pot of coffee.

Jeremy sat back in his chair, relaxing and inhaling the aroma of the pie mixed with the smell of fresh-brewed coffee. He began reflecting on how late 20th century man was denied the everyday smells his ancestors took for granted.

"You look like you're deep in thought, Jeremy."

"Just thinking about your pie," he said. As she passed out pieces, the talk shifted back to golf, Ben saying that he'd heard the yacht owners talking about golf and he figured it had to be a rich man's game.

"What do you know about photography?" Mrs. Ingalls asked, changing the subject, directing her question to Jeremy.

"Really not a lot," he answered evenly," but I worked in an office in Indianapiolis that was next to a photographic studio." This conversation, he realized, was related to the discovery of his wallet, and he didn't—just yet—want to alarm her.

"I wanted to show you something," she said, hauling her bulk over to the sideboard. She opened a drawer and rummaged around, finally handing Jeremy two post cards, watching closely as he took them. "Do you know these scenes?" There was the slightest rise in her voice.

"*Ma*, you're showing them old post cards of the Fair *again?*"

In fact, Jeremy had seen similar post cards. They showed two scenes of the Columbian Exposition. The first was a shot of the Midway. People were crowded together, and in the background was the huge Ferris Wheel. The other featured the "Administration Building" with the "Columbian Fountain" in front. Both photographs were crudely colored, likely by a commercial sketcher. Jeremy guessed the photos, after being painted, had been put through some kind of a lithography process and copied by the thousands. He passed the cards to Ben.

"I never got to the Fair myself. Did you?"

"Earl did," responded Mrs. Ingalls. "His aunt took him while I stayed out here. I was so proud he was able to send me those cards." Jeremy looked over, noticing the childish scrawl on the backside of the card that Ben was examining.

"Did you know that they made such pictures in color like this?"

"Another of the wonders of our century of progress, Mrs. Ingalls," said

Jeremy mildly, giving her an opening.

"Well, do you think these can be improved upon?" she asked, as she took back the post cards, tapping them on the table, studying Jeremy.

"Why, I wouldn't be surprised, not at all. Just look where photography has come in the last thirty years," he said, reaching down to feel his wallet. He wondered what she had thought, seeing Amy in her red-striped jogging suit or Danny in his purple Viking football jersey.

Jeremy folded his napkin and glanced at the hall clock. "Oh, it's seven-thirty. I forgot I have to check on some deliveries down at the freight house. I won't sleep easy until I've tended to things tonight. Excuse me," he said, getting up.

"It's good you're looking after things," Mrs. Ingalls said. "Constable Lowery told me when I saw him…in town the other day…that there are thieves and brigands about, like as not attracted by the Observatory."

Once outside, he walked briskly along the shore toward the depot and freight house. *So Mrs. Ingalls knows the constable. I might have guessed.* He crossed the now-deserted tracks of the small rail yard, deciding to double back to the Observatory. He would have enough light by the full moon to see or, he realized, be seen. He put up the collar of his jacket against the night chill.

Once at the Observatory grounds, he circled the construction site, finally satisfying himself that he was the only one still on the grounds. It was a continuing surprise to him, but in 1895 construction projects were left unattended. The machinery lay silent—with no guard dogs or security on the site.

He selected a spade from several that were lying near the power house, and hoisting it on his shoulder, walked over to the makeshift offices and unlocked the door. Inside, he lit the hurricane lamp on the table and almost immediately found an empty mason jar. After learning his wallet had been tampered with, he knew he'd have to hide it but in some place where he could retrieve it if needed.

Certain control parts for the generators had arrived during the week. They were particularily delicate and had been carefully packed in tissue paper. "Now if that box and it's stuffing haven't been thrown out," he said aloud. He searched the shed. Sure enough, sitting near the door, ready to go out in the morning's trash was the box filled with the tissue paper. Jeremy carefully used some to line the glass jar. His wallet lay on his desk, and he opened it to the pictures of his children. After studying them closely for several moments, he sighed and returned them to the wallet.

Carefully placing the wallet in the jar, he pushed more paper on top of it. Then he put the jar into the box and locked the office behind him. Once outside, he picked up the spade and quickly walked to the south side of the building site, the quiet side away from the driveway.

The moonlight was filtered by occasional drifting clouds. Jeremy listened to the distant sounds of the men's easy laughter coming from the dormitory down the hill. He set the box down a few paces from the newly-planted saplings. There was little or no construction activity on the south side. The grass that must have been planted last year was already thick under his feet.

Jeremy was going to have to measure where he buried the box as exactly as possible so that he would be able to recover his things when he needed them, whenever or if ever that might be. The south stairway to the building had already been laid out and he walked to the steps, squinting back through the moonlight to sight the little sapling. As carefully as possible he stepped off the sixty paces to where the box sat. He backed up and paced it again. Fifty-nine. Maybe he had swerved in the moonlight, but his measurement would have to do.

The spade bit into the dirt. Quickly he scooped out a two and a half foot hole. Jeremy was starting to lower the box when a door to the dormitory banged closed. He froze at the sound of voices. The speakers were coming up the hill directly toward him. Holding the box, he was about to slip back toward the steps of the Observatory, aware that he likely could be seen in the moonlight.

The voices had stopped getting any closer, and he set down the box and knelt, wishing the sapling were larger. One of the workers was talking excitedly. "The hell you say! You mean to tell me you had *both* of those girls the same night? Elmer, I think you get to be a bigger liar every time you tell a story." Jeremy smiled. Their attention would not be on him. He leaned against the spade, listening. After a few minutes, their voices retreated down the hill until he heard the dormitory door close.

Jeremy picked up the box and lowered it into the the hole, shoveling the earth back on top and then stamping it down until he was finally convinced the digging would go unnoticed. With his shoulders slumped, he walked back toward the site of the power station where he dropped the spade and, without looking back, headed toward his rooming house. *Had he glanced back, he might possibly have seen a figure in the shadows that moved from behind a tree and walked over to where he had been digging.*

9

The westbound *Pennsylvania Limited* began to slow for the outskirts of Fort Wayne. The dining car steward moved off, having seated the young women for lunch. Enid Yandel stretched and covered a yawn as she opened the menu.

"Lora, only because you're such a good friend am I ever going to forgive you for insisting we take the coach out to New York and back. It's no wonder George Pullman got rich marketing sleeping cars."

"You've been a good sport about not filling Pullman's pockets." Lora reached across the table to give her friend's hand a grip. "I'll never be able to thank you enough for going out east with me. I hate to guess what this trip has done to your schedule.

"When I wrote you about Clarence and me—about needing to get away for awhile to think, I didn't dream you'd put everything aside and come up from Nashville."

"Darlin', your letter said you needed help," Enid drawled, "even if you couldn't bring yourself to say it. Didn't I answer you by sayin' that a trip out east, and a visit to old Karl would be good for you? And seein' as I introduced the two of you in the first place... I read somewhere, probably in some novel, that 'old lovers make the best friends.' Was that so wrong?"

Over the last couple of years, Lora had almost forgotten the startling directness with which artists like Enid—and Karl as well—spoke. "No, it wasn't wrong. Karl still knows me terribly well." A blush began to cross her face. "Thanks to your giving us yesterday afternoon alone, we were able to talk. I should say *I* talked. Karl mainly listened. I told him about Clarence.

"Karl's advice wasn't very different from Doctor MacDougal's, and that's something I'll have to keep in mind." Outside the train window, passengers and porters were scurrying about the Fort Wayne platform.

"I don't care what you say about Pullman and that old strike of yours," Enid said as they finished their meal. "I've put up with that awful day coach, the crying babies and especially that foul smell. What *is* it? sausage?— that's surrounded our seats for long enough. We are going to finish this trip in the parlor car with no argument from you, either. It'll be my treat so your conscience can stay clear."

In the parlor car, Lora took a seat at the writing desk, pondering the start of a note to Clarence. Enid settled into the plush easy chair alongside. "That's better," she said with an exaggerated sigh, lifting her feet onto the hassock.

"Have you run into that little red-haired girl from the Fair? You know, the slim, pretty one who modeled for Karl. She had the husband and children and looked like she was about sixteen. I think she lived out at Pullman."

"Jeanette Reilley," Lora supplied the name. "We keep in touch by mail. I wouldn't go near Pullman myself. She and her family still live there. I can tell from her letters that things are hard for them. Her Tim lost his job when he took part in the strike. He had to all but crawl back to management and turn in his union card to get re-hired at half wages." It had been easy-going Jeanette, along with Karl and his probing observations about the "model town," Lora knew, that had sent her back to school in the fall of 1892 a changed person. *Someday, George Pullman ,* her lips tightened, *you'll get justice.*

Enid's eyes had closed. On her own note pad, Lora had absently drawn the giant Ferris Wheel from the World's Fair. She let her mind drift... to early June of 1892 and first meeting Enid.

Pullman School had closed for the summer and Lora had gone to visit her father at his Woodlawn Avenue home. Her old friend Judy from Art Institute classes had looked up Lora. Judy had been hired as one of Mrs. Potter Palmer's secretaries for the Women's Building project at the Columbian Exposition, or simply the Fair, as everyone chose to call it. Judy had insisted that Lora, with her art credentials, should try for a summer job at the exciting fairgrounds.

Lora, with sketches in hand, had been introduced by Judy to Enid Yandel. Enid was the twenty-two year old sculptor who was chosen to provide the caryatids for "Women's." Enid's studio was placed in a partitioned-off corner of the skeletal building. Her account of an artist's life, delivered in her southern drawl as she worked high up on a scaffold, had fascinated Lora.

"The door. Would you get it, honey?" Enid called down from her perch. Lora, at first startled, walked to the door. She pulled back the latch to find herself looking into a pair of dark eyes. The man at the door wore a checked shirt—and was strikingly handsome.

"Can I come in, ma'am?"

"Certainly," she said, letting him pass as she closed the door.

"How is my favorite sculptor today?" He directed the question to Enid.

With her Waterford background, Lora knew the accent as German. But his sounded different, nothing like the heavy strains from her Wisconsin hometown.

Enid set down her chisel and introduced Lora to Karl Bitter. "Karl," she winked, "is Vienna's very own gift to the World's Columbian Exposition." And Enid provided him with Lora's background, shamelessly puffing her resume while Karl examined the figure she was working on. He rubbed his hand across it, appraising some detail, seeming not to be listening, but a minute later he surprised Lora, asking questions about her work. He sat on one of the scaffold steps, idly working some clay with his fingers, his eyes on her as he spoke.

Karl was in charge of the decorations for the Administration Building. "Administration," Enid explained, would become the architectural centerpiece of the whole Fair.

The *Limited* slowed to a crawl and then to a stop. Lora had been half-dozing with her recollections and she shifted forward in her chair as the brakes were applied.

"Nothing to worry about, ladies and gentlemen," the conductor put his head in the door to the parlor car. "Just a local freight ahead. We'll be going slow for a little while until he pulls into the yard a few miles down the road." The smiling Negro attendant took that as his cue to begin serving his patrons coffee. Lora took some, stirring in sugar as the train restarted. Her thoughts went back to meeting Karl.

Thanks to Enid, Lora had been offered a job by Karl. His own preparations for the sculpture that would decorate "Administration" were running behind. Karl had put his new assistant right to work sketching and refining his earlier renderings of "Fire Uncontrolled." He had confided to her how dissatisfied he was with "Uncontrolled," the counterpoint to the serene "Fire Controlled" piece. The two works would be placed opposite each other on the main portico of the Administration Building. The speeches and receptions would take place right there.

During that first week, Karl left Lora in her own alcove of the studio to work alone while he finished sculpting the clay model of "Controlled." Over work breaks, Lora became friendly with Jeanette Reilley, the child-like model Karl was using for the figure. Jeanette, Lora learned, was a neighbor of hers from Pullman.

With the completion of "Controlled," Karl turned his attention to Lora's work. She spread out her sketches for him, growing nervous as he slowly thumbed through them. Lora watched as he studied without comment her progressively more spirited renderings of the primitive female figure. The girl was shown striving against a hostile nature that threatened her, the "uncontrolled" flames licking at her feet. Lora had let the girl's body posture and facial expression suggest that she could control the forces of nature. The ultimate outcome, however, was in doubt—left to each viewer's imagination.

"So much, I see, for my allegorical figure," Karl said at last. His own figure had been a contemporary male worker symbolically trying to turn fire to man's advantage. After two days of sketching, trying to reconcile her ideas with his, Lora against her better judgment had jettisoned Karl's idea, deciding to employ instead a cave girl, boldly fighting back against nature.

"Mr. Bitter," she started, "it's only a rough idea, really a refinement of your concept. Perhaps…"

"Lora. I didn't say I didn't like it. As a matter of fact, *this* ," he held up her sketch, "is exactly what we're going to go with."

Two days later, Helga, Karl's statuesque professional model appeared at the studio, ready to model for "Fire Uncontrolled." She had worked with Karl on an earlier classical piece for the opposite side of the building.

Lora shifted in her chair at the parlor car's writing desk, smiling as she pictured Helga's dismay at being shown the non-glamorous final sketch of Lora's very rustic, very naked cave girl she would portray.

Helga quickly guessed the role that Karl's new young assistant had played in the changes. "Hmmph *I* think the sculptor is letting the *madchen* create his works for him. A helper who looks so much like her own cave girl too, ya? The same cave girl who cannot remember to hold up her clothes."

Lora had to respond. "This girl lives in a wilderness, before any civilization, Helga. Clothes are meant not to be important to her. As far as creating anything, I work for Mr. Bitter. I'm happy I was able to give him an idea or two for 'Uncontrolled,' nothing more. If you give this work a chance, you'll see that this girl is strong, a worthy person, and a woman you can portray with pride."

"Helga, it's plain you're not happy," Karl had spoken for the first time in several minutes.

"Of course I'm not happy with *this*." Her voice had risen. "I will not be part of such a travesty." Helga left the stand and disappeared behind the screen. When she reappeared dressed, Karl handed her some folded bills. Over her protests, he pressed them upon her.

She turned at the door. "You told me only last month how important this panel was, being at the very front. 'It will be,' you said, 'the first look at our Fair for most.'

"Something—or someone—has suddenly caused a change in your work, Herr Bitter. You ought to recover your senses before it is too late."

The studio was quiet with Helga's departure. With the model gone, Lora sighed and took a seat alongside Karl. "I'm sorry if I caused her walkout. I never meant…"

"Stop. What we have here—it is more important than one model. She wouldn't have been right."

"I do have some difficulty seeing Helga living in a cave, starting a fire." Lora was uplifted by Karl's laugh. He seemed to her to be curiously unfazed by Helga's leave-taking, and he leaned back, rolling up a sketch and rapping it on the stand. "I'll put out a call for a model. We'll lose a few days while we find a girl. It will be hard securing one right now. But there's work enough to keep us busy." He fell quiet.

"Yes, I could." Lora suddenly answered the unasked question.

"You could indeed. You *are* 'Fire Uncontrolled.' " From somewhere outside on the grounds, a foreman's whistle broke the stillness.

"Just suppose, well…suppose someone were to walk in on us?"

"That door will stay locked whenever you're up on the model stand."

Lora picked up her final sketch. "Do you really believe I'll personify the girl far better than Helga would have?" Karl nodded somberly. "Then I ought to get ready to become that ancestor of ours."

"Not before I can say 'thank you.' " He took her hand in his.

Lora gazed out the parlor car's window at the switching activity in the train yard they were passing. Once past the yard, the *Limited* resumed its pace. She sipped at her coffee. *Was it my modeling as the "Fire" girl and the easy-going, sensual atmosphere that pervaded the Fair's construction season, or was it really all just Karl and I and our intense feelings for each other that let us slip so naturally into becoming lovers,* she wondered again.

The sculpting of the clay figure began and proceeded ahead over the next few days. Even with all the new hurts and muscle cramps she had gotten from posing for long hours, Lora felt she was living out a glorious dream. At night, with work finished, they would retire to one of the near-by cafes. Radiant despite her stiffness, Lora learned to take in good-natured stride the mild teasing she and Karl received from their fellow Exposition artists. All too fast, she remembered, their idyllic summer season had slipped past.

"Now doesn't this beat that old coach?" Enid had stirred, awakened by the train's high speed swaying. She looked over at Lora. "I suppose that's a letter to the great lawyer himself. Maybe it's for the best that I won't get to meet him. It wouldn't do for me to ask him something about Jessie, now, would it? Oh, don't worry, darlin', that's the last I'll say about him, I promise. It's his good fortune I have to change trains in Chicago and leave for home right away."

Yesterday, their last morning before returning, Karl had taken the two over to "Eldorado," his almost-completed home and studio across the Hudson River in Weehawken. After their return to Manhattan on the ferry, Enid had suddenly "remembered" that she needed to shop for her nieces. Telling Lora she'd meet her at the Pennsylvania Station, she said goodbye to Karl, leaving the former lovers alone in the cafe.

"All right," Karl sighed, "suppose you tell me about this maligned socialist leader, and especially about your Darrow, too."

I really do still love you so, Karl, she said to herself, *even if no longer in the same way.* And Lora started with a description of Debs and his introducing her to Darrow. She recounted her early days of working for Clarence, through the glamour and excitement of preparing for the trial; how their attraction for each other had evolved. Karl's questions were candid.

Lora at length glanced up at the clock on the cafe wall. "Karl, I'm sorry to have made you listen to this melancholy journal. There's very little of this last year you don't now know. Whatever must you think?"

Karl brushed his hand lightly across her cheek. "What I think is that you're the very same girl, the one who caught my eye, and then my heart at the World's Fair—and never let go. And now here we are, talking like some brother and sister.

"So Darrow has problems in his marriage. And he's sure enough made some for you—and for Jessie as well. Those problems don't have to be yours, Lora. You didn't tell me he'd get divorced, or what's more important, that you'd still have him even if he did. I got the impression that you might not.

"Do you have any idea how unique you are?" He laughed at his question. "Of course you do. You never lacked for self-confidence. And you have to know you're much too precious to waste in the situation you've described.

"Someone is waiting for you." Karl looked aside momentarily. "I wish it could have been me and I'm frankly jealous of Mr. Darrow: jealous of the effect he's had on you. But that someone who's out there, he won't be married, and he'll be right for you."

Lora's eyes were wet as the two searched for a cab. At last one responded, the horse clomping to a stop at the curb. She bit her lip hard, brushing back tears. This might well be, she knew, the last time she would ever see this man again—this person who had shared so many emotion-filled days and nights with her—and so many private thoughts.

"Karl, I..." She looked up, but he had turned away, having his own trouble speaking.

Goodbye my lover, my friend, she said to herself, crying and clinging to him for a last moment before she climbed into the cab.

Karl reached up, paid the driver, and stepped back as the carriage

71

pulled out into the traffic. Lora watched out the back window until the angular, bearded figure had receded into the crowd.

10

May 19th, 1895...

Few people were awake in Williams Bay so early on a Sunday morning. It was another chilly day, and out on that lake it would be downright cold, *if* they ever succeeded in getting Paul's boat started. The red ball of the sun rose over the east side of the bay. It would offer some help if it stayed out.

Jeremy made his way along the shore toward the boat docks opposite the depot. Work at the Observatory was going well. Just as he guessed, he had slipped into an easy routine of keeping the books at the office and spending the rest of his working time at the freight shed, and Paul seemed to enjoy his company.

Life at Mrs. Ingalls' boarding house had settled down. Jeremy knew she'd found out he had moved the wallet, but he vowed to remain cordial to her until he could find somewhere else to stay in the little boom town.

Paul had returned from Cleveland on Saturday and surprised Jeremy just as he was finishing up and getting ready to leave work. "Well, I finally got it. My boat was delivered this morning and we just launched her."

"A boat?" Jeremy looked up from his desk. "What kind, a sailboat?"

"Oh, no, a real power launch. She's a beauty, but you'll have to see her yourself. Say, how would you like a ride on her tomorrow? I want to see how she runs, and then go across and look over my house, too. Will you join me?"

"I'd love a ride."

"One small detail," Paul said. "I've got to do some work on her, a few last-minute changes before I start her up and I'll need some help. Can I

73

count on you?"

"Of course you can. What time do you want me down there?" he asked, then groaned when Paul told him just how early.

Now, as he got closer to the two large yachts tied to the main dock, he could read the name *Thetis* on one. Making it ready for summer seemed to be a family project. A man stood on *Thetis's* roof, directing two boys, likely his sons. A pair of women were on the afterdeck, polishing. Their good-natured banter carried across the water on the crisp morning air.

I remember all those good, family times. And where did they all go? A sharp pang of remorse swept back over him, remembering his own life prior to the break-up of his marriage. He hitched up his shoulders and walked out onto the dock, determined not to let the depression settle upon him. As he reached the second yacht, he was startled by a shrill whistle. A small steam launch was putting in at the dock. A line was thrown to him and he looped it around a post.

"Much obliged," the young boatman called, jumping across the gap to the deck. He stepped back to look with pride at the boat. It was newly painted, and its roof was adorned with a snappy red and white canopy.

"Well sir, how does he look?" he asked. This newcomer was little more than a teenager.

"How does *he* look?" Jeremy echoed. But with a wave of his thumb the skipper pointed to the bow of the craft. There in brass letters was the name, *Wilbur F.* " And when did you put *him* in the water?"

"Just this week and none too soon what with Kaye's Park opening up next week and all of the gawkers flocking out here to see the Observatory."

"What's Kaye's Park?" Jeremy asked, searching his memory for the name but coming up empty.

"Why, now I know when you ask that question that you're new around here. Look, right over…there," and he pointed almost directly across the lake. "That's Kaye's Park. It's got rides, games, and some of the best music around. I expect I'll be making a lot of trips over and back, picking up folks from the train, but," he paused, a worried look crossing his face, "it won't be as easy as it used to, what with Kaye's having their own yacht. I suppose I'll have to cross the palms of some of those rotten conductors to steer the folks to me," he said, seeming to think out loud. "But just see how narrow my boat is," he continued, back on track. "Well

74

sir, when the ladies get in, see, I stand right there," and he pointed to the wheel in the smallish cockpit. "I can all but sit in their laps. And sometimes," his acquaintance continued, "if *Wilbur* and I are up to it, I'll let him roll on the waves a bit for them. You ought to hear those girls squeal."

Jeremy noticed the young boatman was talking in that fast, clipped cadence that marked the conversation of workingmen. It was an affectation, he guessed; meant to show a crisp, businesslike style.

Paul's shout cut their conversation short. Saying goodbye, Jeremy hurried down the shore to where Paul was standing on a small pier. At first glance, his boat looked vaguely like the *Wilbur F,* being narrow-beamed and around twenty-five feet long.

"How do you like her?" Jeremy answered the question with a "thumbs up." Paul studied the gesture for a moment, then smiled. Jeremy admired the boat, an open cockpit launch with very clean lines. Unlike *Wilbur F,* it was trim and free of a smoke stack which lent Paul's craft a decidedly modern look.

"She's a beauty," he said, climbing aboard. He examined the engine which sat exposed on its mounting near the boat's middle. Jeremy was, or at least had been, familiar with engines but he feigned surprise as Paul went about enthusiastically describing the power plant. The boat, one of the water taxis from the Columbian Exposition, had been bought from a storage service.

"I couldn't make do with her the way she was. She was run on storage batteries. Every night they charged up the batteries and then put them back in the next morning. Why, she could barely move. That was all right for those lagoons at the Fair, but for here I put in this gasoline engine and today we're going to try her out."

The boat had just been painted white and the deck wood newly stained. Its role as a water taxi was hardly recognizable. Paul had removed the rows of benches. In place, he said, giving Jeremy the captain's tour, he'd be putting in some comfortable chairs. Eventually he would even add a little buffet at the rear. "One of these days she'll have nearly everything those two yachts over there have and she'll run rings around them."

They shared sausage and bread that Paul cut up. Reaching down, he brought up a pair of root beer bottles that were dangling over the side in the still-cold water. He showed off some of the improvements he'd made, demonstrating how he'd taken out the primitive steering system.

"See this?" He reached for the new steering cables that ran through tubes on both sides of the boat, holding them up.

"I rigged these in the storage yard in Chicago this April. Don't mind telling you I attracted some attention from those fellows, too."

But Paul wasn't finished describing his improvements. "If you lean out, you'll see the new rudder I put in. It's the latest—a balanced rudder. The weight is in the center, closer to the propeller where it belongs for control. I'll have to work out the ballast. I'm afraid she'll be a little light at first."

Jeremy leaned out over the stern. The man had done his homework, all right. The name *Lora L* stood out in bright script.

"Your daughter?"

"She is. And won't she be surprised and proud! Lora worked at the Fair as a guide and likely rode on this very boat. She knows I bought one of the water taxis, but she'll never dream what a keen little boat she's become."

Paul handed over a wrench and a pliers-like tool, showing Jeremy how to thread the steering cable through the tubing and around to the wheel. "You catch on fast. You ever been around boats?"

"Just seeing one..." he shrugged, "reminds me that maybe I have," he answered. Jeremy indeed remembered getting his own boat ready for the summer seasons.

"I almost forgot. Malcolm told me about your loss of memory." Paul proceeded to tell Jeremy a story of a person he knew years before up in Waterford, Wisconsin. The man had fallen into the river while fishing near the dam and had been swept along. He'd dashed his head on some rocks before he could be rescued. *His* memory, Paul observed, looking out across the bay with his chin resting in his hand, had taken months to return. "You'll be all right." He patted him on the shoulder.

Paul began tinkering with the engine while Jeremy went to work on the cable. "Are you from Waterford originally?"

"No," Paul answered, grunting as he turned the wrench. "I came from Racine. At least that's where I grew up." He sketched out for Jeremy his past in Racine. He had gone into business right after his marriage, as a builder. About the time his daughter Lora arrived, he went into partnership building small homes for the J.I. Case workers.

"Our business was by word of mouth—first one little cottage and then another and things kept picking up for us. I would have stayed there for the rest of my life, likely, but I heard about an opportunity over in Waterford. That's a town maybe twenty-five miles east of here and about the same distance from Racine. It's on the Fox River.

"I went to my partner, Duke, who's passed on now. Duke was the only partner I've ever had," Paul said, straining as he turned the wrench. "He tried to talk me out of it, reminding me how well we were doing, and in just a short time, too. But I saw the move as a chance for something bigger. Both Celia's parents and mine had died, and Duke finally bought me out.

"Things went well in Waterford. I got all the work I could handle and the bank was generous in giving me a start." He stood up, seeming to concentrate on the engine. "It was 1875," he started slowly, "almost twenty years ago to this day. Her coughing started early in the spring with the dampness and the cold, and it just got worse. It was consumption and it took Celia within a couple of months." He rubbed his teeth across his lower lip, the distant memory still fresh and painful.

"Lora was only a child, seven years old. After the funeral, I'd stay up nights wondering how I could look after her, but the neighbors were wonderful. Everyone pitched in to help out. Eventually, I learned about a housekeeper, a Negro lady from Burlington. You know a number of Negroes had come through that way on the underground railway.

"Martha joined us and we lived in Waterford for fifteen years. Then, one day, a man I'd done some construction work for looked me up. He had heard of a family business for sale in Chicago. They had started getting into electrical construction when a feud had broken out among two of the brothers, and they had almost run the business into the ground, even though there was plenty of work.

"I didn't want to leave Waterford. We'd made a place for ourselves. Lora had grown up there and nearly all my friends were there or close by. She was just then finishing college over at Normal School in Whitewater. She was going to be an art teacher," his pride showed on his face. "I'd had this dream that I wanted to get into electrical construction for, oh, at least ten years.

"I felt, and still do more than ever, Jeremy, that it's the future. When Lora came home from school, I asked her advice, and she told me to go.

77

She knew this was what I wanted. Then she surprised me—told me she had applied to teach near Chicago herself, out at Pullman. I sold my business and the three of us moved there.

"I haven't been sorry I got into electrical construction," he continued, "but sometimes these days I find myself tiring so easily. Maybe it's just old age," he smiled ruefully. "You know, there's really more of this business than anyone can handle. It seems every small city around here is, or soon will be, electrifying. Lake Geneva has started work on its own power plant."

He had set down his tools and was looking directly at Jeremy. "Do you know why I wanted Malcolm to find someone for me? Oh, to get a local person if possible, yes, though I doubt you'd qualify as a local. I asked him mainly because I *trust* him. I knew if *he* suggested someone, it would be someone I could trust as well."

"I'll try to earn that confidence," Jeremy answered.

Paul stood up in the hold, stretched, and walked up to the front of the cockpit where he sliced some more sausage. "I told you how much I worried over my little girl," he said as he leaned against the railing. "How I wondered if I'd be able to raise her. Well, if it hadn't *been* for her, and thanks to Martha, I'd have gone to pieces."

He gazed out across the bay. The sun had once more ducked behind a cloud just as it had done all morning as they worked. A cold gust of wind swept down upon them, rocking the boat against the pier.

"Did I hear you say your daughter is out east now?"

"Yes, she's gone with a friend to New York." He filled Jeremy in on Lora's work. Jeremy noticed his description was neutral; he took no side, despite his daughter's involvement in the Pullman strike.

Paul described Lora's befriending Eugene Debs, and confirmed that she had been working for Clarence Darrow during the past year. Jeremy was finishing his work on the steering cable and put down the tools to listen, fascinated, as Paul told him he didn't know much about Debs' case, but that Lora had said that she and everyone were sure Debs was about to be acquitted. Then one of the jurors took sick and, according to his daughter, through some shenanigans the trial judge ruled for a mistrial. He found Debs guilty of contempt of some injunction, though, and ordered him to jail.

"Mind you, now, this is Lora's view of the trial, not mine. Lora always swore to me that she was sure the judge was in cahoots with the government. I'm not sure whether that's her idea or Darrow's.

"I'm too small a businessman to really *have* any labor problems. I can't say I agree with this American Railway Union of Debs. They shouldn't be able to stop all the trains. Lora and I have had many an argument over Mr. Debs and that strike. Most of my daughter's political beliefs I don't agree with at all, but I raised her to think for herself and I'm proud that she does."

Paul glanced up at the darkening sky and ended his narrative. He came over and tested Jeremy's work on the cable and gave it his approval. "Now you're about to witness the finest little engine on all of the lake."

He took a can of gasoline and squirted small amounts in the petcock of each cylinder. Then he gave the crank a couple of turns, getting noticeably redder until Jeremy was about to offer to help. Just as he started to speak, the engine coughed into life, making him homesick with its familiar odor.

Paul seemed overall a man of few words and Jeremy bet he seldom opened up the way he had.

"I'm hoping Lora will want to spend some time, maybe even the whole summer, up here. You know, she's the one who supervised most of the design of *Bluffside* last year. That's what we call our place." Paul, he noticed, had succumbed to the tendency of Lake Geneva owners to give fanciful names to their summer homes. "Lora should arrive next weekend," he called above the engine noise as he backed the boat out into the bay.

11

The sun, which had been in and out all day, had disappeared behind the low dense clouds. Spring comes reluctantly to southern Wisconsin, especially when the weather turns back on itself, as it had on this Sunday, bringing the winds down from the northeast. As the launch headed out of the bay, past Cedar Point and into the open lake, they felt the sting of the cold wind on their faces.

Paul was enthusiastic about the success of his gasoline engine. He was alternately listening to it and talking about the *Lora L* and his new home on the lake. Jeremy pulled his jacket up about his neck as he listened, noticing as he did that Paul was oversteering the boat. He glanced up at the clouds passing low over their heads.

"There's Black Point," Paul called out, indicating over the rocking bow the heavily wooded prominence that angled out from the south shore. Jeremy had seen Black Point, known for its sheer drop offs, countless times before, but now with the dense woods that covered the point it was darker and more foreboding. Just off shore the depths registered over a hundred feet, he remembered.

He was staring out through the cutting wind at the familiar landmark when Paul called out to him over the engine. "Can you see that house on top?" Jeremy nodded, noticing above the distant trees a large house topped by a tower.

"It was built about seven years ago by Conrad Seipp. Have you ever heard of Seipp brewing?" His companion shook his head.

"The fact is, old Conrad only lived a year or two after that house was built. I never met him, but his widow, Catherine, is one great lady." He was now shouting over the noise of the engine and the waves slapping against the hull as the boat wallowed in the open water.

"Catherine is his second wife. He left a huge family, children and grandchildren. Matter of fact, they're going to let me keep the *Lora L* in their lagoon over there," he pointed, but Jeremy couldn't make out any feature. "And our own place is just down the point."

With growing anxiety, Jeremy looked up again at the sky. The wind had picked up. He couldn't tell if it had yet started to rain or they were being pelted with spray, but the *Lora L* was confirming his earlier worries about her. The narrow launch may have been a fine water taxi at the World's Fair, but it wasn't designed to be out in any storm on this lake. Worse, he thought, while Paul was a gifted engineer, he made a lousy sailor. Jeremy was beginning to wish he would cut his story short and concentrate on running the launch in this heavy weather. Their situation was getting more precarious by the minute as they neared the middle of the lake.

The launch, made to carry an electric motor and a brace of heavy storage batteries, was now riding light, much *too* light and much too high on the water. The wind funneling down through the Narrows had built up high waves which were striking the boat broadside at critical intervals.

Paul was still making a straight line for Black Point. He was steering the craft along the troughs and the boat was heeling over from the waves and then righting itself only to repeat the process with the next broadside.

The white foam on the caps of the waves washing past contrasted with the water, which had turned nearly black under the dark sky. Paul was oblivious to the jeopardy they were in, and the rain now began sweeping down the lake in force, coming in at them from their left side.

The launch had begun to swing like a pendulum, with each swing getting longer. He called out to Paul, "Turn into the waves, dammit! Turn!" Paul turned toward Jeremy, his confusion now mirrored on his face as the *Lora L* barely righted herself after the last wave.

Jeremy grabbed for the wheel just as the boat began another sideways roll, but before he could reach the wheel, the boat literally fell from the crest of the wave, knocking him off his feet.

Crawling to the helm, he gripped it and brought the boat into the wind just as another wave passed under them. He couldn't see Paul as he looked about the hull. He was gone.

He'd have to turn back with the wind behind him and try to find Paul in the dark water. Good God, he didn't even know if Paul could swim. Suddenly he heard a voice, more a moan than anything and saw a hand around one of the stanchions. Letting go of the wheel, Jeremy dashed over and tried lifting him back into the boat. He couldn't budge the heavier man, nor could he get any leverage from the rolling boat under him. Paul's hand began to slip its grip on the stanchion.

"Hold my hand!" he shouted as Paul clutched, releasing his grasp on the stanchion. With his right hand Jeremy grabbed his shirt, and reaching down, took hold of his pants. He tried again to lift Paul over the side. Still no use. As he strained, they were again met broadside by a wave and lifted. As the boat dropped into the trough, Paul was again picked up, and with all his strength, Jeremy gave a last heave.

Paul flopped over the rail and into the hull as the water in the hold swirled back and forth over them. Jeremy got to his knees, and struggling for his breath, he grabbed the spinning steering wheel again. He brought the bow into the next wave which broke over them, sending a torrent of water into the boat.

Normally a boat could have ridden out the waves, taking them head on, but he discovered a new problem, the trim of the launch. The low, pointed prow, so practical in the lagoons, was plowing the water in front of them. He could feel the boat almost trying to act like a submarine as waves broke over the prow, with the engine roaring as the propeller came clear of the water with each wave. Jeremy knew that with a few more repetitions, if they didn't dive to the bottom, that roaring engine would stall, and they'd be left drifting at the mercy of the winds.

Jeremy contemplated his dilemna. If he kept the boat straight it would either dive or be left engineless. If he ran the troughs, it would eventually capsize. Then he remembered something Paul had just told him back at the pier—about how well he believed the boat would steer. They were about to find out.

He spun the wheel before the next wave hit, so that the windward side of the bow took the force of the wave. As soon as the rolling crest had passed, he turned and ran down the backside into the trough. It worked. The *Lora L* responded. He tried it again, and once more the boat rose up on the swell and ran down the backside.

As he got the feel of the ungainly little craft, they began working together, rising and falling, plunging through the waves. Paul was right in one respect, the boat's steering was responding perfectly. At least so far. He prayed he'd threaded those cables through correctly. As he turned the craft to face the next wave, he lost his balance, and grabbed at the rail to keep from being swept over.

They literally fought their way across the lake and he began to think that they might just beat the storm if only the engine would hold out. He checked Paul, sprawled in the hold with the water sloshing around him. He'd be safe if the boat didn't heel over too far, and he had no intention of letting her do that.

By now they were east of Black Point. He peered out at the storm. It seemed to him that a few hundred yards beyond, the waves were smaller. If they could just reach that area, they might be in a lea from the Narrows. After a few minutes, the *Lora L* did begin to settle down. They'd passed out of the worst blast of wind. He turned them into the relatively calmer waters and began running parallel to the shore.

At his first chance, Jeremy cut the throttle, letting them idle as he left the wheel and knelt in the buffeting, freezing water where he managed to lift Paul to a sitting position. "We made it!" he shouted. Paul managed a weak smile in return, the icy water still running over him.

Jeremy went back to the helm and squinted ahead to see the opening to the Black Point lagoon. Finally, he caught sight of the drawbridge and idling the boat off the entrance, put over the anchor. He played out their fifty feet of line, but it failed to catch, even though they were only fifteen or twenty yards offshore.

"You okay?" he asked, looking down at Paul and reverting to slang.

"Okay...yes, I'm okay," he answered, adopting the jargon, as he slowly drew himself up out of the knee deep water. He put his arm around Jeremy's shoulder.

"You saved my life," he said in little more than a whisper.

"You can give some thanks to that steering you rigged and that engine. If she'd quit or gotten flooded out there..." Jeremy looked out at the whitecaps, letting them finish his thought.

Just then he saw people on the shore waving as the little drawbridge was raised. He lifted the anchor and tried his best to steer the boat through the narrow opening, barely able to hold the wheel as he was shaking so violently from the cold and a delayed case of nerves.

Finally, the sodden *Lora L* drew alongside an elegant yacht named the

Lorely. He threw the bow line to a man on the slip who secured them. As Jeremy helped Paul out of the launch and stepped onto the slip himself, someone began shaking his hand.

"Great job of bringing her in. We all thought you were going over," the man exclaimed, as he helped Paul to stand up. "I'm Henry Bartholomay," he said to Jeremy. "Paul, you *do* know how to make an entrance to start the summer season.

"Come on," he said heartily, "let's get you two up to the house, warm you up and get you something to eat."

Bartholomay led the way up a flight of wooden steps. Jeremy noticed they seemed to stretch endlessly above. He took a final glance over his shoulder at the whitecaps, still frothing out on the lake, and then looked over at the boats gently bobbing, tethered to their slips in the calm, dark lagoon.

"Your new boatman can really handle himself," Henry Bartholomay said to Paul as they started to climb, "but wasn't he reckless crossing in that storm?"

"*He* wasn't reckless. I was," Paul answered, "and that fella saved my life…both our lives."

Jeremy *did* feel proud, catching his breath as they climbed. But now that they were safe the thought crossed his mind—*If we had capsized—and died—would I have returned home? Would I be erased from the 20th century completly? What about my children? About everyone I knew?*

Proud to have accomplished something for his new friend, Jeremy was still filled with ambivalence.

12

As they reached the top of the slope, Jeremy stopped for a moment, staring up at the Seipp house. From ground level, the tower made the house seem much taller. The water-logged pair followed Henry Bartholomay up the front steps. What looked like a small army had gathered on the front porch, and Jeremy felt himself the center of attention as arms encircled him and he heard choruses of "bravos" and "well-dones." Apparently, someone had been up in the tower and having seen them out on the lake, had called to the others.

In no time the tower had filled with many of the residents and guests of the huge house who crowded together to watch the drama. It was witnessed, he learned, by some very experienced and skilled boatmen. He and Paul were led into the huge living room. The most welcome sight to greet Jeremy was the crackling blaze in the fireplace.

Catherine Seipp ushered her newest guests over to the fireplace. Someone put a steaming bowl in Jeremy's hands. They were still shaking so much he had to steady one with the other as he tried to taste the soup. He hoped no one was looking too closely as he lowered his face closer to the bowl, hardly able to hold the spoon. It was the best he'd ever had.

"Here it is, late May, and we're gathered around a roaring fire," said Catherine Seipp, as Henry set another large log on the fire. Jeremy watched the sparks shoot out against the metal screen, the heady wood smell filling the living room.

Someone had thoughtfully offered him a blanket which he put over his shoulders. As he started to thaw out, his mind began to roam. He had almost drowned out there—or had he? Was he immune from harm? Did this new life of his present him with some form of charmed existence?" A woman was speaking to him. "As I said," she repeated, "you do seem to have a knack for seamanship, though I feared for a few minutes that you were going to flounder. I'm Clara Bartholomay, Henry's wife. I was one of those up in the tower. Was that Mr...?" she hesitated.

"Slater," he supplied the name.

"Have you boated much on the lake before?"

"Yes," he started. "Excuse me. No, ma'am. I'm still a little confused. No, I haven't been on the lake before. I've been working for Mr. Lockerby at the Observatory, and I just happened to be along when the storm came up," he finished.

"Well, nevertheless, you showed your mettle, and that's what we like around here." She delivered the statement with an easy ring of authority. Jeremy thanked her, his modesty couched by his caution.

"I guess I just had some beginner's luck." At this expression several heads close by turned toward him. He realized he may have just coined a phrase, new to them, and he knew he had better not push that luck.

"Will you be staying on here when the work at the Observatory ends?" another woman asked. She walked over and placed a snifter of brandy in his hands and gave one to her husband who lifted his glass. "Cheers," he offered. The woman, an attractive brunette, was introduced as Elsa Madlener, another of the Seipp daughters.

Elsa had remained quiet while he and Paul were questioned about their adventure on the lake, but Jeremy had noticed her watching him closely. Her gaze was steady and thoughtful. He wondered whether she had picked up something about him, and the thought made him slightly uneasy. This was the first real social situation he'd found himself in. What, he wondered, had sparked her curiosity? Was it some mannerism, perhaps some slang phrase like the one he'd just used, or had this observant woman noticed something else about him?

"I don't know, Mrs. Madlener," he answered, addressing her formally, grateful he'd remembered her married name. "I like my present job—and this area. I'll have to decide, I suppose, when the work is finished."

"And what did you do before your...position...at the Observatory?" Her melodic voice almost cloaked the probing nature of her questions. He sipped on his brandy, feeling the warmth spreading over him and sensation returning to his fingers.

"I've worked as a bookkeeper and store clerk in the Indianapolis area.

Nothing too exciting, I'm afraid."

"Have you ever played 'Authors,' Mr. Slater?" asked Elsa. Had she noticed the practiced way he'd been holding the brandy snifter, he wondered?

"It's a new card game, and it's sweeping Chicago. We were about to play when the excitement started."

He shifted the glass. "No, ma'am. I'm afraid I don't know the game."

"Well, each player," she started to explain, "receives a number of cards and each of the cards has an author's name and picture on it. Oh, for example, Dickens, Cooper, Poe," she went on. "After that, the players are dealt other cards marked with titles of various authors' works. You trade with the person to your right. The first to match all of the titles with the correct authors is the winner."

Jeremy was soon enjoying himself and could almost imagine he belonged here. He drained the brandy and he and Elsa continued to talk on for a few minutes about authors, saying more than he should have, but at the same time feeling the need to talk to someone.

Paul moved over next to him. "We'd better leave, my friend, before they start the game. We want to get over to the house before dark."

"Well, since you won't stay for dinner, I won't let you leave without some nourishment to take along." Catherine Seipp had stepped out onto the porch with her guests. She took a huge covered hamper of food from a servant and handed it to Jeremy. Thanking her as he took it, he noticed that the others back in the living room had gathered into a lively circle to start "Authors." The two made their way eastward and downhill, stepping carefully through the growing darkness.

"That's where the pier will go. It will be a sixty-footer with a "T" at the end so we can receive boats and berth *Lora L* at the same time. Eventually I'm going to put in a parallel arm with a roof shelter."

Until Paul stopped and pointed over the water, Jeremy didn't realize they'd arrived. It was only a short walk eastward from the Seipps. He looked out again over the pier site.

"And when will it go in?"

"They'd better have it finished this week or else, and no more excuses, either. I want everything in place by the time Lora arrives."

Paul led the way up the bluff. Heavy log stairs had been cut into the side, and Jeremy could hear his boss panting as they reached the top. "I see where you get the name for your estate," he said, looking back down.

As they turned around on the crest, he caught his first sight of the house. Even in the weak light it looked beautiful. It was a large, white-framed house, in no way as grand as the Seipp house, but far larger than Paul had let on.

On the first floor the house was surrounded by a veranda. Sets of double columns were spaced around the front half of the house, supporting an upstairs porch with a dormer above. The house itself sat on the highest ground. Tall oaks were in the front and on both sides. Jeremy examined the house as they walked up the flagstone sidewalk, aware all at once that Paul was watching him, waiting for some reaction.

"It's gorgeous, Paul." He said it simply, without elaboration as they both stopped in front of the house. No architect, Jeremy couldn't place the style.

"I can thank my daughter for the design. Oh, I can build and engineer, and you know I've had a hand in some of the houses up here, but it was her artist's touch that made the place." He pointed. "See those sets of arches in between the bannisters around the porch? Well, they were Lora's doing. I showed her the basic plan, and she looked it over and studied it. That was just about a year ago. Her drawings kept to the original design, but she'd rounded and softened it and lowered the roof line. And do you know what her inspiration was?" By now they had stepped up onto the veranda.

"It was the Women's Building from the Columbian Exposition. She managed to find sketches of it, and she had adapted that exposition hall to this house. Thank God the interior needed few changes." Jeremy smiled, noticing Paul's practical side had shown through.

"You know, you can talk about your Crane or Seipp estates, but here's the only true Italian Renaissance on the lake," he beamed proudly. Paul opened the main door and led them inside. The furniture, all new, had been stored in a corner and covered with sheets. Paul lifted off some of the covers and they pulled out chairs, the same white-painted wicker type that he had seen at the Seipps. Dusk was closing in and he found candles.

"Never dreamed I'd own a summer house like this," he said, holding a lighted candle as he led Jeremy through the living room and out into the kitchen, opening the door to the downstairs bedroom. "Martha's. She's our housekeeper I told you about. Martha was up here during the end of the construction and helped with the furnishings. In a few days, she'll arrive for the summer."

Walking back out onto the veranda, they sat on the steps and looked down over the now-peaceful lake which had threatened their lives such a short time before. Jeremy opened the cover of the picnic hamper and found slices of ham, boiled eggs and bread. He also uncovered a metal growler of beer and discovered that Catherine had even included mugs. As they finished supper, their conversation drifted from the Observatory to the boat trip.

Paul thanked him again for saving his life. "You've got to promise me something...that you'll give me some lessons in handling that boat. I can see now there's more to owning one than just paying for it and tinkering with the engine—but let me show you the guest room. You've got to be just as tired as I am," he said, as they put away the remains of their dinner and went inside.

Walking up the stairs behind Paul, Jeremy noticed the house still had the smell of newness about it as well as a trace of that musty, closed-up smell he'd remembered from opening their own summer house so many past years at Lake Geneva.

"Get yourself a good night's sleep. I've got another surprise or two for you tomorrow."

Jeremy, too tired to even guess, soon fell fast asleep. Paul stayed awake for some time, unable to quiet the thoughts of his own close call out in the storm. Somewhere in Jeremy's forgotten past, he had learned seafaring lessons that had saved their lives.

13

Jeremy's dream seemed as though it would never end. Amy and Danny were on the launch. The three of them had fought their way through a storm and were docking, but while he tied up the boat, someone was leading his children away.

"It's all right! It's all right, Daddy," they called back as he struggled with all his power to break away and follow them.

"It's all right. It's all right." Paul was standing over his bed. His big hand was on Jeremy's chest. "You've been having a nightmare."

Jeremy sat bolt upright in the big four-poster. "I'm fine now." He slowly shook his head. Actually, he was more disturbed to awaken and realize that he had *not* escaped from his time prison.

What did I say in my sleep?

"It's just as well we were up, anyway," Paul said, looking concerned. "Why don't you get dressed. We'll have some breakfast and finish the tour. I'm no cook, but my coffee is the best you'll ever drink, and I found some cinnamon rolls Catherine put in the hamper."

A few minutes later, Jeremy walked down the stairs. He had smelled the coffee, and could hear his host in the kitchen. As he stepped into the living room, his attention was drawn to a pair of framed photographs on the mantel above the fireplace. He must have been so tired last night, or it had been so dark that he had missed them.

The first picture was of a woman he took to be Celia, Paul's wife. She had her hand on the shoulder of a child about five who was riding a stick horse. He studied the other picture of a young woman in her mid-twenties, her hands held in her lap. He looked more closely at the photograph. *Have I seen her somewhere before? Of course I couldn't have.* He'd always found it hard to judge looks, particularily of women, in old photographs. Was it just a different standard? Most of the subjects he'd seen had looked so severe. This woman did not. She was looking directly at the camera, with an expression not really bold, but frank. She had large, round eyes, and her mouth was formed in a mirthful half-smile, as though she'd just heard something that amused her. Still, she looked familiar. "That's Lora," Paul said. He had come in from the kitchen without Jeremy hearing him. "The other is a picture of Celia, with Lora there in the background." He handed Jeremy the coffee mug. "It was really not her best. A public photographer took it. You can see that he stood too far away. He barely caught her features." Jeremy saw that the child was laughing, the image of her face blurred. She had no doubt moved.

"It's the last picture that I have of Celia. She died the following year."

"Your daughter is very beautiful," he said as they moved into the kitchen. "I know why you're so proud of her."

"Just look around at this kitchen, the way it is now. When Martha arrives, you'll hardly recognize it. There'll be two or three pots going at once and that oven over there will be red hot." He offered Jeremy a cinnamon roll, taking one himself.

"Will your daughter also be arriving?"

"Lora will be up later, probably next weekend or thereabouts. Before she left for New York, she surprised me by saying that she'd like to spend more time up here this summer. After all the time she put in for Darrow on that Debs trial, before and after, well, she was only up for two weeks last year…just when we opened the place in August. I'd like to see her get attached to this house, since she designed it and all. But," he shrugged, "how long she stays is anyone's guess." Paul seemed to want to say something more but cut himself off.

"Well, there I go again, going on about Lora," he said, taking another roll. "Just the doting father in me. But if you ever have a daughter, Jeremy, you'll see what I mean."

Paul's words cut him. *Where are my son and daughter now? Marooned almost a hundred years ahead of me somewhere in time. What did I say in my sleep?*

"Well, I'll be glad to have her up here anyway. Now, though, it's time we completed a tour of the grand 'estate.' I want to show you that surprise I have in store."

Opening the side door off the kitchen, they stepped out into the drive—really more a rustic path behind the house. There were still more large trees overhead and heavy woods to the west of the property. Paul pointed to a new white cabin, built to resemble the main house, but on a much reduced, single-story scale. The little cabin had the same porch across the front with the same railings and arches between the pillars.

"Like it?"

"It's a caretaker's cottage?" Jeremy wondered aloud.

"Right. Lora designed this one, too. She wanted the same influence carried out."

"Where is your caretaker? Is he still in Chicago?"

"That's my surprise. If you want it, the job is yours, and this house in the bargain. No, don't say anything now. I've noticed that you're handy with tools and things. I know you're thinking that with work at the Observatory and with the traveling back and forth across the lake that you can't possibly hold two jobs, but hear me out. You need a place to stay, correct? If I'm not mistaken, you're none too happy at Mrs. Whats-her-name's house." Jeremy nodded, surprised at how very much Paul had taken in.

"I'm going to have to be away quite a bit, in and out of Cleveland and Chicago this summer. Martha and Lora will be out here soon, and I need someone to look after the place. The boat can be at your disposal most of the time. Lord knows, you've shown you can manage it, and we may even be getting a horse and carriage later in the summer. For now, though, we'll be using one of the Lefens' horses and carriage. They're great neighbors. Next year, I'm going to put in our own stable back near that tool shed and complete the drive around the back of the house."

Jeremy didn't have to weigh the offer. He'd love nothing more than to move into this pretty little cabin. "I don't know what to say Paul, except 'yes' before you have a chance to change your mind. I am worried, though, about keeping up these grounds," he glanced up and around at the trees and the expanse of land, realizing how large it suddenly looked, "and doing my job at the Observatory."

"Don't worry," Paul answered, leading him up the steps and onto the porch of the cabin. "I've watched you and the work you're doing. It doesn't *begin* to fill your day even now. Does it? Well?" Jeremy nodded in agreement, leaning against the porch railing.

"I'll tell you something. Our electrical work is ahead of schedule, and if I have my way, by God we'll stay ahead of the rest of the construction team, too, so as the summer goes along, there will be lulls in the work. Mark my words, come August and we'll be slowed by deliveries.

They had been walking through the cabin, and Jeremy had seen enough to know he loved it. It would give him what he most wanted, somewhere he could live by himself, away from others. "When should I move in?" he asked as they started down the path.

"Why don't you come over with Martha on Thursday." As they reached the main house, Jeremy turned to take a last look at his new home, at least for the summer.

"I'll go go down and see about the boat. She'll need a lot of bailing and some cleaning up." From the pantry he picked up a pail, a sponge and some rags. He followed the shore path, retracing their route from last night. In the daylight, he got a clear look at Bluffside. Its simple, graceful lines were in marked contrast to the huge Victorian homes sprouting along the shores of the lake.

So Paul's daughter would be spending time, maybe the whole summer. He found himself wondering what she was like. Very good-looking for one thing. He tried to put together a picture of her: someone who was or had been an art teacher, had participated in one of the most famous strikes in history—had even been a cohort of Eugene Debs, and had worked for Clarence Darrow. At the same time there seemed to emerge from this picture a person who wasn't above enjoying the good life at the lake. Yesterday the Seipps had spoken of her as someone they knew well, as someone who knew how to play as well as work. He was pleasantly absorbed, wondering just what Lora's presence would add to his life.

14

Later that week, on his last day at Mrs. Ingalls', Jeremy hitched a ride down from the Observatory. He was going to meet Paul at the boat dock, pick up Martha, and return to Bluffside. As the driver was passing near the boarding house, he had him pull over and he hopped off. Mrs. Ingalls would have to be told he was leaving. He didn't want that big mouth saying he'd up and left without so much as a goodbye. The last of his belongings had to be cleared out as well.

The day was warm with just a faint breeze, the smell of the last blossoms hanging in the air. Climbing the stairs, he crossed the porch and entered the house. No one was at home. Just as well, he thought. It was impossible to tell if Mrs. Ingalls had been snooping around his room or not. Her daily cleaning was a ritual, but he no longer had anything of value left in the house.

He quickly gathered up his things into the old grip, inspecting the room one final time. Jeremy sat down at the hall desk and proceeded to scribble a farewell note. He'd slipped the note into an envelope and was standing up when Earl came in.

"You leavin'?" Earl seemed disappointed. He saw the grip next to the desk. As simply as he could, Jeremy told Earl about his new job. There was no secret about it and he didn't know how much Earl would retain, anyway.

"We're going to be seeing each other. I'll still be working out at the Observatory," he reached out and took Earl's big hand in his.

As they shook hands, Earl shifted from one foot to the other. "You been nice to me," he started. Jeremy was touched. All he'd shown was nothing more than a little courtesy, but he guessed it had been more than

Earl had received in a long time.

He crossed the porch and started down the stairs, the old suitcase in his hand. "Jeremy?" Earl had followed him out onto the porch. The soft, little-boy voice contrasted with his size. "Are you really a lawyer? Cause I never met one."

Jeremy stopped and turned. "No, Earl, I'm not," he hesitated. "Why? Do I look like one?"

"I don't know," Earl paused, deciding whether to go on. Jeremy waited for him to continue. He was about to learn something, he felt sure.

"Ah overheard Momma sayin' you was a lawyer."

"Well, I'm sorry Earl, but I'm not," he answered, leaning against the rail. "But when did your mother say this?" he asked as easily as he could.

Jeremy held his breath for a couple of seconds. "Who did she say that to—to you?" She seldom ever addressed her simple-minded son, and he knew she wouldn't have discussed anything with him. Earl waited a minute and then answered, possibly out of gratitude.

"I was on the porch the other day when the constable, you know, Lowery?" Jeremy nodded. "He came by. He said Momma had left word that she wanted to see him, and I went in and got her. She met him out on the porch and then they went down to the kitchen together. She got him some lemonade, I think." Jeremy wished Earl would hurry his narrative. Mrs. Ingalls might return at any moment.

"Then they came back into the living room and sat down. I couldn't hear what they was talkin' about at first, so I got up next to the screen door." A woodpecker began tapping away just then, and Earl looked up. He seemed to lose his way.

"You got near the door," Jeremy prodded gently.

"Well, Momma doesn't think I have any sense, or that I ever listen to her. She told the constable that you was a lawyer, that she was sure of it—that she'd seen some papers of yours. She said..." he hesitated, trying to remember her words, "...that you lived in Chicago. She thought your name was something else. She said it, but I can't remember, and then she told him you had some colored pictures of children, like they was your own. Do you have any kids?"

Jeremy shook his head in a gentle lie. "What did the constable say?"

"Well, mostly he just listened while Momma talked. She said somethin' about you havin' some funny cards or tickets."

"Then what happened?"

"He asked if he could go through your room. I couldn't hear no more, but when they came back to the living room, Momma gave him that card. She said she found it in your papers, that she put everythin' else back, but she kept the card." Jeremy silently cursed the snooping landlady.

"The constable looked at the card," Earl continued. "I saw him readin' it, then he shoved it into his pocket.

"He thanked Momma. 'I've seen that fella, and I'll be keepin' a sharp eye on him. You've been helpful before, Mrs. Ingalls. I need your eyes and ears, and don't you forget you'll be in line for any reward money.' "

Jeremy knew that Lowery would not let the matter drop. He thanked Earl, promising him a tour of the Observatory later in the summer. Walking to the depot, he tried to sort out what Earl had overheard. This situation would bear watching.

He reached the depot just as the afternoon train was pulling in. Watching it slow down, Jeremy told himself there was nothing he could do—the constable had what he had and that was that. He'd just have to live with it, but he pictured Lowery studying whatever card he'd been given. *I hope it was that computer system salesman's card. Let him figure that one out.*

"Jeremy, this is the Martha you've been hearing so much about. And when I said I raised my daughter, I really meant Martha here did." Jeremy looked up to see Paul and a middle-aged black lady on the platform. "She's been with us for…just how long is it now, Martha?"

"Oh, Mr. Lockerby, don't remind me of the years. These grey hairs here ought to answer you." She took Jeremy's hand. He noticed she had been studying him. "Mr. Lockerby wrote me a note about his new assistant and caretaker, too. Are they both you?" He laughed along with her, and hoisting up her bag, led the way across the road. He put the bags aboard and helped Martha hesitantly step onto the launch as it bobbed on the quiet water.

Once aboard, she looked around, taking in the Lockerby's new addition as Jeremy lifted the small can and began squirting gasoline into the petcocks of each cylinder. Paul watched with silent approval, noting his assistant had picked up the starting ritual in a hurry. He looked on as Jeremy took the starting bar and turned, repeating the motion a second time, bringing the engine to life, and causing Martha to move further away at the sound. They cast off, backing slowly away from the pier.

"Over there." Paul was pointing out on Williams Bay. A hundred or so yards away, Paul's friend, George Bernard, was standing at one side of his boat, the *Topsy B*, holding a megaphone. Smoke was starting to pour from her red-topped stack.

"Let's see what that little dinghy of yours can do," George called through his megaphone. Jeremy saw the foam had begun to churn behind the heavy white yacht as it got under way.

"Let's race him!" Paul exclaimed, taking up the challenge. Jeremy let the engine idle for a few moments while they turned, the oil circulating. Then he pushed down the throttle, listening to the engine. Every cylinder was hitting perfectly. He throttled back, putting the *Lora L* into forward, opening the throttle again as they began moving.

The *Topsy B* was already far ahead and growing smaller. It was obvious George was not about to wait for the little launch. The surface on the bay was perfectly smooth, the very kind the launch was made for. The water began to fly beneath them and the wind whipped their faces. They peered ahead, their eyes full of tears. Jeremy was sure they were beginning to narrow the gap. He decided to stay behind the bigger boat, drafting on its wake.

The *Lora L* was closing the distance between them at a rapid clip, so rapid that Paul glanced over, worry showing over his face, their adventure in the storm very much in his memory. As they reached the mouth of the bay, Jeremy cut to the side and shot past *Topsy B*, so closely that their spray struck the side of the yacht. A thoroughly startled George Bernard, now holding his yachting cap in his hand, could only stare over as the *Lora L* passed.

George gave a shrug, raising his hands as if to say, "I'm giving her all she's got," as *Topsy B* rocked in the launch's wake.

They ran at full power for a few minutes on the open water before Jeremy cut back on the throttle. The big yacht was far behind and turning off for the Narrows. Paul and Jeremy were quiet for a few moments, both surprised not so much that they had beaten the big yacht but at the ease with which the launch had won.

"Congratulations. I guess this means you have the fastest boat on the lake. There's sure nothing wrong with your engine. You have her purring

like a kitten. If we just move her back a little and add some ballast, well
…."

"Isn't she something?" Paul's face was flushed with excitement. "A little jewel! Everything I wanted in a boat. I can't wait until her namesake sees her."

"And you sure enough know how to introduce me to yourself and this boat, Mr. Jeremy," Martha called out from the rear.

He pulled the boat up to the slip in the lagoon and helped her out, watching the two start down the shore path, telling them he'd be along with Martha's bag in a few minutes after he'd secured the canvas. He was unprepared for Martha's speech. She spoke with only a trace of dialect. He just assumed all Negroes around the turn-of-the-century would have had heavy drawls, until he remembered what Paul had told him. Martha and her family had come to Wisconsin, he thought he'd said, about 1850, by way of the underground railway. She would have been a young girl when she arrived and, away from the southern influence, would of course have lost the drawl.

He finished covering the launch and leaned against a post. "That's just wonderful," he said aloud, giving himself a pinch. "I'm still not dreaming. I've just won an old yacht race, and I have an obsessive policeman out to get me. How the *hell* can I get out of here?" He shook his head and started up the path, feeling every bit as helpless as he did on his first day in 1895.

The two were just reaching the house as he joined them. Paul must have labored again getting up the hill. His face was even more flushed than with the excitement of the race. He leaned against the edge of the veranda as he caught his breath.

Martha was by his side. "I'm gonna take good care of you now, Mr. Lockerby. You come inside and rest while Î fix you a dinner like you haven't had in the weeks you've been up here." Jeremy just hoped he'd stocked all the things on the long grocery list she'd mailed up to Paul. He parted company with them, humming to himself as he walked back toward the little cabin.

"A big dinner is probably the very last thing he needs," he said out loud, "but I'm going, at least for right now, to keep my big mouth shut."

He stood in front of the cabin, seeing it as his own for the first time. Then he reached down, and picking up his grip, walked up the steps and sat down in the three-seater porch swing. Jeremy relaxed, letting the easy motion of the swing rock him, just as the one he remembered from childhood had done.

15

"Here's what we did, let me show you." Following Ben Hazelwood down into the hold, Jeremy saw that the engine had been moved back at least two feet and new mountings added. "Your boss knows something about engines, I'll grant that, but he doesn't know boats or their design." Ben had shortened the driveshaft and re-attached it to the newly-mounted engine.

"Look down here. This will make her a little more seaworthy." Ben pointed to the double steel rails that he had secured to the hull with bolts. He'd also braced the rails against each other with heavy timbers.

"That's the best I can do. She won't wallow so easily, but I'd keep her out of any heavy weather. Let's take her for a run."

When they were out in the bay, Ben studied the angle critically, ordering more throttle, and then signaled when to stop. They put *Lora L* through her paces for twenty minutes or so. "I like the way she steers, quick and easy, but she's still going to roll in the waves." Jeremy noticed the launch did ride lower, the bow rising slightly at speed as a result of the weight shift. Ben had been leaning out from the bow and now came in, wiping his wet hands on his pants.

"That still feels mighty cold." Jeremy ran his own hand through the chilly water, agreeing as he turned and pointed the boat toward the Jewell pier. "I'll bet you don't miss ol' Miz' Ingalls' place, do you, Jeremy. By the way, I was going to work the other day when that constable—what's his name—Lowery, stopped me. He just stood in front of me and blocked my path."

Jeremy raised his head at the mention of Lowery's name. "He asked me how well I knew you; did you ever talk to me about where you'd come from, things like that. I told him you'd only been there at Mrs. Ingalls' a couple of weeks. That we talked about, well, everyday things. I tried to get past, told him I had to get to work. He put his hand out. 'I have a couple more questions,' he said, just like that—wouldn't let me by. I don't like that fellow," Ben said, shaking his head as he remembered the encounter.

"He asked me if *you'd* ever spoken about him, or asked any questions about him. He finally told me, 'you can go. That's it,' just like that. But I had to walk around him. The bastard stayed right out in the middle of the street."

They had reached the pier and Hazelwood slapped Jeremy's shoulder and hopped to the pier from the launch. "You watch yourself around that one. And tell your boss if he ever wants a *real* boat, to see us. We'll build him one—we'll even put one of these," he held his fingers over his nose in disgust, "gasoline engines in her."

Jeremy docked the launch at Paul's spot. Waiting for his boss to arrive from the Observatory, he decided to walk over to the freight house and check on arrivals. When he reached the shed, Bill pulled him away from the small crowd of people gathered around the freight depot. They were watching the workmen on the dock loading bricks onto the wagon for the last trip of the day out to the site.

"I think these chains are going to have to go back, but I wanted to check with you," he led Jeremy over to the corner.

"Well of course they're going back. We talked about them this..."

Bill cut him off, whispering, "I wanted to see you." He bent over, pulling out one of the chains. "Lowery was in here this morning. He must have waited for you to leave. He came in here like he owned the place—asked me where you were. I said you was at the Observatory."

"What else did he want?" That was twice in one day Lowery had been asking after him.

"He wanted to know if you talked to me about the places you'd been. I said no. Watch that guy there." Bill pointed out a small, wiry workman who was going in and out of the freight building. As he entered or left, his eyes darted over to them. "We think he's Lowery's rubberneck. The boys at the dormitory had some of the girlies from town out for a party last week. Not long before Lowery arrived," Bill nodded toward the brick-carrier, "he got up and left the dorm."

"Thanks, Bill," Jeremy said, starting to rise.

Bill put his hand out. "There's more," he said, pulling out the chain farther and holding it up. "Tommy Napper, the station agent, he ain't got no use for him either. Tommy said Lowery sent a couple of telegrams about you to some town in Illinois. And from what I hear of the talk at the dormitory, he even asked Ernie Walker about you."

God, thought Jeremy, *Ernie is the Superintendent of the Observatory and a friend of Paul's.* He'd have to hope Ernie would have given him a boost, and doubted Ernie would have any special liking for Lowery, who was always poking about the Observatory on some petty mission, making trouble.

Bill replaced the chain and they walked out of the shed and along the tracks. "I had me a wife out in Iowa once. Finally had to up and leave." Bill paused, sifting the memory. He bent down, picked up a hunk of cinder and threw it, sending it bouncing over the tracks and into the weeds beyond.

"I like you. I've had straw bosses I couldn't take to, but—well, you play the game fair. Fact is most everyone, least all of us working for Lockerby, like you. We knew we was getting a straw boss but he coulda' been a louse. All's I'm sayin', Jeremy, I don't know what your story is. We all got stories. But if I was you, I'd be wonderin' what that bird was up to. I've got to get back. See you tomorrow." He'd abruptly turned and was walking away before Jeremy could say anything.

Paul arrived a few minutes afterward and inspected the changes on the boat. After they'd cast off, he steered, putting the boat through its turns, satisfied with the new trim. "Now if only I can dock it without destroying either the boat or the pier."

"Why don't you ease back on the throttle," Jeremy offered as they moved along. Paul looked over at him, doing as he suggested until they were barely moving. "How about that lesson now?" Jeremy asked.

"Out here in the middle of the lake?"

"Why not, no piers to take out." He went to the stern and picked up a couple of cardboard cartons he'd gotten from Ben Hazelwood. Following Ben's suggestion, he first set one of the cartons overboard and a few seconds later the other. The cartons floated twenty feet apart. "There's the Bluffside pier. And you are going to practice docking."

For the next thirty minutes Paul brought the launch up to the cartons while Jeremy called advice to him, occasionally reaching down to reset the cartons. Finally, as their waterlogged "pier" sank, they were both satisfied with Paul's progress—so satisfied that they headed over to the real Bluffside pier where Paul managed to dock the boat with only a minor bump.

16

The train that had delivered Lora was still steaming at the depot. Only a handful of passengers boarded the *Ripple,* and as it got underway its ancient steam engine labored loudly.

She had not informed anyone of the exact time of her arrival, telling herself she didn't want Martha and her father making a fuss. She didn't acknowledge that her lack of notice had also given her the opportunity to contact Clarence had she weakened. She hadn't, and as the boat backed away from the pier at Williams Bay, she leaned against the stiff bench at the stern. As she looked out over the water, the sight of familiar Lake Geneva began to have a calming effect. Lora had boarded this delivery boat along with her luggage, having missed the regular passenger one.

"We'll deliver your baggage, ma'am, and you can follow on the next passenger. You'll be more comfortable," the mate at the dock had said, glancing at her stylish dress as he hoisted her luggage on board. But the *Ripple,* with its haphazard schedule and well-worn livery suited her fine on this day as it slowly moved out of the bay and around the shore of the lake.

She stood up and leaned on the rail as they rounded Conference Point, knowing it would be useless to look for the dome of the Observatory. Construction had barely begun and it wouldn't be visible above the trees until the end of the summer.

The *Ripple* nosed in at a small pier. Four men in denim work clothes boarded, glanced toward her and then away, electing to sit in the bow section. She guessed they were from the Observatory—probably going into one of the villages for the night—and she wondered if they might be some of the workers from the power station. Lora was proud of her father. He'd told her all about the project last autumn as they'd toured the site of the Observatory. As they'd reached the edge of a small incline, he had pointed out the future location of the power station. He had described how the motors, *his* motors, were going to raise the floor and move the huge telescope and the shutters on the dome. Father and daughter had walked around the grounds, kicking an occasional pile of leaves, until dusk and a frosty wind had driven them to hail a passing wagon for a ride to the depot and their return to Chicago.

She had been so busy with events in her own life over the past year that she had spent very little time with her father, and she felt badly about that. Her job at Darrow's firm and her relationship with him had made increasing demands on her time and energy. The long days at the office with Clarence had been physically and emotionally draining.

The boat pulled in to another pier, where a housekeeper and a male servant were waiting at the end. The Chicago newspapers and groceries were handed over, and the boat pulled away again. This boat performed a variety of chores, especially on a Saturday. The workmen at the bow had produced a deck of cards and were sitting in a tight circle, engrossed in their game. Someone might have lost his pay by the time they reached town, she guessed.

Lora wondered what the summer would hold for her. At twenty-six, was she becoming too old for all the Lake Geneva socializing? Could she really throw herself into the frivolous summer out at the lake? For the past three years she had spent little time up here. In '92 and '93 she'd worked at the World's Fair, only coming up for two weeks at the end of the season, and then last year with the strike and boycott, she was up for an even shorter time.

The *Ripple* drew up to the first of the double piers at Kaye's Park. The resort had already opened and children were playing on the wide lawn. Kaye's had a charm all its own, and Lora always looked forward to visiting. It was a place where she and her father had vacationed for years before "Bluffside" had been built. "Bluffside," she said it out loud. The name still didn't roll naturally from her lips.

The boat rounded Black Point and she glanced up to see their new house, partially hidden among the large oaks in front. After docking, the porters unloaded her suitcases and trunk and carried them down the long pier, eyeing the bluff that stretched above them with a visible lack of enthusiasm.

"Whoever named this Bluffside wasn't kidding," she overheard one workman grunt to the other as they started their climb. At the top she thanked and tipped them before rapping on the front door. Within moments, a beaming Martha was beckoning her in.

"Child! You always have to surprise us, and here I thought you was comin' up tomorrow or Monday. Your daddy's still at work over at the Observatory." Clucking and scolding all at once, Martha swept her inside, looking her up and down in an open appraisal. "Too skinny," she pronounced, "and you look too tired, too. You sit right here while I get you a cold root beer. Then I'll take you on a tour of the house."

Later, sitting in the kitchen watching Martha stir and chop in preparation for dinner, Lora allowed her mind to drift. It *would* be nice, she mused, to revel in the luxury of Bluffside for a while. And it would be especially nice to spend some time with her father.

She started, "My trunk! It's still on the porch. I've got a present in it for Father. And one for you, too, Martha." A mischievous smile pulled at the corners of Lora's mouth. "You'll never guess what it is."

"You shouldn't be spending money on me, child." Martha was scowling, but Lora knew she was pleased. "And don't worry about the trunk. Jeremy, our caretaker, will bring it in. He'll take those big suitcases up to your room, too. You just take what you want for the night and he'll do the heavy lifting later."

Lora brushed her off. "At least help me bring the suitcases in. I'll leave them here in this closet." She opened the door to one of the huge downstairs closets. A fishing pole was standing in the corner.

"Father's?"

"Well, Mr. Lockerby bought it in Williams Bay but I haven't seen him use it yet." Lora remembered her father taking her fishing at Kaye's Park. He'd make a game try at fishing, but he had far too much energy to enjoy it and Lora would wind up doing the fishing while he paced up and down the pier.

"And what's your opinion of our new man?" Lora's tone was offhand as she stood next to the closet, but she was dying to hear about him. "Our own caretaker." She laughed. "Martha, that sounds so grand when I say it, it makes us sound like—I don't know—the Sturgesses or Cranes or some family like that."

Martha moved across the kitchen, setting down her chopping knife and facing Lora. "I know your daddy's written you about Dr. MacDougal taking him in and referrin' him. Well, this Jeremy, he's real nice enough. Keeps to himself and polite and all, but from what I can tell he sure hasn't been a caretaker before. Like for instance the other day. Oh, I know he's workin' for your daddy at the Observatory too and it's not like he's a regular caretaker but, well, I saw him out by the garden plot—remember?" Lora nodded. She and Martha had planted a vegetable garden for the rear of the house last summer.

"He tilled it and all but then didn't seem to know what to do next. I watched him from the window. Finally I'd had enough and went out to show him just where and what to plant. But I noticed he seemed to pick up on what I'd showed him right away. He's smart, and he's a good-lookin' man too, though he's a little too old for you." Her back was to Lora as she opened the oven door.

"And how old is too old for me?"

"Mr. Darrow. He's too old for you."

"Now please, Martha. Don't start."

"This Jeremy though, Miz Lora, he's different," the housekeeper continued. "He has a, well, a look like he may be about to tell you somethin' and then he won't. It's almost like he has—I don't know—a spiritual side, though he don't seem too religious."

Spiritual, thought Lora, would be Martha's word. And probably not an accurate description, either. She knew Martha sometimes thought both Lockerbys, father and daughter, were too practical, too worldly and not spiritual enough. "From the way you describe him it almost sounds like we have some sort of a medium for our caretaker," she said, picturing the expression she'd seen on his face and the strange outfit he wore that day at Malcolm's. She considered but dismissed any thought that he would have remembered her as well, given his condition.

The two had moved to the kitchen and were still talking when they heard the door slam. Her father walked to the kitchen and Lora ran to meet him, throwing her arms around his neck. He was breathing heavily from the climb and his face was flushed and moist, even on the cool evening.

"I didn't expect you, darlin'. We could have brought you across—and on your own launch, too," he said, lifting her and twirling her around.

As her father set her down, she looked out the rear window. In the gathering dusk she saw Jeremy. He was slender, about six feet tall. She thought again about the glimpse she'd had of him in May, recalling the troubled, searching look. And how had Martha just described him? Almost spiritual? Allowing for Martha's exaggeration, it would be interesting to meet him. She watched the figure turn off the path and climb the steps of the cabin.

At dinner, she and her father talked away, interrupting and laughing as they filled each other in on their doings of the last month. Near the end of dinner her father brought up Jeremy, telling her about his cool action on that stormy crossing and how he had saved them.

"And Malcolm thinks he has some sort of amnesia?" she asked as she served up Martha's tapioca pudding for dessert.

"That's what he said, but you know me, darlin'. I don't ask a lot of questions." He told her what information Malcolm had supplied: details of the bicycle accident, and the fact that he'd been from Indianapolis originally. "But Jeremy's smart and he does his work. I think you'll agree when you've met him that we're lucky to have him with us." She knew, even discounting Clarence's flattery, that she'd become adept at sizing people up during the last couple of years and she began to look forward to their meeting.

After dinner she and her father continued their conversation until at last, noticing that he seemed to be tiring, she got out of her chair and walked over to kiss him on the forehead. Martha, about to retire herself, stood at the door of the kitchen.

"You have some letters on the mantel. And Miz Lora, I almost forgot, that Todd Brinkley has been over here asking after you." Martha's distaste for Todd was plain by the way she spat out his name. Her "almost forgetting" was no accident. "He said he was gonna drop over here tomorrow about noon in case you arrived. He wanted to take you for a ride on his yacht."

Lora picked up a couple of envelopes from the mantel, examining them as she climbed the stairs. One was from Jeanette Reilley, her old friend from the World's Fair and Pullman. The other had no return address. She recognized Clarence's handwriting at a glance.

She read Jeanette's note first. It was short, written in her slow, precise style. They were still at Pullman. Baby Matt was two and getting into everything. The other two children were so big that she doubted Lora would recognize them. Tim had been getting more work of late. She dearly hoped they'd get together soon. Lora made a mental note to respond to Jeanette the next day.

She tore open the other envelope as she kicked off her unlaced shoes and flung herself across the bed. As she read the letter, she could almost hear Clarence's voice. "Over and over, I have had to ask myself," he began, going on to question the wisdom of their continuing to see each other, concluding, of course, that they should. Lora read the letter' through and then reread it. She'd soon have to let him know whether she'd return to work for him in the autumn. She ran her fingers through her hair as she thought about her reply. Perhaps she should go to Chicago in a couple of weeks, have lunch with him. And nothing more.

She put the letters on her dresser and opened the door to her own porch. The night was chilly as she looked out over at Black Point and the lake beyond.

"So Darrow has problems in his marriage. And he's sure enough made some for Jessie—and for you as well. Those problems don't have to be yours, Lora." Karl's recent words of advice sounded in her ears.

17

The days of June were long and dawn came up quickly. Jeremy, always an early riser, was up before the sun, building a fire in the stove and putting on coffee. Sunday would give him a chance to get caught up. He retrieved his list of things to do, sitting down at the kitchen table. He'd taken this caretaker job as an opportunity to get away from Mrs. Ingalls, but he was learning how much this extra job entailed, especially for someone with almost no knowledge of landscaping. During his marriage, Mary Kaye had done the gardening on their suburban home, kidding him about killing every plant he touched. His only contribution had consisted of mowing the lawn. He was just plain lucky Martha had helped him with planting the garden.

Paul didn't seem particularly religious but Jeremy didn't know how much he should do on a Sunday. He decided he'd first sharpen the mower and do the lawn at the rear of the grounds, out of sight of the neighbors, before he worked on the garden. That should take him about three hours. Then he'd take a look at the boat and check out the engine and the improvements. The pier would also be the most likely place to cross paths with the mistress of the house.

He hurried through his grounds-keeping chores, then changed into a clean work shirt, picked up a wrench and screwdriver and started down the path toward the lake front. The rustic path weaved from his cabin around the garden and past the main Bluffside house. There was no noise or sign of life, and he was cautious about Paul's daughter. *She must be a pretty good sleeper,* he thought, wary as he set about tinkering with the engine. *Get on the wrong side of her once and you'll be out of a job or worse.* Still, he'd be living next to her all summer. She'd probably be a disappointment. Of course her father and Martha would have built her up beyond any reasonable expectations.

He squirted gasoline in the petcocks and cranked the engine. On the third try it turned over, coming to life. After listening to it for a minute or so, Jeremy cast off, opened the throttle and headed out into the lake. With the exception of a few fishing boats, the lake was all his. Even with the addition of the ballast, the craft was still overpowered. He opened the throttle all the way, trying to see if the boat would raise itself out of the water even on this calm day. It was improved but it still wanted to plow. Boat building was definitely an evolutionary art and true speedboats would be a long time in arriving. Still, the little boat went through some tight turns at the Narrows with more confidence than it had shown before.

Jeremy was heading back toward Bluffside when he saw a girl dressed in a red-checkered summer dress on the pier. She was standing at the end observing the boat. His pulse quickened when he realized who it was. He brought the launch in smartly, easing off on the reverse and cutting the engine to an idle as he coasted to the pier. He looped the bow line around a post.

"Why don't you hand me the other line," she offered. He did and she drew it around another post. "How does the boat run?" she asked simply. He climbed out onto the pier, taking the rope.

"A little better than before. She's been a bit light and we had to add some ballast." Hearing her speak surprised Jeremy. *How silly. Of course she's flesh and blood.* He guessed he'd expected or feared someone very stuffy or formal.

The black and white portrait had not done her justice, either. The oval face was far prettier in person, her brown eyes larger and much more expressive than he'd imagined. Her nose was just slightly tipped and her full lips parted in an expectant half-smile. For just a moment, a flicker of memory made him think he'd seen her somewhere before...but he dismissed the thought. It must have been the portrait Paul had shown him.

"So you're the other Lora," he said. She knitted her brow, not sure of his meaning, until he pointed to the name written in script on the boat's stern.

"And I'm the original, too," she laughed as she offered him her hand. "You have to be Jeremy. Martha tells me you're our new caretaker. And you're keeping father's books at the Observatory?"

"Well, Miss Lockerby," he took cover behind the formality, "your father seems to think I can manage as a sort of caretaker. I hope he's not wrong." She stepped to the edge of the pier, leaning on a post to inspect the boat.

"I can't believe father picked these out," she said with an almost private chuckle, running her hand over the green and white striped curtains which were folded up, barely protruding from the roof. "These curtains are just so unlike him," she shook her head. "Maybe he's changing in his old age.

"I heard you start the engine up and saw you leave and I said to myself, "I'll see if I can get a ride when he returns."

He held out his hand to her, inviting her aboard. She took it, stepping easily into the boat. He cast off and headed out. "Where would you like to go?"

"You're the engineer," she answered, her voice rising above the engine, "or is it captain?"

"On this boat it's both, and steward too, when your father puts in provisions for food and drink." He noticed the dimple in her chin when she laughed. Jeremy headed straight out, letting the boat knife swiftly through the still water. With the throttle almost wide open, he glanced over at his passenger. She'd taken off the straw hat, letting her auburn hair stream back in the wind. He wondered whether he should say something or wait for her to speak.

"Would you like to take the wheel?" he finally called. She moved over, setting down her hat as she grasped the wheel. She handled the boat far more naturally than her father had. When they were off Cedar Point, she cut the throttle, letting their wake catch up and propel them ahead.

"Do you know the history of the boat?" she asked, pushing her hair from her eyes. He decided he liked her voice. It had a musical quality and was lower than he'd imagined.

"Your father told me he'd purchased it from some company that was selling the Columbian Exposition boats."

"And did he tell you I gave him the idea?"

"No,"

"Well, I worked at the Fair and I knew these launches." She patted the wheel affectionately. "I was a kind of guide or hostess. Often I rode through the waterways on these, quite possibly on this very boat. They didn't have names though, only numbers." He noticed Lora refrained from applying her own name to the boat.

"Did you ever operate them?"

"Yes," she nodded with a faint smile, looking over at him. "We weren't supposed to, but at the end of the day it would be a long walk back from where the tours ended and we'd be tired. We often hopped on for a ride. These were battery boats and at night they charged them in the South Pond. The boatmen used to let us take the wheel. There was a covered tunnel that led from the basin into the South Pond. If they trusted you enough, they let you keep the wheel through the tunnel. It was dark and not very much wider than the launch. It was exciting—and a little scary." She moved away from the wheel and was leaning back against the railing, talking about her job as they drifted.

"I suppose you met quite a few important people over the summer?" he asked.

"Oh, yes, I did. The Fair was so beautiful and exciting, but so transitory. When I went back to teaching school in the fall, it was almost as though the summer had been a dream." She was standing at the rail looking into the water, her chin cupped in her hands, a mannerism she'd no doubt picked up from her father. Then she turned to him and grinned. "Here I go again, talking too much. Did you get to the Fair?"

"No, I'm afraid I didn't, but I feel as though I did. I've heard so much about it."

"I'm sorry you didn't get there. There really hasn't been anything like it before nor, I fear, will there be again."

"Your father," Jeremy ventured, not sure how far he should push this conversation with the boss's daughter, "told me you're active in the labor movement—in the Pullman strike?"

"I was. Old George Pullman might think he had the last say from the strike but we're going to come out on top." She paused. "You know I lost my teaching job at Pullman."

"Because of that strike?"

"Without a doubt." He knew she worked for Darrow in his law office but he didn't know that she'd lost her job as a direct result of the strike.

"The Pullman strike and Eugene Debs. It was because of everything last summer. Have you heard of Debs?" Jeremy nodded before he thought to catch himself.

"Anyway," she said, "here I just met you and I'm telling you my life's history. Is that how you get all the women to tell you all their secrets, Mr. Jeremy?" She tilted her head, beckoning him to take over the wheel.

He smiled in reply and headed back to Bluffside. It was a perfect cloudless day, and Jeremy was pleasantly distracted, thinking about their meeting when Lora cried out in dismay.

"Oh, heavens, he's here already."

Jeremy eased the launch in at the opposite side and helped Lora onto the pier. As he reached down to retrieve her hat, he heard voices from up on the bluff.

"There's our little anarchist now." Two young men in fresh-pressed whites and a young woman with a parasol were coming down the steps.

"Todd! And Frank and Charlotte!" She met the trio, greeting them warmly. Jeremy couldn't hear what was being said but the one she called Todd briefly put his arms around her. He turned away and stepped back toward the launch as the four walked out onto the pier.

"Jeremy is my father's assistant at the Observatory, and he's also helping us out by stepping in as caretaker here at Bluffside this summer." *That was certainly a generous job description,* Jeremy thought. Frank waved a friendly hello. Todd studied him closely for a second or two before raising his hand.

"Let's go, anarchist," he said, turning back to Lora and leading her towards his gleaming white boat. He was about thirty, Jeremy guessed, and looked to be in good shape.

"Todd, I'm not ready. Why Martha..."

"Don't worry about Martha," Frank cut in, laughing. "Her old friend Todd explained we were whisking you away for a cruise."

"Good meeting you, Gerald," Todd called back. "Will you be a good fellow there...and give us a hand," he gestured toward the rope. It wasn't a question but a casual command. Jeremy cast them off, watching as the stately yacht backed away from the pier. He read the name *Ariadne* as it turned and started away. As Jeremy stepped down into the launch, he heard Todd call for the champagne to be opened. And in spite of the heat of the sun, a chill spread over him as he covered the *Lora L* with its canvas.

18

As the *Ariadne* glided off with Todd calling to Frank to open the champagne, Lora turned to wave goodbye but Jeremy's back was to her. Martha was right; Jeremy was a good listener but gave away little about himself. In the past two years Lora had become adept at drawing people out, and given time, she was certain she'd be able to learn more about him. He *was* attractive, she thought, though perhaps Martha had exaggerated his looks. He was friendly enough, and surprisingly at ease. There was something about him...her thoughts were cut short by the sound of Charlotte's voice. She turned, embarrassed to realize the other girl had been chattering.

"Anyway," she continued, "I told everyone at the club, 'this is our own Lora.' I mean, it's like we know a celebrity! You're just going to have to tell us what you've been up to this past year. We can't wait to hear about everything."

"We mean *everything* too, anarchist," Todd called over, one hand on the wheel.

"Todd, you hush!" Charlotte scolded. Frank emerged from the cabin. He held a champagne bottle in one hand, balancing a tray with crystal glasses in the other.

"Listen, Lora, we've all summer, I hope, to hear the details of your past year. On this very first day you're going to relax—and celebrate." He filled the glasses, letting champagne froth over the tops. Unlike most of Todd's friends, Lora mused, Frank had a warmth and a generosity that was totally unaffected. He was one of those people who never really changed. You could be away for a year and come back to find him just as you remembered him, infectious laugh and all.

"A toast to Lake Geneva and the summer of '95," he boomed. In her mind's eye, Lora could see Frank many years into the future—a genial, fumbling grandfather surrounded by little ones. His family, the McClures, had had their money for ages. Both he and Charlotte had a relaxed gentility that the new money on the lake lacked. She guessed she'd be classed with the new money herself—or at least on its edges. Todd would be too. His money had come from his Aunt Harriet. It was Aunt Harriet's boat they were on and his wealth and station depended on her good will.

Frank's old-fashioned manners were frayed sometimes, she remembered, by the champagne and his association with Todd. Partly, he was just being swept up in the frothy spirit of the '90's. Frank steadied himself against the gentle roll of the yacht as he topped off their glasses. He toasted again, at the same time pulling a blast on the *Ariadne's* whistle.

"Here's to our friendship," and he looked at Charlotte, who tilted her head in expectation. "Here's to the girl who's made me the happiest fella on this lake—on this earth!"

"Certainly," Todd turned to him, "to the girl who made you so happy. I'll drink to..." he paused, "Gertie Potter." He laughed broadly at his own joke.

"Todd, I'm going to throw you off this boat," said Charlotte and she smacked his shoulder. "Why, Frank hasn't laid eyes on Gertie since 1893. *Have* you, Frank?" She raised her champagne glass above his head.

Listening to the three banter, Lora remembered how she had felt on guard the few times she had been out with Clarence and his friends. They were all so damned witty, particularly the women who seemed to be measuring Lora. She had held her own, but at the end of a long, social evening she was drained. She and Clarence had once ended up in a pointless argument over something that had been said. Maybe in this company, annoying though it might sometimes be, she could at least let herself relax.

Todd and Frank looked sporty, both dressed in their whites and dark blue engineer caps—the standard uniform of the professional yacht engineers. Wearing that garb, she guessed, was the newest seasonal fad for the wealthy young men of Lake Geneva.

"Give me a refill, my duchess," Todd called, his voice too full of bravado as it rose above the noise of the engine. Lora took the bottle from

Frank and refilled both their glasses.

"Where are we going today, my captain?" she asked as she poured, forcing herself into the spirit of the outing.

"Well, madam," he said, dropping his voice and pulling on his mustache, "I thought perhaps we'd steam around the Cape and maybe come up the west coast of Africa. Or, maybe perhaps the east coast of Williams Bay." A sudden, deep pang of longing gripped Lora. *Good Lord! The emptiness of this fellow. And I wanted to try to forget you, Clarence.*

Frank and Charlotte had moved over to the railing and were holding onto each other as the yacht, now running at full speed, had begun to shudder under them, a large wake fanning out behind. "It really is good to see you again," Todd said. "I...well, I very much missed you. I thought to come down from Milwaukee to pay you a visit, but when you didn't answer my letters..." She couldn't explain why she hadn't answered him. She had been busy, but mainly it was indifference.

Lora had regarded their acquaintance of last year merely as a late summer diversion, nothing more. She had come up for a couple of weeks at the end of August on the heels of the Pullman strike and its aftermath and had needed to relax. Her father had wanted her help to finish their move to Bluffside. She'd been reintroduced to Todd at a party—they had met the year before. Lora hadn't thought to write to him when she went back to Chicago and had been surprised to receive his letters.

She had been mildly flattered that he had written, but was so busy working for Clarence—going back and forth to Pullman, getting ready for the Debs trial—that she just hadn't found time to answer. She would think of an explanation later. *Lora,* she chided herself, *you're up here to try to get over that nagging ache of being separated from Clarence.*

"If we're going clear around the Cape," she lifted her glass, "I'll have to check on provisions," and she tapped on the nearly empty bottle, joining Frank in the cabin. In a minute or so Todd cut the speed. The graceful yacht slowed to a drift. In the distance, another yacht rounded Cedar Point and headed into Williams Bay. With the engine idling at a murmur, the stillness on the lake was magnified. The four of them moved through the cabin to the afterdeck. Frank had gotten another bottle and, holding it out, he popped the cork, letting it fly far from the boat.

"Whew! It's sweltering in that cabin," Frank exclaimed. "Do you know you have the heat on?"

"It's that exhaust steam pipe." The annoyance was plain in Todd's voice. "It still runs through the cabin. It was supposed to be rerouted last winter. The damned thing keeps the cabin too hot to use. Aunt Harriet must have forgotten to tell the people at the boat works."

As the morning slipped by, Lora was coaxed into recounting some of her activities of the past year. She tried not to get preachy about the strike, its aftermath or Debs' trial. Given their families and wealth, she knew how her friends would feel regarding the American Railway Union. But to her surprise they did want to know all about Debs and Pullman. Charlotte seemed honestly shocked by some of the incidents Lora described, in particular one that involved a heartless eviction of a family down the street from her. She described in stark detail the expressions on the faces of the starving children.

And Eugene, that shy, kind, complicated man, she thought, it's time they heard the truth about him. She set about explaining him, but after a few minutes gave it up. The public had been sold the image of a person playing god with the commerce of the country.

There might be a time later to defend what Debs is about, but not now. Besides, any long narrative would be sure to make Todd even more ill at ease, she knew.

"That Pullman! He's nothing but a damn fool!" Frank exclaimed, surprising her. He suddenly came forward in his wicker chair, slamming its legs on the deck. "Why couldn't he have met his men halfway?" Even Todd nodded at that. Lora felt encouraged. Maybe the message of the strike and the basic unfairness of the government during Debs' trial—maybe some of that had gotten through.

Todd stood up. "We'd better tell these fair maidens what we have in store for them."

"Are you going to make us walk the plank?" Charlotte asked.

"I have something much worse in store for you. That's right, ladies, you *should* look frightened. We're going to take you to Kaye's Park where you'll be made to dance with us!" He and Frank exited through the cabin and pointed the drifting yacht toward the resort.

Charlotte moved into Todd's chair next to Lora. Her somberness at hearing about Pullman was replaced by a cheery glow. "You don't know how happy I am. I haven't had a chance to tell you, but Frank and I are going to be married!"

Lora hugged her friend. "Wonderful! When? And here you let me go on and on about myself. Is it still a secret though? I mean Frank, he didn't say..."

"Oh, you know him—twenty-eight and still doesn't know how to tell his mother anything. But we'll get married next spring or summer." And the two began discussing Charlotte's wedding plans as the *Ariadne* eased into a berth at one of Kaye's Park's two piers.

"Lora, you've something on your mind, haven't you? And it's not Pullman, either."

"Does it show so readily, Charlotte?"

"Only to me. Not to the boys." Two neatly uniformed attendants were securing the yacht at the already crowded double pier. "Oh, I shouldn't ask, but...is it a man?"

Lora started to answer but Charlotte took her arm. "Not now. We'll have a chance for a good talk." The two stepped out onto the dock.

From the pier, Lora noticed that the Crane yacht *Passaic* was moored adjacent. The Crane family was fond of taking their first-time guests over to Kaye's Park. How different Richard Crane is from Pullman, Lora thought as she shielded her eyes, searching to recognize anyone on deck. Crane had been a pioneer in paying a percentage of his company's profits to its employees—with good worker relations to show for the effort.

"Listen to that music," Charlotte said as the two young men joined them on shore. "I'm telling you, Frank, you better not have had too much champagne, because I'm going to dance your shoes off." How handsome Todd and Frank look, Lora mused, and even with those silly hats perched to the sides of their heads that somehow seemed to fit.

They crossed the tree-lined circular driveway near the lake. There was a clamor of horses and carriages wheeling around. Ahead were the resort buildings. "What's first, girls?" asked Frank, sliding his arm around Charlotte's waist. "Are you ready for a waltz lesson?" He began to whistle, mimicking the orchestra in the hall.

"Let's just stroll a bit," said Charlotte, as a carriage careened near them, drawing a menacing scowl from Todd.

"Judging from the smells," he looked off to his right, "we must be near the zoo." A crowd, mostly families, had gathered in front of the cages. By now the foursome had moved up from the shore area and were walking among the smaller buildings containing the shops. A passive Indian sat out in front of one, selling beaded moccasins.

The main hotel building was ahead. Lora was surprised at the number of people gathered on the veranda, some talking, or some just sitting, enjoying the music. *If it's this crowded now, imagine what it will be like for the Fourth of July and afterwards,* she thought. If there was any financial crisis in the country, it wasn't apparent at Kaye's Park.

Lora saw a young girl, about sixteen, standing with her parents. She was leaning against the railing, swaying to the music. At the same time, she was trying hard to act reserved, mustering all the sophistication she could.

Lora had been the age of that girl when her father had first brought her to Kaye's. She's stood on that same veranda, taking in all the sights, imagining she was one of the ladies with an escort on her arm. The pace of the resort was still the same. The rich and the not-so-rich bustled about, enjoying the park, but without the shuffling and rudeness she'd noticed at carnivals and fairs.

She had loved the resort the moment she'd seen it, and dearly hoped her father would, too. She couldn't remember him ever taking a holiday before. He needed a rest and this had seemed like the perfect place. Once there, however, he was unable to slow down, whisking her one moment to the zoo and the next over to see the gruesome collection of freaks and oddities Kaye's had assembled. She remembered being both fascinated and repulsed. Inside a tent was a man who could pull his skin almost a foot off his arm and snap it back. Next door was a sword swallower her father convinced her they should stay and see. Lora almost gagged anew as she pictured him. Most of all, though, she remembered the scary, exciting sailboat ride. She'd been seated on the edge of the cockpit, the boat skimming along with the water inches away.

The "skipper" was really just a teenager, only a year or so older than herself. She remembered him shouting to lean out over the water as the boat heeled on its side, threatening to overturn. Her non-swimmer father had held onto her with one hand while the other clung white-knuckled to the gunwale. He'd glanced at her with a tight smile, trying not to show his fear. And she remembered his smile as they'd gone ashore, watching as his daughter and the youthful seaman had exchanged quick, hopeful glances.

The next summer at Kaye's, her beloved skipper had departed. She asked discreetly about him, all to no avail. Her father insisted that summer that if she wanted to continue taking sailboat rides, she'd have to take swimming lessons as well. And learn to swim she did, in spite of the clumsy bathing costume she wore. By the season's end, she was swimming out well beyond the piers, back and forth along the shoreline, frequently bringing out the lifeguard in a rowboat to coax her back.

"Lora. It *is* you!" She turned at the sound of her name. "I didn't think you'd be back this summer." Lora recognized Victoria Koch, who lived at the estate down the south shore between Kaye's and Black Point—Lora couldn't recall its name. Victoria, a slender, pretty girl knew Lora's companions as well, and they all fell into talking, their voices rising above the orchestra in the pavilion.

She told them she had been working at her father's manufacturing plant. And *her* news was that she'd be getting married in the fall. The marriage would likely take place right at Villa Thekla. *There*, thought Lora, *she's supplied the name herself.*

The other three had followed the music inside the pavilion. Victoria was about to part, then pulled Lora close. "Who is that caretaker staying out at your place this summer?" She cocked her head. "I heard about him from the Seipps last week when I arrived." Victoria recounted the event where Jeremy had saved her father and himself. Lora wondered if this tale wasn't getting blown out of proportion, though her father had given Jeremy full credit.

"I've only just met him, Victoria."

"Well, by the way the Seipps described him, he sounds very singular. Mrs. Seipp thought there was something about him that was..." she hesitated, trying to recall the word. " 'Enigmatic,' I think she said."

"Victoria, I think Mrs. Seipp is given to high drama. At any rate, you all make him sound very mysterious, indeed. I'll try my best to solve any mysteries this summer." They laughed and parted. As Lora moved away, she felt perplexed. The perilous story and description of Jeremy intruded on her carefree mood.

"There you are," Todd called. "We're going to dance this one." He guided her out onto the crowded floor alongside Frank and Charlotte and the four danced, changing partners back and forth for nearly an hour, until, happily glowing, they sought the benches along the wall.

Todd found a waitress who returned with a pitcher of beer and steins for the thirsty dancers. They watched as a polka band replaced the orchestra. Lora had tried the polka last spring in Chicago. She urged her friends back out onto the dance floor and they attempted the steps, moving with more spirit than skill while out across Lake Geneva the afternoon sun dropped closer to the Fontana hills.

Frank announced that dinner would be on him. This earned him a round of cheers as the others followed him into the dining room, laughing and talking as they entered. An older woman seated at one of the tables motioned Charlotte over. Lora stepped behind her.

"You must be a little less boisterous, dears," she said, smiling tightly.

"And just who…" Lora started, but Charlotte turned and guided her away, smiling sweetly as she did at the matron whose mouth was agape.

"Lora, darling, you're going to have to relax, and remember you're not still with those strikers."

Fried chicken with all the trimmings, a Kaye's Park specialty, arrived. Charlotte, her eyes glowing, raised her stein and offered a toast. "I love this place and I just hope we all come back here often through the years, and that Kaye's lasts forever and a day."

"And us with it," joined in Frank as the four touched mugs. Todd placed his hand on Lora's.

Deciding she should get into the spirit, she reached over, pulling his engineer's cap—he was still wearing it at the table—down almost over his eyes. "If you're going to wear that, Todd, at least wear it like a real engineer."

"Why don't you lead *me* on one of your strikes? Maybe Aunt Harriet will give me a raise."

"What are you going to threaten not to do?" Frank cut in with a good-natured laugh. "You don't *do* anything anyway."

"Oh, dear," Charlotte said, peering out across the lake at the setting sun. "I hate to spoil any afternoon as good as this, but if we're going to get back home, well, Todd dear, we'd better get started." Frank signaled the waiter.

When they arrived back at the shore, Todd and Frank readied the *Ariadne,* shoveling on coal and building the steam. While the pressure built, Todd uncorked another bottle of champagne. The bottle was warm and the wine sloshed over their glasses, dripping on their hands. The warm bubbly liquid tickled Lora's nose and she set her glass down.

Just as Frank was about to cast off the lines, Todd was hailed by a well-dressed young man on the pier. Lora recognized him from the previous summer. His name was Doug something, and he was an obnoxious pest, one who could sober up enough to be nasty. He was an old friend of Todd's from Milwaukee. She wouldn't soon forget his manner of leering.

Todd called to Frank to hold the ropes and he sauntered over to join his friend. Doug leaned over on a post, his arm on Todd's shoulder, laughing loudly as he responded to something Todd said. Todd laughed as well and they both turned their gaze toward the *Ariadne*. Charlotte sized up the situation and roused Frank to cast off. Doug slapped Todd good-naturedly on the back before he ambled out along the pier.

Grabbing his champagne glass, Todd settled back behind the helm. He called goodbye to his friend as he backed the yacht away—one hand on the wheel, the other holding both the glass and throttle. He drained the glass and pitched it over the side as he turned the big yacht, narrowly missing the incoming *Arthur Kaye*. How a fellow like Doug could bring out the worst in people, she thought.

"Good lord, Todd!" she cried. "You know..." and she started to tell him that the crystal he'd casually thrown overboard would have equaled a full week's wages at Pullman—doing the kind of hard work he'd never done in his life. She felt Charlotte's pull at the puffed sleeve of her dress. She let herself be hushed. Tonight was the start of the summer and she wasn't going to mount any soap boxes.

"What is it, my goddess?" he asked after they had backed out into open water.

"I don't like it when you act childish, and you can remember that, too."

He gave the wheel a practiced spin, pushing the throttle forward as they moved out into the lake. "And how would you like me to act on a night such as this, with a sea goddess—correction—lake goddess in my mortal presence?" he asked as he tried to take her hand. She pushed his arm away. Frank and Charlotte were looking back at Kaye's, watching the glow as the newly-installed electric lights flickered on. Rocking arm in arm to the fading strains of a Strauss waltz, their attention was on no one but themselves.

Within a few minutes, the vessel had pulled in at the Belvidere Park landing. Frank and Charlotte alighted and the four exchanged goodbyes. A half moon had risen and as the *Ariadne* backed away, Lora went to the stern and set out a lantern as darkness closed over the lake.

Todd had run at nearly full speed to Belvidere Park, but now, with just the two of them aboard, he let the yacht serenely slice the water as they headed toward the south shore. He took off his engineer's cap and looped it onto a chair at the front of the boat. Lora paused for a moment, not wanting to give him any false encouragement. Finally, she shrugged, then removed her own hat, sailing it into the same chair.

With no warning, he reached over, letting go of the wheel, and drew her to him. She pushed him away, crying "Look out, you'll wreck us!" He looked up and saw nothing but darkness ahead. Then he spun the wheel and turned the yacht, no more than a hundred feet from shore.

"See what you do to me." He refilled his glass and drained it. Lora quickly moved to the side of the yacht, collecting herself as she watched the shore, occasionally glancing at Todd, her anger rising.

In a minute or so, as they drew opposite the Harvard Club, he cut the throttle and let them drift to a stop. Moving to the bow, he heaved the anchor over, letting out the chain until it secured on the bottom. Then he sauntered back, pausing before he stepped unsteadily down into the hold. She leaned over to watch as he used a long-handled shovel to push the coals to the back of the firebox, effectively banking the fire.

Climbing back to the deck, he filled his glass again, then waved the bottle toward Lora. Thanks to the champagne, his earlier uncertainty had disappeared. "Come on, join in on the fun." She shook her head. "Well, we were getting to be good friends last summer weren't we? And you certainly seemed happy enough to see me." Todd turned away, stifling a hiccup. She wasn't afraid of him, at least not yet, but she had never seen him drunk. Then he suddenly gripped her arm, pulling her close. He reached for her chin with his free hand.

"I told you to *stop*…damn it." There was a real edge to her voice. "Do you want me to pull that whistle?"

The look was hard, but it flickered off his face, replaced by a smile. "No I don't, so I'll have to fix it." He reached up and neatly detached the whistle cord, stuffing it into his pocket. "Those folks over on shore don't want their sleep disturbed." He took a long swig from the bottle.

"I heard all about you during the Debs trial, that you were working for that Darrow, being real important and too busy to answer a letter," he slurred. "And I thought we were friends last summer."

"Todd, we still can be friends. It'll be a long summer"—she looked to the shore—and it would be a long cold swim in this dress with some embarrassing explaining when I arrived, she finished the sentence silently.

Todd raised the bottle to his mouth again. In another moment, he'd resume his menacing attentions. Reasoning with him in his condition would be out of the question. Maybe she could use his ego to her advantage; a little cold water would cool his ardor. She walked to the rail, glanced up at the moon, and then knelt down and reached a hand into the water.

"What a beautiful night. It's too bad it's too cold for a swim."

"Too cold? Don't be silly. You felt how warm a day it was." He joined her at the rail, scooping up a handful of water. Lora saw him wince from the cold as he turned away from her.

"And if I were to be goin' in, might my lake goddess be escortin' me?" he slurred.

"Oh, Todd," she looked down, "I...don't know." Her measured hesitation lasted a moment too long.

He stood back up, trying to slip an arm around her once again. "On second thought, I believe I'll just stay dry up here and renew an old friendship."

Lora half-twisted away as he reached for the bottle. "That's right, let a little chill in the water frighten you off. Or is it," she paused, remembering from last summer that Todd was a poor swimmer, "that you're afraid because the water's over your head here?" It was a low trick, she knew, born of her alarm, but Todd took the bait.

"Afraid of some cold water, am I? Is that what you think? You just watch! Let me get these clothes off and you'll see some swimming!"

Lora watched the door of the cabin slam after him. She heard a chair being knocked over, followed a few moments later by a loud splash. He was paddling a few feet off the side of the *Ariadne*. "This isn't so bad. You had a good idea after all, even if you won't join me."

With Todd in the water she could pull the anchor and start the yacht. There was probably still pressure in the boiler. She knew enough about boats to take it as far as Bluffside. Looking down at Todd, however, she doubted if he could make it to shore. He was almost straight up and down in the water, struggling awkwardly to keep his head above the surface. He was an even worse swimmer than she'd remembered. The cold water would have deflated him enough to make him unthreatening. It was time to get him aboard.

"Todd, come on up. It's too cold to stay in there."

"You thought I'd be scared being over my head, eh?" His teeth were chattering so badly that she could hardly understand him. "Watch this!" He began to paddle away from the boat and toward the open lake.

"Stop! Todd, do you hear me? Stop!" She thought he might turn back after a few yards, but he continued and she quickly lost sight of him. When she heard his frantic splashing a few minutes later, she was just able to make out his shape, dangerously far from the boat. He started to call but gagged suddenly on a mouthful of water.

Lora looked for a life preserver. *Damn! Where does he keep them?* She heard a muffled cry, this time for help. She pulled off her shoes and stockings, throwing them aside as she searched. There were no life preservers to be seen.

"Todd! Keep yourself afloat. I'm coming!" She tore at her clothes, racing to get them off. The next sound from Todd was a pitiful, choked gurgling, which carried frighteningly well over the water. Lora threw off the last of her clothing and climbed up onto the rail. She held the stanchion, straining to get a glimpse of him.

Seconds later, she arched over the side in a dive that carried her deeper than she wanted. When she surfaced she set out stroking for where his head had last bobbed on the surface. Down in the water it was impossible to see anything. There was no sound except for her own splashing. She panicked for a moment, wondering if she was too late. Then she touched cold flesh. Todd had come to the surface alongside her. Lora was just reaching for him, about to give a sigh of gratitude, when she was suddenly seized and pulled under. Caught by surprise, she swallowed water. In his desperate fright, Todd had pulled them both down, straight toward the bottom. Her ears were ringing and she knew that in a few seconds she would pass out. Pushing against him with all her strength, she wrested herself from his grasp. Then she grabbed his hair and with her lungs bursting, at last broke the surface, gasping desperately for air. Todd was now too far gone to fight her as she held on to him, floating, slowly getting her breath.

Lora knew she had to get him to the boat and out of the water. Weakened from being dragged and still coughing water, she searched for the *Ariadne*. When she saw it, it looked to her to be a mile away. She rolled Todd onto his back and got a hand under his chin, pointing him toward the boat.

She had been so focused on keeping Todd and herself alive that she hadn't really felt the cold of the water, but as she started for the boat, it overtook her. It was bone chilling. She realized that her feet were already numb; she couldn't even tell if they were still propelling her. Her legs were growing numb as well. When she looked up, the boat seemed no closer. Even if she's had the voice to cry out, she knew there was no one to hear her. And then, ringing in her ears, she imagined she heard music. She forced her head out of the water. It wasn't some trick of her mind. It was the polka band at Kaye's Park! The sound was traveling more than a mile across the water on the still night. *And we were listening to that music less than an hour ago,* she thought as the water washed over her head.

It had been nearly a year since Lora had done any swimming and she found herself tiring fast. Her arms were stiffening and both hands were completly numb. How stupid he was, trying to show off! It was going to cost them their lives. The water no longer felt as cold. The numbness that had started in her hands and feet was spreading all over her body.

Lora was tempted to relax, to give in to the water which began to seem less threatening, but something inside her rebelled, demanding she hang on to Todd, to try to swim just a little further. She began lying to herself, telling her spent body that she need only swim another three or four strokes.

Her hand was so numb she barely realized she had touched something. Looking up, she saw they had reached the *Ariadne*. She grabbed onto the bumper that projected two or three inches out from the side. Todd made a low moan. "Oh, please, Todd. Don't die. Not now. I'm *sorry* for what I did. Please, God, don't let him die!"

Lora knew she wouldn't be able to lift him on board. She glanced at the shore. It wasn't more than seventy or eighty feet away and at fifty feet she could touch bottom. But she realized that she—they—couldn't make it. If she let go of the boat she wouldn't have the strength to swim another stroke.

Hanging onto the bumper with one hand and Todd with the other, she slowly moved around to the front of the yacht. Lora could find no place to climb aboard. She remembered seeing a ladder near the bow. "Why didn't I think to put it over the side?" she cried. The *Ariadne* was tugging gently at its anchor, the chain pulling back from the bow. There was only one thing she could do. She pulled Todd to it.

"Can you hear me? *Please, Todd*, can you *hear* me?" He finally gave a small groan. She draped him over the chain as best she could, his head out of the water. "You'll have to hang onto this chain," she said, feeling herself go under as she put his arms around it. When she surfaced, she saw him nod weakly.

"You can do it." She patted him and then let go, watching. He stayed in place, but for how long she couldn't guess. Lora looked at the chain, leading tantalizingly up to the bow. *Damn! I can't pull myself up on it,* she realized, tears filling her eyes.

She made her way back along the boat to the middle, where the deck sloped closest to the water. This would have to be her spot. She tried to pull herself out of the water but her arms were like lead. At last, in desperation, she got a knee up on the bumper strip and managed to grab the railing with her unresponsive hands. With one final effort, she raised herself and tumbled head-first over the rail and into the boat.

Lora fell hard onto the deck, hitting her nose and her leg. That would hurt later on, she realized, but she was too numb to feel anything at the moment. She crawled forward on her hands and knees until she reached the ladder and dragged it over to the side. Once it was in place she paused for a moment to catch her breath. Then she forced herself back down the ladder and into the freezing lake again.

She found Todd still hanging over the anchor chain but with his head barely out of the water. "I've got the ladder down. The ladder! Can you hear me?" His eyes were open, staring ahead. "Listen to me, let go of the chain. We've got to get into the boat. Let go, please!" He was frozen. She would have to pry his fingers off the chain, one at a time.

Her own hands were so stiff that she couldn't feel them. But Todd didn't resist her efforts, and with his hands finally loose, he started to slip back into the water. With one hand, she held his head as high as she could, knowing if he got any more water he'd panic and pull them both under the surface for good.

They finally reached the ladder. "Hold the ladder." Feeling the boat seemed to put a glimmer of life into him. She repeated, "Hold on!" and he managed to wrap his fingers around one of the rungs. "Now pull!" she screamed, "Pull, damn you, pull!" She could feel the icy water wresting away the rest of her own strength. She stepped on the bottom of the ladder. She couldn't feel it under her feet but she wasn't sinking so she guessed that she was standing on it. Her hands pushed on his buttocks.

"Pull!" she gasped. He gave a little pull as she shoved with her last energy, dumping him head first over the rail. She leaned against the boat, gasping for breath, and finally dragged herself aboard, landing in a heap next to him.

Her breath came in short, painful pants. Todd's was barely audible, and becoming fainter. *Don't let him die now. Please, not after all this,* she prayed.

Lora and the other guides at the Columbian Exposition had been required to watch a demonstration on lifesaving, in case a child fell into one of the lagoons. Lora had been one of the volunteer "victims." Now she desperately tried to recollect what she'd been taught as she rolled Todd onto his back and pushed on his chest. He began to vomit what seemed like gallons of water. After a time, he began to breath more regularly. He even began protesting.

"Stop," he whispered feebly.

She felt dizzy and began to get sick herself. Standing up and holding the rail, she retched over the side, trying to keep the water out of her airway. At last she collapsed back on the deck. When she looked over, Todd was staring dully at her.

"I thought...I...was dead."

She reached over and clasped his hand, feeling her own dizziness begin to die down. Then she pulled herself up again and stumbled toward the cabin, still not able to feel her feet beneath her. She opened an ornate chest and reached in to find blankets. She wrapped one about her and bent down to pick up the other. She dimly perceived heat coming from a pipe. And then she remembered Todd's earlier complaint about the heat from the boiler circulating through the cabin.

She got back to Todd and wrapped him in the blanket. With his arm draped over her shoulder, she managed to get him inside the cabin. She pulled the little cot out from the wall. They were both now shaking so violently that she could just barely set him onto the cot. She found one of the cork life preservers and put it under his head. He tried to talk but she quieted him, and in moments he fell asleep, breathing heavily, his mouth slack. She wrapped the blanket tightly around herself and stepped outside.

There was no sign of life on shore. Todd's half-full champagne bottle was standing next to the wheel. She took it back into the cabin and curled up in one of the wicker chairs. Holding the bottle with two trembling hands, she lifted it to her lips, feeling some go down her throat as more of the bubbles ran down her chin. After a long while her breathing began to return to normal and her shivering subsided, thanks to the heated cabin. She tried to put their close call with death out of her mind—to think instead about getting home, about her soft, warm bed, as sleep overtook her, and the bottle slipped from her hands and rolled across the cabin floor.

19

As Lora awoke, she let out a low groan. She ached all over. Even the slightest movement caused pain. The nightmare of the evening before flooded back. Todd was still asleep. His breathing was regular, the light snoring a welcome sound. Lora stood up slowly and stiffly, glad to be able, at last, to feel the engine's low vibrations under her feet. Then she noticed blood on her blanket and discovered that her shin was gashed and her knee was bloody and swollen from where she had bumped it on the railing. Hobbling painfully across the cabin, she looked into the mirror.

"Good God!" She stared at the deep circles under her eyes, then touched the bridge of her nose, where blood had caked. "How will I ever explain this?"

The wooded shoreline was visible from the windows. They were just off the Harvard Club and the shore, so out of reach last night, was less than a hundred feet away. From the angle of the sun, she knew it must be nearly seven o'clock. People would be stirring, and the *Ariadne* would be a familiar sight. She made up her mind; they couldn't be discovered, at least not in their present condition. She looked for her clothes and remembered stripping them off at the front of the yacht. She'd fetch them and then attend to Todd. Lora opened the door and stepped out to hear the newly awakened birds chirping on shore. It was a welcome sound and a beautiful morning to be alive. She spotted her clothes and went to collect them, then stopped in mid-step

On the lake side of the *Ariadne*, not fifty feet away, was a small rowboat. It held a lone fisherman who was facing the lake with his back to the boat. Absorbed in his fishing, he hadn't seen nor heard her. She drew the blanket about her and hurried the distance to her clothes. She scooped up her dress and underthings, the blanket half falling from her as she bent over. Starting back, she stepped over some deck ropes when she heard a *plop* on the surface nearby. She looked over to see the fisherman's eyes following his cast—until they met hers.

He dropped his pole and stared open-mouthed at her. Lora managed a quick smile before hurrying the rest of the way to the cabin. She turned at the door to see him nearly overturning his boat as he lunged to retrieve his pole.

After dressing, she checked Todd for any obvious breaks or cuts. Except for a lump on his forehead, she could find no sign of injury. He stirred and opened his eyes. "Lora. You saved my life. Oh, God…"

"Can you stand up?" she asked, cutting him off and looking away. She got his clothes from the stern and tossed them to him. He seemed to be in remarkably good shape, without all her aches and stiffness.

After putting on his clothes, he went out to see about getting up steam. Lora found a towel, dipped it into the lake and started dabbing at her face. "And isn't this summer off to some start," she said under her breath. "Maybe I ought to go back to Pullman for a rest."

Todd had drawn up the anchor. She watched him from inside the cabin while he stared for a long moment at the chain which had support-ed him as he'd hung wrapped around it. When they had at last gotten underway, he steered along the south shore. He'd retrieved the whistle cord and put it back in place. Lora pulled up a wicker chair and sat down gingerly. Some of the stiffness might have begun to ease but she knew her knee was going to be painful.

He kept his eyes on the lake ahead. "Lora, I can't thank you enough. I don't know how I got into such trouble. One minute I was swimming along fine and the next, I had this terrible cramp."

A terrible cramp indeed! She had seen him flaying through the water before he went down. His old egotism was coming back.

"But I liked the idea of a moonlight swim," and he turned and gave her a wink. She closed her eyes tightly.

"We'll have to do it again."

"The next moonlight swim we go on, Todd, will be in two feet of water and no more."

He passed off her remark. "We're going to take up where we left our friendship last year, aren't we?" There was uncertainty in his voice.

132

Lora paused before answering, weighing her words. "I don't know. I'm just up here to relax—that is—I *was* up here to relax a little, and to see what I want to do," (and after last night…).

"Well, you see the way Frank and Charlotte were—around each other—so close."

"Todd," she interrupted, "Frank and Charlotte are engaged." More than ever she was realizing she wanted no romantic involvements this summer, certainly not with Todd.

"When I wrote you about this summer, I thought about us, about…" he cleared his throat, "well, even about our future. Lora, I'm maturing. Oh, it may not be so plain to notice…"

It's not, she said to herself.

"…but I have. Besides, everyone up here around this lake seems to be settling down. Why, do you know that I'm thirty and you're twenty-seven."

"Twenty-six," she corrected. She glanced over at the shore to see they were just coming up on Kaye's Park. It seemed like weeks ago that they were here, not yesterday afternoon, and a little shiver went through her remembering the eerie sound of the music coming from the park as they struggled in the water.

"And over there," he pointed toward Villa Thekla. "Victoria. Didn't she say she's getting married, too?"

Oh my god! thought Lora, *this is a proposal coming.* She'd have to cut him off or at least parry him without hurting that immensely fragile self-regard of his. "Todd," she started, "I've tried to tell you, so much has happened to me. I need time to think."

He was quiet. "Is there someone else?" he asked finally.

"Maybe," she said carefully.

"You didn't answer my letters," he started.

Lora stood up and put her hand on his shoulder. She *did* feel for him. When she had seen him yesterday, she remembered liking his easy company and offhand demeanor. And his taking the moonlight swim was, after all, in response to her dare. "It's all right, Todd."

"Needless to say, I'm starved. Suppose we steam down to Button's Bay for some breakfast," he said, his spirits returning. He reached for her hand.

"Do you see how we look? We look as though we just lost a fight."

133

"I think you look rather dainty, rather cute."

"I just want to go home."

As they rounded Black Point, she saw the *Lora L* leaving the Bluffside pier. Instinctively, she crouched down by the side of the boiler, away from the launch. She was about to tell Todd to go on, to just steam past Bluffside, when he caught her reaction.

"So, is it that you don't want that surly 'caretaker' or whatever he is to see you coming home after spending the night on a yacht?"

"Of course not, and that's my business!" she snapped, staying out of sight as the launch moved away from the pier.

"Well you can just stay down there because I'm going to let him know I'm around." With that, he shoved the throttle ahead full. Billows of black smoke began to rush from the stack and she could feel the big boat shudder as it picked up speed. She didn't know what Todd planned, except he was going to take out his anger and humiliation on Jeremy.

Lora glanced up and saw that Jeremy was alone in the launch. Her father must have stayed in the house. Jeremy had let the *Lora L* drift and he was bending over, checking something. He didn't see the *Ariadne* swiftly closing the distance.

Lora stood and pulled twice on the whistle cord before Todd could push her away. Jeremy looked up, dumbfounded at the sight of the yacht under full steam bearing down upon him. He grabbed the throttle, opening it all the way. The engine responded and the little gas-powered launch leaped forward just out of the path of the yacht.

"I wasn't going to ram her. I only wanted to give your domestic a scare." Todd turned in for the pier at Bluffside. "And you shouldn't have blown the whistle. Now your jack-of-all-trades caretaker can be left to guess when and how you spent last night." Todd's face was flushed.

"You apparently have forgotten just how *you* spent last night."

Jeremy had certainly seen her and would have no reason not to think the worst. She was furious, but drained. She'd settle things with Todd at another time.

The yacht was slowing. "You *know* that I owe you my life and that I'm embarrassed about—last night." He hung his head, then slowly raised his eyes. "Lora, this is a poor time to ask you, but everyone we know is going to the new Country Club site for a season-opening party on Saturday night. Let me escort you. Don't refuse me, please."

"You're right about one thing, Todd. It's a very poor time indeed to ask me." In fact, during dinner at Kaye's, Charlotte had mentioned the party. She could go with the two of them. "Possibly I'll see you there," she answered, not wanting to discuss the matter any further.

When he pulled in to the pier, Lora told him not to dock. She didn't want to call any more attention to the yacht than necessary, and docking and backing the big craft would take several minutes. "Just pull alongside and I'll get off."

She looked down, frowning. Earlier, she'd slumped in the wicker chair without first bothering to put on her shoes or stockings or hat. With the distractions of their conversation and the near collision, she'd forgotten to retrieve them from the front of the vessel.

Todd had slowed the yacht. "Can I bank on seeing you then, at the Country Club?"

"If I go, perhaps. I forgot to pick up the rest of my things from the bow of the boat. Just leave them with Charlotte." With that, she gathered her skirt about her and hopped to the pier.

The launch was all but out of sight as she turned and walked toward shore, feeling the pain in her knee and wondering who might have seen her as she climbed the steps of the bluff. "A few hours ago, I was just glad to be alive and now I'm worried about conventions."

As she neared the house, she fussed with the tear in her dress, then stepped off the walk and went to the side door. She was bone-tired but also starved and thirsty. The screen door swung open just as she reached it.

Martha took in her appearance in one glance. "Child! I thought you'd disappeared, that you was lost out on that lake. Get in here!" Lora stepped into the kitchen, then went to the door and cautiously looked into the living room.

"Your daddy's still upstairs. He wasn't feeling well. He thinks you're asleep. I checked your room and told him that was where you was." She went to examine her nose but Lora pulled away.

"It's all right. It's nothing."

"Nothin'! Did that Todd give you that?" She shook her head, then her eyes widened in disbelief. "My God! Your dress is all torn…and where is the rest of your clothes?"

Lora lowered herself slowly into one of the kitchen chairs, trying to hide the pained expression on her face. "How about some breakfast," she asked, hoping to sound nonchalant. "Do I get any?"

"Huh. If you was a few years younger, I can tell you what you'd get. You'd get a good hard strappin'! Here, take this coffee," she said, setting down a cup. "I been prayin' for you and you been out…the lord knows where, all night," she went on, but stopped when she saw how tired Lora was. She set some hot bisquits down on the table, then stood behind Lora and gently rubbed her shoulders.

After a minute of silence she said, "Jeremy stopped by the kitchen this morning. He was lookin' to take you over to the Observatory. I think he wanted to show it off to you. I had to tell him I couldn't wake you so he went on." She started the eggs and bacon and then picked up an envelope from above the stove. "You must have been in such a hurry yesterday that you missed this."

The letter was postmarked Elgin, Illinois. Turning it over, Lora saw it was from Kittie Hogan. She had met Kittie and her husband Jack at the World's Fair, where she had been their guide. Since then they had become good friends and had visited each other back and forth. The Hogans had a little two year old, Jimmie. Jack treated the mentally ill at the state asylum in Elgin.

When she had last seen Kittie in March, Lora had told her about Bluffside being finished and had made Kittie promise to visit. She hoped the letter was a response to the open-ended invitation. Kittie and Lora were the same age. Kittie had met her husband when he was a new young doctor in her hometown of Joliet. Jack was quiet, and like Kittie he had red hair and a full face of freckles. Kittie told Lora that people had joked at their wedding they'd probably produce nothing but oversized leprechauns.

When she'd last seen Jimmie, he had, in fact reminded her of a leprechaun, dashing around their house on the asylum grounds.

Lora tore open the envelope and began reading:

> Dear Lora, trust this letter finds you and yours
> well. I do hope you are getting some rest this
> summer. (Lora smiled wearily). Your schedule the
> past couple of years has been so hectic. I do want
> to hear more about Eugene Debs. What do you
> plan next, another appeal?

Jack stays too busy. Sometimes he's just all worn
out at night. It bothers me that he's starting to
look older than his thirty-three years. It seems
the asylum keeps getting more and more patients
and never any more nurses or doctors. Oh, dear,
there I go again. Before I run on, let me tell you
our news. All of us—me, Jack, Jimmie, my brother-
in-law Father Jim and sister-in-law Mary—the whole
bunch of us are getting together at Kaye's Park for a
holiday near the Fourth of July. The three of us will
stay for two weeks but Father Jim and Mary will have
to return earlier. We will arrive on Saturday, the 6th of
July. No, we won't stay at Bluffside, thank you in
advance. That's just too many Hogans.

Kittie went on to explain that her brother-in-law was a Catholic pastor
in nearby Harvard and that his sister Mary lived there also. Did Lora perhaps know a fellow she might meet if she coaxed Mary into staying on?

How about Todd? Lora thought wryly.

Martha set down the bacon and eggs and refilled the coffee cup. Lora
thanked her and began to devour the food without looking up from her
letter. Martha shook her head. Lora, she saw, was apparently reviving
from whatever ordeal she had gone through. She was sitting at an angle
on one of the kitchen chairs, absorbed in the letter. Both of her bare feet
had been scraped raw and one of her toes was cut. And when her dress
rode up, it looked like she might have gotten a nasty gash on her leg.
Where has the girl been, she wondered.

Knowing Lora, she knew she would hear no complaints—nor explanations. She just bet that Todd was responsible. Maybe now Miz Lora will
see what a worthless good-for-nothing he was, she said to herself.

Jack has even promised a "surprise," though I finally
coaxed him into telling me what it is. He's
chartered a boat, the "Dispatch," for us Sunday
afternoon. I can hardly believe it, since Jack fears
the water so.
I've run on, but Lora, please say you'll join us
for the boat ride Sunday. I suppose you're probably
used to huge yachts, but if you are, don't tell me. I look

forward to seeing you. We'll be at Kaye's July 6th, a
Saturday afternoon. Please bring a friend with you.
Much love, Kittie and Jack and Jimmie.
P.S. Are you still seeing a certain C.D?
Can't wait to talk.

Lora felt better just thinking of a visit from her friends. She reread the letter to Martha, omitting some references, elaborating on others.

"What she mean about her husband bein' scared of the water?"

"Well," Lora answered, glad Martha's attention was directed away from herself, "she told me last year about Jack's fear of the water—almost a terror of it, really. This spring he said it was an irrational fear and that he wanted to meet it head on." She replaced the letter in its envelope and stood up, stretching.

"Martha, I'm going to take a hot bath and go to bed. Would you wake me please at three o'clock?" With that, she started for the stairs. Martha watched her slowly cross the living room, certain Lora was hiding a limp.

20

Back on the *Lora L,* Jeremy was still sorting through the incident. "What was that all about?" he wondered out loud. He pictured again that lethal prow bearing down on him and the blank expression on Todd's face as he passed—that fixed, straight-ahead stare. And what about Lora? She had to be the one who sounded the whistle, but why did she wait so long? Did the near collision start as a joke? Was he maybe in some way in the middle of a lover's quarrel? His stomach tightened at that thought.

"One thing's very certain. She spent the night with that s.o.b, and that means Martha had lied when I asked for her earlier this morning. Could Todd be jealous? Is that why he buzzed me? And would he even have turned in time to avoid cutting the launch in half if Lora hadn't sounded the warning?

Oh, what the hell, he told himself as he veered around some fishermen in rowboats off Cedar Point, *none of her carrying-on should have any effect on you, anyway. You're only a caretaker, and a pretty poor imposter of one at that. Whatever forces have put you here aren't going to be enough to let you win a girl like Lora from her rich playboy boyfriend.*

It was just that he had been looking forward to meeting this girl, and then yesterday things had seemed to go so well. But he had obviously read more into the Sunday meeting with Lora than actually existed. She was being friendly to an employee, nothing more.

He tried to shake himself out of his gloom, watching the *Chicago Express* give off clouds of black smoke as it rounded the bend and disappeared. Things would be quiet until the freight delivery later in the morning. He angled the *Lora L* toward the dock space Paul had leased. As he eased the craft in, vivid images of Lora frolicking with Todd all night

139

on that damn yacht kept assaulting him.

"Nice morning, heh?" Jeremy was down in the hold when he heard the voice above him. He had been securing the canvas, and when he glanced up, the constable was standing on the pier, looming over him like a tower.

Jeremy offered as friendly an hello as he could muster, stepping up onto the pier, checking himself to weed out any modern slang as he talked.

"You know, most everybody calls me Gene," the large man said as they walked down the pier. Lowery seemed even bigger than when Jeremy had last seen him. He stood six-two at least, not so muscular as heavy-boned. He looked indestructible. In a fight, Jeremy thought to himself, he would be. Wind and cold had put deep lines on his stony face. Jeremy tried to size up the constable out of the corner of his eye as they tramped along toward the shore.

Lowery's broad chest stretched the buttons on his ragtag uniform coat. Jeremy guessed that the uniform must have been assembled from police surplus. The pants and coat didn't go together, nor did a single button match any other on the coat. His instincts told him the constable wasn't at ease in his uniform; he seemed too conscious of it. Jeremy placed his age at early fifties. The hair under his billed hat as well as his drooping mustache were salt-and-pepper colored. The two started across the road. Jeremy stopped short as a driver coming down the road jerked his carriage to a halt in front of them. Lowery seemed oblivious to the driver as he crossed the roadway and Jeremy noticed the driver had no curses nor even a dirty look as he started his horse again.

"How are you finding it, working at the Observatory, Mr. Slater?" Still monitoring his speech, Jeremy described his duties as they approached the freight station. As he talked, he noticed Bill standing on the platform, glancing over at the two of them.

Bill gave the constable a brief wave and then called to Jeremy. "Can you come up for a minute? I have to find out what goes back on the afternoon train." The constable settled in, sitting on the edge of the platform and looking down toward the passenger depot. He wasn't going anywhere. Bill hoisted a barrel onto his shoulder as they entered the freight shed.

"He was here again earlier. Wanted to know when you'd be over. That bird is showing a heap of interest in you."

"Thanks, Bill," Jeremy said, helping him roll the barrel into the far corner. "I'm not worried about him. He's just got a nose problem." Jeremy used one of the workmen's colloquial phrases, hoping he sounded more casual than he felt. He took a box of electrical parts from Bill. "I've got to get them out to the Observatory. I'll be back down this afternoon."

When he emerged from the shed the constable had disappeared. There wasn't a wagon in sight, either; he'd have to walk. "I'll send a team back for the rest of the freight," he called to Bill, putting the box under his arm. As he reached the end of the platform, the constable reappeared, limping out to him.

"I heard you say you're going to walk. I had hoped to hook a ride from you but it looks like if you walk, I walk. I'm checking a dog bite report out on Geneva Street." He smiled as he hobbled along. The smile was forced and it faded in an instant.

"Glad for the company," Jeremy lied. He thought that it might at least be an opportunity to learn something about Lowery's suspicions. Thanks to Bill and Ben Hazelwood, Jeremy was on his guard—and nervous as well. Lowery had an intimidating presence and Jeremy was sure he was smarter than he let on. The telegrams he'd sent through Tommy Napper would have had to do with the business card he'd been given. For a moment, Jeremy considered digging up the wallet, but he quickly dismissed the idea as stupid. At any given time, he would have had at least fifteen or twenty business cards with him. He'd never know which card was missing and there would be too many risks attached to the digging.

"So," Lowery started as they approached the blacksmith's. "I understand you're a caretaker, too."

"Not really. Paul Lockerby has a beautiful home but it's not a large estate or anything like that. I cut the grass, do some gardening and run the boat. If he's expecting much of a gardener, I'm afraid he'll be disappointed." It was Jeremy's turn to smile as he extended a small confidence to Lowery.

"Well, they can't expect everything from one part time servant." Lowery's tone was fraternal. "But I know you can handle a boat, though."

So Lowery has heard about the incident in the storm. Jeremy shrugged. "I only did what most anyone would have done."

"That boat you arrived in this morning is the same one you saved, right? And it's a modern gas one, right?" Jeremy nodded again.

"And you saved it from capsizing in a bad blow. Well now, how many workmen at this Observatory are going to be able to do that? You're too modest, Mr. Slater. But however did you learn to handle a boat like that down in Indianapolis?"

He was a smart one, all right. Jeremy kept his voice even. "Like I said, I'm from Indianapolis—but I've spent some time in Chicago," and on a whim he threw in, "I've done some boating over on Lake Huron." Perhaps he could fudge up his trail.

Lowery persisted. "I've been down through Indianapolis. I had a sister who lived there. I haven't been back for quite a while, though. Is that…what's his name, Conrad, is he still mayor?"

So here's where we play a scene right out of Columbo, thought Jeremy. "I haven't been there for a time and I'm not much for politics, but that name doesn't ring a bell."

Lowery laughed, slapping his good leg. "Doesn't ring a bell! I like that. I've never heard that one before. That's an expression I'll have to remember. Yes sir, 'doesn't ring a bell.' I'm going to have to get down to Chicago. Up here," and he waved his arm back toward the village behind him, "you don't hear many new expressions."

Jeremy decided he'd better ask a question or two himself to distract the man. He figured he'd guessed right on the question about the mayor—Lowery had been too careful with the name. He'd made it up trying to trip him, but if Jeremy kept fielding his questions, he'd find himself in a no-win situation.

They'd almost crested the hill. Lowery was a surprisingly spry walker for a large man with a limp. Even walking uphill the limp seemed not to bother him. In another five minutes or so, they'd be at the Observatory drive. He shifted the box of parts to his other arm. "How did you happen to arrive here, Gene?" he used his first name. "I mean you don't…" Jeremy tried to experiment with a little flattery, "…you don't act like a small town policeman."

It was a mistake. He'd no sooner gotten the words out than he knew it. Lowery didn't respond immediately. He was looking at the ground as they walked. The birds chirping above in the trees were the only sounds.

"And what do you think I look like?" His voice had a hard edge. The conversational tone had disappeared.

"You…well, you seem like a businessman, maybe the owner of a store," Jeremy said lamely.

"I don't look like a store owner and you *know* I don't. What *do* you think I look like?"

It was more a challenge than a question. He'd stopped walking and had turned around to face Jeremy. There was a cold glint in his eyes, but something else was there, too, an uncertainty. A buried fear maybe? Lowery might well be some sort of fugitive himself, Jeremy realized. A *real* fugitive.

"I meant you don't look like a constable from Williams Bay." He decided he'd be better off leveling with this guy, at least as much as his instincts would allow. "You look like you might have been…" he paused, "like you might have been a detective, maybe in a big city. That's my guess, if you're asking." *There*. He'd gotten it out.

"Sometimes it doesn't pay to guess too much, Mr. Slater…just as it doesn't pay to butt into police business." He let Jeremy know he had in no way forgotten the circumstances of their first meeting out on the Lake Geneva dock. They were walking again and he was making no effort to keep the edge out of his voice. "And I imagine you want to know where I got this limp?" Jeremy didn't answer the rhetorical question. "Well, you're right, mister. I *was* a detective. And I had you pegged for a smart one, too. Right from the start. And something tells me you've been around some. I can't tell what *you* were, not yet. But I know you're not a caretaker."

"Look here," Jeremy cut in. "I'm not making any secret about not being much of a caretaker—I told you that. I only…"

"I got this bum leg," Lowery continued, dismissing Jeremy's protest, "because I let my guard down. I had this fellow in custody. He didn't seem like much…" He looked Jeremy in the eye, as if to say, 'about like you.'

"I let him go over to his saddle and the next thing I knew he'd pulled a gun and got off a shot. Right here," he tapped his thigh. "Another half inch more and I'd have lost the leg. His second shot went wild. Then his gun jammed before he could fire it again. I got one off myself, right in his belly." He had a malevolent grin on his face that seemed much more natural than the earlier smile. "You know, he had to beg me for the next bullet."

Jeremy turned his face away. The constable was likely not only deranged but far more ruthless even than he'd figured. He didn't want Lowery to see either the fear or loathing he knew he showed. When a housewife with a basket balanced on her shoulder suddenly appeared on the other side of the road, Jeremy felt strangely relieved, as if he had been rescued.

"Where's your dog bite case?" he asked, his voice surprisingly calm.

"Right down that way." The constable pointed toward a little farm cottage down the road. Jeremy said goodbye and started toward the Observatory drive.

He had already reached the entrance to the drive when Lowery called his name. "Mr. Slater." Jeremy turned. Lowery was still standing where Jeremy had left him.

"I might have to go down to Chicago in a week or so—some business. Do you know any lawyer in Chicago—or say in any towns north of there I could look up?"

"Sorry," Jeremy answered evenly. "I don't know a single one."

21

Jeremy tried to turn his attention to work, starting through the list of orders and rejected parts that would have to be returned. Jim Keane, Paul's construction foreman, banged through the door. He had been overseeing the construction of the power station. That building was fully erected and the next phase would be the assembling of the generating equipment.

Jim ticked off the parts he was impatiently waiting for. "The boss sick?" he paused finally to look around the shed.

"Uh huh," Jeremy answered. He was bent low, trying to fish purchase orders out of the rear of the drawer. "He might take a public boat later," he said, raising his head.

"I watched you come in today. You look a little peaked yourself—like you've just seen a ghost."

"You're close. Constable Lowery kept me company on the way out."

"You ever cross him? He really has something in for you." Jim had pulled up a stool.

"Never. I'm not sure, but I'm starting to get an idea why he dislikes me."

"Oh, I forgot. Ernie Walker wants to see you." Ernie Walker was Warner and Swasey's general superintendent of the whole Yerkes Observatory project. In effect, he was Paul's superior as well.

"He wants to see *me*? You mean, because the boss isn't here?"

"My friend, he said *you*."

Jeremy got up uncertainly, smoothing his hair. Walker wanted to see him? He started for the door, with Jim following.

"Don't let that Lowery bother you," Jim said. "Most of us here rolled up our rugs at one time or another."

"Thanks," he answered. "Oh, you'd better send a team down to the freight depot. Your turbine shaft is down there."

"I'll go myself," Jim said. "There's a new clerk at the grocery store. Name's Tillie O'Neill. Someone should welcome her to town."

"Tillie O'Neill?" Jeremy repeated, "Sounds very Irish to me. You'd better watch out." Grateful for Jim's friendship, he started toward the main building. The fact that Jeremy had been given a nominally higher position in Paul's operation didn't seem to bother Jim. Their duties were separate and Jeremy went out of his way to let him know how valuable he was. He admired Jim's facility with the grapevine. He'd bet Tillie hadn't been working down at the store more than a day or so.

The Observatory building, he saw, was beginning to assume the shape he remembered. In the past week, new teams of masons and bricklayers had appeared on the grounds. *More snooping material for Lowery,* he thought.

As he rounded the main dome, he almost bumped into Ernie Walker. Even on this mild June day, Ernie wore a dark suit with a high collar and vest that emphasized his tall, slender frame. He had been talking to a man who carried a scroll of blueprints. They parted, the man rolling up his plans and hurrying off toward one of the two smaller domes under construction.

"Just the person I'm looking for." He beckoned to Jeremy to follow him around the main dome to the east side to show him the well site. Jeremy saw the big, steam powered jackhammer was standing idle, a bad sign. It was used to dig the core. The problems in striking water were becoming well—documented in the *Herald.*

Why in the world does he want me? Jeremy wondered.

"Another broken drill bit," Ernie began. "That's the fifth one we've lost on this bore and no adequate flow of water yet. This is our third separate boring for the well."

"A boulder?" Jeremy was familiar with the problem. The area had once been covered by a huge glacier, leaving after it boulders on and below the surface.

Ernie nodded and leaned against the jackhammer. He could probably work all day long in a ditch and emerge looking spotless, a contrast to all the dusty machinery and men everywhere. Watching him, Jeremy realized how much he resembled pictures he had seen of Connie Mack, the legendary gentleman-owner of the old *Philadelphia A's*.

Jeremy glanced down again at the bore and machinery, not sure why he was summoned or what he could contribute. "I'm afraid I have a request of you," Ernie started. "I called you because, frankly, I thought you'd be easier to talk with than Paul. We've been hauling up water in tanks from town and getting by. Oh, the men are sure enough grumbling, but I've been telling them we're going to hit water. But now this. Do you know that even if the new bore comes in, it will take three weeks to set the casing and deliver water? And now, with the mortar for the stone and brick we've been using, do you realize how much water we'll need? Over 40,000 gallons a day, all of it hauled up in wagons," he paused. "That's why I have to tell you that we'll be requisitioning every wagon to haul water. All we have here and all we can find."

"Mr. Walker," Jeremy started, forgetting caution, "we're getting all our heavy parts in the next two weeks. They *can't* be handcarried. If we can't haul, we'll have to close down."

"That's what I was getting to. The water will have to come first. I'm afraid you'll have to stop your work and idle some people until the well comes through."

Now I know why he wanted to speak to me! Jeremy thought. He could picture Paul or Jim Keane receiving this news. Paul would be storming up and down right now, his face red, his arms waving. He stopped a few feet away, thinking.

"Mr. Walker, thanks for having enough confidence in me, but I'm only an assistant. I don't hire or fire anyone on my own. Paul is sick today, but I'll tell him tonight—no, I won't either. I'll wait until tomorrow morning. But you know our men are highly skilled. They're *electrical* workmen. We can't just hire them anywhere. Paul did well to assemble and train this force. If he has to idle them..." he shook his head, "I don't know if Paul can get all or any of them back. Right now the town of Lake Geneva has started wiring up for electricity for next year. They could all get jobs right *there* tomorrow. If it weren't for their loyalty to Paul..."

"I know what I'm asking. I'm not happy with the artesians, believe me; it's been one excuse and broken promise after another. But if we have no water, we have no construction. I know all the schedules, yours included, were based on well predictions..."

Jeremy had been looking off through the trees. In the distance below was the lake. *Of course.* "There's your water, sir. Right there. How far are we above the lake?"

"One hundred and twenty-five feet." Ernie had the precise figure.

"Well, there's the pump," he pointed to the useless machinery, idly waiting, "and pipes." There were mounds of piping around them. "And you certainly have the hands. Suppose you were to make pipe layers out of your bricklayers and masons."

"Look at that incline," Ernie said, thinking aloud, gazing down toward the lake. He was quiet for a few moments. "You know, it could just work, though. That *is* a huge machine over there. I ordered one bigger than we needed." He examined the pump. "You wait." He walked away and in a few minutes returned with two of the foremen. They were huddled together, listening to Ernie.

When they strode over with him, Jeremy was surprised that they actually took his suggestion. He figured they'd give four or five good reasons why his idea wouldn't work. It would be a big job, running a pipe all the way to the lake. Trees would have to be cut out, parts of the hill leveled. But they could have lake water in under a week and be guaranteed their supply until the well was brought in.

"Jeremy, I'm going to be sure Paul knows that it was his assistant who saved the day. *How* did you think of that, and why didn't I?"

"Well, I think fast when my job is at stake, Mr. Walker. When you told me about the problem, the first thing that came to my mind was, '*I'm* surely more expendable than those electrical workers.'"

Paul didn't get out during the day and at 5:00 p.m., Jeremy, satisfied with himself, headed out in the launch. He decided to take the long way home, going around the lake past Fontana instead of cutting across. He rounded Conference Point and drew opposite the Observatory pier, looking at where the water pipe, *his* water pipe, would go. He moved slowly along the north shore, looking up toward where he'd been circling the lake on his bicycle just a few weeks before. *And here I thought I'd had some problems back then, coming off that trial.* He let the boat drift and closed his eyes tightly, concentrating on the bike trip, trying to *will* himself ahead in time to where he really belonged.

After five minutes or so he slowly opened his eyes. The water was just as dark green as he'd always remembered it, but he was still on the launch listening to the low rumble of the engine. He stared up at the shore and, except for a lack of piers, it could have been the late twentieth century. A primitive sailboat was near the middle of the lake and a pocket-sized yacht approached, giving him a friendly toot on its steam whistle. He sighed, looking up at the blue sky. "What I wouldn't give," he said aloud, "to see just *one* jet contrail up there."

Going back to the wheel, he gunned the boat ahead. Thinking about the constable again, he decided it was time to see Malcolm. He owed him a visit and while there he might ask about Lowery. Perhaps the doctor could shed some light on him. But he told himself that he needed to put the prying policeman's threat in perspective. *Stop being so paranoid. Lowery is just a snoop. He's not threatening your life or your liberty, at least yet.*

The rest of the week went by routinely. Paul, feeling better, accompanied him back and forth to work each day, impressed to learn of his assistant's "saving idea." The turbines arrived and were transported up to the powerhouse for installation, keeping them on schedule.

He'd mailed the letter to Malcolm. It was brief and brought the doctor up to date on his life at the Observatory. Jeremy had also brought up Paul's health in the letter. During the crossings and at work, he'd had time to study Paul's appearance more closely.

Without playing doctor, he could see that what was fatiguing his boss and jeopardizing his health was the day-to-day stress he put himself under. It could have been Jeremy's imagination, but Paul seemed to have aged in the last month. Perhaps Malcolm could suggest something.

Friday, during the trip home, he tried to give him an opening to talk about his health, but he wouldn't discuss it and Jeremy guessed it was a subject he couldn't face. On their arrival, tying the launch to the pier, he bid Paul good night and began securing the boat. From down inside the hold, he watched as Paul climbed the long series of steps, stopping now and again to catch his breath.

Jeremy had finished the last of the canvas when he heard the familiar sound—the whistle of the *Ariadne*—the same sound he'd heard as the boat had borne down on him just a few days before.

The *Ariadne* was heading straight for Bluffside pier. He jumped out of the launch, his blood rising. "If that bastard pulls in…" the consequences of taking out his revenge for the near-miss had escaped him. He looked again. It wasn't Todd at the wheel, but whoever it was, he was coming too fast. For a second, Jeremy thought he'd ram the pier. He heard the yacht strain in reverse and at the last instant it swung out and the graceful yacht's stern slammed hard against the post of the pier.

"You," the uncertain skipper bellowed, as the boat finally halted, bumping again along the post. A chunk of the boat's side had been gouged. "You work for the Lockerby's?"

Jeremy nodded. At first glance, he appeared to be one of the professional engineers, wearing that blue cap and dark, nautical jacket. But any similarity ended with the affectation.

"Give me a hand, there. I don't have the time to dock," he called. Jeremy reached for the rope and looped it around the post, holding the boat from drifting. The other man had stooped and was picking up a box.

"I didn't realize that docking was what you were trying to do, sir."

The operator flashed an angry look. "Here, this is for Miss Lockerby from Mr. Todd Brinkley. She'll find a note inside. You see that she gets it." Jeremy took the lightweight box.

"And cast me off." He pushed the throttle forward. He must have forgotten the rudder was turned as he raked the flank of the yacht on the post pulling away. Jeremy stood holding the package, watching the yacht.

As he climbed the first step of the bluff, a fold of the box came open and he started to close it. On top was a woman's straw hat. Underneath were a pair of black hose and shoes. He remembered seeing the same hat on Lora last Sunday. An unsealed white envelope was next to the hat. He glanced up toward the house, obscured now by the bluff.

Pausing, he sat down out of sight and opened the envelope, reading the scrawled handwriting of the note.

> "Dearest Lora, please forgive my actions of Sunday.
> I must have gotten a mouthful too much of water. Much
> embarrassment—and much thanks to you for your swift
> actions. I have a lot to thank you for and will upon our
> next seeing each other, Saturday at the club, I hope.
> I've had to go to Milwaukee for Aunt Harriet this week
> on some very important matters she has entrusted me
> with—seeing her lawyers. Perhaps this will give us some-

150

thing to talk about.

I've sent Doug to deliver your belongings. Hope you
got in without any explanations. Lora, forgive my
misfortunes in the water. What a beautiful, fond moon-
light swim we would otherwise have had. Saturday? —

Todd.

Jeremy scanned the contents of the note again, replaced it, sealed the envelope and put it back in the carton. On reaching the house, he walked to the side entrance, sniffing the aroma of Martha's stew as he knocked.

"Western Union, ma'am. Package for Miss Lockerby from Mr. Todd Brinkley." He watched her nose wrinkle at the sound of the name.

"Ah didn't give you your tip yet," she said as he started away.

She ladled out a big helping of the stew into a pot and cut off half a loaf of her homemade bread, handing it to him.

Thanking Martha, he trudged to his cabin, a new troublesome image of Lora in the moonlight forming in his mind's eye.

22

From the shed behind his cabin, Jeremy wheeled out the lawn mower. Surprisingly, it was almost identical to the modern-day hand mower he'd owned and always preferred. So many Saturday mornings just like this he'd gotten up before everyone in his family, slipped outside and used the push mower on his suburban lawn, enjoying what little physical exercise he got.

He cut a long swathe between his cabin and the main house. On each pass as he neared the house, he found himself looking up toward Lora's room and the flowered curtains moving in the breeze, rereading Todd's note in his mind...*the moonlight swim.* Before he realized it, he'd mowed the entire back stretch of the lawn, feeling better as his muscles loosened.

He went inside and drew a glass of water. Later, he'd get a public boat schedule from Martha. He'd hail a boat and be in Lake Geneva by noon. If he could catch Malcolm at his office, he would be able to spend part of the afternoon in town and return by nightfall.

Jeremy set the glass down and walked outside. Lora was standing in front, partly in shadow from one of the oak trees. Her hair, brushed up under her hat, looked reddish in the light. She smiled, shifting her weight a little uncertainly. "Good morning."

"Hi," he said, stepping off the porch.

"Jeremy, I have to go to market this morning and I was wondering if you'd be able to take me?" he saw her glance at the lawn mower.

"No problem," he said. "I'm finished mowing for the day." In spite of his resolve he could feel the blood rise as he talked to her. "Just give me a minute to change and I'll meet you down at the pier." *This will work out perfectly. I'll save boat fare and be able to see Malcolm while she shops. And*

152

I'll have her company as well.

"Oh, we can't use the boat. Father took it. He's meeting someone from Warner and Swasey at the train and they're going out to the Observatory. But don't worry. We'll use the Lefens' carriage and one of their horses. Until we build our own stable next year, they'll let us borrow theirs."

He nodded numbly, a panicky feeling coming over him. He hadn't gotten around to learning about carriages or horses. When he rode on a wagon at work, he always did so as a passenger. The fact was, he knew nothing whatever about horses. *He had never been on a horse in his life.*

"Bring the carriage around to the back. I'll be there in a few minutes. And Jeremy," she said, smiling, "thank you ever so much." She turned and hurried back to the house.

"Thank you ever so much," he repeated to himself. "*Now* what am I going to do?" He started across the lawn. The estate next door was owned by Theis Lefens, the son-in-law of Mrs. Seipp. Maybe, he thought as he crossed through an opening in the hedge, he could get Emil, the stable-boy, to hitch the carriage for him. Like Bluffside, the Lefens' estate was only a year old, but it had been furnished with a complete stable at the rear. He didn't even have any idea which horse they were to use.

"Emil," he called, hearing a crack in his voice, as he rounded the front of the stable. Emil appeared from behind a stall. He was in his early twenties, short, with a square build and scraggly hair.

"Don't yell," Emil groaned. "I heard you cutting the grass this morning and I rolled over and said to myself 'what does this fellow do on Friday nights?' " He pulled a bottle from his pocket and drank, giving a shudder as the dark liquor hit bottom. Jeremy turned down the offered bottle, explaining as casually as he could that he was here for the loan of a horse and carriage.

Emil walked him inside the stable. Jeremy sniffed the odor of the horses, something he still hadn't gotten used to. "You're supposed to use old Magnolia here." Emil went to the stall and unhooked it. He led the mare out and handed over the reins. Holding the reins like a rattlesnake, Jeremy jerked them, pulling the animal's head down. Magnolia, surprised, tried to back away. Emil hadn't seen this as he walked ahead out of the stable, taking another swig on his bottle. Jeremy followed, leading Magnolia.

"Mrs. Lefens has the carriage out herself over to Fontana, and she likely won't be back until late afternoon. I can let you have the wagon, though. It's clean enough." Sensing his opportunity, Jeremy handed the reins back to Emil. "I'll have to check with Miss Lockerby. Maybe we'll have to postpone the trip. I'll be back," he said, turning and stopping dead in his tracks. Lora was walking down the path toward him, softly whistling a tune and twirling a parasol over her shoulder.

"See how fast I got ready," she said. He told her about the carriage being in use, suggesting they wait until her father returned.

"What about this?" she asked, walking over to the wagon and patting it. "Can't we use this?"

"Well, I didn't think that you'd want to, that is…"

"Jeremy," she cut him off, "who do you think I am? You flatter me," she chuckled. "But I'm not some princess. This wagon will be fine. Besides," she pulled out a list, "look at all the groceries we'll be hauling. This will even be better. I've ridden in lots worse than this."

With no recourse, he took back the reins from Emil and led Magnolia over to the wagon, as Lora and Emil began chatting in the doorway of the stable, their backs to him. He realized, breaking out in a sweat, that he had no harness for the animal. He looked around stupidly at Magnolia, then walked over to the two. "Sorry for the delay," he smiled weakly at Lora, feeling the sweat pouring off him. He pointed toward the mare. "Harness?"

"Oh, sorry," Emil said, disappearing inside and emerging in a few minutes to hand over a maze of leather straps and gear. Jeremy took hold of them and walked back to the horse and wagon.

"Let me see your stable," Lora asked. "Maybe I can get some ideas for ours." The two went inside, leaving Jeremy and Magnolia alone.

Feverishly he tried to hitch the wagon before they returned. He put the harness over and around the animal who had begun to grow uneasy, pawing the dust as she sensed his confusion. At last he picked up the shafts on the wagon, secured the harness to each shaft, letting it rest across Magnolia's shoulder.

The two emerged from the stable and Emil said goodbye, ambling on down toward the lakeshore. Lora nimbly climbed up on the seat next to Jeremy, setting her parasol behind her. She studied the shopping list, checking items with her finger. When she looked up he was still sitting. "Ready?"

He applied the reins as he tried to remember seeing it done. Old Magnolia promptly strode away from the wagon, the shafts falling to the ground. Had he not let go of the reins, he would have been pulled right off the seat.

If he'd ever had a more humiliating moment in his life, he couldn't remember. Lora looked at him for a long moment, her brows knitted together in disbelief. Ahead the gentle old mare looked back, waiting.

Jeremy heard her laugh. It was uncertain at first and then seemed to burst from her. He only wished he could join her. He got down from the seat and picked up the reins. Lora stopped laughing, her eyes glistening with tears. She cocked her head, seeing his spreading scarlet blush.

She realized he was not joking. This man who'd seemed so self-assured; who became her father's first assistant and had saved his life on the storm-tossed lake, was standing there blushing and foolishly holding the reins. He could not, apparently, hitch a wagon.

She could get an explanation later, she decided. She jumped down, picked up the shafts and with his help, pulled the empty wagon the few feet over to the horse. Jeremy numbly watched her loop the harness around the shafts, over and under the animal, pulling it tight and securing it with buckles. The whole operation, he noticed, hadn't taken two minutes. And as she finished, she did something he'd remember for the rest of his life.

She gave him a little grin and wink. And she walked over to him, resting her hand on his sweat-soaked shoulder. "It's all right. Let's go shopping," she said, handing him the reins and climbing on the wagon as he meekly followed.

Magnolia knew the way to town and fortunately all he had to do was sit with the reins in his hand. They rode in silence as the wagon rumbled down the road. Jeremy wanted to tell her his whole story—to get it out no matter how crazy it sounded. How could a man in 1895, he thought, not have any conception of how to handle a horse or hitch a wagon?

It would be like, no it was even worse, he decided, than for someone in the late twentieth century to be hired as a chauffeur—and then as he held the car door have to admit he not only couldn't drive, but he didn't even know where the key went! They continued in silence, Jeremy's mood getting darker.

When she spoke, her voice was lilting and casual. "How is it you don't have any experience with horses?" There, she'd hit it, he realized. She'd said, "how is it you don't have *any* experience," leaving no room for even the slightest doubt.

"Miss Lockerby, it probably sounds unbelievable, but I guess…that is, I just always had," he hesitated, unsure of how any of this was sounding, "well, someone else to do it for me." She listened silently, seemingly wanting him to go on. Magnolia didn't even pause as the wagon crossed the road to Linn Pier. He looked over at the wooden sign pointing down the road, recalling how many times he'd driven the same way. He decided to come to the point.

"I know a big part of my duties are to drive a carriage or wagon. Not being able to, I'll move back across to Williams Bay." She took the reins from him.

"Whoa," she spoke, and Magnolia stopped, bending to nibble some clover at the side of the road. Lora wet her lips and knitted her brow in a kind of frown.

"Jeremy, I *don't* know exactly what you're saying. Maybe you'll remember everything later—or I'll just understand better. But I'm going to tell you something right now. My father *needs* you, here and at work. He can barely operate that boat on the best of days. And only the other day he told me you solved the water problem at the Observatory—kept everyone working.

"We both need you at Bluffside, and Martha too. Finally," she continued, "who knows where you've been, out at sea or what, but before we get back today, I'm going to teach you how to hitch and drive a wagon. And you're going to laugh at how easy it is." He smiled as she spoke, starting to relax for the first time since he had gone to the stable.

They started off again, Lora driving while he sat almost transfixed, knowing in spite of all his warnings and lectures to himself and the jealous feeling she'd inspired in him, he was falling in love.

The balance of the trip to town was spent in conversation. She pointed out small things to him, tips about driving a horse. He listened intently, afraid even to ask a single question and show any further ignorance. Jeremy was tempted again during the trip to blurt out the story of his origin to her to be done with it. Maybe, he thought, he just needed to assert himself.

As they neared the town of Lake Geneva, she gave him back the reins and had him practice stopping. The gentle mare, with an occasional look back, seemed to grow a little more confident in the driver behind.

"Pull up there, in front of Johnson's," she pointed out the grocery store on Main Street. "Stay with the wagon. I'll place the order and be out. I thought we'd take a drive around town. And don't," she said, nudging him playfully as she bounded down from the wagon, "go racing this old mare through the streets while I'm gone."

Lora reappeared in a few minutes. She stopped to give Magnolia some sugar from her hand and then climbed onto the wagon, handing Jeremy an apple while she bit into her own. "You have seen *these* before haven't you?" the dimple was back in her chin. "We call these apples."

She took him on a tour of the town, again both familiar and unfamiliar to him. They went by the school building where she stopped the wagon. The building and playground were deserted for the summer. "I almost taught here. There was an opening four years ago and it seemed like such a peaceful, pretty town I thought I'd like to live here all year around."

"Are you sorry you didn't?" Jeremy asked as they watched a pair of bicyclists teetering on their high-wheeled "bone breakers" go by.

"No, I'm not sorry at all. As pretty as this town is I wouldn't have traded it for all the experiences, good and bad at Pullman or at the World's Fair. I loved Waterford, too, when I grew up there, but I don't think I could ever go back to a small town to live—not after Chicago."

"How did you like working for someone as famous as Darrow?"

"Oh, it's been exciting." Lora gave him a short description of her duties. She was, he decided, something that in the 1990's would be a cross between a law clerk and a para-legal. "Clarence, I mean Mr. Darrow, wants me to become a lawyer. Can you imagine?"

"You sound like you'd be a devastating lawyer." Now it was her turn to blush if just slightly.

"But it takes ever so long to become one, and..." she hesitated. He sensed she was weighing the words she'd use. "I think I may be better off if I leave his office, and go back to my art teaching. Art teachers can get rusty too, you know."

They were rolling along by the lakefront park, nearing Malcolm's. "Could you stop a minute?" he asked. "I just want to see if Doctor MacDougal is home." She pulled up in front of his house, and Jeremy stepped out, ringing Malcolm's door. No answer. Gertrude must have gone for the weekend. He fished a piece of paper and stub pencil from his pocket and quickly scribbled a note.

After they had arrived back at Johnson's and the groceries were loaded, they headed out of town, veering away from the lake, about to climb a small hill. Jeremy had been musing that a hundred years in the future this same stretch of the town would be renovated and, interestingly, would look much like it did now. The run-down miniature golf courses and carmel corn stands of the 60's and 70's would be gone—giving way to a Victorian restoration.

"How do you find father's health?" she asked, breaking into his thoughts.

"Since you asked, you must be concerned."

"I am. Father seems to have aged so much in the last couple of years. I thought having Bluffside would help him relax. And getting the work at the Observatory was such a prize."

"Your father enjoys work. He'd be worse if he didn't. I think he keeps a lot bottled-up inside him. He's a perfectionist—and that type of person can pay the price. But to answer your question, I have noticed that he sometimes has difficulty catching his breath. And his face gets very flushed when he exerts himself."

By now Magnolia had crested the little hill and was almost in a trot, glad to be on the shady lane. "I think he should see Malcolm. The doctor might have some help for him." On a hunch, he continued. "Let me ask you a question. Does he eat a lot of meat?"

"Yes, of course. He practically lives on steaks and chops. Why?"

"How about vegetables?"

"He says," she laughed, " 'I let the cows eat all the vegetables and then I eat the cows.' "

"I think he eats too much meat. Why not try to switch him—more fish, more vegetables." He knew he was pressing into an intrusive area, but Paul looked like a perfect bypass candidate in another age.

"Maybe, but...ugh!" She made a face. "Fish? He wouldn't eat a fish if his life depended on it—not me either, I'm afraid."

"Where did you learn ideas like that? I was raised by hearing 'eat your meat, chile' ", she parodied Martha.

He shrugged. "Just a guess. But if he sees Malcolm, if he could cut down on worries and stress…" She listened, watching him closely.

They began descending another long hill. She pulled on the reins and Jeremy reached over and applied the brakes. The road curved back toward the lake. When the grade at last leveled off, she stopped the wagon along the shore of Button's Bay. Magnolia took advantage of the stop to lap up a drink.

She was staring quietly out over the water. "Lost in thought?" he asked.

"It was about you," she replied. "How is it, I was thinking, he can use words like he does, think as he does, and not even know how to hitch a horse? I'm sorry, I don't want to embarrass you but you *did* ask what I was thinking."

On an impulse, he answered truthfully. "I don't know how to hitch a horse because I don't think I've ever done it, nor even, save for this morning, watched it being done. And," he added, "I doubt I've ever even been *on* a horse." Her eyes widened, but she met his look, saying nothing.

"At any rate," she drew on her pet phrase, giving Magnolia a tap with the reins, "before we reach the house, just like I promised, I'm going to show you what you need to know."

True to her word, when they were out in the country, she got down and meticulously, step by step, showed him how to hitch a wagon. After she'd run through it a few times she had him do it until he surprised himself at how good he'd become.

The rest of the way, she peppered him with questions about the Observatory. He was surprised how much she knew about the project. Lora even drew out of him his concern with constable Lowery. She chewed thoughtfully on her lower lip as she listened. "You'll have to point him out to me. The last couple of years I've had encounters with 'peace officers' who sound very much like him."

At the Lefens' stable, Lora watched approvingly as he unhitched the wagon and led Magnolia into her stall, and at the side entrance, she held the screen door while he edged in and set down the boxes along the kitchen sideboard.

"Look at the time!" Martha said. "I thought you two went to Chicago for groceries. I have to rush to get your dinner, since you're goin' out tonight, I s'pose." Jeremy was just setting down the second box and saw

Lora flash Martha a glare. "There is a letter for you. I think you'll want to see it."

Lora picked it up. "It's from Eugene...Eugene Debs! He's mailed it from Woodstock. Poor Eugene, still in jail there." Forgetting the other two, she tore it open.

"Well, he's feeling good, but oh, he hopes the appeal is successful." She turned over the envelope, looking at the date mark. "He wrote this before he learned it was turned down."

Jeremy remembered reading in the *Herald* that Debs' appeal had been denied. He paused at the door, saying goodnight.

"How rude I am, letting you stand here while I read." She replaced the letter in the envelope and followed him out the door. "Some day," she laid her hand on his arm, "you're going to be able to tell me where you come from—where a person needn't know anything about a horse. Good night, Jeremy."

He heard her talking to Martha as he started down the path. Did she really suspect his origins were very different, he wondered.

He finished a quick supper and went back out on the porch. He tried to read the *Lake Geneva Herald* but couldn't concentrate. He knew why, thinking about his afternoon with Lora, and her going off for the night. He found himself walking along the low hedges that separated Bluffside from the Lefens' property, following the meandering border until he reached the lakeshore path atop the bluff.

Jeremy hadn't admitted it to himself, but he was down at the lakefront wondering if Lora would again leave by yacht. Sure enough, after a few minutes a yacht did round Black Point, heading for Bluffside. He had positioned himself behind a large oak tree, and he watched as Lora crossed the lawn. She'd changed to an apricot shaded dress with white lace and a straw hat. He saw her board the boat, greeted by the same couple he'd seen on Sunday. Light laughter drifted over the water, and he felt a dull ache as he watched them pull away from the pier.

"I bet you like her, don't you." He had been concentrating on the boat and at the same time not being seen by anyone on board, and the question startled him. The little girl was standing next to him. A small cocker spaniel was with her.

"This is Nero," she said, "and you're the caretaker at Bluffside, aren't you? I've seen you when you come and go in the boat." Nero had come

over to Jeremy, sniffing and let himself be petted, his tail wagging vigor-
ously.

"Nero is a nice dog," he offered. The dog pricked his ears at the sound
of his name.

"I'm Marie Lefens," she said. "I live over there." He guessed Marie was
eleven or twelve, just about Kim's age. Allowing for the difference in
dress, the child reminded him of his own daughter.

"I have a sister, Catherine," she said, sitting down on the edge of the
bluff. Nero settled at her side, his head in her lap. "Do you know her?"
she asked, more to herself than to Jeremy. He shook his head.
"Sometimes I hate her. Do you know what she did? She told mother that
Nero and I had run through the flowers," she pointed to a flowerbed,
"and trampled the gladiolas."

"And did you?"

"Yes, but she didn't have to tell. Nero's ball went in there and I stepped
on some old gladiolas. Mother was already mad at me from the morning,
and Catherine knew I'd get it." She winced at the painful memory.

"Well, think about all the fun you have with your sister, though,
right?"

She had gotten up and they were walking slowly along the path toward
Bluffside. "Do you have any children?"

He was caught off guard by her question. "You can call me Jeremy.
No...I don't have any children, Marie."

"I think that you do. Yes you do. I can tell by the way you answered."
She was looking directly at him. Marie's intuition had cut his defenses.

"Yes, I do," he admitted for the first time to anyone. "Two, a little boy
eight and a little girl, ten, just about your age."

"I'm eleven. Where are your children?"

"Far away. Very far away."

"That's too bad. Can they come up here this summer?"

"No, I'm afraid not." They both stood gazing out over the lake. The
yacht carrying Lora and her friends had disappeared beyond the Narrows.

"When can you see your children?" And before he could respond, they
heard a woman calling her name. "My mother," she said. "I'd better go
before I catch any more trouble. Could I go out with you in the boat
sometime? We don't have one yet except for *that*..." she wrinkled her
nose at the rowboat pulled up on their pier.

"Sure, you can go if your mom and dad say it's all right."

"Don't worry," she grinned. "I can swim like a fish," and she made a stroking motion as she turned to leave.

"One thing, Marie. I haven't told anyone about my children. Can we keep that a secret?"

She stopped and paused for a minute, thinking. "That can be our secret, but I hope I can meet them. Goodnight, Jeremy." He watched Marie and Nero run down the path.

23

Jeremy hadn't slept well, tossing in bed until well after midnight. Now he was up early and put the coffee on, throwing on a workshirt and pants. "To hell with Sunday," he said, remembering how formally even peons like him dressed on Sundays. He hadn't finished cutting the lawn, but if he got an early enough start, he could be through before any visitors would notice he'd worked on the Lord's day.

He took his coffee cup out on the porch and sat there, looking off through the trees toward the main house. In spite of himself, his eyes traveled up to Lora's window. Doubtless she'd be sleeping in late. His mind drifted back to the previous afternoon. He chuckled at the sight he must have made—with the old mare unharnessed, ambling away from the wagon, and then stopping to look quizzically back. He heard Lora's laugh again and pictured the prominent dimple on her chin. He thought by now he would have been able to sort out what had happened to him and what direction he might take for the future, but no answers had come.

On the plus side, this time regression or whatever had at least left him in a place he was familiar with. Added to that he'd been lucky, very lucky, to have met someone like Malcolm almost immediately, when he was most vulnerable. And Paul. And Martha. Even Lora, though his growing attraction to her seemed a mixed blessing.

What should I do? He tried to concentrate as images of Lora laughing, taking his arm, intruded on his concentration. *I'm a successful lawyer— well, at least fairly successful—now working as a part-time bookkeeper and caretaker. And with the prospect that neither job will last beyond the first frost.*

He ought to return to Chicago in the fall, he thought, and see about a law license. Maybe he could clerk and dispense with law school. The very thought of going back to law school, even if he could afford it, was unbearable.

On the other hand, why *not* use all that he knew to become a kind of "superseer"? He would have to compile all the history he could recall about this period. What a golden opportunity!

He refilled his cup and rocked in the swing, alternately exploring the idea of using his knowledge of what surely would be coming events and conjuring up images of Lora. But what if, he suddenly thought with a start, events *didn't* unfold the way he'd learned them. Just suppose history did not repeat itself.

Oh hell! This is ridiculous. Whatever happened to me is not science fiction, and events do seem to be unfolding according to sequence. The very Observatory where he worked, and Lora talking about the Pullman strike and Eugene Debs. But could he change history? Could he alter events he knew about? Should he dare try?

Finishing his coffee, he stretched and still yawning, walked down to the shed. He took out the mower and then reached in the rear to find the flat scythe he'd need for cutting the grass on the bluff.

It was going to be another beautiful day. And minutes later his spirits lifted as he stood on the edge of the bluff. A few early fishermen and a solitary sailor were the only boaters out on the lake. Jeremy squinted at the low sun, rising above the trees near the Narrows.

He began moving along the top of the bluff. He'd finish and then take the scythe to the side of the bluff. He'd finished the topside mowing when he heard someone hailing him.

A man in a rowboat shouted "Ahoy!" in a loud voice that carried up the bluff. Jeremy waved at him to stop shouting, pointing back at the house. He didn't want this guy's foghorn voice waking up the family. With the scythe in his hand, he clambered down the hill to see what he wanted, ready to tell him there was no fishing from the Lockerby's pier.

Jeremy could see that the man, who was about his own age, had pulled his boat against the rocks on the shore, leaving the oars outside. "Hi there. Dave Dumser's my name. What do you call this place?"

"Bluffside."

"Well, I'm up here scouting a place for my missus and family. We're going to camp for a couple of weeks. Know any spots around here? I rented this dinghy back at Linn Pier, and they said to try over near Black Point."

"You're at Black Point, but it's mostly all private," he said. But he didn't want to put the fellow down. He must, after all, have rowed a couple of miles. Jeremy smiled and snapped his fingers.

"You know, come to think of it, I *have* seen people in tents over there," and he pointed east, beyond the Lefens' estate. "Down there, oh about a quarter of a mile or so. You can camp on this same bluff. It's a great view of the lake if you don't mind the climb."

"I'm the only one who uses the lake unless I can talk my oldest into fishing with me. Much obliged," he said, pushing off. "Nice launch there," his voice carried over the still water. "Yours?"

"No. I just work here," Jeremy answered.

"Well, she's pretty, but I wouldn't want to be on her during a storm." Jeremy agreed, remembering his own recent adventure. Dumser spun the rowboat with a practiced dip of the oars and started to row away.

Jeremy waved. "Hope you find something."

As long as he was down here at the shoreline, he decided he'd begin cutting from the bottom and work his way to the top. He wielded the scythe with a vigor that surprised him as he progressed up the side of the bluff, easily mowing the thin grass. *I sure wouldn't want this job in two or three years when this grass has grown in.* He stopped to mop his brow as he neared the end of his chores.

He caught sight of the yacht as it rounded Black Point, well out from shore. His anger began to rise once more as he watched it slow. There was no mistaking the *Ariadne's* majestic lines for any other as it turned in. The boat seemed to hesitate, as though the operator couldn't decide where to go. Finally it nosed into the pier not at Bluffside but at the Lefens. Jeremy made a pass with his scythe as he watched. Todd was at the wheel. After a minute, he reversed the big boat and headed back out toward the center of the lake, letting go with a couple of mighty blasts on the steam whistle, loud enough to wake up everyone for a mile.

"You damn idiot!" Jeremy muttered, watching as the yacht grew smaller. Todd gave two more blasts on the whistle as if for good measure.

"Todd." Lora spoke. "I guess everyone's aware he's been here by now." Jeremy hadn't noticed her come down the walk from the house. He didn't know if she'd heard him. "I can imagine what you're thinking, Jeremy."

"I just work here, ma'am," Jeremy answered. He had shifted the scythe to his left hand. He started to finish the mowing, not knowing what else to say. Lora, he could feel, was still standing near him.

"Could you use some breakfast? I could." He started to beg off. "I'm going to get something and bring it out. It's too nice to eat inside—and I, Jeremy, I need to talk with someone." He heard the catch in her voice as she spoke.

He busied himself with the lawn, wielding the scythe on the last of the bluff. "If I finish before she comes back, maybe I ought to call it a morning and head back to my cabin," he said. But his decision was made for him. Just as he was finishing up, the screen door to the kitchen slammed. Lora was walking slowly down the front lawn, balancing a silver coffee pot in one hand and a laden tray in the other.

"Come and sit," she invited, settling on the grass and smiling up at Jeremy. He took the tray from her. She'd filled it with Martha's frosted muffins, slices of ham, and had even remembered a creamer and sugar bowl. "I can vouch for this being hot," she shook her hand, putting her finger to her mouth to cool it. The two sat along the edge of the bluff. "Sugar and cream?" she asked.

"Please," he said, beginning to smile in spite of himself, as she primly put out their breakfast. She set the silver coffee pot down on the lawn. Lora sipped her coffee and leaned back, letting her legs stretch out over the edge of the bluff as she gazed across the lake.

"It's beautiful here this time of day and I've never done this—that is I've never had breakfast out here. I'll have to try to talk father into building a little gazebo up here. What a beautiful spot to look out over the water. Here, have another," she said, handing him a second muffin as she took a bite of her own. He took it from her, embarrassed that he'd already wolfed one down. He'd forgotten how hungry his labors had made him. She was too busy devouring her own to notice his discomfort.

She took a second herself and passed the tray over to him. He hesitated, and then with a grin he shrugged and took another. "What a pig I am," he said.

"Nonsense. You look like you've earned it," she gestured down the side of the bluff. "You did all that this morning?"

"Well, it was either that or saddle up Magnolia and go for a gallop.

Thanks for your help yesterday, Miss Lockerby."

"Oh don't thank me, I was glad to do it. I just hope that you'll be able to tell me someday how an accomplished person like yourself could have gotten so far without ever having ridden upon a horse." A few minutes earlier she had turned away, trying to stifle a big yawn. Now, as she finished talking, she turned her dimpled smile on him.

"It's a promise. I'll tell you someday," he answered, meeting her eyes.

The two sat drinking coffee in virtual silence for a few minutes. They made some very small talk about the few boats out early. Lora cleared her throat. "Last Monday, you saw me coming in with Todd. I'm so sorry about his actions. And now, seeing him here in front of the pier," she shook her head. "I don't know what..." He started again to say that he was just a caretaker, but she waved her hand and continued.

"I just hope you don't get a wrong impression—well an unfair impression from this that all I do is to party on yachts." He started to answer, but realized she was going to continue so he decided to become a good listener. He leaned over and refilled her cup from the silver pitcher sitting on the grass, remembering she took one spoon of sugar.

"Thank you," she said, taking the cup. "You've met Todd."

"Have I ever," he said. And she laughed at his idiom.

"I met Todd a couple of years ago. He seemed so totally different from...all the people I'd been around. He has such an amusing, light way of talking. I imagine this all sounds so shallow to you. But I'd seen so much poverty and turmoil, and then arriving back here at the lake where everything was so tranquil, it just felt natural to go about with someone who seemed so much a part of this setting...the yacht and all."

"And this year?" he asked. He should have checked himself, he knew, but if she was going to take the trouble to explain Todd to him, he was damned if he was going to make it that easy for her.

"He'd written me several letters over the winter and just appeared on the pier last Sunday. He is, or was," she added "a good introduction to the summer society here."

"Was?"

"We've had arguments ever since I arrived." Lora paused before going on. "And the very last thing I wanted this summer was to...to have disagreements with anyone while up here." She went on to tell Jeremy about the Kaye's Park incident and even about his swim afterwards, being very sketchy on details, careful not to run down Todd nor to give Jeremy too close a picture of the evening. She *did* say that he'd had trouble in the water and that she had to help him back to the boat.

"Look, Miss Lockerby, there's no need for you to have to tell…"

"Please," she stopped him. "I just want to explain—to talk to someone. And would you please call me Lora instead of *Miss Lockerby*? I'm not very used to formality. *Miss Lockerby* doesn't sound right.

"Jeremy," she started again. "I shouldn't have gone with him last Sunday. I'd forgotten how possessive Todd was. I knew he'd become enraged when he saw you."

"Now that's crazy." It was Jeremy's turn to say something. "I met him for all of two minutes on the pier."

"It was the timing," she interjected. "You see, he had started to propose when I tried to change the subject. It was that plus his humiliation from the swimming incident the night before. It was at that very moment that you came into view, and he decided to take his feelings out on the first person he saw."

"The first *servant* do you mean?" Jeremy asked.

"But anyway," she disregarded his remark, "last night I went with Frank and Charlotte—you remember them from Sunday?— to the dance at the new Lake Geneva Country Club. Todd was there as well. After a dance, he asked me to go for a stroll with him along the path that leads to the little offshore island. It's connected by a causeway. I should have noticed that he'd been drinking again. After we were out on the island, he brought up once again how our friends around the lake are getting married. I told him I wanted to get back to the others. On the way we ran into some acquaintances, and Todd was downright rude." She reached over and flicked an ant off the tray.

"We left on Frank's yacht, with Todd insisting on controlling it. He began drinking more heavily once we were out on the water, and he went around the entire lake, stopping to dock at the town of Lake Geneva. Frank is easy-going, but he even got mad at Todd when he saw how nervous Charlotte and I were becoming.

" 'Todd! For God's sake! It's almost two o'clock,' Charlotte said. 'You've *got* to get us home.'

"He finally agreed, after opening another bottle of wine as we steamed along the entire length of the lake down to Belvidere Park." Lora went on, telling Jeremy how Todd had suddenly wheeled to face her at the pier, saying that she had better be careful because he would be watching who she was seen with. With that he charged off the boat and Frank and Charlotte had brought her home.

Jeremy reached over and took her hands in his. "He put you through a lot last night, Lora," he used her first name. "But if he bothers you, let me know." At that moment, it didn't matter to him that Todd was bigger and ten years younger than himself.

He was so absorbed in her story that he was startled by the tinny sound of a whistle as a steamer rounded the point and pulled into Bluffside. "Doctor MacDougal is here!" Lora exclaimed, spotting the doctor first as he stepped gingerly from the excursion boat.

"I got your note," he said to Jeremy, "and I thought I should come out and see the great caretaker myself." He and Lora had greeted each other warmly and Jeremy saw the doctor bend close and speak to her. She shook her head.

"Since it was such a beautiful day," Malcolm continued, "I decided to hop the *Admiral* and ride around the lake, just like one of the tourists," he chuckled, putting his arm around Lora and starting up the steps.

Jeremy took the doctor's bag. "Father should be awake by now. Doctor, do you think you could take a look at him while you're here? You know he would never take the time on his own to visit your office." Lora briefly explained to Malcolm her father's symptoms: the shortness of breath and tiredness.

He nodded. "As a matter of fact I should like to see him." Jeremy had stopped and gathered up the vestiges of their outdoor breakfast and when Malcolm caught his eye, seeing the dishes, he gave him a wink. At the house he handed the tray and pitcher to Martha and returned to busy himself with the lawn while Lora and Malcolm went inside.

Later, Jeremy was down on the pier cleaning the woodwork on the launch when he looked up and saw the two descending the steps. He climbed down into the boat as they reached the end of the pier. "As I was telling Lora, Jeremy, we don't know all we should about the heart and how it works or doesn't. Years from now, maybe, medicine will have the answers."

"He thinks father's heart is…" Lora started, plainly worried.

"Now, now," Malcolm interposed, patting her arm, "I don't mean he's going to collapse or die tomorrow, but he should relax more. My colleagues might say I'm into quackery, but I think that the effects of strain and worry take a heavy toll on the heart.

"I told Lora and Martha as well that they should see that he gets his rest and takes the medicine I left him. I'll see him in a week. Now then, how about a ride in this craft Paul's told me about?"

Jeremy started the launch while Lora and Malcolm went over one more time the directions he'd given her for her father's care. Jeremy climbed back on the pier and helped Malcolm on board. "With a nurse like that, who couldn't get better?" Malcolm said, as Jeremy handed him his bag.

Lora stepped over and squeezed his hand tightly. "Thank you for *everything,* Jeremy," she whispered. He wanted to answer, but could only manage an awkward smile as he pushed the launch out from the pier, jumping on board.

Malcolm raised his voice over the steady thrumming of the engine. "He's sick. The heart sounds are very irregular and I believe there may be damage to one of the major valves. I'd like to observe him for a couple of days. Lora will try to convince him to come to my office, though she doesn't know the extent of his illness."

Jeremy cut the engine, letting them drift to the north of the pier arms that jutted out from the large Lake Geneva 'Y' pier. Jeremy brought up the subject of the constable. He told Malcolm about the man's snooping, and his inordinate interest in him. "I'm getting concerned about Lowery. I don't have any idea why he has such curiosity about me except for the incident with that young prisoner of his."

They tied up and walked down the pier to the shore. "I haven't spoken to you in about a month. Has your memory come back at all?" Malcolm asked.

"No," Jeremy answered, wishing he could tell Malcolm the truth. He didn't know how much longer it would be in his interest to keep up the pretense of amnesia.

"I've done some studying, my friend. Do you find you still have no further recollection since early May?" Jeremy shook his head. "You should have had some more, even total recall by now." Malcolm stroked his beard, thinking. "Are you worried about your amnesia?"

"No. I'm not worried about the amnesia." His answer was simple and direct. He'd let the doctor wrestle with its meaning. Malcolm invited Jeremy in for a cup of tea and had him sit in the living room while he heated the tea and rummaged about the kitchen. Gertrude was gone off to her relatives for the weekend.

Jeremy stared up at the wall calendar; it was June 23rd. He'd arrived "here" just over seven weeks ago. He almost hated to admit to himself how acclimated he was getting.

When the doctor returned, they sat and talked until almost dark. Jeremy described the progress at the Observatory. Malcolm interspersed their conversation with an occasional question, but Jeremy, ever on guard, retreated into his amnesiac's shrug. However, when Malcolm talked first of Paul and then his daughter, Jeremy opened up. He told the doctor about his feelings for her and even repeated much of what she said.

"She's quite a woman," Malcolm said, weighing his words. "Maybe a trifle unconventional with her independence, but all the same she's a gem, and with a loyalty you won't find in a generation. Her father worries some about her labor involvement. I believe he's concerned," he burred, "about that Debs and his bunch."

"I think she's one person who can handle herself, Doctor, though I'd sure like the opportunity of doing some looking after her." Jeremy rose. "Look at the sun. It's almost setting. I'll have to be off." He bid Malcolm goodbye at the door and strode across the street and down toward the boat dock.

Malcolm watched the receding figure. There was no doubt Jeremy had real feelings of affection for Paul's daughter. The two were clearly attracted to each other. Malcolm and Lora had earlier been talking, first about herself and then about her father while they sat on the front porch. She mentioned nothing further about Clarence Darrow. Their conversation had shifted to Jeremy. "Has he been a help?" he asked, knowing what her answer would be. But he was unprepared for her very obvious affection for him. Escorting him across the lawn, she stopped and turned to him.

"Doctor Malcolm," she asked, "you've known Jeremy…longer than I have. Does he sometimes seem to you to be, well, different?"

Malcolm saw that she had picked up the same feeling he'd had, but he decided to extend his faith in Jeremy again. "I guess we all of us have a few imperfections," was all he said.

"Well," laughed Lora, "the Lord and you certainly know I have mine."

Perhaps these two deserving young people had been steered to each other by fate, he hoped. Malcolm closed the door and walked back inside. He went to his office and sat down at his desk. He opened the drawer and once again removed Jeremy's articles, first picking up the undershirt with the strange markings, turning it over as he examined it. Setting it down, he picked up the black watch which was still placidly shooting up numbers. The face, he noted, read "Su 6 - 23". His friend's gift was still passing out information on the day of the week and the date, though *how* it did, he hadn't the faintest idea.

He absently fingered the strange, oversized lenses with the dark green glass. Putting the glasses on, Malcolm looked out the window toward the darkened sunset. He didn't know what malady his friend was suffering from, but he was convinced that it was not amnesia.

24

On Tuesday, Paul and Jeremy left early for the Observatory, buoyed by Lora's company. She tried stifling her yawn as she stood next to Jeremy in the front of the launch while Paul sat in back, going over papers.

At Jeremy's invitation, she took the wheel, steering with little effort. Lora was plainly excited about going to the Observatory, listening as Jeremy described his duties, sharing inside stories about construction on the rising structure.

During the crossing, she told him about Kittie Hogan, her husband, Doctor Jack, and their two-year old son, Jimmie. They were coming to the lake, arriving on July 6th for a week's stay at Kaye's Park.

Lora was going to try to get Kittie and the baby to move over to Bluffside after Jack went back. "We have plenty of room and she'll be great company. I've only seen Jimmie once, last Thanksgiving. I probably won't recognize him. What a little dickens," she laughed, recounting some of the toddler's antics.

"You don't think it would be dangerous for him at Bluffside, do you?" she furrowed her brow.

"If he's only two, that would be a lot of watching near the pier and all," he said, remembering anxiously watching over his own children when they were Jimmie's age.

Lora quietly regarded him before answering. "Well, Kittie's a careful mother, and I know we'd have some great times together."

At Jeremy's question, she said she'd met Kittie and Jack at the Fair, serving as the guide for their group. They'd hit it off right from the start, and when their tour was over the three of them—no baby Jimmie yet—had headed over to the Marine Cafe.

"I was famished. I'm surprised they didn't think me a glutton, but I'd overslept and hadn't eaten breakfast. At the Fair I met so many people, hundreds or thousands, really, but I seldom had a chance to get to know anyone. You gave either a two or four hour tour unless you escorted some really prominent people." She stepped away from the wheel, letting Jeremy take over.

"We sat on the porch of the Marine Cafe," she held tightly to a stanchion as the *Lora L* canted with a wave. "It had all those pointed spires and gingerbread architecture. I don't know *what* in the world it was supposed to represent, but the view was magnificent. You were next to, was it the Fisheries Building?" she frowned. "Oh, dear! Only two years and already I'm starting to forget. A sure sign of old age.

"At any rate, the cafe was on the lagoon overlooking the footbridge to the Wooded Island and across from the Women's Building. There were crowds of people crossing the bridge, with launches like this and gondolas slowly gliding by.

"Did you ever meet someone—or a pair—you instinctively liked right away?" he nodded. "That's how I felt about Kittie and Jack. I could relax around them and that's not usual for me with new acquaintances.

"They were from Joliet. Jack had taken a job at the state asylum in Elgin. That's about fifty miles outside Chicago on the Fox River," she supplied. "Oh, the stories Jack told about that place."

Jeremy docked and Lora turned to talk to her father while he secured the boat to the pier. Jeremy was going to take Lora up to the Observatory while Paul checked some outbound parcels. When they reached the freight depot, Jeremy helped her onto the seat of the wagon and stepped over to Bill Wheeler.

Bill gave him a look that said "well done," and handed over a pair of boxes that Jeremy placed on the wagon. He slipped the reins from the hitching post with a motion he hoped looked practiced. Climbing onto the seat next to Lora, he gave the big dray horse a gentle slap with the reins. "How am I doing so far?" he asked as they started the long climb up the hill.

"Perfect. You know, I'd ride with you on any wagon as long as I was sure you weren't the one who hitched it," she laughed softly, holding onto his arm as they bumped across a rut.

"You were telling me about the Hogans," he edged her back to her story. She continued her narrative, pausing after a few minutes to glance back over her shoulder. "Jack took Kittie and me down the 'Street in Cairo.' We had our pictures taken on a donkey. We were afraid to ride that camel, though. Have you ever seen a live camel?" He shook his head. "Are you sure you haven't? In that case, I can tell you it was that high!" She pointed exaggeratedly at one of the newly installed telegraph poles along the side of the road. "Do you know what else Jack saw? The *Danse du Ventre*," she rolled her eyes at the phrase. "*Those dancers*. He made us wait outside while he went in. You can guess what Kittie said to him.

"The three days went by so fast. I wanted to take them out to Pullman, but we never found time. Kittie did come out that fall. She had just found out she was expecting their baby. I got a chance to take her around George's model town. There was already trouble in the air out there."

"Did she like it?"

"Like most people, Kittie loved Pullman at first—the cute row houses, the little apartments and tidy streets. When she was there the trees were just changing. As we walked along, she saw something that I'd never noticed.

" 'Look,' she said, 'it's the middle of fall and there isn't a single leaf anywhere.' And do you know, she was right. No sooner did a leaf fall to the pavement than one of Pullman's sweepers would have it up.

"It was one of those little things about Pullman I'd overlooked. After I'd told her about some of the incidents that were taking place: the on-the-spot firings, the labor spies, I think she began to see the town in a different light. It was a balmy Sunday and we found ourselves walking past the Florence Hotel.

" 'Oh, Lora. That hotel is so pretty,' she said. 'Let's go in and I'll buy us tea.'

"That's when I had to tell her I didn't go there, that residents weren't welcome. I don't think she believed me at first. The Florence did look inviting with its big porch facing out on the park. I told her about Ned Greenwood—how he'd been sacked just for having a few drinks in the hotel bar and being 'discovered' as a resident of the town.

"I could tell you so much about Pullman," she tugged on his arm, "but there'll be other stories for other days."

"I'm glad those stories you're going to tell me are piling up," he said, trying to hide his stirring at her touch.

"*No!*" she cried under her breath. She had been glancing over her shoulder. "Is that the fellow you told me about?"

Jeremy turned around to see the constable. He wondered how Lora could have noticed him, even as she'd been chattering on. Lowery was following on horseback some distance back. "It's him," he said.

"He looks like one of those railroad detectives. Small town police don't skulk like that. The last year and a half have broadened my education," and she gave a short laugh. It was strange, he thought, that she right away thought of Lowery as a railroad detective. It was just what Jeremy had guessed about him.

They turned down the Observatory drive and Lora took one final look at the constable. "I've just decided something else as well, Jeremy. We're going to have a party on July 6th to welcome the Hogans."

"Wonderful," he said, not at all sure where he fitted in to any party.

"And you're invited, of course, my..."

"Caretaker?"

"Well, for sure you're not my horseman. How about simply my friend? Would you settle for that?" Her dimple was distracting him again.

"Whatever you say." They were drawing up in front of the Observatory. Lora gazed up at the building before stepping down from the wagon. The central building was rising and the main dome that would house the forty inch telescope had even begun to take shape.

"I hear that when this is finished, Lora, an observer will be able to see a quarter," he made a small circle with his thumb and forefinger, "a thousand miles distant from the scope here."

Just then Ernie Walker rounded the unfinished south side of the building. Jeremy introduced them. "I'm pleased to make your acquaintance, Miss Lockerby. I've heard from your father that...that you've had a most exciting year." Ernie had started to blush as he spoke.

The three walked the few feet to the steam pump which was noisily puffing and turning near the new pipeline storage tank. "That working pump is your friend here's contribution. Did you know that?" Ernie tipped his hat before hurrying off to confer with some new arrivals hailing him from a wagon.

"You're such a celebrity," Lora said in a soft aside, brushing her hand against his as they were joined by Paul. After a few minutes of descrip-

176

tion, their tour returned them to the front of the main building.

"Quite a change from last fall, isn't it, darlin'? Does the place meet with your approval?"

"Just like the newspapers say, Father, it's stupendous. But I'm much more impressed with the people in charge," and she stepped between them, taking each of their arms as they strode down toward the almost-completed power house.

With Lora's arm over his, Jeremy pushed any more thoughts about constable Lowery to the back of his mind.

25

"Father, I won't hear of you going alone or putting it off until next week. I've already asked Jeremy and he'll delay his mowing until tomorrow. Besides, I can shop in town while we're there." Lora stated it flatly, leaving no room for Paul to argue.

They were taking him to Malcolm's office for an examination, much more thorough than the one he had gotten the week before. Malcolm had written to Lora two days earlier, suggesting she bring her father for a weekend visit. "Nothing to worry about, but it will give me an opportunity to observe him over a few days, and give two old bachelors a chance to catch up." As far as transportation back to Williams Bay was concerned, Malcolm had to check in on a couple of Observatory workers on Monday, and he and Paul could travel back together.

"Darlin', I don't want to be any trouble," Paul started. "I could go in next week and..."

Lora held up her hand. "Do you hear that? Jeremy's already started the boat. Come on, father, we'll take a leisurely trip down the lake."

"But I don't have anything packed. It will take me..." Lora had turned the corner of the living room, returning in a minute with his grip.

"I took the liberty of having Martha pack everything you'll need."

"I see I can't win," Paul shrugged, smiling in defeat. "You go down to the pier and I'll be right along."

Lora started for the boat, glad that she had taken extra care with her outfit. The previous evening she had gone back to Jeremy's cabin to ask if he would take her father to see Malcolm in the morning.

"Of course. You know I've been wanting him to go." He was more than willing to take Paul, especially since Lora would be going along on the trip.

As the launch moved down the lake, Lora reached up and took off her hat, letting her hair catch the breeze. Listening to the engine humming and to Jeremy and her father talking, she lapsed into a reverie about Clarence, and about her recent trip to New York with Enid. She pictured Karl enthusiastically leading the two of them around New York, showing off the Brooklyn Bridge, dashing to the Battery, taking them to an offbeat artist's party in Greenwich Village. He also took the opportunity to show his guests his work at Trinity Church as well as his expected pediments for the new Stock Exchange building. On their final day, he had brought them across the Hudson River to his new, still-unfinished home and studio, the former "Eldorado" amusement park on the palisades overlooking Manhattan.

"It looks like Lora's drifted off to sleep," she heard her father say as she stirred awake from her daydream.

"What is it, father?"

"We were talking about the new country club going in over that way, darlin'."

Lora glanced over at the temporary, tent-like clubhouse, remembering her recent Saturday night there with Todd. Two golfers wearing ostentatious knickers strode along near the shore. Lora didn't know the first thing about the game, but she did think that the area picked out for the club seemed to be an uninviting, flat lowland. What pictures she had seen of golf courses showed players on hills and highlands.

"Careful," Paul warned. "It gets shallow in there." The idling craft was steered away from the shore. Lora trailed her hand over the side in the water as Jeremy and her father resumed talking.

How did Jeremy get up here, and where was he coming from before his accident? And why can't I place his speech pattern? The other day, while she and Malcolm were on the veranda, she had discreetly asked if anyone had inquired about him. No one had. And too, there was Jeremy's advice about her father, and about Kittie's son needing watching. She remembered his angry reaction to Todd. Their new caretaker's poise meant he'd been something very different before his puzzling accident. *But what?* Lora indulged thoughts of Jeremy as she watched him driving the boat.

Her own fixed thinking about Clarence had diminished in the last

179

couple of weeks. That was a large part of why she was up here, she knew, but she was surprised at how little she had been dwelling of late on their romance.

"Someone is waiting for you," Karl had said to her on their last day in New York. "I wish it could have been me, and I'm frankly jealous of Mr. Darrow...but that someone who's out there, he won't be married, and he'll be right for you."

She felt a sudden buffet as the *Lora L* picked up speed, leaving the country club behind and heading into Geneva Bay toward the busy municipal pier in the distance.

The large double-decked excursion boat *Harvard* blasted its steam whistle. Jeremy had headed for the spot it was vacating before someone else could take it, and the *Harvard's* captain, who'd stopped reversing and was about to start his trip, angrily responded as their launch cut in front.

"We weren't even close. He's just throwing his weight around with that big double-decker," Jeremy said as he hopped onto the pier, reaching to help Lora and Paul. The three walked to the end of the dock and toward the doctor's office, following the promenade along the shoreline.

Lora caught up to Jeremy as they left the pier. "Throwing his weight around! I declare, you find a new expression every time you open your mouth." She laughed, shaking her head as they walked. The village had started to crowd with the tourists in for the day, the weekend or longer. When they arrived at Malcolm's, the doctor met them himself and sensing Paul's uneasiness, immediately took charge. Assuring Lora her father would be fine and spend only a couple of nights with him before being returned, he sent them off.

The two walked together along Main Street toward the center of town and the market. Jeremy felt both familiar and displaced. Most of these houses had survived through the 1980s, and after the restoration movement they actually looked nearly the same as they did on this day.

"I'll stop worrying about father. He's in good hands. And I'll let you in on something, Jeremy." Lora's voice brought him back to the present—or the time at hand. "This party has me nervous. I've been away from Lake Geneva so much, and my life has been so different of late..." she paused, considering her next words.

"You know, I never became that much a part of the lake's society. If the

Pullman strike hadn't taken me away maybe I would have. When I told you the other day about my idea to have a party for the Hogans—well I *do* want to entertain Mary and Jack, but I thought that the party also would give me a chance to sort of reconnect with Lake Geneva." As Lora spoke she took Jeremy's arm.

"Do I seem too pragmatic?"

Jeremy was touched by her confiding in him. "Of course not. The Hogans will appreciate the party. It'll be a change of pace from their life at the Elgin asylum and if a party helps to re-establish you up here, well, so much the better."

She regarded him before answering. "Thank you. That's what I felt but I needed that reassurance." A smile lit up her face. "I want to tell you all about those plans, too. Let's go over to Arnold's drug store for an ice cream soda. If they're as good as last year, you're in for a treat." Lora led him kitty-corner across Broad Street's intersection with Main and nearly into the path of a nattily dressed bicyclist. He was riding another of the enormous high wheelers. She ignored his glare as he swerved his awkward device around them.

Jeremy followed her into the drug store. Arnold's formal front window, with its mortar and pestle and colored jars, belied the friendly socializing inside. At the rear of the narrow store was a raised mezzanine where the real pharmacy work was apparently being carried out. The rest of the store, at least what he could see of it, was given over to an ice cream parlor. On the left was a marble counter with all of its stools occupied. Behind the counter an attendant was hustling up concoctions.

The pair sat down at one of the half-dozen or so small round tables, each with its own wire-backed chairs. An enthusiastic teenager in a candy striped skirt took their order for strawberry sodas. Just as she left, a young man in a jaunty white sport coat and holding a straw sailor hat approached.

"Lora Lockerby! I thought you'd be kept too busy by old George Pullman to be up here this summer." Lora brightened seeing him.

"You look better than ever, Rob Allerton, and you're just the person I want to talk to." Rob's companion, who had stepped around from behind him, was introduced as Callie Braddock. Callie was a cute young deb from nearby Lake Delavan, whose parents, Rob said, he'd almost convinced to move their summer address to Lake Geneva. He shook Jeremy's hand as Lora explained that he was "working for my father out at the Observatory and staying with us this summer." Jeremy mused at his change of status from part-time caretaker to that of a sort of guest. *I've just gotten another upgrade.*

Lora invited Rob and Callie to sit down at their table, and began to tell them about the Hogans and the party in their honor, soliciting Rob's advice in helping with the guest list. Jeremy started to order two more sodas.

"Please, no," Rob said. "We just finished. Two more sodas and some-one will have to carry us out." Rob, it turned out, lived across from Bluffside and down the lake at the Narrows, at a property both he and Lora referred to as "Folly". Jeremy got this story, and a short history of the Allerton's large estate from Callie, who filled him in while Rob and Lora went through names. Rob eagerly threw himself into the project, and with the aid of a borrowed pencil and some paper, they came up with a list of fifteen or twenty people. Todd Brinkley's name, Jeremy noted with satisfaction, was not included.

"Lora," Rob said finally, standing. "Callie and I have to be off. Father's up for the weekend. He hasn't met Callie yet and he'd better not try to steal you, either," he circled his arm around her waist. Before they left, he bent to Lora and lowered his voice. "I heard about your rotten luck at Pullman with your job and all. That man's a devil, but you know I'm on the board at the Art Institute now. They're going to be opening a chil-dren's school in the fall and I happen to know they're looking for an art teacher. And as a matter of fact, she ought to be someone like you. I'll do what I can. Please keep it in mind, Lora."

Lora's gaze followed the two as they walked out of Arnold's. "Lord, Jeremy, did you hear what he said about the Art Institute? What a god-send it would be if he could do something..." she trailed off, thinking.

Jeremy remembered the day they'd ridden around town behind Magnolia and Lora had told him that she probably would not be return-ing to Darrow's office. He was puzzled at her reluctance to go back there. *Why,* he wondered. Of course, Darrow wasn't yet the mythic character he would become. Maybe he was a hard taskmaster. With time, it was a sub-ject he might pursue with her.

She turned her attention back to the guest list. "Kittie is so down-to-earth that I wanted people who weren't snobs or goody-goodies. Rob's given me some useful ideas. Did you hear him say his sister Kate is up here? He's sure she can come. Kate's married to a doctor and that will be perfect for Doctor Jack. This party's going to be fun, you'll see, Jeremy, now that we've got ourselves a guest list." Jeremy put down twenty cents for the two sodas.

"Let's go over to Johnson's and stock up on our groceries now." They had emerged into the warm summer day. The two crossed main Street in front of a farmer driving his wagon, which reminded Lora to ask Jeremy if he had been working on his horsemanship.

"As a matter of fact, I *have* been doing just that. I've been practicing with the harness and drawing on Emil's advice, hopefully without his realizing it. Wednesday, I hitched Magnolia to the wagon and rode to Fontana and brought some things back to Martha. I really think she's starting to believe I have a head on my shoulders."

"Oh, nonsense, she has lots of affection for you. She just...well, she *is* a little puzzled by you at times."

"Like you?" Jeremy asked, testing.

"No, I have you all figured out," she said, taking his arm as they walked along. "You come from some place far away, Mars, probably, where there are no horses or anything of the kind."

"How did I get here?" he asked, picking up on her jest. She looked at him pensively for a moment, furrowing her brow.

"I believe," she started slowly, "You had some kind of an accident and landed here in little Lake Geneva and even right now, you're trying to find a way to get home. Does that sound fanciful enough?"

"It does," he answered, "but you forgot to mention why I'm working at the Observatory. You see, I'm going to steal that telescope when it's finished," he said, laughing along with her as they entered Johnson's grocery. He wondered what she'd think if she knew how close to the truth she'd really come.

Once inside the grocery, she gave Jeremy half the shopping list and set him to work finding a clerk. In Johnson's store, the customers stayed in the center by the cash register, talking to each other or walking down aisles if they wanted to look at produce or canned goods. It was young teenage boys who hurried around filling the orders. They pushed the sliding ladders back and forth, scurrying up and down. Sometimes one of them would take a prong-like device and reach up to the top shelf to snatch a can. To Jeremy, the system seemed far superior to the huge supermarkets of the future, where the shoppers did all the work. What paths progress takes, he mused, as a quick-moving clerk dodged around him.

In no time they had two large sacks of groceries. Lora left Mr. Johnson an additional huge delivery order. "The rest of the food for the party," she added as they left the store. Jeremy was balancing the sacks as they took her "shortcut" to the dock, an ancient footbridge that crossed the outlet from the lake.

They stored the groceries in the launch and cast off, heading out into Geneva Bay and along the south shore of the lake. "Look ahead," Lora said, pointing to an enormous house on the hill, topped by a red pagoda. "That's the *Ceylon Court*. I never dreamed I'd see that here at the lake!" She told him the building was a reproduction of a Buddhist Temple brought over for the Columbian Exposition by the government of Ceylon. After the Exposition, it had been purchased by an American family and transported to Lake Geneva for use as a summer home.

"At the Fair they called it the *Singhalese Villa*. It sat at the end of the midway and it was one of the most popular exhibits. I couldn't even tell you how many people I took there on tours. I have a warm spot in my heart for the Villa because I could get off my tired feet for twenty minutes or so while the Singhalese guides took over my parties."

"There must be an unfinished addition," Jeremy said, noticing scaffolding around the building. He slowed as they pulled opposite the estate.

"Todd knows the people who own it. I think their name is Chandler. They aren't moving in until next summer. Can you see any workers around?"

He couldn't see any activity. "It's Saturday afternoon, Lora. It looks like they're all gone."

"Do you feel like an adventure?"

"Sure," he answered, "why not?" She apparently had another surprise up her puffed sleeve, he thought. He watched as she studied the shore, knitting her brow, her chin in her hand.

"I don't want to pull into the pier. We'll have to anchor the boat somewhere, but not in front of the estate. Pull ahead and around Manning's Point," she said. "At least we'll be out of sight from anyone in the house. We still have to figure someway to get ashore. How close can you *get* to the shore?" she inquired.

"This boat sits pretty high but she probably needs two feet of water under her, at least. What do you have in mind?" Lora didn't answer as she chewed pensively on her fingernail, but just as they rounded the point, she saw a dilapidated rowboat along the shore. It was tied to a tree and seemed to give her an idea.

"How close can you get us to that boat?" she asked.

"About fifteen feet, I suppose. I wouldn't want to bring us any nearer."

"Do you think if I took the wheel and brought us that close, you could possibly wade over to the dingy?"

"And?"

"I could take the boat out aways. You could come out, anchor us and row to the shore. I want to see the house. There's something I have to show you. Please?"

He threw up his hands in mock resignation and sat down. He took off his shoes and socks and rolled his pants up to his knees, thinking how comical he must look.

"All right," he said, crawling out on the bow of the launch. "Head her in *easy*. When I tell you, put her in neutral and get ready to reverse. If the bottom is anything like that shore, it's all boulders under us. I wouldn't want to explain to your father how we put a hole in this hull."

Lora let the boat idle in forward gear until he gave her the word and then she shifted into neutral. He leaned over the bow, peering into the water but with the light chop on the surface and the sun's angle, it was impossible to see below. When they were about twenty feet from the rowboat, he decided that it probably was not more than a foot-and-a-half or so deep and he climbed over the side and let go. He was wrong. The water was over his waist. He looked back. Lora's hand was up to her face covering a laugh.

"Are you all right?"

"It's only water," he mumbled, as he started towards the shore, wincing at the sharp boulders underfoot. When he finally reached the rowboat, he discovered that there were several inches of water in the bottom and, of course, no oars. *Little danger anyone would want to steal this*, he thought, shaking his head in disgust. He untied the rope and just managed to lift one side enough to rock the water out. Unlike himself, it was at least reasonably dry, and he pushed off. He had to lean out over the bow and paddle with his cupped hands. At last he drew up to the launch, and tying the rowboat to the side, he climbed up and threw over the anchor.

Once again, he marveled at her agility as she climbed over the side— long-skirted dress, puffed sleeves and all and dropped easily into the dingy. With both of them back inside, he reversed the journey again, paddling towards shore.

"Can't you go *any* faster?" she teased, reaching over and tickling his foot.

He pulled the boat up on shore and helped her out. "I really hope this is going to be worth it," he said, glancing back at the *Lora L* as she led him along the shore path.

They rounded Manning's point. From land the building was more imposing. And even by the standards of the lake in the 1890's, this house was going to be something very special. The path began to veer away from the shore and climb up the terraced hillside in front of the estate. Lora had him wait as she left the trail and scrambled down almost to the water, disappearing from view. In a few minutes she reappeared and gestured for him to join her below.

"This is what I wanted to show you." She pulled back a piece of canvas and he found himself looking into the mouth of a cave. He hadn't noticed it at all from the water.

"What in the world is this?"

"It's going to be the latest thing around the lake. This tunnel leads all the way back to the house where you're taken upstairs by an elevator. Jeremy, I know it's way beyond our means, but wouldn't something like this just be grand for father?" He nodded, agreeing, as he peered inside the tunnel. He didn't remember ever hearing about any underground tunnels to the houses and he knew that Lora's prediction that they would become the latest rage would never be proved true. Cost, he guessed.

She stepped into the tunnel and he followed. It was high enough for a person to stand, wide enough for two. Large boulders were at the sides and overhead, giving the impression they had been piled there by nature but on closer inspection, he could see they'd been carefully set into solid masonry. The tunnel abruptly turned left, plunging them into darkness. She took his hand and he led, putting one foot carefully in front of another.

Their passageway angled again but Jeremy noticed by feeling the wall and the smooth surface under foot that the tunnel had apparently been finished.

Obviously the tunnel would be lighted for use but now the darkness and windings were disorienting. The two hardly spoke and when they did their voices sounded so hollow that they whispered as they felt their way along. They reached what felt like a fork in the tunnel but discovered it was a room carved out of the earth.

"I read about this," Lora said. "I think it's going to be the root cellar. Can you imagine? It was described in the *Herald* as being near the elevator. We must be almost there." They moved a little further and sure enough, after another turn they reached a metal door. Jeremy could feel it was on a hinge and was fitted with a window.

"I wonder if the elevator is working?" she whispered. Her finger found a button and she pressed. Immediately there was a loud clank that echoed down the tunnel, followed by a whir of machinery and the clanging of chains.

"I think you just answered your question," Jeremy said. Lora, surprised by what she'd set in motion, grabbed his arm tighter. It was certain that if there were anyone around, they'd for sure be alerted by the clamor. In a few moments an elevator car slid into view and stopped with a thump. A single bare electric light inside lit up the area around them.

"We know it's working. Isn't this something, Jeremy?" She opened the door and pulled on the lattice-metal inside screen. "We won't go up. I just wanted to see it. This is like you would find in one of the office buildings in downtown Chicago," she said as she stepped in, holding back the collapsible screen.

"Wait, listen." Jeremy touched her shoulder. Lora stopped to listen, then looked at him, her mouth open. There were voices at the end of the tunnel. Jeremy scanned the passageway. They would either have to go up the elevator or face whoever was coming. The house at the top might be locked, but even if they were to get inside, it would be the end of a very embarrassing prank for two people their age to be caught in someone else's home. Better to face whoever was coming down the tunnel.

Lora let the door close quietly and took Jeremy's hand, leading him down the tunnel. She ducked around the corner, pulling him after her and entered the root cellar. They were again in total darkness as they

187

heard the voices growing nearer.

"I know I closed that opening, Hank. I swear I did," said the first voice.

"Go on, you never bothered to close it behind you. It's a wonder half the tramps in the county haven't taken up living here," said a second and older voice.

Jeremy couldn't see them but from the sounds of their shuffling and panting, they were carrying something very heavy between them. "Look, the car's at the bottom!" said the younger. "It means someone came down from the house and went out. I *told* you I didn't leave the entrance open." They could be heard struggling to open the door. "Where does this damn thing go?"

"Well now, and just where do you *think* an icebox would go? And if you minded the tunnel, how would you like for us to have to carry this up that hill out in front? Come on, let's get this up there. I want to get through for the day," said the older voice.

They heard the door shut and the car start its noisy upward trip. "Phew," Lora blew out a breath and leaned against him. Then they both laughed, shushing each other at the same time. Their foreheads bumped in the dark. One minute they were laughing and the next moment his arm was around her and he brushed his lips against hers, And all the pent-up feeling he had for her was suddenly there in his kiss, in their embrace. At last he pulled back and searched to read her expression in the pitch blackness.

"I," she started, her head still against his chest. "I guess we'd better get back before we get more company." He could think of absolutely nothing to say but took her hand as they retraced their steps through the tunnel. At one point, he bumped straight into the wall at one of the windings. His mishap broke the tension. "See what you've done to my sense of direction?"

"Go hitch a wagon," she answered, giving him a little shove ahead toward the last turn and the light from the opening.

They paused at the entrance to see if anyone was outside. There was only a large rowboat at the end of the dock which the men had doubtless used. She stopped him at the entrance. Putting her arms around him and looking up, she nuzzled him. "I'm glad that happened."

"So am I, Lora. I've wanted to do that since I first saw you." There, he'd spoken his wishes, even if he'd been trying not to think them. They were both quiet, then stepped out, blinking at the afternoon sun. The delivery men had left the tunnel entrance open, obviously intending to exit in a few minutes.

"Wait," Lora said as they were about to start down the shore path. Jeremy watched as she replaced the oilcloth, carefully covering the entire entrance. "There," she turned, at last satisfied with her work. "Just one more mystery for them to unravel," she took his hand as they started for the rowboat.

26

During the first week of July, Lora's party plans heated up. Glad to be included in those plans, Jeremy worked diligently at sprucing up Bluffside's grounds. Thursday was the Fourth of July, and Lora, Jeremy and Martha sat around the kitchen table drinking coffee. Martha was fretting over each of Lora's new ideas when the caretaker from the Koch's estate down the shore knocked on the door. Jeremy followed him out to the wagon where the two unloaded the most recent of Lora's inspirations—dozens of Japanese lanterns on electrical cords. The colorful lanterns were the latest '90s outdoor decorating fad and Victoria had donated them for the party.

Emil had been recruited to help with the stringing and he handed the strands up to Jeremy who wove them through the branches of the oaks. Jeremy was much higher up on the heavy wooden ladder than he wanted to be as he leaned out to circle the lanterns around the branches. On hearing conversation below, he glanced down and saw Klaus, the Lefens' gardener, at the base of the tree talking to Emil. Jeremy knew him as the most meticulous groundskeeper he'd ever seen, and he was glad the Lockerbys demanded no such level of gardening from him. Each weekend, as he mowed the lawn, trimming and weeding as best he could, he watched Klaus kneeling in the long gravel driveway. The elderly German would painstakingly pluck weeds hour after hour. His progress was slow, and at times he seemed not to move at all, but at long last he would finish weeding and then spend as many hours carefully raking and leveling every inch of the driveway's ornamental gravel. Klaus was friendly enough but because he spoke so little English and never stopped working, their dialogue was minimal.

Jeremy called down to say hello. "You're in luck," Emil shouted up. "Klaus wants to help. He'll put in some flowerbeds for the party."

"I help," the old man said, peering up through the branches at Jeremy. Before he could say anything, Klaus had turned and was gone. Jeremy backed down the ladder.

"You watch Klaus. He's like nuthin' I ever seen before," Emil said as he helped move the ladder to the next tree. As they were setting out the string of lights on the ground, Klaus reappeared, pushing a large wheelbarrow filled with spades, hoes, a pitchfork—almost every garden tool existent in 1895. "Just watch," Emil murmured. Klaus had a big grin on his face and spoke in German to Emil.

Emil was second or third generation and his own German was halting. "He says he wants to help. Klaus has an idea…" Emil hesitated over the right word. "…an idea for flowerbeds." Already tufts of sod in the front lawn were being torn up and flung aside. Jeremy walked over to the spirited gardener.

"Klaus," he started, "you want some help?" Klaus paused and leaned on a pitchfork, a light sweat trickling down his forehead. "Work—alone," he smiled, turning back to his labors.

After Jeremy and Emil finished stringing the lanterns across the branches, they moved the ladder against the side of the house where Jeremy climbed to the second floor porch. From there he could see why people considered Klaus to be the top gardener at Lake Geneva. He'd already cleared one flowerbed with a graceful oval contour and he was busily digging out a matching one on the opposite side of the walk.

Jeremy found the electrical outlet or what in the 1890s passed for an outlet. Like many estates at this time, Bluffside was wired with direct current from its own generator. Paul had installed the small kerosene-powered unit at the rear of the property. Ever conscious of appearances, Paul had buried all the wires in the ground, just as the wiring at the Observatory was underground. Carefully wrapping the uninsulated cord with a piece of rubber, he inserted the plug. Even at midday, as he, Klaus and Emil stood watching, the lanterns seemed well worth the effort. Then he unhooked the lights—time to show Lora later.

By the end of the afternoon, two large flowerbeds had sprouted. Pansies, marigolds and flowers Jeremy couldn't identify had been transported from the Lefens' terraced back gardens. Incredibly, Klaus had even

191

transplanted large gladiolas. Someone coming upon the beds would have sworn they'd been there for two months instead of two hours. Jeremy was as touched by Klaus's generosity as he was amazed that one person could produce such a miracle in less than half a day. *Would I have seen this in the 1990s,* he wondered? Possibly but not likely. Was it all the sophistication of the future that interfered with people's helpfulness to each other? As the two volunteers departed, Jeremy pumped their hands, thanking them earnestly

Jeremy then went to fetch Martha. Lora and Paul had gone over to visit the Seipps for a Fourth of July celebration and weren't due home until after supper. "Don't you think I'm improving as a caretaker? Come see what I did," he said, pointing to the flowerbeds.

"Oh Jeremy, that's unbelievable, especially since I been at the front door and saw ol' Klaus out here."

"I can't get the better of you, but isn't this an improvement?" he asked. "Now you wait here. No, back up a little. There." He hurried back up the ladder and turned the lanterns back on. In the fading light of late afternoon they came alive. "Is this going to be some party or what, Martha?" he called down as he unhooked the cord.

"You come on in, Jeremy. You must be starved, even if you *didn't* dig those flowerbeds." After he had washed up and reappeared at the side door, she had him in for a dinner of her baked ham and sweet potatoes. After dinner, he sipped a cup of the strong black coffee she brewed as she sat down at the table, pouring herself a cup. That was another thing he noticed. Martha never ate. Not so much as a bite in front of anyone, except for coffee or a rare donut. He hadn't been raised around servants. Did she perhaps stay up late and eat then?

Jeremy was relaxed, and with a full stomach, he listened to the fireworks at Kaye's and began thinking of other Fourth of July's he'd spent, once in a cablecar climbing Lookout Mountain at dusk, his daughter asleep in his lap, her head resting on his shoulder after a long day of sightseeing. He remembered other times, lying on his back along with his family on St. Petersburg Beach, watching skyrockets abruptly burst, the ache of his separation beginning to return with force. Martha started talking.

As he listened, she slowly began to sketch her history for Jeremy. He sat back, sipping the coffee as she told him she'd been born in northern Georgia, on a small plantation near Rome. Her father was a freed slave who had worked diligently, finally saving enough to buy freedom for the rest of the family—her mother, her sister and herself. They stayed on the plantation afterwards, working for small wages. She recalled how her father had come home one evening and how her sister had heard him talking to her mother in a worried voice. It was puzzling that he should be concerned now that they were free. They crept over to the curtain to listen, aware of what being caught out of bed would mean in the strict household.

It seemed that Mrs. Dexter, the mistress of the house, had taken sick with "breathing problems." Her daddy had learned this in whispers from the house servants. Mr. Dexter, a man her father had always respected, was being forced to sell and move his sickly wife to her sister's in Atlanta. He had planned to tell the workers, she heard her father say, but Mrs. Dexter had talked him out of it. They could, she said, get much more money from the Rumseys if the Negroes didn't find out who the purchasers were.

Her father's next words had struck real fear in her, as young as she was. Mr. Dexter was going to sell everything, including two not-yet-freed slaves, to the Rumseys. All the Negroes in the area knew the name Rumsey. They were notorious for the way they treated their slaves and it was rumored that they were buying up land as fast as they could. When you worked for the Rumseys you didn't leave, freed or not, and you took the wages they wanted to pay.

Jeremy got up and poured more coffee. "What year was that, Martha?" he asked, trying to fix in his mind when this could have taken place.

"1853," she answered, remembering clearly. "You ever hear of the 'Fugitive Slave Act?' " she asked. He paused, then shook his head. "I expect that'll come back to you. It was passed in 1850 but what it meant to the slaves as well as us freed people was that we could be chased and followed up north and that U.S. courts would issue warrants for 'fugitives'." The marshals, she told him, weren't too choosy about who they picked up on the owner's affidavit, which a supposed fugitive could not even testify against. He could then be brought back. The Rumseys were said to have gotten back several of their workers this way, even ones who had already been freed. A bitterness had crept into Martha's voice that Jeremy hadn't heard there before, and her face grew uncharacteristically cold.

Her parents decided to leave before the Rumseys had a chance to take over. They set off a few days later after dark. Her father instructed Martha and her sister to come along and be quiet; nothing more was told the girls. She was just then still more afraid of her stern and very real poppa than she was of the willowy Rumseys, whom she'd heard of but had never seen. She remembered her mother's tears as she left her few possessions behind in the cabin. This would create more doubt about the permanence of their leaving. They also left a cover story at the Negro church that they were going to a cousin's baptism.

That night, their first on the road, they waited in the woods until a wagon that her father had hired came by. In response to a low whistle, her father hurried them out of their hiding place and into the wagon and they set off, traveling all night to put as much distance behind them as they could. During the daytime, they waited back in the trees until dark, when it was time to resume their journey. Once out of Georgia, they sometimes traveled during the day since they were freed, but more often than not they were passed on at night through the hills of Tennessee and Kentucky by mountain people.

The only whites she'd seen until then, with the exception of a few slave handlers, were the genteel, well-scrubbed southerners. These new people they were meeting in the hills were strange and alien. The family occasionally stayed at night in their cold cabins, which were even smaller and far dirtier than any of those on the plantation. She hadn't known any white people lived like that. These folks were unfriendly and rough in their talk, what little there was. Her father told them not to be afraid of their rough talk, that he'd heard they were unfriendly toward everyone but honest nevertheless. It was true. They were as gruff to other whites as they were to Martha's family. For days the travelers made their way through the hills until at last they crossed the Ohio River, beginning to breath easier as they went north.

"The Underground Railroad?" Jeremy asked.

"Poppa never let us say those words, even years later. He wouldn't let us say we arrived by the underground. 'That was for *slaves*' he'd say 'and we was no slaves'.

"My daddy was handy with tools and I thought we could settle. We was livin' in a nice cabin out on a big farm near Marengo, Illinois. Then one night Poppa comes home, just like in Georgia. He told Momma a

194

marshal had hauled away some folks down the road. They swore they were freed. 'Were they?' Momma asked.

" 'Don't know. Don't care. Don't make no difference. We're movin' on!' "

Her parents decided they'd go on to Wisconsin. There were cities there where a freed man could get work, and then her father said something about—she hadn't followed it exactly at the time, but it seemed there were more whites who stood up for Negroes up there. The marshals seldom went above Illinois into a court in Wisconsin, she said, telling Jeremy how strange and foreign "Wisconsin" had sounded on her tongue.

She recalled asking her father several times along the way if they could settle down, especially if a town where they stopped seemed friendly and pretty. " 'No honey,' he'd say, putting his arm around me, 'this is just a waystation. Look up at that ol' North Star. We're still followin' it a little further'." And that was how, after a series of starts and stops, they arrived at Racine. They settled there until after the war when she moved over to Burlington, becoming a housekeeper.

"My Mrs," she went on "had just passed on and she left me a little, and I was straightening up, clearing things out, getting ready to go back to Racine. It seems some folks told Mr. Lockerby about me. He had just lost his wife. When I met him, I said to myself, that poor, sad man. I thought I'd finished with domestic work—I could get a job at the J.I. Case factory in Racine—but he brought his little girl along. She'd been in the wagon but she slipped out and walked up to the porch while we was talkin'. She was seven years old, a quiet little thing and she had the biggest, saddest brown eyes I ever seen. I found her a cookie or two and that was that. She just stole my heart.

"I been with Miz Lora almost twenty years and I seen her grow up. I've cooked for her, washed and dressed her, stayed up with her fevers. I've scolded her and a whole lot more than that even when she had it comin' and I've worried some over her as she got older."

Martha stirred her coffee slowly, then looked over at Jeremy, fixing her steady gaze on him. "I like you, Jeremy. But I've seen enough of life to know you've been places—you have a look to you like you been keepin' things to yourself. Now that's all right," she hurried to add. "What I'm sayin' is that if Bluffside is only a waystation, you'd best move on. I don't want my Lora to be any waystation. I know how she feels about you.

She's fond of you, maybe even *too* fond."

He looked down to the floor. He was going to tell Martha just how he felt. She'd leveled with him, confiding how Lora felt, and he was reeling with happiness. Euphoric, he decided to tell her his story. Not the time travel. He'd make up a story around it and give her as much of the truth as he could about himself and about his own feelings for Lora.

As he started to talk, they both turned, hearing Lora and Paul cross the porch and enter the house. Lora walked into the kitchen and seeing Jeremy, she paused, hesitant.

"If everyone walks out front," he said, standing, "you'll get a preview of the party." Once again, he turned on the Japanese lanterns, now glowing brightly as they swayed from the branches above.

"Oh, it's so beautiful! Thank you," said Lora. Paul smiled his approval and crossed to Martha to speak with her. Lora led Jeremy by the hand across the lawn. "I'm sorry I didn't see you earlier. I wish you could have gone—with us—the Seipps asked for you. Elsa and Al Madlener are the only ones who can come to the party. The rest are all back in Chicago and Catherine says she's too old for the party; she wants to stay put. Can you imagine?"

They had walked around to the side of the house out of sight of Paul and Martha. Jeremy put his arms around her. She lifted her face to him, rising up on her toes, circling his neck with her own arms. They kissed for a long moment, drawing against each other. "I love you," he whispered at last. "No," he followed up, placing his finger over her lips, knowing what she'd respond. "Don't say anything now. There's time tomorrow and afterward." They kissed again, his arms still around her, before reluctantly parting for the night. He hadn't said those words to any woman in years.

27

The *Lora L* was filled with more cut roses than Jeremy had ever seen. Lora had just returned with him from "Folly", where Rob had thoughtfully provided them with every color and description of rose imaginable. The two had climbed the steps, their arms loaded down with flowers. "Do I seem nervous, Jeremy?" she asked when they reached the top of the bluff.

"No. Excited maybe, and why not?"

"Well, I *am* nervous. Sit down for a minute. We have some time." Lora went over the guest list with him once more, giving him short descriptions of each person. "How many is that?" she finally asked.

"Ten, so far. I just ran out of fingers." Jeremy felt more at ease as she ticked off Rob Allerton and Callie Braddock. "And Rob said his sister Kate and her husband would come over," he reminded. "That's fourteen."

"Remember I told you about the General Managers Association?" she asked. As she spoke, she circled her arms around her knees, drawing her feet under her.

"At Pullman?"

"Yes, well, not exactly at Pullman but in connection with the strike. General Strong was very active with the Association. He's President of the Santa Fe." He started to say something but smiled and shrugged. Lora was off on a story. "I went to their house and met him last summer. You know, we moved here not long after the strike when the government was doing all that investigating. I was up here for a few weeks and I saw Janet Strong in town one day while Todd and I were there.

"I'd met Janet the year before. This was a Saturday afternoon and she asked us over to her estate. Her father was an organist and was giving a concert that afternoon. It never occurred to me on the way over who he might be until we'd arrived. Jeremy, there were over a hundred people. The Strongs used their own boat to bring people over from the town.

"We all sat in a large open building near the lake. And then, suddenly, a curtain was pulled aside and her father stepped out before a huge organ. He was introduced as *General* Strong. *That's* when it came to me! General Strong was one of the insiders, one of the ring-leaders for the Association, who only a few weeks back and maybe still even, was conniving with Olney, the U.S. Attorney and all the rest of that pack of jackals—to crush our strike—and jail us or as many as they could."

Lora's eyes twinkled with humor as she remembered the day. "He really is quite a good organist from what little *I* know. At least it sounded good and his choice of songs was surprisingly modern—he even played 'After the Ball is Over' and some others from the World's Fair. At any rate, when the concert was over, most of the townspeople drifted back to the yacht for their return trip to town, but Janet asked a few of us to stay and meet her father.

"I'd only seen a picture of the General before. He's much more striking in person. He looks…" Lora paused, "Very robust, very commanding. I could easily see him pounding tables and getting his way with that mousey government attorney, his hired hand," she squinted as she talked, picturing the General.

"He seemed fatigued, though. He'd played this huge organ without any break for well over an hour on a hot August day. After a few words of welcome, we were led over to a table where the servants had brought down a barrel of beer on ice.

"A line formed to meet him and when it came our turn, Janet introduced us. 'Father, this is Lora Lockerby.' He took my hand, then studied me closely, slowly repeating my name." Lora's voice had taken on that slightly husky tone Jeremy had come to listen for. "His eyes never leave your face as he talks to you.

" 'And where are you from, Miss Lockerby?' he asked.

" 'Her father has just finished a house at Black Point,' Todd offered, introducing himself.

"Actually, sir," I said, "I'm only visiting. I live, or lived, in Pullman, Illinois."

"He nodded with a smile of recognition. 'Meeting you makes me won-

198

der again why our adversaries always seem more charming than our friends. It also makes me realize what a surprisingly small world this is. We must talk together some time, Miss Lockerby,' he said, turning to someone else and ending our interview.

"Jeremy, I suppose I should have been flattered, his placing who I was and all, but that measuring stare. I tell you, I was damp with perspiration as we walked out to his pier. But I've made this story too long," she said, rising up and stretching, her eyes meeting his as she took his hands.

"Look," she pointed across the lake at a smudge of smoke, "there's the Hogan's train. I've made arrangements to pick them up at Kaye's Park in three hours, so let's get these flowers someplace," she said as they walked towards the house, between Klaus's elegant flowerbeds.

"Oh, yes, there is another couple," she added as they crossed the veranda. "Frank McClure and his fiancee, Charlotte. You saw them on the pier when I left with Todd. They're also the couple I told you about the other morning."

The rest of the afternoon sped by with Martha taking control of the arriving caterers. Jeremy had gone home to change. His mustache was fully grown out and he gave it a last smoothing before trying on the stiff, four-button coat. He noticed he could hardly move his arms in it as he started across to the main house. As he rounded the side, he heard screaming and laughing and saw a small child dart out onto the lawn with young Marie in hot pursuit. She waved to him as she plunged after the high-spirited toddler. Paul was on the veranda with a man about Jeremy's own age.

Paul introduced them. Doctor Jack said he had heard of Jeremy—what a good seaman he was. "That lake was so calm coming across this afternoon, and not as large as I'd imagined. I've always been afraid of being on water. It's the stuff of most of my nightmares. A phobia we'd call it. But tomorrow I'm going about defeating it. We've chartered a boat, the *Dispatch*. Really my brother, Father Jim, has." A white-coated waiter appeared, passing out champagne glasses from a silver tray.

The Dispatch, Jeremy repeated to himself. He couldn't place seeing the boat either at Williams Bay or Lake Geneva town. There was something unsettling about the name, but he dismissed it. "Is that a kind of confrontation therapy?" Jeremy asked. Both Paul and Jack turned to him at his question.

"I guess that's a good term," he hesitated for a moment, "an excellent term." Doctor Jack seemed uncertain about what to say next.

Probably, Jeremy mused, *it must be difficult for someone at the turn-of-the-century to think of something appropriate to ask a friend's caretaker-date.* Doctor Hogan's eyes fell upon the flowerbeds and he suddenly brightened. "Your work?" he moved closer to the balustrade to get a closer look.

"No," Jeremy said as he took a sip of champagne. "That's the work of the man next door. I'm not the best caretaker, I fear."

"Jeremy primarily works with me," Paul said, helping. "He's my assistant and is in charge over there when I'm gone, which has been too often of late." Jeremy mentally thanked Paul, wondering how many more awkward scenes there might yet be. But the conversation veered over to the Elgin Asylum and Doctor Jack's career.

He'd been there two years—working on the men's side—his own first experiences with mental patients. Jack was struck by Jeremy's interest in the asylum in general and in his work. Jeremy didn't know how much, if any, Jack had been told of his "amnesia". At the turn-of-the-century, he remembered, insane asylums and work with mentally ill patients, "lunatics", as he'd seen them openly referred to in newspapers and even by doctors, was not popular medical work. A return to normalcy by any of these patients was rare.

The young doctor's dedication showed through as he talked about his patients. This was someone, Jeremy thought, who would never be heard making glib references to his patients as lunatics. He told them about a patient of his who had been brought in raging and violent and who just the other day had been released back to his family.

Paul had been listening closely. "Might that not be very dangerous, Jack?" he inquired gently. Jeremy was more convinced than ever that the recovery of a mental patient must have been thought of as a rare event in 1895.

"Yes, it could be," Jack answered carefully. "He's being returned to his wife and children, not to mention to society in general. But I believe we were able to learn about his rages—the causes—by listening to him and counseling him. I think I was able to show him how to recognize his feelings and how to channel them. We have to get these people back to their families and to society. I don't want to retire forty years from now and..." he paused, "and feel that all I did was help preside over a kind of warehouse for the insane." Just then, he was interrupted by the laughter of the women as they came through the doorway.

"Oh, and get off your soapbox, Jack. You're at a party." It had to be Kittie Hogan, Jeremy guessed, with that short, reddish hair. Her blue eyes shone and her pixie face was dotted with freckles. Jeremy was introduced. She gave him a friendly, appraising look and with a sigh to Lora, put on an exaggerated Irish brogue. "It's handsome he is and not nearly so fat and homely as you told me.

"Seriously, Jeremy, it's glad I am to meet you." He took her offered hand, put at ease by both of Lora's friends. They all sat down in the veranda chairs while Kittie proceeded to tell about meeting Lora.

It seems they were assigned a guide for their World's Fair tour and were just about to leave. Kittie, as she told it, spotted Lora. She was in her guide's outfit, leaning against a railing, talking and laughing. Kittie recounted how she nudged her husband "This is the great Columbian Exposition, Jack. What are we here for if not for fun. Let's just wait and go with *that* guide over there. She looks a little naughty', that is, begging your pardon Mr. Lockerby and you too, Jeremy. I only meant 'naughty' in the best sense," she added, while Lora laughed, raising her eyes.

Just then, two-year old Jimmie reappeared and climbed the veranda, slipping under the balustrade and plopping onto his mother's lap. Marie followed a few steps behind, glad to sit down for a minute. She poured herself a lemonade from the big pitcher, and one for Jimmie as well. "You look like you're a little weary, Marie," Jeremy said.

The twelve year took a long drink. "Well, I chased Jimmie through the flowerbeds at our house. That was when we found the old rope swing out in the back. I hadn't seen it before. It must have been the people's who lived in the old cabin. I tested it first and it held me so I gave Jimmie a swing."

"She swing me," he piped up as he lifted a cookie from the table.

"What is it about an old rope swing," asked Paul, "that when you hear someone talk about it, it takes you back over the years to your own first rides. Here's to all those summers and rides that are ahead of you, Jimmie," and they lifted their glasses as the toddler, giggling at the attention, slid off his mother's lap and took another cookie.

"Oh, look!" Kittie cried, pointing out across the lawn toward the lake below. A large, dark yacht with a high smoke stack turned towards

Bluffside, caught by the rays of the setting sun.

"Let's all go down," said Lora. "That's the Allerton's boat. Come on." Paul told them to go on and he'd stay put as the rest started down across the grass. Jeremy looked down at Jimmie, who had just snatched another cookie from the plate, just as his son Danny had done at that same age.

The little boy caught his eye, and gave him a tentative smile. Reaching down, Jeremy picked him up and placed him easily on his shoulders. "Now you can have the best view of all, Jimmie." They started across the broad lawn. Lora looked back at him as they approached the side of the bluff, and smiled, giving his free hand a squeeze. "I think he's found a friend, too."

The *Time* glided into the pier and Rob and Callie stepped off, followed by his sister Kate and her husband who'd emerged from the cabin. With a cheery whistle, the engineer backed away and was off as the new arrivals met the rest of the party half way up the bluff.

Rob and Callie greeted Jeremy familiarly. "Say, have you been hiding a little child?" Rob asked, reaching up and very solemnly shaking Jimmie's hand. As Jeremy pointed out the boy's father to Rob, he realized Lora was right, seeing that Kate's husband, Doctor Papin and Jack Hogan had already gravitated together as they stood at the top of the bluff. A soft summer breeze stirred the leaves above as the Japanese lanterns, glowing against the gathering dusk, swayed back and forth.

"There's still two more yachts," enthused Kittie as she looked out. A boat was pulling into the pier as still another came around Black Point and waited for the first to unload. Jeremy was introduced to Janet Strong and her escort, Floyd Baxter, a young lawyer from Chicago. Janet's brother Gordon shook Jeremy's hand warmly as their yacht *Alme,* puffing black smoke, pulled away sharply. He watched a young lad, barely a teenager, waving to the party as he pulled on the whistle cord.

Gordon nudged him, pointing to the *Alme* which fast picked up speed and almost took out the Lefens' pier. "A fourteen-year old. Can you imagine? That's my nephew, Ned Sheldon." He shook his head. "Ned's quite a boy, and you should see the stories he writes. That ability must come from his father's side of the family. But by God, Jeremy, you ought to see him in charge of that yacht."

"I think I just did."

"Well thank heavens we'll be picked up tonight by the engineer,"

Gordon watched the *Alme* turn away from shore, keeling sharply.

Jeremy had returned little Jimmie to Marie and joined the others on the bluff. By now, another couple had arrived by the shore path. "That's Victoria Koch and her fiance," Janet Strong said to Jeremy. The new arrivals had their arms entwined as they came into view, not knowing they'd be seen by so many as they rounded the turn in the path from Black Point.

"Dan and I decided to hike. It's close, and such a beautiful evening," Victoria said, brushing close against Dan. They were both slightly winded as they reached the top of the bluff and gratefully took the punch glasses, laughingly accepting teasing about their walk as well. This certainly was the season for engagements and romance, Jeremy thought, as he glanced out at the yacht approaching the pier. He looked again. It was the *Ariadne,* and as it nosed into the pier he saw someone wave. The operator was waving to *him.* He stepped onto the pier and as he did, he recognized the operator.

"You!" Todd called. "Give a hand. Help these people off." He walked out to the end of the pier and took the rope Todd was impatiently holding out for him. "Don't you work here?" he asked, as the young couple with him embarrassedly began to step onto the pier.

"You're right," he answered immediately, "sometimes I do work here." He took the hand of the girl. "Would *you* like my hand also, or were you just leaving?"

Todd watched him with a look of hate and said nothing. He shoved the throttle forward and again the *Ariadne* screeched her sides against the pier posts. "I'll be back to pick you up," he called to the couple, riveting his eyes on Jeremy who had already turned away.

"Sorry to be of any trouble," the stocky young man said. "It wasn't necessary to give us any help. My friend's just a little...he's a little out of sorts," he swiped the blue engineer's cap off his head as he introduced himself—"Frank McClure, and this is my fiancee, Charlotte. Didn't we see you on the pier a few weeks ago?"

"You did and you have a good memory for faces," Jeremy said, as they reached the top of the hill. He fetched two glasses of punch from a waiter and handed them to Frank and Charlotte.

"You see," he said, "like I told your friend. I *do* work here sometimes," he said, hoping his remark would break any ice.

As he started over to Lora, he glanced out at the lake and saw the *Ariadne* a half mile or so out in the growing dusk, idling along under her brooding skipper's hand.

The party was a grand success. Lora, despite her worries, was a gifted hostess and Jeremy found the guests amiable and friendly. His work at the Observatory was a natural target for their curiosity and through the buffet supper he tried answering their questions. "How far could one see?" was asked. "I can't wait to see closeups of those Martian canals," Rob said. "What do you think, doctor?" he asked Jack Hogan, who had been buried in conversation with Doctor Papin.

Jack thought for a minute. "I'm more interested in what we may find right *there*," he said, pointing to the bright moon. Their eyes looked up through the trees. "I don't think we'll find much on Mars, but maybe we'll be up *there* sooner than many think." The conversation drifted around to when they thought man would go to the moon. It was obvious, thought Jeremy, that the building of the Observatory and all its publicity had fueled people's imaginations, at least up in this area.

Paul had joined the group of younger people around the buffet tables on the front lawn. He listened with interest to the opinions about moon travel. The consensus seemed to be that a large cannon ball would be the vehicle—with the main problem being to find a way for the voyagers to survive the force of the shot.

Jules Verne's novel "From the Earth to the Moon" was discussed, and the huge cannon used to launch Verne's space travelers had obviously inspired most of the opinions. At last the question came around to Jeremy. He wouldn't have offered much in the way of an opinion, but the easy warmth of the group as well as the punch had loosened his caution. A small skyrocket across the lake gave him his cue. "Over there," he pointed to the dying rocket. "There is your means."

"But how big do you think it would have to be?" Frank asked. He had just offered an opinion himself about a huge cannon shot.

Jeremy thought for a minute, trying to recall some of the dimensions of the "Apollo" program. As the details started to come back to him, he began, with the aid of 20/20 hindsight and against his better judgment, to sketch out how such a trip to the moon could be accomplished, complete with his "guess" about relative gravity pulls. When he finished, he had clearly won their attention. A little flustered at being the center of attention, he shrugged. "At least it's one theory."

Kittie had circled over next to Lora. "Your fellow is a bright one sure enough and you didn't tell me just how *cute* he was in your letter. But I remember how you said he was, what?—different? Well, glory be! You could say that again. What's he doing after this summer?"

"He hasn't—well, we haven't discussed…Oh, Kittie I've only known him a few weeks." She paused. "I don't know. But listen," she pulled close to her friend's ear, "isn't he *something?* I so wanted you to meet him."

"Well, Lora darlin', I'd say he's worth some pursuin'. Listen, I want to hear more about him," she said, pointing to Jeremy, who was surrounded by a small crowd. "And," she added with a wink, "I also want to know all about Mr. Darrow."

"Shssh," Lora put her finger to her lips, glancing in her father's direction.

"Well, I can see we'll have a lot to talk about on the *Dispatch* tomorrow. I've just decided to talk Jack into letting us stay with you for another week after he goes back. Oh, Lora, we'll have so much time together, but right now we have to get back to Kaye's Park. Look over there at Jimmie, still going strong and he's worn little Marie out. She looks as though she's about to drop. I thought for sure he'd go off to sleep after dinner. We've got to get him to bed."

Paul Lockerby listened at the edge of the circle of conversation as his assistant had sketched out his concept of space travel. He lit his pipe as he studied him. Lora worked her way around the guests until she reached Jeremy. She placed her hand on his shoulder, saying something softly to him. He listened and nodded. After that she spoke to the gathered guests.

"The Hogans are leaving to take their baby home, but they'll be up for a full week at least, so everyone, please stay."

Paul made his goodbyes and walked up to the porch, relighting his pipe as he sat enjoying the night and contemplating the strangely illuminating projections he had heard from his employee.

At Lora's request, Jeremy had guided the Hogans down the steps to the pier. Jack seemed truly frightened at the prospect of the boat trip. "I promise to go as slow as possible and stay near the shore," Jeremy assured him, holding their sleepy toddler in his arms.

He handed Jimmie to Lora, stepped into the launch, and started it on the first try. He helped Kittie in and taking the baby from Lora, handed him to his mother. Doctor Jack was hesitant to board the gently bobbing boat. With Jeremy's hand out, he climbed clumsily aboard. "Come on," Jeremy called over to Marie Lefens, standing next to Lora. "You certainly earned a boat ride." The youngster hopped lightly aboard and took the heavily lidded Jimmie from his mother. He looked around, smiled, yawned and settled back in Marie's arms as the "phhrumm" of the engine worked on him like a lullaby. The launch backed out slowly. Lora blew them a kiss, then walked toward the party. He kept the launch at little more than an idle as they rounded Black Point and headed for the resort a mile down the shore.

The night was beautiful; the lake was calm. An occasional late sky-rocket or distant yacht with its twinkling lights were the only distractions. Poor Jack Hogan sat stiffly mesmerized by the dark water passing beneath them. Kittie put her hand on his. "We'll make a sailor out of you yet, dearest," she soothed him, squeezing his hand. "As for you Jeremy, you either are quite a predictor of the future or a good storyteller," she was scrutinizing him as she spoke.

"I think it's more of the storyteller, Kittie."

"And you are going to join us on the boat tomorrow for sure, aren't you?" she asked.

"Well," he said, hesitating. In fact, Lora hadn't yet said anything about it to him.

"Well then," she said, finishing for him, "It's settled. You'll go." she stated, just as they approached the double piers of Kaye's resort. A pair of skyrockets arched out from the shore, high above and beyond them.

"Oh, just listen," said Marie as they could hear the band playing a waltz. The piers were crowded with yachts and smaller craft which had been hired for the Fourth of July weekend, and the shore was strung with lights. Jeremy picked his way to a small opening at the far pier.

Marie transferred the sleeping baby to his mother and jumped to the pier with the line. Jeremy stepped out and took the youngster, then helped Kittie and Jack onto the pier. Jack had regained his composure as soon as his feet touched the pier. "Sorry to be so quiet," he said, "but I promise I'm working up to this. Tomorrow will be a breeze."

They bid each other good night and the two cast off to return home. Once out from the pier, Marie begged him to stay and hear one more melody, and he let the launch idle off the pier while the sleepy child, listening with her chin in her hand, gazed back at the glimmering dance pavilion.

As Jeremy and Marie rounded Black Point, he saw the *Ariadne* parked at the pier. A bad sign. He eased in to the other side and sent Marie on ahead, saying good night. Spreading the canvas, he covered the boat and started on down the pier, wondering what was in store with Todd's apparent arrival. He'd nearly passed the big yacht when he heard the voice.

"Just look who's here."

28

Todd had been sitting on the opposite side of the boat alongside the boiler and until he'd stood up, couldn't be seen. A bottle was in one hand as he walked over to the railing.

"Pretty sure of yourself, aren't you, pal?"

"How is that?" Jeremy asked, trying to keep any edge out of his own voice. *He isn't even due back for over an hour, yet here he is—and drinking to boot.*

"You know what I'm saying. You damn well know what I'm saying." Jeremy started away from him up the pier. "Wait, my companion," Todd called. "I'll go up with you." He belched and let his bottle drop into the water in the space between the boat and the pier.

The two said nothing as they walked up the stairs. Reaching the top, Todd looked around, trying to focus. Jeremy saw he'd pulled himself together and his white flannels gave him an easy, casual appearance. He felt his own arms cramped inside the pinched jacket he was wearing.

Todd hailed the waiter over, taking a glass of punch. "And one for my old friend here." The party, Jeremy noticed, had dwindled while he'd taken the Hogans back. Elsa and Al had already left as well as the Strongs group. Todd moved away, in the direction of the partygoers. Jeremy stayed at the table. Lora, he saw, detached herself from the group and walked toward Todd.

"And how's my favorite little anarchist tonight?" he heard Todd call. "Even if she did forget to ask me to her party." Jeremy tensed, wondering if he'd be needed, but to his surprise Lora stayed unruffled, even walking Todd over as he greeted the other guests. With the exception of Callie and Dan Cerny, Todd already seemed to know them all.

He was about to start over when he saw Lora and Todd talking. He couldn't hear what was being said but they had moved a short distance apart from the group. The rest had gone back to talking, accepting Todd's presence. Doctor Papin was telling a story and they'd closed around him. *That bastard has casually crashed in, and gotten away with it.*

Lora and Todd were conversing, walking slowly in front of the veranda. Todd was taking pains to use exaggerated gestures, touching her arm for emphasis. But whatever he was saying, she didn't seem particularly bothered. Their voices, at least Lora's, were low and Todd seemed to be standing overly close, straining to hear her and laughing. Dan Cerny had moved next to Jeremy. He'd gotten another refill of punch and was questioning him about the launch.

"You know, I've been interested in those gas engines. Everyone says they're going to take over. Could you show it to me?" Unsure at first, now Jeremy was certain. Dan was trying to distract him, get him away from a confrontation with Todd.

"Sure Dan, in fact how about going out on the lake tomorrow? You can take the wheel—see how it performs. Only now, I just want to walk over there for a minute," he pointed toward the two, now standing together on the front walk under the cheery glow of a lantern.

"Look, Jeremy," Dan said, his voice steady, patient even. "I only met you tonight and that fellow—I don't even know him. I saw what he did, but why don't you just ignore him? He's trying to get your goat. Victoria knows him and said Lora is probably just trying to get him to leave without making a scene. Now how about showing me the boat?"

"Tomorrow, Dan," Jeremy said, setting down his glass and walking across the front lawn. When he arrived next to them he was suddenly flustered. He'd counted on Todd or Lora seeing him and reacting but they both had their backs to him.

"Really, Todd. You're terrible! And you embarrass me so! Here you're practically drowning and you mean you were thinking *such scheming thoughts?*" He heard Lora's small laugh. "But let me get you back to Charlotte and Frank."

They both turned, seeing Jeremy at the same time. Lora started to speak but Todd called, "Oh, there you are. I was just thinking about you. Shouldn't you be turning in? You'll have to be getting up early to clean up these grounds."

"Todd, stop!" Lora looked uneasy.

"As a matter of fact," Jeremy said, "I just came over to invite you to leave."

"Invite me? Listen to him, Lora," he said, moving next to her. *"Invite me?* I didn't hear the *lady* invite me to leave. Do you own some part of Bluffside now, that you can order people about? I meant to tell you," he said, turning to Lora, "this fellow is a fortune-hunter. It's written all over him. He's the type to try to own the place if you so much as let him."

"Todd!" she cried out, "that's uncalled for and you know it." Heads in the group had started turning their way. "I'm sorry for what he said," Lora looked to Jeremy but he cut her off.

"Don't say anything. I understand. This sponge hasn't had enough liquor in him yet to think straight or get his courage up."

"Now that's enough, both of you," she cried, stepping between them as Todd moved toward Jeremy. "Todd's come here to pick up Charlotte and Frank and take them home."

"Yes, and he happened to arrive an hour or so too early," Jeremy snapped, wishing he could have recalled the petty words as soon as he'd said them, forgetting the enormous social gap that existed between himself and the others.

"If that doesn't beat all! Now your gardener tells me when I can arrive as well as leave." He looked at Lora, "and I didn't hear the lady tell me to leave, but...I don't want to make any scene so I'll depart." Lora seemed to visually relax. "And please, Lora," he continued, "send Frank and Charlotte down when they are ready. I don't want to rush them. I'll be on the boat and if I arrived too early, I apologize to you for that." His sudden conciliatory tone had caught Jeremy unprepared.

Lora said she'd talk to Frank and with a look toward Jeremy, she turned to walk back to the guests. He stood for a moment, uncertain. Todd was beside him. "I'll leave but where do you come off, being so rough on me? I used to be her..." he let the phrase hang too long, "...her beau." He'd started walking along the bluff. They were sixty or seventy feet from the knot of guests who had turned their attention to Lora.

"You can even walk me over to the steps to make sure I've left and then see off Charlotte and Frank." Todd was talking too easily, glancing as he did at the guests and noticing that they had gone back to talking. Jeremy should have kept his guard up. The next moment he'd been slugged as hard as he'd ever been before, across his left eye and forehead and he staggered from the blow.

He nearly lost consciousness, reeling backwards. As he did, Todd was on him again, raining blows on his shoulders and chest. Jeremy just managed to block a punch aimed right at his nose. Todd's face was contracted in rage as he swung again and Jeremy was just able to slip the punch. He remembered telling himself that Todd outweighed him, and not to start grappling with him. But Todd also hadn't very fast fists. Jeremy had been able to block and duck what should have been his put-away punches. *If I can only clear my head,* he thought, surprised at how controlled his own rage was.

Todd had stepped back, panting and gulping quick breaths before he came in to finish off his opponent. Then Jeremy remembered a trick he'd learned in a quickie judo course he'd taken almost ten years before. It was a simple maneuver, one of the first they'd taught and one of the few he'd mastered.

Facing his adversary, he backed up, realizing as he did that the edge of the bluff was close behind him. He dimly remembered hearing voices from the guests as they turned to see the commotion. A smile slowly spread over Todd's face as he saw Jeremy backing up, apparently cowering, not realizing that he had stopped. He lunged forward. Jeremy, quicker than he had dreamed and faster than he had ever done it before, raised his leg and drove his foot into Todd's knee. Todd, off balance, began to collapse, and Jeremy drove his fists into his ribs, hearing the air explode out of him. But Todd had gotten an arm around him and lunged forward, trying to bring him to the ground. Just as he did, Jeremy suddenly turned, throwing him over his hip. Todd's forward motion caused him to leave the ground and he arched clear out over the edge of the bluff, suspended a moment before hitting halfway down the side, rolling over and over until he reached the bottom. Jeremy stared down into the darkness at the limp figure below.

It seemed a long time before anyone moved. Frank was the first to reach Todd, racing down the steps and along the shore to his friend. The rest were at the steps staring down, still some distance from Jeremy. Fred Papin spoke to the others and hurried down with the waiter behind him, joining Frank. Jeremy, worried, was about to slide down the bluff but checked himself. They were raising Todd, or trying to raise him. He was on his knees and a groan came from him, a sound Jeremy was relieved to hear. The doctor and Frank had helped Todd to his feet but with another louder groan, he fell back against the base of the bluff.

Jeremy saw Rob had also reached the scene and they all surrounded Todd. After a few long minutes, Doctor Papin stepped back as the others half supported, half carried Todd along the shore. "He's going to be all right, it looks like, folks," he called up to the others standing along the top of the stairs. "There don't appear to be any broken bones. We're going to take him out to the boat where I can have a better look at him."

Jeremy walked slowly along the bluff above them. He noticed his own eye for the first time and saw the blood on his shirt and hands. He took off the tight coat, holding it over one shoulder, stopping before he had reached the others.

Victoria and Dan moved next to him. Kate had tried to hold Lora back but she'd pushed herself away and run down the steps, following the others out to the *Ariadne* with Kate behind her. Victoria put her hand on Jeremy's shoulder. "He's going to be all right. You heard the doctor."

Dan nodded, standing on the other side of him. "I didn't see the fight," he said, checking Jeremy's eyes and forehead. "I just saw our friend go sailing out over the side."

"I know Todd, Jeremy," Victoria said, "...well enough to know he probably started it. Lora may be mad now but one thing I've learned about her, she gets over things." Callie had joined them, standing silently behind.

The four stood together watching the yacht below. Finally, some of those that had gone down to the *Ariadne* started back up the stairs. At the top, Callie met Lora and Jeremy walked over. "Doctor Papin thinks he'll be all right," Lora said in a flat voice. "He's been very badly shaken up," she turned to Jeremy.

"You don't mind if some of these other people stay on, do you, or must they leave too? Have you decided yet who can stay?"

"Lora, now please," it was Victoria. She prodded Lora aside. The others had begun to come up the stairs with the doctor. A good sign, Jeremy thought as he saw Frank cast off and the *Ariadne* slowly back away. He turned, watching Victoria standing with Lora near the house, debating with himself whether to try again talking to her.

"How did you do that?" It was the waiter talking. "Listen, I saw what he did to you. While they was all talking, I kept my eyes on you two. I said to myself, that 'swell' with the engineer's cap, he's going to pull a fast one. Then sure enough, I saw him sock you, but—my god! That kick and then..."he trailed off.

"Are you sure he's all right?" Jeremy asked.

"Him? Why do you care? He got what was coming. Listen, I have to close up, but in the next fight, I want to be on your side."

The Allerton's yacht had docked and was waiting. Doctor Papin beckoned to Jeremy. "I wanted to assure you that he will recover. He'll have some bad bruises and a swollen ankle and knee but nothing appears broken, though I want him checked tomorrow. Let me see that eye." Jeremy flinched as the doctor touched it, feeling around. "The bleeding has stopped. Try to keep ice on it. It will nearly swell shut on you, but there isn't much to be done for it. I surely don't see how," the doctor said, lowering his voice, "how someone your size could throw that fellow. If I hadn't been watching, well..."

Apparently, thought Jeremy, only the waiter had seen Todd throw the first punch or punches.

"Look here, Jeremy, it's none of my concern what's between you and that Todd though it's easy enough to guess, but I'll tell you this. He came very close to getting a broken neck or back and being paralyzed. You'd best be very cautious about that...that skill you have. You seem too fine a gentleman to have to answer for...," He didn't get to finish as Rob stepped over.

"Jeremy, I don't want you to worry. The waiter told me that he saw Todd start it. I know Lora will get over this. It's just—you know how she was looking forward to the party—how she wanted everything to be perfect. Give her a day or two; you'll see that she'll be fine." He patted his back before starting for his yacht.

Jeremy watched the *Time* leave. Turning around, he noticed he was alone. The waiter had cleaned up and unplugged the lanterns, leaving Bluffside in darkness.

29

Jeremy sprang awake. He'd been dreaming. But now the dream, though vivid, had stayed just outside his recollection. He remembered that Lora was in the dream, and she had been in danger. Then he felt the searing pain at the side of his head, interrupting his thought, bringing last evening back to him. He got up, let the tap run for a minute, drew a glass of water, downing it while walking to the porch. It was still pitch dark outside as he sat down on the steps.

Try as he might, it was no use; he couldn't recall the dream. He cautiously rubbed his fingers over his left eye. It was already swollen and would be almost shut by tomorrow. He tried to focus on the events at the end of the evening, finally deciding he'd have done everything the same way again, only maybe next time, he smiled tightly in spite of his throbbing head, *he'd* have thrown the first punch or at least have kept his guard up.

He felt awful. How angry *was* Lora? Well, only time would tell. *But what the hell,* he was feeling glum. *Maybe it's time I looked for something else to do. I should move on to Chicago anyway. It might be a mistake to stay here much longer. First there's the nosy constable; I've acquired Todd for an enemy and I've for sure alienated Lora.* He got up and walked into the kitchen, and opening the door of the icebox, took the pick and chopped a piece off the block and returned to the porch steps. He sat down and pressed the ice to his eye.

The moon had departed and the night was now pitch black. It was still and warm. He ignored the melting water running down his cheek. Paul, he knew, would keep him on at the Observatory—and at the house. He'd just not be able to see Lora, at least not socially anymore. And come fall, he'd move back to Chicago.

His thoughts turned back to his dream again. It had something to do with his knowledge from the future. That much he was sure of. He sat thinking for a long while, with a sense of something impending about him. *Ah, the hell with it,* he couldn't remember. Jeremy felt tired and depressed. He stood, stretched, and walked to the screen door. As he opened it, the first faint rays of the new day came through the trees. He lay down and fell into a deep sleep.

The sunlight was in his face. He got up and strained with his one good eye at the ancient clock. It was almost eleven o'clock. He studied himself in the mirror. That was an ugly shiner, and it would stay with him for a few more days at least. In another era that cut along his eye might need a few stitches but it would heal, nevertheless. He put coffee on. With Lora and the Hogans on the boat, there'd be time at least to straighten up out in front and return the Japanese lanterns. He was just setting his coffee mug down when his dream suddenly materialized before him. Kittie Hogan had said they had chartered the *Dispatch* for their outing. He couldn't put his finger on it before, but now he suddenly remembered from his research; the *Dispatch* was the name of the boat that had sunk! It had taken all aboard to their deaths. He couldn't recall precisely when but it was a mid-summer outing. He tried to visualize the events of the sinking as he had read them in that yachting book. With a feeling of growing dread, he realized that the year of the disaster, he was *sure*, was 1895, and the fateful date was around the Fourth of July.

He checked the clock. It was nearly eleven-thirty. Kittie had said they were leaving at noon. He threw on some clothes and dashed to the main house. Without bothering to knock, he flung open the screen door, calling for Martha. She appeared and catching sight of him, she shook her head and said softly, "Ooh, ee, that's looking bad! That nasty Todd got in a good one on you."

"Where's Lora? Has she gone?" He dismissed his damaged face.

"Let me tell you something," she said. "I know that girl. She gets very mad but she gets over things. You'd best…"

He interrupted. "I don't care about last night. Has she left?" Martha nodded, starting to say something. "When did she leave?" he demanded.

"Well, she left about an hour ago. She was going to walk down to

Kaye's Park and meet the Hogans. Then they were going to take a charter boat. That priest brother had it chartered. Jeremy, if I was you I wouldn't follow her now. She'll be fine when she cools off. I know that."

"I have to get her, I have to get all of them off that boat." And he started out the front door and across the lawn with Martha following.

"Mr. Lockerby is upstairs not feeling good today. If you do something foolish down there, you might ruin it all.

"I didn't tell you everything the other day, but I *know* Miz Lora's in love with you. Doesn't that mean anything to you? What happened last night, that was a lover's fight. She told me about it this morning. But if you make a fool out of yourself now…besides, have you just *seen* how you look?" she called behind him as he scurried down the bluff to the pier.

When he was at the bottom he shouted up, "I have to get her off, get all of them off that boat. It's going to sink!" He couldn't stop to listen to what she was shrieking.

He threw the canvas back just enough to let himself board, then turned the ignition on and cranked the starter. Nothing. He swore and cranked again, then stopped to squirt gasoline on the cylinders. The engine wouldn't catch. He realized with desperation that he might have flooded the engine by opening the throttle too much in haste. He closed the throttle and said a short prayer, waiting. Then he took a breath and cranked the engine. It caught, died, and then caught again, blue smoke billowing out.

He jumped back on the pier, untied the ropes and cast off, kicking away from the pier as he opened the throttle slowly so as not to kill the engine. As it responded, he let it out until the engine was roaring. He took the straightest line to Kaye's, cutting dangerously close to the shore as he cleared Black Point.

Jeremy began to have doubts as the wind whipped into his face. He was *sure* it was the *Dispatch* that sank, but when? *Was it really in 1895? In fact, did any of this happen?*

The docks at Kaye's Park were as crowded as the night before. He didn't even know what the *Dispatch* looked like. The *Arthur Kaye* was backing out for a trip across the lake to pick up train passengers. There were two other yachts, a number of rowboats, and…then he saw it.

It was a launch much like the *Lora L,* only bigger, and it was ready to

216

leave the dock. Jeremy cut around the *Arthur Kaye,* drawing an angry hoot on the steam whistle along with some curses. He turned in front of the launch, cutting her off.

Lora and the rest were staring open-mouthed at him. He read the name *Dispatch* on the bow as the *Lora L* bumped up against the other craft.

He couldn't know what, if anything, Lora had told the Hogans about last night, and the events after they left. "Don't go out on the lake!" he shouted over, realizing as he did how stupid he must have sounded. The young engineer was the first to speak.

"I don't know who you are, but I'll thank you to get away from this boat. This is a charter boat about to leave." Lora put her hand on the engineer's shoulder. Jeremy couldn't read her expression, but when she spoke, he knew last night hadn't been forgotten.

"What is it you want? We're just leaving."

"I need to talk to you. The boat isn't safe." As soon as he said that, he realized he'd taken the wrong approach.

The young engineer was glaring at him, trying to grasp who this person was, and why he was trying to end his charter. "I mean," he started again, "the weather. It's not going to be safe out there." In truth, he'd hardly noticed the weather. Now, as he spoke, he turned to look up, as did all his listeners. The sun was dazzling in a bright blue sky.

The engineer had heard enough. "Look mate, these people are out for a cruise and to be frank with you, you look like you'd feel better if you slept off whatever is bothering you." He glowered at Jeremy as if he wouldn't mind shutting his remaining eye.

Jeremy looked again at the party. The two he didn't recognize were obviously Father Hogan and his sister Mary. Father Hogan seemed a little amused by this scenario. His sister was talking to Lora. Lora nodded and then walked to the rail a few feet from Jeremy. She lowered her voice when she spoke.

"Don't do this. I'll talk with you when we get back. I realize you were provoked."

Baby Jimmie had just then broken out of his mother's hold and recognized Jeremy. "What happened you?" he asked. Jimmie was wearing a blue cap the engineer must have given him for the trip, and it almost covered his little face.

Lora made a quick introduction to Father Hogan and his sister. The priest wore a black shirt, with its Roman collar removed. He smiled at Jeremy. "Sorry we missed the party. You know Saturday night is kind of a working night for priests, though. It looks," he said, "like you walked into one of those low-hanging Japanese lanterns I've heard about."

This brought a few good-humored laughs from the party. The engineer looked balefully at Jeremy and then around at the party, anxious to start. "Seriously, Jeremy," said Father Hogan, "we'd like to get underway. We're going to have lunch at Lake Geneva. Would you join us?" It was clear they weren't about to call off the cruise.

For a moment, Jeremy thought about pulling Lora onto the launch and charging away. *Maybe the dispatch won't sink for another couple of years. Maybe it'll never sink. Maybe events will never unfold as I've known them.*

An idea came to him. Without even thinking, he beckoned to Lora. She leaned toward him. "I didn't want to alarm you or upset your friends," he said in a lowered tone, "but your father told me an urgent telegram came after you left. It was from Eugene Debs."

Her hand went to her chin and her brows knitted up. She chewed on her lower lip for a moment, then turned and spoke to the Hogans.

"Something's come up. I'm terribly sorry, but I'll have to go home." She took Father Hogan's hand as well as Mary's. "I hope I'll be able to see you later this evening." She tousled baby Jimmie's head, pulling the cap still lower on him. "As for the rest of you, well, we have at least another week or two. Mr. Preston, I'm sorry for any inconvenience to you."

Jack Hogan spoke up. "You know, if it's all the same, maybe we should just cancel." But before Jeremy could jump in and urge them to do just that, Kittie cut him off. "Listen here, Jack. You are going for a boat cruise and that's that. We'll see Lora tonight."

Lora stepped out of the *Dispatch* and into the *Lora L,* waving goodbye as the two launches parted. As the distance between them grew, Jeremy looked back, undecided whether to make another try to persuade them to call off their trip. His last sight of the group was of baby Jimmie waving back.

He headed back toward the house, anxious at least to put as much distance between them so that when Lora learned of the ruse, she wouldn't be able to rejoin them.

"First of all, thank you for coming for me," she said. "I'm sorry about last night." She ran her fingers gently over his eye. "Can we talk about it later?"

"Sure," he answered. *Oh brother, and wait until she finds out I made up this whole story.* He glanced out the corner of his good eye and saw the *Dispatch* moving across the lake toward the north shore. In another ten minutes they would be out of reach. The lake seemed alive today with all sorts of craft. Jeremy had never seen it more crowded. Ahead in the middle was some kind of sailboat race, and fishermen and young couples in rowboats were strung along the near shore.

"I don't think you're going to be invited to any parties that engineer Preston throws," she said. "But did you really have to try to talk him out of the boat trip? I would have gone with you." He just shrugged and kept their course, taking them farther away from the other launch.

"I can't imagine what the telegram says. Did father read it or give any clue?" he shook his head. "It must have something to do with the sentence. Maybe old Judge Woods changed his mind. Oh my heavens! Maybe Gene's afraid of more violence. But why would he send *me* of all people a telegram? Maybe he wants to see me over at the Woodstock jail right away."

From her tone, he thought, she was canvassing possibilities in her mind, but she was *ready* to be flattered by Debs calling on her. *Oh God,* he thought, as they rounded Black Point and headed for Bluffside. Out across the lake the *Dispatch* had disappeared from sight.

Lora jumped out, took the rear line down to the end of the pier, and held it for him while he secured the bow, using an extra line for good measure. He took the rear line from her, looped it around the post and doubled it back to the boat.

"You look like you're expecting a typhoon," she called over her shoulder as she hurried up the pier.

He finished securing the boat, and had reached the top of the bluff when he saw her stepping quickly off the veranda, walking toward him. "Martha knows of no telegram and father has been ill in his room all morning. She just brought him some breakfast." He nodded. Her lips, drawn together, quivered before she spoke. "Then there *was* no telegram?"

"No."

219

"Then you took me off the boat to get even for last night," she said it with half a question in her voice. She was still perplexed, still fighting back, he saw, a growing fury.

"No," he said simply.

"You knew what this trip meant. You knew that only a," she paused, "a *monstrous* lie like you told would have gotten me off the boat." She scrutinized him closely. "So why? Tell me why," she demanded, her voice rising.

"I think," he started weakly, feeling the strong sun beating down on him, "at least I feel, that the *Dispatch* is going to sink." *There, I said it.*

"What? When is it going to sink?" her anger growing.

"I don't know," he shrugged, "maybe this afternoon, and maybe it never will."

Hurt, confused, she began to cry. Her shoulders were shaking. He reached for her but she slapped him, hard, just missing his puffed eye. "Don't touch me! I don't know why you did this. But I know you've played on my trust," she said between sobs, "and on my *vanity* too, and I'll never forgive you for that. I was going to make you take me to Geneva just now, but I don't even want to be around you for that long."

She turned, and bursting into tears, she ran up the steps and into the house. There was nothing to do but walk back to his cabin.

Jeremy tried to collect himself. He'd talk to Paul tomorrow, to tell him he'd had a premonition or something about his daughter, apologize, and then find a room over near the Observatory. *Was it only twenty-four hours ago everything had seemed so right with us, but first the fight, and then this!*

He went in and studied himself in the mirror. He was looking worse all the time. He washed up, shaved and ate a couple of Martha's biscuits, washed down with the warmed-up coffee he hadn't finished in the morning.

Back out on the porch again, he lay down on the swing. He opened the magazine, and tried to get into the *Harper's* Civil War article he had started.

After a few minutes the swing began to gently rock and a cool breeze had come up. He stood up and walked down the steps to the path. The sun was still out but clouds were gathering and the wind had picked up. It was now coming from a northerly direction.

The feeling he'd had when he woke up from the dream had returned, that feeling of something impending. He held his palms out, feeling the change in the air, the dream coming back to him.

He put on his boots, laced them up and donning a work jacket over his shirt, he walked down past the still-quiet house to the bluff. By now the clouds had filled most of the sky. They were heavy and were going in one direction at one moment, and then turning, moving back in the opposite way. The wind seemed to let up for a few minutes.

There were still dozens of boats of all kinds on the lake. The *Lorely* came into view. The big yacht was making for Black Point. Some of the sailboats had had enough of the choppy waters and the ominous sky, and were heading toward their docks, many with their sails down.

Jeremy saw the lightning still in the distance as the first drops of rain hit him. He went down to check the *Lora L.* She was safely moored. He looked again at the sky, which now had turned purple. The lightning was coming closer.

He loosened the canvas and took out the oilskin, slipping it on as the rain began to come in sheets. Climbing the bluff, and with the hood of the mackinaw up, he sat down, oblivious to the rain, watching the boats making for shelter. When Lora spoke he didn't know how long she'd been standing next to him.

30

"It's bad, isn't it?" she asked.

"And getting worse. Here," Jeremy took off the mackinaw and put it on her shoulders with the hood over her already soaked and matted hair. "They probably stayed in Geneva," he offered. She nodded slowly, unresisting as he put his arm around her. He was about to say something when he saw a little, flat-bottomed rowboat come around Black Point. The waves were behind, sweeping the craft forward. A single person was rowing mightily, trying to get out of the force of the wind which was blowing the boat at an angle away from shore.

Jeremy raced down the pier. The boat would pass close. "Unlock that oar and hand it to me!" he shouted. "Now! Give it to me!" The rower stretched out the oar and Jeremy, hurrying out along the pier, just managed to grasp the end of it. He nearly lost hold of the wet oar, but hanging on they both finally pulled the boat over to the side of the pier.

"Thanks for the hand," the boatman called. He was now out of the main thrust of the wind, and putting the oar back into the lock, he was able to row the small craft alongside the pier. Jeremy helped pull the rowboat onto the shore. He recognized the man as the one who'd been off the pier a week or so ago, the one he'd given a tip to about where he could camp.

He thrust out his hand. "Dave Dumser. Much obliged. If you hadn't caught the oar, I don't know when I could have put in." Jeremy looked down into the little rental boat, resting on the shore. Its stern was filled with four or five good-size crappies now revived and swimming contentedly in the punt.

"Come on up," he said, as the two climbed the bluff. At least with someone else along, conversation with Lora would be a little less nervous. Lora met Dave and asked if she could get him anything, but he shrugged off the offer, thanking her. The three declined to take cover up on the veranda but stood on the edge of the bluff, ignoring the rain and watching the last of the boats head for safety.

"You can be glad you're not out in that storm," Dave said, glancing discreetly first at Jeremy's black eye and then at Lora.

The wind had whipped the waves into unbelievably high whitecaps for an inland lake. Even the gale Paul and he had been through was like nothing compared to this. He saw Paul and Martha were wisely standing on the veranda out of the brunt of the storm, but still getting soaked by the wind-whipped rain. The huge trees along Bluffside were nearly bent over by the wind.

Lora tapped his shoulder. "I have to get something." She disappeared, returning in a few moments with a long spyglass under her arm. A lightning bolt cracked across the lake, striking Cedar Point. Dave shouted to Jeremy, pointing west. The sky was a menacing purple and black and the clouds were so low and heavy that they seemed about to fall.

"We're in for a tornado. I'm sure of it." Dave Dumser's voice was being carried away by the wind. Strangely, Jeremy noticed as it got darker, the opposite shore nearly two miles away stood out in relief, as though it were moving closer. He held the lid of his puffed eye open as best he could. With relief, he noticed there were only a couple of scattered boats still out on the lake and they were all near shore.

"The *Dispatch!* There it is!" Lora called suddenly. She had been sweeping the far shore with the spyglass.

"I think they're tying up," she said. He could see distant figures on the boat. It was still making heavy steam. At that moment the storm seemed to go into a lull. The wind on the lake eased, though the lightning continued, and the booms of the thunder were now continuous.

"Can you make out if they're leaving the boat?" he asked as Lora pressed the glass to her eye.

"No!" she shouted. "Oh, no, no!"

He looked across, not believing what he saw. The boat had moved away from the pier, with puffs of black smoke coming from the stack. They were going out onto the lake! They must have thought the lull in the wind signaled the worst was over.

"They're all still on board," Lora gasped. "No one's gotten off. God almighty! I can see Kittie. She's holding Jimmie to her." He took the glass from her and looked. From their vantage point, he turned the glass to the west. The wind had picked up again. The water in the middle was foaming, hurled back at itself by the cyclonic winds.

"Those damned fools have the curtains down!"

Dave was right, and Jeremy knew that meant the boat would capsize as soon as they hit the full wind.

"They're putting them up now," Lora said. She grabbed Jeremy and turned him toward her. "Will they sink? *Will they?* "

"If they turn back, I think they can still get in. But past Cedar Point, they'll get the full force." He guessed that, down in the water, Preston wasn't able to see the height of the waves.

Dave tapped him again and Jeremy looked to where he was pointing. A large funnel-shaped twister, the first he'd ever witnessed in person, dropped from the low clouds. He couldn't see it touch, only guessing that it was somewhere in Williams Bay, moving out on the lake. Lora, still watching the pitching boat, hadn't seen the funnel.

By now, the *Dispatch* was nearly in the middle of the lake and had suddenly caught the brunt of the storm. It rolled, nearly capsizing. Then Preston apparently decided he'd have his best chance by facing into the storm and turned the wallowing boat.

Lora screamed. She'd been looking through the glass. "Someone's been blown off, one of the girls. I can't see her anymore!" Just at that moment, the funnel with its path of foam swept toward them.

Etched in Jeremy's memory forever was his last glimpse of the *Dispatch.* There was no smoke. He guessed the engine had gone dead. The boat lifted high up on the billows of a cross wave and then plunged, the dangerously low prow knifing downward into the water. He blinked, straining to see the boat in the enveloping foam.

Lora spoke first. "Where is it?" she wailed. "I've lost sight!"

Jeremy took the glass from her and scanned the water. He saw only the boiling surface. The funnel had moved down the lake, So absorbed with the boat were they that they hadn't even noticed the roar of the tornado as it passed out onto the lake. Just then, no more than thirty feet behind them, a huge tree snapped and fell.

Jeremy stared at Dave. "She's gone," he said. He looked out again.

There was nothing on the surface of the lake, as though they had all simply imagined that the *Dispatch* had been there moments before. He clutched Lora to him. They'd have to get back to the house. They were right in the line of other trees that might go.

Lora resisted him. No!" she shouted. "Leave me alone!" She was still squinting at the empty lake through the spyglass.

Together with Dave, Jeremy half-lifted, half-wrestled her back across the lawn. Jeremy got his feet entangled on the way to the house and nearly fell. He looked down to see a forgotten strand of Japanese lanterns had wound around his leg. The lanterns had been blown loose and were swinging haphazardly from a tree branch. When they reached the house, the two carried Lora inside. She was ashen under the hooded oilskin. Martha took off the mackinaw and laid her on the couch. Jeremy rubbed her hands, which were as cold as ice.

"Get her some tea, she's not hurt," Dave said, kneeling alongside Jeremy. He looked closely at her. "I haven't seen this since the war. She's in shock. Keep her warm and get her something hot to drink."

"What the hell is going on?" Paul demanded. "My daughter wasn't hurt, but you say she's in shock. What's happening?" he asked, watching Lora who was quietly staring across the living room.

"The *Dispatch* went down in the storm. One minute we were watching her being tossed about, and the next she—they, were all gone—disappeared." Jeremy filled him in, feeling helpless.

"Are you sure?" he asked. Dave glanced up from Lora, nodding.

"Everyone?"

"Everyone on board," he answered.

Martha brought some tea, catching the news from the rest. "All?' she asked.

"Yes," Dave replied.

"Even the little boy? Did he go down too?"

Dave nodded to her. He stood up and tugged on Jeremy's sleeve. "I've got to be off to my campsite. My boys should be big enough to look after themselves, but..." his worry showed. "I ought to be back with them. Sorry," he started, "I'm so sorry about your people," he was looking from one to the other of the shocked, grief-stricken group. He shook his head and turned to walk toward his campsite.

Paul and Jeremy sat in the living room for a time, keeping watch on

Lora. "I saw the boat go almost straight down, like it was diving," Jeremy pointed his hand at an angle to imitate the path of the doomed boat. Paul nodded slowly and stood up, his shoulders more hunched than usual, the sorrow and fatigue of the day etched on his face. For someone in his health, it had been a long day. He stopped to bend over and kiss his daughter.

"I'm feeling better, father. I want you to take care of yourself. Please get some sleep.' Lora seemed improved. She sipped the brandy Jeremy had handed her.

A few minutes after Paul had left, Lora addressed Jeremy. "Tell me again," she began, her voice quiet and lower, "how you came to know that the *Dispatch* was going to sink."

"I just thought, well," he faltered, "the weather and that the boat was unstable," he was searching for words but she cut him off.

"Horse feathers, Jeremy!" Her eyes were intense. "It was a beautiful day. There wasn't a cloud in the sky and that boat wasn't anymore unstable than ours. And you threatened my feelings—*our* feelings for each other—by inventing that story to get me off. You knew how I'd feel when I found out you lied about Gene Debs." She lifted the brandy snifter and drank, holding it near her lips as she watched him.

"Why? You wouldn't have risked such a thing unless you *knew* that the boat was going down. So how did you know?"

He was quiet. Any answer he gave—except the truth—would be lame. "By instinct, Lora." He stood, preparing to go back to his cabin. Lora reached her hand out to him and he pulled her to her feet.

"I'll walk with you," she said and they started down the path. The moon was bright between the trees and only the broken branches scattered about the lawn bore witness to the previous storm. The quiet midsummer night and the sound of insects mocked the fact that any tornado had ever swept through. When they reached the cabin, she sat down on the top step of his porch and he settled next to her.

"Let me see," she said at last, trailing her finger over his puffed eye. "You know, I really wasn't all *that* mad at you. I just have a quick temper, although you scared me with the way you seemed to throw Todd out into the air. I don't know where you learned tricks like that."

She grew quiet for a few moments. "Jeremy, I just can't believe," her voice faltered, "they're gone. Tell me it's a bad dream. Don't you think *any* of them might have gotten out? What about life preservers?"

He weighed his answer. "You saw the boat go down." He realized that his recollections about the *Dispatch* were perfect and there would be no survivors.

"Promise me," her voice was out on the edge of control again, "that one day soon—you'll tell me things you feel or see and why." Before he could answer, she let her lips brush up against his before she started back down the path.

31

On Thursday, the *Dispatch* was located. It was found to be lying off Cedar Point in over one hundred feet of water. Jeremy and Lora were out on the lake early. Alongside the *Majestic* at the center of the operation was a flat-bottom barge with several people on board. Jeremy could see a diving suit, a helmet and piles of line. He dropped the anchor and they drifted a short distance away.

The diver walked about the scow, giving orders. He could, Jeremy reflected, have been provided by central casting. About twenty-five and muscular, with curly blond hair and a handlebar mustache, he seemed at home with his companions. They made jokes and small talk as they prepared for the dive. At last he donned the bulky diving suit. The helmet with the little front porthole was placed over his head and secured. Apparently satisfied the air supply was working, he was lowered off the edge of the scow.

The air bubbles roiled the surface as he disappeared. Jeremy noticed the line being played out. The colored markers indicating depth and the amount of line brought home how far down a hundred feet was.

In a few minutes, the diver broke the surface and was brought onto the scow, The assistant picked up a megaphone. "Mr. Nelson has found the boat," he said, talking and sweeping the megaphone in an arc. "He believes he sees some of the bodies and he'll be going down again, but we'll be moving to the south a bit. So please stay clear," he said, finishing the announcement.

His next dive seemed to last forever. The small circle of bubbles trailed around the surface. At times the bubbles would stop for a few seconds, giving Jeremy real cause for alarm—only to start up again. He guessed the diver had been down almost a half hour when they began to reel him up. As he broke the surface, he thrust a body onto the scow, drawing an audible gasp from the watchers. Jeremy could see it was not yet bloated. The body was transferred to a launch which left in the direction of Lake Geneva village.

He was watching the body being transferred to the launch when he glanced back to see that the diver had already returned to the bottom. After a short interval, he hoisted another body from the wreck. This time Jeremy could make it out as Doctor Jack. Lora pulled herself against him as the body was turned, facing them, and Jeremy felt himself shudder, remembering the doctor talking about his fear of water. Jack's worst nightmare had gruesomely come true.

The diver climbed out of his suit and slumped on the deck, fatigued, as the second body was placed aboard another launch. The assistant, megaphone in hand, gave another bulletin. "Mr. Nelson's through diving for the day. The two bodies were recovered outside the boat. There were none within. The boat itself is intact," he continued, leaning down to get more information from the diver, then straightening up and clearing his throat. All this time Nelson lay propped up against the pile of ropes, puffing on a large, well-earned cigar.

Rob called over that they would follow to Bluffside. Once there, Lora and Jeremy boarded the *Time.* Kate and Robert greeted them in an upbeat, if serious mood. "As ghastly as it is, Lora," he said, handing them glasses of wine, "at least the bodies are going to be recovered and decently buried. You'll see that you'll put this behind you. We all will."

"They haven't all been found. There's still some hope, Rob," she said.

So she's going to cling, thought Jeremy, *to any smallest thread of hope.* They moved out on the afterdeck and Lora momentarily stepped inside the cabin. The conversation between Rob and his sister drifted over to the Columbian Exposition. Jeremy found himself looking out over the lake, only half listening.

"And don't forget," Rob's voice lowered, "when we reached the Administration Building...right up in front..."

"Enough, Robert," Kate quickly interrupted. She turned to Jeremy, remarking on how long the diver was under water. *Something she'd rather I didn't hear,* Jeremy noted to himself.

As the Allertons prepared to leave, Rob took Jeremy aside. "I'll be by to pick you up tomorrow. Kate thought if she stopped by she might take Lora's mind off…" and he jerked his thumb out toward where the boats of the diving operation were anchored, the bright pennant still visible above the buoy.

The next morning Jeremy saw the *Time* glide up to the pier. Starting across the lawn, he passed Kate on her way to the house, telling her Lora was still asleep.

"It's all right. I'll have breakfast with Martha and wait. That scene yesterday was too grisly for me. You and my brother can be the ones to go."

He and Rob pushed off for the diving area. Jeremy was surprised at how easily Rob handled the large steam yacht by himself. "Help yourself to breakfast," Rob pointed to the large cabin behind as he lifted a mug to his mouth. In a minute, Jeremy joined Rob with his own mug and a donut in hand.

"Look at the bow," Rob said. "I got an extra long line over at Judge Withrow's. There's at least a hundred and fifty feet there. We'll be able to anchor on the bottom, no drifting."

In a few minutes they were on the scene. The *Majestic* was already there and Jeremy could see Nelson on board talking to the captain. He appeared very unhappy. The nearby barge, carrying all of the diver's equipment, was empty of people. Captain Johnson recognized Rob and hailed them over. "Andy Nelson seems to have been rather deserted by his crew, " he said, as they drew alongside

"That's the word sure enough," said Andy. "One's gone and gotten dead drunk, and the other took off in a carriage with some wench. I think she took a shine to him with all that announcing he was doing and carrying on yesterday. Lord knows when he'll be back."

"Can we help?" Jeremy asked.

"Nah," he said, looking amused and probably thinking, 'Here's a couple of playboy dandies.' Then he scanned the serious, self-assured pair once again.

"Can you learn fast and follow directions?' He paused. "That'll be my life down there." Seeming to have decided something to himself, he said, "well, let's try the two of you. You two can't be worse than those other couple of louts."

They anchored the *Time* a short distance away and rode the dinghy over to the barge. Nelson got right down to explaining their jobs. The air

230

compressor was already running. He carefully showed them how it worked and how to operate it, as well as what to watch for.

"This is our communication line." He spelled out the rudimentary code of jerks and pulls, then tested them, not sparing any swear words, but after a few times through, grudgingly giving his approval.

"She's directly below us, the bow facing that way," he said, pointing toward the Elgin Camp. "She's in a hundred and ten feet of water, lying in a shallow ditch across the bottom. That stuff on the bottom is blue clay—as bad as anything you could work in. It reminds me of the god-damned Detroit River, but at least here there's no current. That muck likes to grab you, though, so remember, if you feel two yanks, then you start to pull me up."

"How's the visibility?" Jeremy asked, feeling cowed in the diver's presence.

"Twenty feet, no more, and a damned sight less if that sun goes in. You got everything? Let's go to work."

He put them once more through the entire routine before he let them clamp the helmet on him and then tested the air flow. Satisfied it was working, he eased over the side. When he was below the surface, he tested it again for any leaks. Andy gave them the "all's well" signal, and they began to lower him. Rob worked the winch while Jeremy fed out the air line, the bubbles indicating that Nelson was directly below.

In a couple of minutes the line slackened and they got the three pulls indicating he was on the bottom. The line played out and the bubbles moved away from the barge, showing he was fanning out from the *Dispatch*. Every few seconds, Jeremy gave an "all right?" yank that Nelson answered. Failure to receive an answer would mean they should *immediately* begin reeling him up. Finally, he gave them the three yanks. He'd found something. A moment later he gave the signal to pull him up.

Captain Johnson's mate, Howard, joined them as they reeled in the line. At last Jeremy saw the helmet at the surface. Nelson was holding something out, wanting them to hoist it aboard. Jeremy hesitated a moment and Howard looked away. Finally Jeremy reached down. It was a corpse. As it left the water, he could feel the enormous weight that had built up.

"Give me a hand," he yelled to the mate, who had stood up. The two of them lifted the body of a man on board. He could see the well-preserved body was that of Preston, the engineer. Captain Johnson came over onto the barge, now weighed down low in the water. He cradled the head of his engineer in his arms as he knelt over him, weeping silently.

Andy Nelson had lit up another of his big stogies. He'd climbed out of his suit and was again leaning back against the pile of wet ropes, breathing slowly. He was visibly tired; strained by the terrible work he was doing so well. "I see another body down there. I'm almost sure from the size it's the child. He's off about thirty feet to starboard."

"See anything else?" Rob asked.

"Nothing. No one else. It's very murky stuff. Listen," he said to Jeremy, "you give a lot of yanks on that line."

"Too many?"

"I'd rather have too many than too few. But when I'm busy, I may not be able to answer you right away." Then he stood up. "I'll take the time I need on the next dive. I'll look further out, and then I'll get the child," he hesitated, "and that will be that. No more dives." He picked up some of his diving gear and walked to the edge of the barge, staring down into the depths and thinking. At last he straightened up, flicking his cigar into the water. "Let's get to work." He donned the gear and they secured his helmet, then helped him over the side.

He yanked on the line when he reached the bottom. From the rope, played out almost to its entirety, as well as by the trail of bubbles, Jeremy could see he had worked his way far from the *Dispatch*. The other boats had moved back as Nelson's air bubbles came toward them. Jeremy looked at Rob from time to time.

"It's now been over thirty minutes," Rob said, pulling out his watch for at least the tenth time. Nelson had been answering Jeremy's pulls with his own yanks. Finally, he saw the air bubbles slowly start back toward the barge. Jeremy was dimly aware that a small crowd of boats had gathered. He heard someone say that the coroner had arrived. Then he felt three tugs—followed almost immediately by two. "Pull me up," they said, "and *now*."

Jeremy signaled Rob, who began to crank, picking up a few feet of slack, and then he stopped. The winch would not budge. Jeremy moved over and they both tried to crank. Nothing. Rob spoke in a low voice. "It's that damn clay he talked about. He must be mired in it." They both hoisted again. And again, there was no response from the winch. Jeremy was afraid that if they pulled too hard, they might snap the line and Nelson would be lost.

He felt two more pulls on the communication line, followed again by two more. Jeremy told Rob to crank, as he leaned over and grabbed the line. "Pull!" he called. As he did, he was aware of another pair of hands also pulling on the line. He looked up to see Todd.

He'd come aboard the barge. Jeremy stared at him for a moment— then quickly filled him in. They both pulled on the line as Rob tried to crank, but still there was no movement. Jeremy gave the line a yank. He felt a single answering yank, followed by two quick ones and then two more.

"What does that mean?" Todd asked, standing up, his hands on his hips.

"It means he's all right so far, though he's damn worried. This fellow doesn't scare, but I'm afraid we won't be able to budge him, or else we could snap that line and maroon him down there," Jeremy ran his hand nervously through his hair.

Todd reached down suddenly and began pulling at the anchor line. "Give me a hand. I've got an idea." The anchor line was stuck as well and it took the three of them to pull it free from the muck. They hauled it up. The other boats, carrying spectators out for a gala afternoon, had pulled in closer now, not sure what was going on but sensing some drama.

"Captain," Todd called over in as low a voice as possible "He's stuck down in that clay and we can't budge him. Take this." He and Rob passed over the anchor and line to the *Majestic's* mate.

"When I signal," Todd directed, "move ahead *dead slow.* If I raise my hand to stop, then *stop.*"

"What if your plan doesn't work. Suppose the line pulls out and he's left down there?" Johnson asked.

"Then he'll be left down there, but we can't get him out of that clay any other way," Todd answered. "We have to get him up soon, too. His air could give out at any time."

Johnson nodded reluctantly, checking the line before moving back to the wheel. Jeremy lay flat on the deck of the barge, reaching over to keep the line from snagging while Rob stood by the now useless winch. At Todd's sign, the *Majestic* inched slowly away. The line joining the two craft tightened. "Can you feel that?" Jeremy asked. Todd had joined him holding the line. It had begun to tighten in his hand.

"I can. Let's hope it doesn't snap." Todd paused. "We're about to find out." Jeremy had no idea how much strain the line could take. They both heaved again. He thought he felt the slightest amount of give. He prayed it wasn't because the line had parted, leaving Andy Nelson on the desolate lake bottom. At last they seemed able to pull up a few inches, then a few more. They pulled the line a foot, followed by a few more feet. Todd signaled to Captain Johnson to stop as Rob began to crank the winch.

Slowly they began to pull him up. By the weight, Jeremy was at least sure the diver was still on the line. He watched the colored markings appear. They pulled him to within fifty feet of the surface, managing tense smiles, then forty, and then thirty. The froth of bubbles on the surface increased as the diver got closer—and then abruptly stopped.

The noisy compressor went silent, having shut down. All three began hauling the diver the rest of the way as fast as they could. As soon as the diver's helmet broke the surface, Rob reached down and took the tiny, pitiful armload from him, as Jeremy and Todd pulled Nelson on board.

They unscrewed the heavy helmet, yanking it off. Andy Nelson lay gasping for air for several minutes. Rob was holding the infant's body in his arms, heavy from the water, but otherwise looking as he had a week ago. The coroner took the baby from him and Rob slumped down on the barge.

Nelson, helped out of his suit, lay on the deck too exhausted to move—even to light one of his cigars. At length, as his breath came back, he spoke to them, his voice shallow and raspy. There was real respect on his face when Jeremy told him how Todd had used the *Majestic* to free him.

"I thought I was done for. I'd just picked up the tyke, but I stirred things up so's I was blinded. I was about to signal to be lifted, when I stepped into a patch of ooze and sunk up to here," he indicated his waist. "I couldn't move at all," he gave a shudder at the memory, "and then I felt myself plucked free of that hellish stuff. What happened to the air line?" he asked suddenly, almost as an afterthought.

Told the compressor had quit, he lifted himself wearily and walked to it. He bent over, examining it. Jeremy noticed that most of the boats had dispersed. Todd had also left, having quietly returned to the *Ariadne*. Jeremy watched as he pulled away.

Andy Nelson called to them "See this?" he asked, holding up a valve. "She's totally useless. I'll have to replace this in Chicago. I guess she held out… just long enough." He shook his head. "Well, if you fellows ever need jobs, you've got them with me."

The next afternoon, as he was getting ready to board the *Lora L* for the trip home from the Observatory, Jeremy overheard a conversation on the dock. The last body—that of Mrs. Hogan—had been recovered. *So there's the last sad chapter in the tragedy,* he thought.

He stopped reluctantly at the main house to see if Lora had learned the news. Martha greeted him. Lora had gone to Villa Thekla, she said, to be with Victoria Koch. And yes, she had been told about Kittie's body being recovered.

"Jeremy," Martha added, as he started to leave, "Miz Lora asked if you could go down to Elgin to the funeral with her tomorrow. Mr. Allerton, Victoria, and some of the others at the party are going, too."

"Of course, Martha," Jeremy replied. "I'll be over early in the morning."

32

The little band of mourners docked at Williams Bay without a minute to spare, hurrying across to the train. Frank and Charlotte were waiting for them at the depot. They were much the same group that had attended Lora's party not two weeks before. They all seemed so much older, Jeremy thought as they boarded. Was it merely the black clothes they wore? The women with their black hats, gloves and veils? Or had the tragic events actually aged them? Jeremy gazed out the window as the train started, remembering the last time he had ridden this line with Malcolm. Both he and Rob soon found themselves being peppered with questions from Dan, Victoria, Frank and Charlotte, all wanting to know about the diving operation.

"What did the diver say the bottom was like?"

"How about visibility down there?"

Clearly, deep diving was a new and awesome activity for people of 1895 to contemplate. But he was glad for the talk about diving to distract the group, particularly Lora, from the funeral. He was about to move across the aisle to her when he noticed that she was absorbed in a note Charlotte had handed her.

Their train began to lean into a long, gentle curve, slowing to a stop for a small village. "Ringwood" the sign on the tiny station house read. He remembered riding his bicycle along here. In fact, the whole right-of-way they were traveling would someday become a tranquil bike path.

"How about joining me?" Frank asked as he stood up, taking a cigar out of his pocket. The two walked down the aisle of the coach and stepped out on the open platform at the end. He struck a match and lit up, the billows of smoke drifting behind him down the track. "You don't use these, do you?" Jeremy shook his head. "That was something with the diver."

"For a few minutes there, it was scary," Jeremy agreed. "Can you imagine what it must have felt like for that diver—being marooned down in that black lake bottom?" Frank gave a small shiver.

"If it hadn't been for your friend, Todd," Jeremy continued, "we wouldn't have ever gotten Nelson on board again."

"Do you know how Todd happened to be there? He saw you on the barge and came over. He wanted to say something to you—to apologize for the other night."

Jeremy paused, mulling what Frank had said. "Well, his being there saved Nelson's life."

"He wanted to apologize to you," Frank resumed, "and to tell you that he took that sneaky punch at you because he was so infatuated with Lora—and jealous of the person who's taking her away. I noticed you watching Lora read the note that Charlotte gave her. It's from Todd. He's left."

"Where has he gone?"

"He's left for Puget Sound, of all places. But no one needs to feel sorry for Todd, though. He's managed to talk his Aunt Harriet into loaning him a great deal of money. He plans to open a ferry service between Seattle and Vancouver Island. It's an idea he's had since he visited there three or four years ago. But he also told me to tell you that if you don't take good care of Lora, he'll be back to pick up where he left off before you came into the picture." While they were talking, the train had pulled into McHenry depot and a number of commuters boarded, bumping past them on their way inside the coach.

Leaving McHenry, the train moved rapidly down the line, rumbling across a bridge over the Fox River. It was just after nine o'clock when they reached the Elgin station. The group alighted from the train. The sky had grown steadily darker and a slow drizzle had started. Rob, their unofficial leader, returned from talking with the station agent. "The church is that way," he said.

They climbed the hill, trudging up through the warm drizzle. When they reached the crest, they could see Saint Mary's Church ahead. It looked almost new to Jeremy, its bright red bricks contrasting with the light stone base. He tried to recall if he'd ever seen the church before.

"Over there," Victoria said softly, and the rest followed the direction of her gaze. Coming up the hill from the south, the direction of the asylum, was the procession. Uniformed nurses and attendants were at the front. Behind the marchers were several carriages, each bearing a separate casket.

Many of the people had gone inside but the little Lake Geneva group stood together on the sidewalk. Two young men emerged from the first carriage. Jeremy could tell by their faces that they were the McGraths, Kittie's brothers.

Two days earlier, after Nelson's diving operation had pulled out, they had arrived at the lake and after a long day of dragging the lake's bottom, they had recovered their sister's body some distance from the *Dispatch*. While Frank was waiting at Williams Bay for the rest to arrive for the trip to the funeral, the station agent had told him that he had been on duty and had seen the brothers pull in with their boat, carrying Kittie's body with them and they had asked him to call the coroner.

The pall bearers removed the caskets from the hearses. There was a visible stir among the onlookers as the tiny white casket holding Jimmie's remains was carried along with those of his parents toward the church. Lora held tightly to Jeremy's arm as they followed them in.

She was looking around inside at the statues, crosses and holy water fonts. "I was baptized a Catholic," she whispered, leaning over to Jeremy. "I don't think I was taken to church after my mother died..." she trailed off as the mass started

The sermon was short. The priest paid tribute to Doctor Hogan's service, and remembered where the family had been seated just three weeks before, pointing to a pew almost directly in front.

Fate can strike, he told the assemblage, turning a peaceful, well-earned Sunday outing into sudden tragedy. He asked for understanding —for acceptance of the often mysterious ways of God. In a kindly gesture, he asked that they remember engineer Preston, who, he said, had been the subject of criticism in reports of the event for his venturing out into the storm.

"Indeed, I doubt the final story, the final answer of the hows and whys of the tragic events, will ever be known." He closed the service by reading a moving poem about the sinking of the *Dispatch,* from the *Lake Geneva Herald.*

The funeral director was standing in the middle of the street and announced that the procession would go over to the North Western depot. "Those returning to Joliet for the interment," the hearses had started slowly, "are welcome to join the McGrath family on board the train."

"He said McGrath's," Lora said, as they fell into step with the procession, the drizzle still falling. "It just occurred to me—there *are* no Hogans left. Kittie said that Jack, Father Jim and Mary were the last, and that little Jimmie…" she choked back tears, "…was going to preserve the family name."

As they approached the depot, they saw an abbreviated train made up of a coach and baggage car behind a steaming engine. They were introduced to the McGrath brothers, as well as an aunt and uncle. The brothers had apparently been told that Lora had been on the boat, ready to leave, when she had been taken off.

"It seems you were spared by a highly providential act, Miss Lockerby," said one of the McGraths.

Lora tightened her grip on Jeremy's arm at the comment. "I received a message and reluctantly had to leave."

"And is this the fellow who took you off?" he asked, indicating Jeremy. The attention of the brothers was suddenly taken up by an elderly woman, a neighbor from Joliet, who clasped their hands emotionally.

At the distraction, Lora and Jeremy stepped aside, and moments later, the conductor announced the special train would be leaving. The group watched the train as it rolled away, and Jeremy knew the others in their group, having heard Kittie's brother, would also be wondering to themselves about his taking Lora off the boat.

They found themselves with time on their hands until their return train arrived, and they walked down the single track, avoiding the puddles that had formed until they reached a little cafe. In spite of themselves, they were hungry. Few of them had taken any time for breakfast.

Inside, Victoria and Dan were asked about their October wedding plans. "It's New York for us," Dan replied. "We're going to see all the sights like a pair of rubes."

Frank and Charlotte were to be married the following May, and their plans weren't definite. "But maybe we'll do something unusual for a honeymoon, like go to Niagara Falls," Charlotte offered, tongue-in-cheek.

239

They stayed in the restaurant, asking for refills of coffee long after they'd finished their meal. Disregarding their black mourning clothes, the stocky proprietress finally stepped over, announced she wasn't running a hotel, and asked them to leave.

Outside, the group walked along the banks of the Fox River. Below the dam, Rob and Frank had gotten into a stone-skipping contest. "This dam reminds me of the one where I was raised," Lora told Jeremy, as they watched the competition. "It's even the same river, although it looks much cleaner up in Waterford."

They drifted away from the others, drawing opposite a small island. "A penny for your thoughts, Lora."

"What an expression! I swear, they must nearly speak another language in Indianapolis," Lora exclaimed, then grew somber. "I was thinking about what Kittie's brother said. *Was* it a highly providential act, Jeremy?'

He was about to mumble some answer, but he took her hand instead, turning her toward him. "Lora—I will tell you—I promise."

Once on the train, they turned two of the seats around so that they were all seated together, facing one another. In spite of themselves and the priest's charitable remarks, they began to speak again about Preston, wondering why he had headed out from apparent safety into the storm. "Maybe from where he was, he couldn't see the size of the waves," Jeremy offered.

"But he could see the *sky*, looking at those clouds and lightning." Frank said, "why would he have tried a crossing?"

"He didn't want to." Callie Braddock had been quietly listening to the conversation. The others turned to her. "I was there, on the pier," she explained.

There *had* been a report in the *Herald*, Jeremy remembered, from unidentified observers. It had alluded to Preston's not wanting to venture out. Callie had been staying with Rob and his sister over at their Folly estate, she said. She and her cousin had gone out rowing, but when the weather suddenly turned bad, they put in at the Elgin camp. The two stayed out on the pier, under the canopy but getting soaked through from the wind blowing the rain on them. There were four or five others out there, wet from the rain and afraid of the lightning but watching intently as the boats battled their way in out of the storm.

Callie was a very pretty, slim-figured girl with short-cropped blonde hair. She was so quiet she tended to fade into the background. When she spoke, she talked fast, as though her thoughts were running ahead of her. "Slow down, Callie," Rob said, and patted her knee.

"Anyway," she continued, stretching her long legs in the cramped seats, "we looked up and saw a larger boat, running near shore. It was a white launch, something like yours, Lora. They came in to the pier. When they got there, I was surprised. I recognized Kittie and her husband from the party. The little boy was with them."

"Did they tie up?" Rob asked.

"Let me think," she said, frowning. "No, not really. The engineer just looped one of the ropes around the post to hold the boat. He and the other men were talking right near us."

"Did you say anything to them?" Lora asked. She had been sitting very quietly. Jeremy knew that hearing this story would be like reliving the whole tragedy for her. He pictured her watching the *Dispatch* at the pier through the spyglass, helplessly crying out to them when they left and started across the lake.

"No, I didn't have a chance. I waved to Kittie and she remembered me, waving back. She was trying to keep Jimmie out of the rain. One of the men I didn't know. He was the priest, I learned. He and Preston were talking. 'You know this thing is really a little toy boat with that kind of wind blowing up, Father,' Preston said.

"Father Hogan seemed concerned and said he needed to get back. He was to do a baptism that night. It was someone important, and he had to be there for it. There was some argument, well, discussion, between the brothers. It seemed like Jack wanted to get off. His brother as well as his sister had to get across the lake and back to Harvard.

" 'Well, you three get off then,' I heard the priest finally say, 'and John Preston can come back for you.'

" 'No,' Kittie spoke up, 'if you go, we all go.' Then there was some more talk. Preston listened. I couldn't hear what was said, but finally he threw up his hands and went out and undid the rope."

Lora asked if she'd heard anything else. "Well, right then Preston said that at least they had a good engine and they'd make a run for it. He took the wheel and...they left." Callie had been fighting back the tears as she recounted the events. She paused, trying to regain her composure.

241

"There was another person out on the pier with us. He wore a yachtsman's hat. 'That boat is going down if it gets out too far,' he said. "We watched, but we could hardly see the *Dispatch* as it reached the middle because the waves were so high. It was there in the waves one minute, and then it just…wasn't there anymore."

Later that evening, after their return to Bluffside, Jeremy sat alongside Lora on the veranda's steps. The sun's last rays were barely visible across the lake. "I feel so awkward saying anything about this so soon after the funeral," Lora started. "Did you see Rob take me aside at the Williams Bay depot?"

"I did."

"Do you remember a few weeks ago at Arnold's when he mentioned a possible job for me at the Art Institute?" Jeremy nodded. "Well, he told me he had followed up on our conversation; he's almost sure now that I'll be hired as head of the new children's section at the Institute.

"Rob is going back to Chicago on Tuesday. He'll let me know by the weekend. Am I too vulgar, Jeremy, talking about a job, and with the Hogans hardly buried?"

"Lora, I'm lucky enough to have met the Hogans. Everything I saw about Kittie tells me that she would be the happiest of all for you." He took her hand. "You won't be going back to Clarence Darrow, then?"

"No. I had been giving it a lot of thought even before hearing from Rob. I'd decided over the last two weeks that I wouldn't return to him—to the office." Her eyes met his. "You played a part in that decision. I can't tell you now what that part was, but I've made up my mind to go back teaching."

I played a role in her decision? What role? Jeremy wondered. Lora seemed to want to talk about her job prospect, perhaps to distract herself from the grief of the last few days as well as to mend fences from her bitter words toward Jeremy.

"I saw that yawn you couldn't hide," she said after a time, giving him a warm smile.

"I didn't want to let you see me. Your caretaker had better get to bed, though. Look at my work for tomorrow," he added, peering into the dusk at the overgrown lawn and storm-damaged flower beds.

242

33

The next three weeks saw the pace of work at the Observatory quicken. Jeremy was taking Lora to the train for the trip to Chicago and her interview at the Art Institute. "I'm so sorry to miss the motor demonstration today. I know how much it means to father, but this was the only day for my interview."

Lora had just asked him once again for his opinion about her outfit during the lake crossing. Did her dress and matching hat make her look too much like a teacher and less like she belonged at the Art Institute? Flattered at her asking, he told her she looked perfect.

"It still seems like a dream," she said as he escorted her across to the train. "You have good luck at the Observatory and keep father from getting too nervous."

After seeing her off, he hopped a ride out to the Observatory. The wagon was loaded with bricks and huge slabs of limestone were now stacked alongside the freight house. Teams of strong horses were going to be needed to get them up the hill.

The Observatory work had progressed to the point where they were ready to show off Paul's pride and joy—the motor mounted under the floor of the main building. On his arrival at the grounds, Jeremy saw that the workers were already gathering around the Observatory. Many had climbed atop the building itself to get a better perch for the test. The large, temporary canvas dome that protected the Observatory from the elements had been removed.

Over at the power station, Paul started up the dynamo-generator and Jeremy listened to it give off its reassuring sweet hum of authority. After a final adjustment, Paul started for the main building. Jeremy and Jim

Keane trailed him, trying their best to look nonchalant as they covered the hundred feet from the power station to the observatory, facing the stares of the workmen.

Paul's successful test of the power system and its ability to lift the main floor of the Observatory would be vital to the success of the whole project. If it failed, they would have to install another dated steam and hydraulic lifting mechanism like those used elsewhere. The beauty of Paul's design was the precise control it would give to the astronomers.

For the test he had rigged temporary controls. The crowd of workmen—carpenters, masons and bricklayers—all pushed as close as possible. Many were on ladders and scaffolding, perched against the side of the building's walls, looking over the top. Others had wedged inside, standing on the newly finished catwalk that encircled the dome. There was a holiday mood around the site, with workers joking and calling to one another across the space.

Paul was going to activate the motors with current running underground from the dynamo at the power house. If all went well, the floor would be raised by as much as twenty-five feet. When completed, the huge telescope would also be controlled by the mere flick of the buttons. When the telescope's weight was added, the motors would have to lift over forty tons. The power house crew had volunteered to stand on the floor and ride it up. "We could use more weight to demonstrate. Come on, fellas," Paul urged. A few of the workmen, dared by others, moved down and out onto the circular floor.

Jim Keane spotted a friend watching and waved for him to join them. "Come on, Lindy, be a part of history," he called. Lindy's face disappeared from over the top of the building where he had been standing on a scaffold. In a minute, he surfaced at the door and tentatively stepped onto the floor, drawing shouts from his own work crew.

"Slater, how far will this thing lift me, or rather how far can it drop me?" Lindy asked.

"Oh, about a hundred feet if it doesn't work," Jeremy exaggerated, "but where's your spirit of adventure?"

Paul stepped to the center and began to give a rundown on the mechanism. Most of the workmen, even those who had been on the site from the outset, knew nothing about the revolutionary machinery that would power the telescope. Jeremy watched their absorbed expressions as Paul, playing on their curiosity about electricity, briefly explained the equipment, deftly relating it to the work *they* had all performed. Then, keeping his persuasive edge, he moved to the portable control board and began to turn dials.

"Do you know any good prayers?" Jim whispered to Jeremy.

Before he could answer, the floor, silently and without the least tugging or jarring, began to rise. A cheer went up as it reached the maximum elevation, stopped briefly and then smoothly descended six feet below the original floor point. The floor was raised and once again lowered to the starting level.

Paul stepped to the center. "Well, what do you know?" He pretended to mop his brow. "It works!"

Ernie Walker stepped over to Paul and draped an arm around his smiling, red-faced engineer's shoulders. "Men," he started, "Paul Lockerby and his crew have just shown us all what can be done. They also showed us what secrets they've been up to. And all the while," he paused, turning toward the power station, "we thought they were building a machine to put themselves on the moon." Ernie drew a spirited chorus of cheers.

"They've also shown us not only what's been done, but what we have to do to finish before winter gets here. So let's get busy...starting tomorrow. Because if you look out in front, you'll see a wagon loaded with beer and pretzels has arrived." The last words met with a scramble down the ladders toward the wagon, where beer was being ladled into metal cups. Jeremy stepped off the movable floor and walked over with Jim to watch the celebration.

"Ernie's a leader," Jeremy said, drinking from a cup of beer. "He's kept the construction going through cold and rain, heat and no water, and he's going to bring her in on time." Jim only nodded, absorbed as he watched the men enjoying themselves, likely remembering when the accomplishment with the motors must have seemed like some distant, unlikely dream.

As Jeremy arrived back at the dock, Tommy Napper waved him over. "I have this wire for you." It was from Lora, asking that they wait to meet her. She would be on the afternoon train and, she added, she had exciting news. He handed Paul the telegram as he joined him on the platform.

"It can only mean that she's gotten the job at the Art Institute," he said.

When Lora stepped off the train, the smile on her face left no doubt she'd been successful. On the crossing to Bluffside, she talked about her interview. "What about Clarence? Did you give him the news?" Paul asked.

"I told Clarence at lunch. He was disappointed, though I doubt he was surprised. I'd forgotten how knowledgeable he was about the Art Institute. He keeps right on amazing me." Jeremy thought Lora was speaking a beat too slowly, measuring her words. "He said he'll have to start looking for my replacement when he gets back from a trip to Los Angeles." She turned to them. "But now here I am, talking all about myself, as usual, the whole time. Tell me about the demonstration. Did everything work?"

As Paul described the successful test, Jeremy listened, glancing across at father and daughter, no longer surprised at Lora's technical knowledge.

"I've got more news, though, Jeremy," Paul said, "which I haven't even had a chance to give you, as busy as we've been. The motor's test performance was everything I could have hoped for and more. As a result, we're ahead of the rest of the project. So for two weeks I'll be in Chicago and then over in Cleveland at Warner and Swasey, consulting about next year's schedule: installing the motors to power the dome and telescope. While I'm gone, you'll be in charge. There'll only be Jim Keane and Bill at the freight shed, plus yourself. The rest of the men are getting the two weeks off with half pay. I expect you'll only need to go over a couple of times."

"That's great, Paul. As a matter of fact, I can use the time for caretaking," he said, staring at the grass on the bluff which was once again embarrassingly long.

Lora caught his eye, giving him an equivocal smile as her father's back was turned. Then she stepped from the boat and walked down the pier, leaving him to wonder just what that smile meant.

34

Jeremy was glad things had slowed down at the Observatory. It was going to be another hot, sultry day. The wind barely stirred as he finished dressing and walked out onto the porch, yawning and stretching. No sign of any activity came from the main house. If she was at home and hadn't gone back to Chicago, he'd work his courage up and ask her into the town of Lake Geneva.

He had been thinking about the two of them; in fact, he had been able to think of little else for the last several days, remembering that look Lora had given him when Paul said he would be gone for a couple of weeks. Now, with time on his hands, well, it *was* the 1890s and *he* needed to take the initiative. Up until now, it had all been hers. He shook his head, inspecting the cabin. He'd have to straighten up the mess that had accumulated or he couldn't dream of having Lora over.

Starting in the kitchen, he washed a stack of dishes he'd let pile up in the sink. Many were sent over by Martha. Returning them would give him a reason for going to the main house. He was just finishing the dishes when he heard Lora's voice.

The water was running and he turned the tap off to listen. Quickly drying his hands on a cloth he'd grabbed, he hurried down the hall, running a hand through his hair. "Is anyone at home?" she called.

He swung open the screen door—too quickly—and walked out onto the porch. "So there you are. I began to think no one was here." Lora was standing out on the path in front of the house, wearing the summery print dress she had been admiring in the window next to Arnold's drug store. She wore a floppy, wide-brimmed hat and over one arm carried a straw basket. She was barefoot.

"Martha's had to go to Racine. Her sister has suddenly taken ill so she'll be looking after her for a week or two. I saw her off on the *Admiral* this morning."

"I could have taken her. I'm hardly working these days except as caretaker," he said, glancing out across the long grass, trying to cover the thrill that was going through him at hearing the two of them would be alone.

"Don't worry," she answered, casually shifting the basket to her other arm.

Oh, that smile of hers, he sighed.

"I know you've been putting in long hours at the Observatory, and the boat will let her off only a couple of blocks from the train. She'll be fine. I thought I'd come over and ask you if I could pick some of your apples." She gave the basket a little swing in the direction of the trees.

"They look about ready and I'm going to try my hand at baking some apple pies. This morning I finally pried Martha's favorite recipe from her." She bashfully scuffed her toes in the dusty path, making a little trench. "I wish you'd join me, Jeremy. I'd like the company."

"My apples? Oh, the ones in back. I'd love to join you. And what a terrible host I am—on a hot day like this, too. Come on up. I'll get us some root beer. I'd forgotten all about those apples."

"Thank you," she answered, needing no second invitation. She was already climbing the front steps. They had sat together on those steps before, but this was the first time Lora had visited on his porch.

"Let me take that basket and you sit right here." He patted the cushions on the swing, sending dust clouds flying out. *Damn! Why didn't I clean up this place yesterday, and with all that time on my hands. Lora will see how flustered I am,* he thought, opening the screen door.

In the kitchen, he took out two bottles, working off the caps with the primitive opener. At least he had some clean glasses. He poured the warm, foaming root beer and began to chip at the block in the ice box, nearly stabbing himself with the pick. He at last dropped a couple of shards in each glass and headed back to the porch.

Lora was on the swing. She had removed her hat and set it on the chair. Had she put it there deliberately so he'd sit on the swing with her, he wondered, handing her the glass. While he was inside, she had unpinned her hair, letting it fall over her shoulders. It was longer than he'd realized. She settled back on the swing, taking a long drink. "That tastes ever so good on a day like this."

Of All the times I pick to go mute, letting Lora lead the conversation again. Jeremy took a quick, nervous sip from his glass. *I was at ease out here before. Didn't the two of us sit on these very cabin steps after the Dispatch's sinking?*

He didn't even hear her comment. He had put his hand on her arm, asking her to repeat it, but before she could get any words out, he closed the gap between them, taking her glass from her. Her face was turned to him and he quickly kissed her full lips, tasting root beer. *"I know Miz Lora's in love with you. Doesn't that mean anything to you?"* Martha's words rang in his ears.

She leaned back, facing him, her expression unreadable. "Am I going to get a tour of the cabin?" she asked.

"Right now," he answered, helping her up. The last few moments had been awkward. Was she giving him a chance to collect himself?

She walked to the railing. "Did father tell you that I designed this cabin?" she asked. She straightened her dress, her back to him.

"No, he didn't. Wait a minute. Of course he did. It was on that very first morning. We were here after the storm." He held the door open for her as she picked up their glasses.

"Lora, before we go in, please don't mind the mess. As you can see, I spend all my free time on the groundskeeping around Bluffside."

"The groundskeeping. How could I help but notice," she laughed easily. "I nearly got lost in the grass coming over here."

Jeremy pulled out a kitchen chair for her. He stepped over to refill their glasses. When he turned he saw Lora's face was knotted in concentration. She was inspecting the sole of her foot. "I picked up a splinter," she winced.

He sat down beside her. "Let me see. Put your foot up here," he indicated his lap.

"No, Jeremy. I don't want to bother you. It's only a little splinter, and no one ever died from one. Besides, that would be much...much too unladylike."

"Unladylike or not, I can see it hurts." he lifted her foot in spite of her protest and examined it. "There it is. Just a minute." He got up and poked around in one of the drawers, returning with a knife.

"That blade looks awfully sharp. Are you sure you know what you're doing?"

"I'll have it out in no time, but if you'd rather not look..."

"When father told you about the main house and this cabin," Lora had looked away, distracting herself as she felt the edge of the knife on her skin. "Did she tell you that I got the design for them from the 'Women's Building' at the Fair? Now let me think," she continued before he could answer, "who do you suppose I ought to tell that you're living in the "women's cabin'?"

"Why don't we make that another of our secrets."

"*Another* of our secrets. Are they mounting up? I'll consider that. I...ow!"

"Hold still. I've just about got it worked out. There! I really think you'll walk again."

"The next thing, you'll be taking Malcolm's patients away from him." She set her foot down. "Thank heavens Martha didn't see me letting you 'operate.' I know what she would have said—in private. But now that I'm as good as new, can I see the rest of the cabin?"

Lora held out her hand and he led the way down the hall and into the tiny sitting room. Jeremy had spent little time there and it showed. It held a single, dust covered chair. "Only one more room," he said, stepping across the hall.

"Good god!" he cried. "I knew it needed a cleaning, but *this*. I'm really sorry." His clothes were strewn all about. Dresser drawers were open and old newspapers and magazines covered the floor. He began to wade into the mess as she stood at the door, her hand resting on the knob.

"You don't have anything to apologize for. This is *your* home and I invited myself. But I'm not all that busy, and if you need help cleaning it up, not that it needs it, of course," she glanced around "but at the rate you're throwing things about, you're never going to find half your belongings."

It was so much easier than it had been earlier out on the swing. He simply put an arm on her shoulder, leaned over and kissed her. He could feel her breasts through the thin cotton of her dress as she returned the kiss, not backing away to ask any questions.

"I've been putting that off a long time—for too long a time, Lora." The words tumbled out as he eased her down to the rumpled bed. She lay quiet and still, the bantering between them stopped.

His fingers traced a wavering line across her face. *If she's going to say something,* he thought, *it's going to be right now,* as he sat part way up and took off his shirt. "I love you." He leaned over and kissed her.

"I love you, too, Jeremy. I'm so very, very afraid right now—of what you must think of me—being so forward," she finished in a lowered voice. He gently brushed away the tears that were running down her cheeks. In the dim light of the cabin, he stripped off his clothes and lay back down, facing her.

"Will you let me love you?" In reply, she nodded her head slowly against his chest, their apple picking postponed.

Lora made love with a straightforward intensity and, he discovered, she moved with surprising abandon, arching her back as she drew him tightly to her, crying out. He had lost all track of time until he looked up, still dazzled, to see Lora alongside the bed. She searched among the covers, at last finding her dress and slipping it on.

"I'll be back in a few minutes," she said, catching his disappointed look and bending to kiss him. He followed her to the door, watching as she lightly bounded down the cabin steps and along the path to the main house, her basket swinging under her arm.

In a few minutes she returned, her face flushed and the basket overflowing. "Wait until you see what I found for us," she exclaimed, pausing on her way to the kitchen. She reached into the basket, taking out bread, preserves, eggs—frowning at one that had cracked and was running over her hand. Jeremy looked in and saw that she had brought peaches, cherries, even a partly crushed cake.

"You just see if I don't turn this cabin into another Palmer House." She pulled a bottle of wine from the bottom of the basket, holding it up triumphantly before she pushed him toward the bedroom to await their first meal.

Afterward, they moved out onto the porch steps, sharing the wine. The chirping of the late summer katydids surrounded them. Lora rested her head against his shoulder.

"Do you know what I wish for, Jeremy?" She was facing him. "That this summer would never end."

Jeremy was torn. He wanted to preserve their idyll, but he knew the time was right to finally get his tale across to her. *Where can I begin? How will she take what I'm going to tell her? Lora is far too smart and inquiring to ever be satisfied with only a part of this story.*

She was quietly speaking and he let the opportunity pass. The two talked into the night, laughing now and then at something said, not even minding the mosquitoes. Finally, Jeremy whispered to her. She stood and took his hand as they walked back inside.

The next two days passed in a soft, dreamy haze. Jeremy had never been with any woman before who had come close to matching Lora's torrid sexuality. Over those days he tried to will his former life away—to let it just recede. He absolved his guilt feelings. Amy and Danny were, after all, somewhere out beyond his reach, weren't they?

While Lora slept one night, he lay awake. Resting on an elbow, he spoke out loud to her slumbering figure. "How am I going to be able to live in this room again without you? Your presence will be everywhere. I'm already lonesome even thinking about your leaving. I've never, ever felt so close to another person." He ran his hand lightly through her hair. "And I don't care—almost—about who you've known before." Right from their first afternoon together he knew she had been trying hard, without success, to conceal her sexual experience. "I love you so, even if this is history's craziest romance.

"Old Martha was right. You do love me too, don't you? Do you know what? I'm going to do everything I can to keep you in love forever." He lay back down. "I'm picturing us right now, in the next century. Would you come with me if we could?"

Hearing his voice, Lora stirred. She sighed contentedly and fitted herself against him. Holding her, Jeremy knew, even if he were somehow offered an escape back to the distant future, what his decision would be— if that escape should mean having to leave Lora behind.

Blinking his eyes from the sunlight, Jeremy awoke on Thursday morning. Lora was in bed next to him, totally absorbed in whatever she was composing. The covers were thrown off the bed and Lora was lying on her stomach with her legs drawn up behind her, her ankles crossed. She would write a sentence or two in her looping, left-handed script, then frown, tapping her teeth with her pencil. Jeremy quietly watched, bemused by her serious expression and its contrast with her casual naked-

252

ness.

"I hope that's not a diary," he spoke at last. Lora halted her writing to lean across the bed and give him a kiss.

"I'm trying to get started organizing lesson plans for the fall. This program is all so new. I'm really excited, Jeremy, but nervous, too. These students at the Art Institute are going to be so far ahead of mine at Pullman. Listen and tell me what you think, but be honest, please."

She scanned her notes, frowning before she picked out an entry. He turned on his side, listening, lazily stroking her back. Lora continued to read as his hand slowly eased downward.

"You're very distracting," she was moving with his hand.

"I don't want you being all nervous even before you start."

Lora pushed her pencil and paper off the bed. "I ought to make you go stand in a corner..." She didn't finish, rolling instead into his arms.

35

Lora was already up on Saturday morning and busy in the kitchen, facing the stove and the crackling bacon. She was wearing only Jeremy's blue denim shirt which she had appropriated over the last few days.

"Guess who?" he put a hand over her eyes.

"Let me think. George Pullman?"

"You're right," he answered, lifting the tail of her shirt to press against her.

"*Mister Pullman!* Does this mean I'll be getting my old job back?"

"That all depends on how good a breakfast you make, but it smells promising, and I'm always willing to negotiate with a former employee."

"Now I *know* you aren't George Pullman," she turned, putting a slice of bacon in his mouth. Over breakfast, she reminded him that this was to be their long-delayed apple picking and pie baking day. Lora had already brought out Martha's recipe, the same one she'd hastily scribbled down while the two had awaited the *Admiral.*

Jeremy straightened up the kitchen while Lora went out to start picking apples. "With her around," he said aloud, "I could very easily forget where I came from." She put him to work, letting him boost her so she could climb to the upper limbs of the trees. From there she threw down the best apples until their basket was brimming.

"How many pies are you going to make?" he asked, lugging the heavy basket into the kitchen.

"Only one for my start, but if it goes well, who can say?" She was leaning over the stove, squinting once more at her handwritten recipe. He'd built a fire in the oven, adding to the heat in the close kitchen. Lora frowned as she worked, muttering that she was sure she had measured the sugar, cinnamon and nutmeg brought over from the main house. At last she finished, trimming the dough from the pie and stood back, studying.

Jeremy was reluctant to criticize but there seemed something wrong with the unbaked pie. "What do you think?" she asked.

It may have only been some minor ingredient that had been left out, but it didn't somehow *look* right to him. "Do you want an artistic opinion or a technical one?"

"Don't sound so much like a lawyer. How does it look?"

"I can't place it, but it seems...to lack something."

"I think so too," she conceded, consulting her recipe once more. "But I didn't leave anything out so..." she slid the pie into the oven. "Martha said that with a good fire it ought to bake in an hour."

"Good. That will give us just enough time..." he tugged at her shirt.

"That will give us enough time to clean up that bedroom of yours." She pushed him down the hallway.

"Jeremy, how in the world could you have collected so many old papers?" The two were in his bedroom, surveying the clutter.

I must be hearing her teacher's voice, he thought, as she directed him to pick up, sort out and put away his clothes. Lora rummaged in the pantry, reappearing with a full bucket, soap and brush. Rolling up the sleeves of the work shirt, she knelt down and began to scrub the floor.

"There," she said after a time, standing and drawing her hand across her brow. "That's a little better."

"It never has looked this good. I'll be afraid to walk on this floor."

Lora sniffed and Jeremy caught the odor at the same time. "Lord! It's the pie! We forgot all about it!" Dashing back to the kitchen, Lora grabbed for the oven handle, jerking her hand away with a scream. She picked up a rag and eased open the door. Thick, choking smoke poured out. The pie had literally exploded and was on fire, its cover blown off, splattered and burning around the roof of the oven.

"Now I remember," Jeremy said quietly as she slid the still-smoldering remains over to the sink. "You're supposed to put holes in the top so it won't..." he pointed uselessly at the sizzling pan. "But stop worrying, who says it wouldn't have tasted good, and your next one is going to take first place at the county fair."

"Thank you. That's a nice, if very bad, lie. Wouldn't that be some fair

255

if a pie of mine won a prize," she shook her head.

"I tell you what," he said. "Go in and lie down. I'll clean up here and make us a surprise picnic. When everything's ready," he gave her a light prod. "I'll come and get you."

"Where is this surprise going to take place?" Lora asked. Jeremy had led her to the bottom of the bluff along the shore. "We're not exactly dressed for a lawn party over at General Strong's." She ran a hand across the shoulder of her sundress she had changed back into.

"The picnic is going to take place right on your own boat. We don't even have to leave the pier. And for a bonus, look over at that 'sailor's delight' sunset!" They slipped under the *Lora L's* canvas. Jeremy opened the basket and began to serve sandwiches and the remaining wine with an expansive flair.

"What an utter flop I am." She turned her wine glass in her hand, studying it. "I used to watch Martha bake when I was little, but I never took any real interest. I suppose I just liked her company. I don't recall a thing she taught me. So much time spent in classrooms. I'm sure most any fourth or fifth grader out at Pullman could have baked a decent apple pie.

"Martha didn't bother telling me to poke holes in the pie because she assumed even *Lora* would know that much," she trailed off.

"Will you put it to bed," he soothed. Lora laughed, her mood lightening at hearing his lapse into that curious slang.

"I don't suppose I should be telling you this, but I wanted to show off for you," she said, taking his hand in her own as the *Lora L* swayed in the soft wake of some distant boat. Jeremy was relaxed, so much so that at first he thought he'd only imagined the sound of music drifting across the water. He shuffled to the rear of the launch. Lora moved to his side, and they pulled back the canvas to peer out.

"The *Passaic*," she said. A large yacht, gaily decorated with small lights, slowly coasted to a stop off Black Point. A group of partyers had gathered on the afterdeck.

"It's the Cranes. They used to come by last year and play their victrola. I was up at the lake for such a short time I only heard it once, but Victoria told me it was a regular weekly occurrence. I guess Mr. Crane has been so busy this summer he hasn't been up much. I'm sure some of the

Seipps are on board." Lora stayed kneeling at the stern for a few minutes, listening until another melody began. When she moved back, she stretched out alongside Jeremy. He had taken the cushions from the chairs and propped them as pillows while they listened. The night was still and warm, with a full moon. The grainy gramophone played on as laughter and talk mixed with music from the yacht.

"Our own serenade. You really have thought of everything for this picnic." She was running her hand across his chest. "A perfect night—if only it weren't so late in August. Can you believe how fast the summer has gone by?" She returned his passionate kiss with one of her own. "We aren't going to have many more nights like this," she whispered.

Time *was* getting short, he knew. This night was as good an opportunity as he would get to talk to her. His mind was made up. "What a time I picked to tell you..." he started, drawing in a breath.

"To tell me what? *Jeremy ...you seem so serious.* Is it that old music?" Lora fingered one of the buttons she had unfastened on his shirt.

At that moment, the shrill sound of a whistle came from around Black Point. The two looked out from the drawn-back canvas. Another yacht was heading straight in for Bluffside's pier.

"Oh my god! That's the *Time!* It's got to be Rob and Callie visiting. What if they find us here like this?" She glanced down the pier and then back to the Time, measuring. "We don't have time to run down to shore, either."

Moments later the yacht pulled in. Rob secured the Time along the top of the pier's "T" and Lora and Jeremy could hear the voices of Rob and Callie as they stood alongside the *Lora L.*

"Rob, it's pitch dark up there. They've probably all gone to Chicago."

"I don't think so. Lora didn't say anything about leaving, and their boat is still here. They'd have taken it to the train. She wasn't at Kaye's. Maybe they took a walk down to Victoria's. I see the *Passaic's* put in at Seipps, but I didn't notice them on board.

"Did you realize you just said 'they'? Is Lora seeing Jeremy exclusively now?" Callie asked. They had begun walking down the pier toward shore, and Lora and Jeremy exchanged nervous glances, self-conscious at what they might hear next. Jeremy thought he heard Rob say something about the World's Fair, but the two had passed out of earshot.

"I'm going to speak to them," Jeremy said, stirring under the canvas.

"You'll do nothing of the kind!" Lora locked a leg around him. "Don't even joke like that! Anyway, I can hear the boards of the pier. They're coming back out this way. Come around here," she moved behind the engine on the side away from the pier.

"That was some unforgettable party, wasn't it?" Rob was speaking. "I can still see old Todd go flying over the side of that bluff."

"So can I, and he deserved it."

"I met him a couple of years ago, and let me tell you something," Rob said. "I like Lora's going with Jeremy a good deal more than seeing her with that rascal. I'll say one thing for Todd, though. He came through when he had to—saving that diver's life. Without him, for sure that fella was a goner."

"From what you've said, Lora seems so much happier with Jeremy than with anyone you've seen her with." There was a pause. Callie continued. "This memory loss of his you told me about. You mean it hasn't gone away all summer? That's really puzzling."

"Who knows, Callie. Lora is one of the most closed-mouth persons I've ever met. If she's learned anything more about his past, she hasn't shared it with yours truly—or my sister either.

"Wait. I'll only be a minute," Rob said. "They've left the canvas undone at the stern of their boat. I'll fasten it." Lora and Jeremy crouched as low as they could behind the cowling.

"They must have been in a hurry and forgotten it," he called out in a loud voice as he returned to the *Time*.

"I suppose we should start back to the cabin," Lora said after a few minutes. Jeremy had helped her onto the pier. She saw he was still standing alongside the launch. He was holding the picnic basket.

"Look inside," he said. "The rest of the apples and eggs have been shifted to one side. And the top's closed."

"Oh, Lord! I wondered, too, why he called out to Callie in such a loud voice." Lora had caught the significance. "That means Rob figured out exactly where we were. What in the world could we have said if we'd been caught? Do you think he'll tell her? Perhaps some day he will," she chuckled lightly before he could answer. She squeezed his hand. "Now, what was it you were going to tell me back there?"

"I...Lora...I need to go over to the Observatory tomorrow," he started, fumbling. The moment for candor had passed.

"So *that's* what you were so serious about? You sweetheart! Well, I'm going to miss you terribly too, even for the day, but I suppose I shouldn't be seen over there with you, so you finish up and hurry home."

36

Jeremy felt his foot being pulled. At first it was part of his dream, but on opening his eyes he saw Lora, fully dressed, standing at the end of his bed. He sighed and rolled over.

"Wake up, sleepyhead. Remember that last night I said I'd have a surprise? Well, get up and put on your suit, I've already been over to see Emil. I put on my best helpless charm to get him to hitch Magnolia to the Lefens' carriage. I had to tell him you were on an errand and would be back. Everything's ready. How do you like me?" Her hair had been put up under a turreted hat and she wore a long dress with a waist jacket.

He sat up, blinking the sleep from his eyes. "Very beautiful, I..."

"What's wrong?"

"It's that I didn't recognize you with your own clothes on." He threw the covers back over his head as she swatted him with her parasol.

When they reached the barn, Emil had brought Magnolia out, already hitched to the carriage. "Tell him you're taking me to the train at Genoa Junction," she whispered.

Lora climbed up on the narrow seat with Jeremy. They wheeled down the drive to the main house. In a few minutes she reappeared, carrying a small overnight bag. At his cabin, Jeremy withdrew from his drawer some money he'd been saving.

Lora directed him off the shore road and down a country lane. Late summer was at its best, with the hot spell broken and with a hint of autumn in the air. "When do I learn our destination?"

"We're going to Woodstock," she answered. "Since you used Eugene Debs to get me off the *Dispatch,* I thought you should meet him."

What an opportunity! Debs! To think I wrote a college term paper about

260

him. Maybe I can resolve—or he'll resolve—those mixed feelings I always had for him.

Magnolia was clomping along at her slow, steady pace and Jeremy realized they had just turned down Alden road, a route he had taken dozens of times before. Alden was a back door, country way to return to Chicago, and except for the lack of paving, he saw that the narrow road would change little in a hundred years.

"You've gone this way before, haven't you?" she asked quietly.

"No. I only knew or thought, Woodstock was off that way." He nodded in a southwest direction. Her question had caught him off guard. He had indeed been looking off to his right with a distracted, faint idea of seeing the familiar microwave relay tower. No tower was there, of course, but the farmhouse and barn looked like the same ones he'd known.

If Lora didn't wholly believe his explanation, she nevertheless allowed him to pry her with questions about Debs and the Pullman strike and boycott. Her first meeting with Debs, she recounted, had taken place on May 11, 1894. She and Reverend Carwardine, the activist minister from the Pullman Methodist Church, had both gone downtown as a sort of subcommittee. They had met Debs in the lobby of the Palmer house. She recalled her disillusionment with him as the three walked through Grant Park. They had requested the meeting after several boisterous sessions over at Turner Hall in Kensington. Debs' American Railway Union representatives had attended and strongly advised the grievance committee of Pullman workers against striking. Debs, she continued, repeated this cautious line when they met.

"He was so serene—such a contrast to all the rough shouting I'd grown used to at our meetings. It seemed out of place. And he had little appreciation of the worker's plight. He even brought up the same old point about Pullman keeping his shops open in the face of the declining car orders. Did we come down here, I wondered, to hear what could well have been spoken by Pullman's own representatives?"

Fortunately, she said, the Reverend had nudged her into silence as she was about to ask Debs some very pointed questions. As they walked along, Carwardine told him that the Pullman workers had suffered five successive reductions in wages, while not one officer's salary had been reduced.

Lora continued her narrative. They had moved opposite the Art

Institute, still under construction. It would equal anything in New York, she had boasted with native pride. Debs asked questions about the building as they stood across Michigan Avenue, but when he came back to the subject of Pullman, Debs was clearly still worried about involving his A.R.U. in any strike. Such a move, he told them, was entirely at the wrong time. The union was only beginning to get its strength. Debs had taken Lora's arm as they started back toward the Palmer House.

" 'All we ask," the ardent young minister pleaded, 'is that you come out to Pullman and see the situation. It's one that will tear your heart right out. Let us take you around town, into some of the homes. You can meet with our residents. You'll see, sir, that these good workers and their families have been victimized.

" 'And with the sub-human conditions he's yoked his own residents with, his profits will always stay the same.' " Bill spoke with passion, she told Jeremy. She hoped Debs hadn't noticed that Carwardine's words sounded rehearsed because they had been—nervously—on the train coming downtown.

"Eugene finally smiled. 'You're persuasive, Reverend. I'll be out there Monday morning. Just give me directions.' As we rounded the last corner, news vendors were shouting 'Pullman Strike! Workers called out of shops! Pullman Works to be closed!'

" 'It would seem that your strike is already at hand,' Debs said.

"Reverend Bill and I were dumbfounded. We'd been sent to induce Debs to see for himself the working conditions. Tom Heathcote and the rest of the committee had sworn that no strike would come for at least a week or more, and might very well still be avoided. It turned out that there had been reports of a spy at the hall meeting. The rumor that Pullman officials had determined to close the plant at noon had spread. It was groundless, but the decision had been made and the strike was on."

"What about Debs?" Jeremy asked. "Did he keep his word and come out to Pullman?"

"He did indeed, though he was still reluctant when we left him. We met him Monday morning at the station. He was with another union official, some portly man who didn't say ten words all day. We arranged for Eugene to meet Jennie Curtis, the daughter of a loyal worker who had died after a long illness. Her family had survived mainly from Jennie's wages as a seamstress. She had to pay the back rent that had accumulated

262

while her father lay in bed, too sick to work. Jennie joined the American Railway Union and even became the president of the women's local. On June 15th, it was Jennie who gave the speech, hurling the fiery rhetoric that launched our boycott."

The carriage bobbed along on the outskirts of Alden Village as she recounted how she had shown Debs the impressive Market Place and the rows of townhouses. He stopped to chat at random with some of the residents though he went largely unnoticed that morning. He was taken through some of the houses and saw for himself the poverty and hopelessness behind the tidy facades.

"We slowly moved north from Market Place until we were met by Mary Alice Woods." Lora let her narrative mark time as they pulled the carriage to a stop. She took the bucket and descended the banks of the small "Nippersink Creek," according to a weathered sign. With Magnolia refreshed, they continued on, passing a small school under construction. They crossed the branch line railroad and moved beyond the outskirts of the little community and back into the country.

"Mary Alice's father, Buckley, was a night watchman at the Pullman main gate," she resumed. "He had stopped a worker who was taking tools out of the plant without a pass. When he tried to halt him, the man took a hatchet and chopped at him, knocking him to the ground.

"Buckley's head hit a stone and he never recovered from the attack. When he died the following year, his widow was assured that she would be taken care of and not to file any claim. Well, she was treated to an eviction notice—for her husband's dedication. She'd fallen delinquent while Buckley lay dying from the attack he'd suffered defending that damn Pullman's property.

"Jennie rejoined us as we moved down the street. Jeremy, with her fantastic memory, she showed Gene *exactly* the way Pullman's books were made to look—how wages and piecework had been cut to less than a third of what they had been. Debs nodded, occasionally scribbling on a pad he'd produced. I remember his high, receding forehead dappled with perspiration on that warm afternoon.

"Afterwards, we stopped at a small cafe just outside Pullman, in Kensington. 'I'll concede,' Gene said, 'it's like a breath of fresh air to simply leave that town,' as we sat in the corner of the room.

"Then, without warning, he broke the brooding silence he'd been nursing for the last hour or so. His feelings exploded from him. George Pullman was 'an evil, hypocritical plunderer and felon,' he said, strong words from a mild-seeming person like Eugene.

"There was a kind of ominous thrill in listening to him. As soon as I heard those words and the impassioned speech that followed, I knew we were in for it—that there could be no turning back from the strike. You could all but hear the blazing rhetoric being composed in his head." Her recollections of Debs were stunning, as though his words had frozen in her mind.

"Yes, we succeeded," she repeated

"You seem almost..." Jeremy was searching for the right word.

"Guilty?"

"All right. But why *would* you feel guilty? You wanted him to learn all about Pullman, didn't you?"

"Yes, until I heard him explode sitting at that booth. He had the enthusiasm of a convert. We had all been steeped in Pullman—in everything the name and the town stood for. Yet here was an outsider with all the perfect phrases for what we'd been thinking. Until his visit, I'd have bet Eugene had even nurtured a certain admiration for George Pullman, the man. You'd be surprised at how many people still do. Gene probably thought him stuffy, maybe a typical self-made, ignorant millionaire. But until he'd experienced first-hand the calculated meanness of Pullman, he didn't appreciate all he'd heard and read. And yours truly was the one who had taken him behind those false fronts of our town and persuaded him to look closely. Pullman isn't just another town, Jeremy, but you've realized that by now, hearing me talk on so."

She reached for the water jug, tipping it up for a long drink. "I think Eugene's seeing the real living conditions and meeting Jennie Curtis that afternoon are why we're going to meet him in a jailhouse this weekend." He took the offered jug and drank, reflecting, while she told him how Debs had pledged to use his own best efforts to unite the still-reluctant A.R.U. behind the workers.

"He did return a few days later. Thousands of people gathered on the shores of Lake Calumet. Gene gave a dramatic, bitter speech about the company in general but against George Pullman personally. He called him a felon again, and a self-confessed robber. I don't know where he got that, though," she laughed. "George Pullman would never have confessed to anything!"

They were approaching a crossroads which he recognized. In years to come, it would be busy Illinois Forty-Seven, but on this summer day it was simply another dusty roadway, only slightly wider than Alden Road they were leaving.

Jeremy pulled the carriage to the side. Nearby in a field, two horses marched in a circle, hitched to a wheel which trailed them. The wheel, in its turn, was connected to some geared machine. It led to still another mechanism on a wagon where two workmen were baling hay.

"I haven't seen one of these before," Jeremy said to Lora as they stepped over to the wagon. Like so many of the 1890s machines, this seemed another marvel of complexity.

"I vow as you've never seen one of these," the farmer on the ground called over, setting down the baling wires. "Whoa." He halted the horses.

"This here's a brand new machine, only got it last week." Lora walked over and began examining the intricate reduction gear. The farmer's son, glad for a rest, grinned down from atop the wagon next to the press. Another farm hand had been feeding hay into the press.

"This contraption is supposed to do near two hundred bushels an hour, but I must be slipping because I can't be near that fast, Do you know what I paid for this thing, mister?" Jeremy wasn't about to hazard a guess.

"Why, she cost me over a hundred dollars! I'll be working it for years to pay it off. Is it any wonder why young folks like him," he pointed to his son, "can't afford to go into farming for themselves. It used to be a man could farm without all these expensive machines."

Saying goodbye, the two started back toward the carriage. The farmer called out to Jeremy. "For that old mare, there." He bent down and picked up an armful of fresh hay. "She looks like she's earned this." Magnolia contentedly chewed on the hay as they watched the operation start up again.

A short while later, they drove around the graceful little square in the center of Woodstock, staring up as they did at the brick courthouse and jail where Debs was housed. The Opera House, an improbable building to be found in a small midwestern county seat, was on their right.

"I've always wanted to come here," she said. "They get some of the best companies. Remember, though, when you register us at the

Woodstock House, I'll stay in the background. 'Mr. and Mrs.,' don't forget," she murmured as a boy took their carriage. Inside the tiny lobby, the check-in was uneventful but for a single, quick glance in Lora's direction by the green-visored clerk.

"Room Twenty-Six, sir, at the top of the stairs." He rang the bell smartly with the palm of his hand. Irritated, he pounded on the bell again and, with no one appearing, he sighed and handed Jeremy the huge brass key. "Sorry, the porter's gone off again. If you go up that stairway, it'll be the fourth room on your left."

"First," she said, fending off his hands after they had closed the door and opened the window to let in fresh air, "we've got to check at the jail for the visiting hours tomorrow."

They crossed the square to the jail where a sleepy deputy took their names. "Who is it you want to see?" he asked. When Lora answered "Eugene V. Debs", he sat up straighter.

"Ma'am, Mr. Debs isn't *at* the jail anymore."

Lora and Jeremy exchanged glances. Had he been released? Did they make the long trip for nothing? "The others has all been let go. They're back in Chicago. You folks are friends of Mr. Debs, I reckon. He's stayin' at Sheriff Eckert's house...over there."

The deputy leaned needlessly close. "You can see him tomorrow. Mr. Debs went with the sheriff over to Harvard. They won't be returnin' 'till late tonight."

"Some incarceration," Jeremy said. They had emerged into the sunlight.

"I'm glad, though. I was worried when he went to prison. There was so much hostility. I didn't know what to expect."

They crossed the square, then parted company as Lora went into J.C. Choate's store to look for fall clothes while Jeremy ambled across the park.

"I have a surprise for you," he said, hailing her an hour later as she left Choate's. He led her to an adjacent store. "J.S. Medlar, Portrait Photographer," the sign read.

"We are about to have our picture taken." He nudged her inside as she began to fuss, stopping to look at her reflection in the store window.

"What an exceptionally fine looking couple and you've come to the right studio, indeed," the tall, pale proprietor enthused.

"We'd ah, like a portrait. Something modestly priced," Jeremy suggested while Mr. Medlar opened his sample book. Lora selected a frame, keeping her ringless hand out of sight as she did.

"You and your wife will love your portrait. You step through here now, folks." Medlar pushed aside a curtain, leading them into a small, totally dark studio. They squinted, feeling ahead with their hands. He seated them on a wrought-iron bench.

The photographer busied himself, fussily sliding frames in and out and making adjustments. Finally he ducked behind the large box camera, covering himself with the drape. Jeremy began to understand why no one smiled in old photographs as Medlar again and again popped out from behind the camera, altering their position. Jeremy tried holding an exaggerated straight face even as he felt Lora's hand reach behind him. At last, Mr. Medlar asked if they were ready, lifting his wand that held the flash powder.

"No, no, *no!* " He charged out. "You *both* moved! When I say 'ready,' you must do *nothing.*" His exasperation was showing. "Ready?" They tried looking suitably stiff as the powder ignited into a mighty flash. He led them to the front of the shop.

The picture-taking behind them, they decided to dine somewhere other than the hotel. "Just a minute," Jeremy disappeared inside a small notions store. "Try this," he said, reappearing. "This will give you some peace of mind." he handed her the small brass ring.

Lora tried to work it onto her finger, screwing up her face with the effort. "It's too tight. It won't go on." She suddenly brightened, putting the ring in her mouth. Taking it out, she worked it onto her finger. "There," she held out her hand. "Getting it *off* will be the problem. Now that we've had our picture for the ages taken, let's go over and have dinner."

The meal, their first one out together, was excellent even if Raymond's Cafe was simple and small-townish. Taking their time over coffee, it was almost seven o'clock when they'd finished. During dinner, Lora had filled him in further on the strike, Debs arrest, the threats of her own imprisonment and being "furloughed" from teaching at Union school. She had been without work and forced to move back with her father. It was at this time that Eugene Debs introduced her to Clarence Darrow. In the fall of

1894 he took her on as an assistant during Debs' trial.

"My salary was small, but living at home, I could get by, and working for Darrow put me on the pulse of Eugene's case."

Jeremy saw Lora seemed to grow detached as she spoke about Darrow. "What an absolute, eccentric genius he is," she said, concluding a story about his absent-mindedness.

Leaving Raymond's, they sauntered around the square just as the opera-goers were pulling up in their carriages. Watching them, it was hard for the two to believe they were in a small, rural village. Walking hand-in-hand, they entered the square, stopping at the deserted bandstand.

"Feel like giving a fiery speech?"

"No." She leaned close and nuzzled her forehead against him. "I want to enjoy being in this pretty little park—with someone I Iove."

They sat down on one of the benches. The gas lights gave off a gentle glow in the darkness and the overture of the opera drifted through the trees. "Summer's nearly finished," Lora was somber as she faced him. "Whatever happens to us…this fall," she discarded the leaf she had been nervously rolling between her fingers. "I want you to know that the very first time we met, and then when you saw me coming home the next morning," he started to interrupt, but she put a finger to his lips.

"Shhh, let me talk. There's things I have to say."

Jeremy felt his heart drop, fearing that she was about to tell him, 'this has been fun, but let's end it,' or nineteenth century words to that effect. Lora gazed off in the direction of the Opera House, now obscured by darkness and the thick trees. She went on to recall some of their times together: his trying to hitch the wagon; their hiding in the cave under the bluff. Taking a breath, she even brought up the party.

"I'm sorry I got mad at you. Let me see that poor eye." She inspected the area of the shiner, avoiding any mention of the memory loss. If she had, he knew with the evening and his mood, he'd have told her all. Her recollections brought her to the recent apple picking morning.

"A girl needs a reason when she comes visiting, and picking apples seemed the best one I could think up."

"You never needed any reason, Lora." He felt the little brass ring on her left hand between his fingers.

Her arms were suddenly around him. "I haven't finished," she whispered. "I know you've not told me things because of your own good reasons. But whichever directions we take," she ran a hand across her eyes. "I want...I want you to know that this summer has been the very best time of my life." He started to answer, then had to stop and clear his throat. Listening to Lora, he had made up his mind.

"Do we have to part ways?" he asked, then went on before she had a chance to answer. "I haven't told you a whole lot about... my background...as it's started to come back, because it's such a long story, but it's not a bad one. There aren't any crimes in my past, nor family ties." Sometime, not that it made a difference anymore anyway, he'd tell her about his children.

"*Were* you going to tell me about yourself—someday?"

Jeremy noticed she'd discounted his amnesia. "Like why I've never ridden a horse?"

"Well, that would be a *start.*" She brushed at a tear, managing a smile.

"I'll tell you anything you want to know, only some things I might want to save."

"Oh? And for how long?"

Here goes, he thought. "I figured I'd want to save some things for, say, our fiftieth anniversary?" Her silence greeted him. He had played his hand too strong, he knew.

"Does that mean what I think it does?" she asked at last.

"It does."

"Then the answer is yes! Lord, yes!" Lora knelt up on the bench, her cheeks wet.

"Come with me." He stood, finally, and started toward the courthouse.

"Are you lost, Jeremy? Our hotel is back the other way."

"I'm not bringing an unmarried woman to any hotel." They had turned down a side street. "I'm looking for a sign I saw before...ah hah! There! "

"The Honorable Oren Weeks, Justice of the Peace. Marriages performed," the sign read.

"My God, Jeremy. Look at the time!" Lora pointed to the clock in the courthouse tower. "It's after ten o'clock."·

"The best woman I ever found isn't going to get a chance to change her mind." They stood in front of the little cottage. Jeremy rapped on the door until it was finally opened a crack. "We're here to be married."

"Yes, I know," he said as he followed the woman's glare up toward the clock. "But I hope you'll understand. We've come from Beloit, broke the axle on my wagon and had to wait all afternoon to get it fixed. We rented a hotel room in advance, thinking to be married this afternoon, before I'm to report in Chicago tomorrow. Called back to the army, ma'am." The last he said with authority.

"You did get our telegram, didn't you?" Jeremy hoped that the wire service's reliability was known to be as bad as it would be a hundred years late.

At that moment, an elderly, white-haired man appeared at the door, opening it all the way. "I'm Justice Weeks. You sure you're both sober?" He looked them over. "And you're willing to give oath you're not now married?

"Well, come on in. It's two dollars." Jeremy fished in his pocket for the fee as they were brought into a small parlor. Each was handed a pen and a printed affidavit. Justice Weeks shuffled back from the closet in his slippers, having put on his black robe. His plump wife was called over to witness the two minute ceremony, and he pronounced them man and wife, even as his eyes traveled to the ring already on the bride's finger. He had talked so rapidly that neither was sure he had finished. They stood together in awkward silence.

"Go ahead there, Slater. Don't be such a puritan. Kiss your bride while I make out the certificate." Oren Weeks shook his head, sitting down to write.

"Come here," he finally called Jeremy over, handing him the certificate. "Everything will be all right." He had lowered his voice. "Don't be so nervous." He gave the new bride an approving glance. "And you a soldier, too."

Exiting the cottage, they recrossed the square. At the little green and white pagoda, Jeremy pumped the well handle while Lora held the tin cup. As the opera's finale played in the background, they toasted their marriage. Then the bride and groom headed to the Woodstock House.

37

Yawning and laughing, Jeremy and Lora held hands in the hotel's dining room, oblivious to the malignant stares coming from the older woman at the next table. They had fallen, finally, into a deep sleep early that morning and hadn't awakened until nearly eleven.

"I tell you they *can't* be married," the woman said to her mate. "And this a respectable hotel, too. Something needs to be done about them."

The two newlyweds finished their coffee and crossed the lobby to check out. "Can we leave our bags here for a couple of hours?" Jeremy asked the clerk.

"Certainly," he said, taking payment for the room. The clerk, a different one from the day before, was about Jeremy's age and stocky with twinkly eyes that seemed to be holding back a laugh.

"Anything else?" Jeremy asked, glancing up.

"Umm, no, no sir," he answered, finally making up his mind. "Just, ahh, did you folks enjoy your stay at the hotel?" *Is he smiling?* Jeremy wondered.

"Very much," Lora said brightly, clutching her husband's arm. "We had a visit we'll always remember, Mr...?"

"Dennis Burrs, ma'am. Glad you folks enjoyed your stay." His eyes followed the couple as they walked out the door. He sighed, recalling his earlier conversation. The stern woman had stood before him, her lips pursed, her husband at her side, wishing he was at least as far away as Harvard.

"I tell you a person could not sleep with that racket going on in Number Twenty-Six. Tell him, Jonathan, you just tell him what we heard," she hissed.

"Well, it was, ahh, the bed, there was quite a bedlam." The words finally out, Jonathan smiled at his unintended pun.

"Tell him what that hussy…" she cut in before trailing off in a rage.

"They *were* quite noisy."

"I see," said Dennis, wondering at the time what the offending couple would look like. Jonathan, out of his wife's field of vision, had given him a wink before following her into the coffee shop.

Jeremy and Lora knocked on the door of the Sheriff's cottage and waited. Just as they were about to knock again, the door was drawn back and Jeremy found himself staring at a face from his history books. There was the high forehead with the thinning hair, the aquiline nose, the bow tie, high white collar and, above all, the enigmatic smile. Jeremy couldn't wait to tell Lora that no man could smile as broadly as Debs just had with his lips closed.

"Lora Lockerby," he said, stepping out on the porch and taking her hand. She introduced Jeremy as her husband and Debs warmly shook his hand. "I had no idea you were married, my dear. I seem to be so out of circulation. Well, come on in. Sheriff and Mrs. Eckert are at church services. They'll be back shortly. As you can see, I enjoy a certain amount of liberty, but I try not to be seen sitting on the front porch. Judge Woods, you know."

"Oh, dear me, Gene. Here, for you." She handed him the package. He took it, leading them through the house and out to a small back yard, surrounded by a high wooden fence. Debs offered them chairs while he opened the package.

"Hawthorne! You dear! My favorite and you thought to remember. Jeremy, it was your wife more than anyone who kept me stable during my trial. I owe her so much." Eugene disappeared inside and returned a few minutes later with a pitcher of punch and some glasses. He filled theirs, topping off his own.

"To a long and wonderful union. May you always stay as happy as you both look at this moment. And may you enjoy the happiness in marriage that I found." They touched glasses and drank. *Whoa,* thought Jeremy, *whatever this is, it packs a wallop.*

He had found the sheriff to be a noble man, Debs related, as Jeremy listened to the man's formal speech pattern. An Alsatian like himself,

Debs continued, Eckert made life as easy as possible for the seven American Railway Union prisoners. From the start, they were kept in a separate wing of the jail and were given clean, comfortable beds and good food, with their cells left open unless unwanted visitors such as U.S. marshals were present. These had to get past the sheriff and his vigilant deputies, he explained. At a preset signal, the A.R.U. men would know to close their cells, locking themselves in.

The excellent food and care were not altogether accidental, it turned out. The A.R.U. sent a draft every second week to sheriff Eckert. When the other's sentences were up, the sheriff generously let Debs move into his own home. Gene caught Lora up on the union's activities before he went back into the house, returning with an armload of letters he had received, along with drafts of his own replies. The two pored over the letters while Jeremy listened, enjoying the sun filtering through the shade on the early Sunday afternoon.

Gene had refilled their glasses and was holding up a proposed article he was sending to a paper. "I speak as a victim from a dungeon tomb, as one who loved his fellow man and dared to raise his voice to mitigate the pangs of famine in a suburb of hell known as *Pullman.'* "How does that sound, my dear?" he asked cheerfully. "Does it seem to you to strike the right note?"

"Bravo! I love that, Eugene! 'A suburb of hell!' Keep that." Lora was a revolutionary again. Listening to Debs, her eyes were glistening as though she were reliving the strike. Jeremy watched the two sipping punch and going over letters. *"I speak as a victim from a dungeon tomb."* He repeated Debs' words to himself, a smile on his face as he was seeing his bride in still another light.

Just then he heard voices from inside. The sheriff and Mrs. Eckert had apparently arrived home. "Pour me one, Gene. I swear that Reverend Robert Williamson gets longer-winded every Sunday." He waved out briefly to the new guests as he took off his tie and stepped back into the house.

"Now George," Mrs. Eckert said as she came down the steps to meet the guests. When told they they were brand new newlyweds, she poured herself a glass of punch and toasted them. "I wish you all the happiness George and I have had. I assume you've asked them to stay for dinner, Gene?"

"No? Well, I know how he gets with all those clippings and letters. You're going to stay. We're having roast stuffed chicken and I won't hear of your leaving."

When the sheriff returned, he'd shed his coat as well as rolled up his sleeves. He met the newlyweds and pulled up a chair, asking where they were from and how long they knew each other. The questions, one leading to to another, rolled on. *It must go with the territory,* Jeremy thought, *lawmen and questions.*

When Eugene heard Jeremy was from Indianapolis, he brightened, relating some of his own days working locomotives on the "Vandalia" line. "I used to fire the night train and lay over in Indianapolis." But he picked up on Jeremy's reticence before Lora could notice and deftly changed the subject.

Sheriff Eckert relaxed, stretching out his arms as he leaned back in the chair. Lora had gone inside to help Mrs. Eckert with the dinner.

"Did you know," he asked, "what a crack shot Mr. Debs is? Why yesterday we went—now mind, Mr. Slater, that you don't *tell* anyone of this—but we went up to Harvard, and on the way back we stopped to do some shooting. Any target I'd pick, Eugene would hit on the first shot. And with those eyes, too." Gene laughed and the two chatted for a minute in a foreign tongue. Jeremy got up and refilled the glasses, listening. They were speaking French.

"Don't mind us. Just a couple of Alsatians. I seldom got a chance to speak French to anyone except the wife until Gene arrived. And listen to this," the sheriff said to Jeremy, and he began to detail how Debs had accompanied him to Harvard. He'd gone seeking information on some thefts and robberies near Woodstock. Similar acts had been taking place near Harvard.

"When we talked to the local constable, he told us about the crimes—tools being stolen. Eugene began asking him questions in that quiet, reserved voice. Before I knew it, he had unfolded a pattern the same as we talked about," Eckert slapped his leg, laughing at the memory as he lifted his punch glass.

"You know what that constable said? He took me aside, 'George, that Dawson fella', that's how I'd introduced Gene, 'he's a first class deputy, don't lose him.' Can you imagine Eugene Debs the lawman? As a matter of fact, though, Gene," he paused, "you *would* make a first class deputy."

Debs slowly shook his head. "I'd once thought of it, but you know my first love, George."

Jeremy squinted into the sun, letting his mind wander as Eckert and Debs talked. *Here I am, in Woodstock in 1895. I've become a new bridegroom and I'm sitting here with Eugene Debs and a local sheriff. I may not be dreaming, but I am getting hammered on this punch.*

Mrs. Eckert called then in for dinner. They gathered around the big dining room table for grace, said in French by the sheriff.

"Mrs. Eckert is giving me some new recipes, darling, but I surely won't promise you anything like this."

"Just keep baking apple pies like you do," he said, taking a kick under the table from his bride.

The afternoon passed quickly, thanks to the sun, the food and the punch, until Lora spoke up, realizing the time. They said their goodbyes. "November 22d, Lora," Eugene noted at the door, shaking Jeremy's hand warmly. "Remember the date. I'll be released and returned to Chicago."

They retrieved their carriage and headed toward home. "My husband. My husband. Let me just listen to the wonderful sound of those words," Lora rested her head on his shoulder.

As they turned down Alden Road, Lora straightened up. "Darling, I forgot to ask you one thing. Will you take me across the lake with you tomorrow? I won't go to the Observatory; I'll stay in Williams Bay and shop and such." She paused. "Do you...remember when I saw constable Lowery before? When you took me out to the Observatory? I had a terrible feeling that I knew him, but I need to see him up close to be sure."

"Lowery? Where could you have known that brute from?'

"I'll tell you tomorrow afternoon if I'm right."

Jeremy started to tell her that he had no intention of letting his wife anywhere near Lowery. "Don't worry," she answered. "He doesn't know *me,* and she squeezed herself next to him, shaking her head at any more questions he tried to ask.

"Tomorrow, dearest," she replied, her head beginning to grow heavy against his shoulder while their carriage clattered along in the moonlight.

38

There was no sight of Lora and Jeremy was worried. She had ridden over with him in the morning to do her detective work. Up and down the street and across at the depot, the usual number of coachmen were standing idly about the carriages, joined by mates from the yachts, waiting for their employers to arrive on the evening trains.

Bill spotted Jeremy and walked over, waiting until they stood together before he spoke. "You're even a luckier bloke than I thought. I met your bride this afternoon. I knew Miss Lockerby—I guess I mean Mrs. Slater—before. Quite some caretaker *you* are."

"Where is she, Bill?" At any other time Jeremy would have taken the kidding, but he had to find her. Bill led them across the road until they stopped on the shore in front of the *Dora*, her mooring lines creaking loudly, straining to hold the big yacht to the dock.

"She told me to tell you she'd be waiting out on your launch. It ain't none of my business, but you didn't send her to watch after Lowery, did you?"

"Of course not. It was her idea. She thought she'd seen him before. Is she all right?"

"Oh, yeah, she's fine. I saw her this morning. It was after you'd gone up the hill. Then this afternoon, when I was out on the platform, she came up to me. 'Bill,' she said, 'do me a favor, please. I'll be waiting down in our boat. Keep a lookout for Jeremy,' and then she told me you two were married. I started to congratulate her, but she pulled on my sleeve.

"At first I thought she wanted to surprise you, but she kept glancing up the road toward town, all nervous-like. 'It's about constable Lowery, Bill. Don't say anything to anyone but Jeremy. Thank you,' and she was

276

off."

"How long ago?"

"About thirty or forty minutes. She's in the boat right now." Bill hadn't once looked in the direction of the *Lora L* while they talked.

Jeremy walked to the pier, checking up and down the road for Lowery. "Lora," he called as he stepped next to the launch. The canvas parted a few inches.

"Get in and cast off. I don't want to be seen." He started the boat and backed away.

"Do you want to tell me about this?" he asked, directing his voice to the canvas curtains. After a few minutes, she pulled them back.

"I saw him," she said, raising her voice over the engine as she watched the incoming commuter train. He throttled the engine down to a low hum.

"It took me a while to find him. After you left for work, I walked over to Williams's store. Incidentally, I had to buy this," she took a blouse from her bag and held it up. Do you like it?" His shrug was noncommittal.

"I don't care for it, either, but I had to get *something* for all the time I'd spent there."

She held onto a stanchion with one hand. "It took me a while to find him. I knew the snoop would be around though, and sure enough, he came by the store at about ten o'clock. I trusted he hadn't had a good enough look at me the day I was in the wagon with you to remember my face.

"I followed him down the street back to the depot, where he met the eleven o'clock. I stayed across the street by the main dock. He paced up and down the platform. After the train had pulled ahead to the yard, he went back toward the crossroads. I still needed a closer look, so when I got up my nerve, I followed and called out to him. He walked over to me and I invented a question, asking him where the Jewell boat works was.

"He studied me so closely that for an instant I thought he'd remembered me. Of course he couldn't have, but I almost thought I saw a flicker of recognition. He gave me a terrible forced smile and said he'd walk me there. By then I'd seen him up close enough: those heavy eyebrows, the small, beady eyes. But mostly that scar on his right cheek—his beard only partly covers it. I gushed on, telling him I wanted to see a yacht.

"Now I just know you're so busy, officer, if you'd only point me in the right direction...I could find the way." He did walk me another half block or so. I wondered if he noticed me glancing at the right side of his face. Finally, he pointed out the boat yard and I broke away, thanking him like some simpering fool. I could actually feel his eyes bore into my back as I walked.

"At the boat works, I looked around, asking silly questions and pretending to be helping my husband decide on a yacht. When I felt I'd stayed as long as I dared, I came back to the store to wait until you returned.

"Jeremy," she pulled him close. "I know him. His name is Stark." Even out in the middle of the lake she lowered her voice. "I'll remember that face as long as I live. He's a murderer! During the strike, he killed Bill Anslyn right in cold blood."

Jeremy felt the muscles in his own stomach knotting as he listened. *This has something to do with why he's been so hostile toward me, I'm going to learn.* "He's not anyone named Lowery. He took that name and whatever he told you was a lie.

"Stark was a railroad detective. He'd been deputized as a U.S. marshal during the strike. God only knows what sort of thuggery he was up to before that. It was July 5th," she continued. She and others on the Strike Relief Committee were at the headquarters with Reverend Carwardine. It was the night after the huge fires, when most of the World's Fair buildings had been set afire and everyone was feeling very down.

After the meeting, they had been working on food bundles when word came of some trouble; there had been vandalism at the Kensington station. The Reverend swore under his breath and they hurried outside toward the station.

" 'Look at those hoodlums,' he murmured. 'They're more of the rabble that's been drifting around town, looting and starting fires.'

"They must have been keeping the stalled train from passing. The only Pullman people," she said, "were gathered like us, looking on.

"Suddenly, a group of those so-called deputy marshals swept down from the north, shouting to disperse. Reverend Bill, myself and all the rest had started back to Pullman when we heard a shot ring out. It was fired from one of those marshals. Bill Anslyn was hit by the bullet. He wasn't part of any mob, he was just standing across the way from the sta-

278

tion, not twenty feet from us. In fact, he wasn't even a striker. Bill was a Pullman foreman himself, but well liked by the men. The Reverend pulled me to the ground. The next thing I knew, right near me two more shots went off.

"After he fired, I'll never forget how he turned over our way. I stared straight into that monster's face. He stumbled back, keeping the gun pointed at us. By this time, the police had arrived, and together with the other marshals, they kept the crowd back and got him away.

"I bent down over Anslyn. His little boy had been one of my students, and I knew Bill from conferences at the school. He tried to speak while the Reverend held his hand. Bill was in the most terrible pain. 'Why... why shoot?' was all he could manage to say—weak and muffled. I still see that tortured look on his face before he passed out. They put him on a stretcher and took him to the hospital, but I knew he was a goner."

Jeremy eased the launch into its berth. They sat at the end of the pier. "Those of us who saw the cold-blooded shooting were joined by dozens who'd heard the shots and had streamed over from Pullman. Until then, the strikers hadn't committed any act of violence. But Reverend Bill knew that a murder by one of those hated marshals was exactly the spark that would light the fires of rage and sweep us all up.

"We marched down to the Kensington police station where he went inside. The crowd was sullen and getting meaner—and bigger—by the minute. I don't know where all they'd appeared from, but many of the men had brought clubs and bricks with them, and they were shouting and cursing at the police, demanding that the marshals come outside. The police brandished their pistols, forcing us back. Jeremy, all I could think of was the Haymarket riot, how shots rang out and some police fell."

He put his arm around his bride. Everything Lora had told him before about the strike and boycott was driven home. He wished he could have known her then and been a part of her struggle. Debs' rhetoric that had seemed almost playful over in Woodstock suddenly vaulted alive, sweeping Jeremy up in the emotions of the strike.

"Finally, Reverend Bill came back out," she continued, "and he announced that Bill Anslyn had been taken to the hospital and was being attended to. He said that any violence on our part would only hurt our cause and play into management's hands.

"As we started back to Pullman, he called me over. I told him what a fine job he'd done, but we were both still shattered over Anslyn's shooting.

" 'A fine job at the risk of my word,' he said, glancing around to see that no one was listening. 'He's in custody, all right, but I don't believe for one minute that they're going to indict him or even keep him. Those police weren't the least bit interested in getting a list of witnesses! He'll no doubt be spirited away. It seems that law and order down here only work in one direction, Lora. I hope I'm wrong, but we'll see.'

"He *wasn't* wrong, of course. The police just bluffed us for two days, while poor Anslyn lay in the hospital, dying. Days later, they finally admitted that Stark—they only then gave out his name—had been taken away by federal authorities."

"And nothing was done?" Jeremy was furious, feeling her frustration. They had begun climbing the steps of the bluff.

"Oh, we tried. First, they said there was a lack of evidence. Can you imagine that? With the weapon, the murder victim and God knows how many eye witnesses. Then, later, they came on with something about federal supremacy, that Stark was acting as a federal officer, protecting mail that was supposed to have been on the train." She'd tightened her lips, the old bitterness returned.

"Clarence later told me he'd found out from friends on the Chicago police force that the U.S. Attorney's office had once again meddled, forcing the police to turn Stark over. They said it would destroy faith in the government for him to be tried, as though a *murder* in front of our eyes hadn't rocked our faith!"

They had drawn in front of the main house. "You've got to promise me something. I'll be leaving here on Sunday and you'll only be staying a few more weeks yourself. *Please* don't tangle with him. He's a cold-blooded murderer! There's nothing he wouldn't do! That's why I waited for you in the boat. I don't want him to put us together.

"When we're back in Chicago we can furnish his whereabouts to… someone. Clarence is running down a tip—it's either from the police or labor sources that Stark may be wanted himself—from some other state. You were right about something, though. He is still very nervous. And that only makes him more dangerous. " Lora put her arm out and stopped him. "You must understand, love. Say nothing to him. Don't have anything to do with him. Do you promise me?" She was looking straight into his eyes, genuine fear on her face.

"Darling, stop worrying. You know I've been trying to keep my distance from that fellow all summer."

39

Their last two days together passed all too quickly. Work at the Observatory had begun getting back on schedule. Lora continued toiling on her lesson plans. Her rustiness at being away from teaching was fading and her confidence was buoyed by Jeremy's praise.

On Thursday evening, they crossed the lake to meet Paul and Martha. With her sister recovered, Martha had gone to Chicago from Racine and she and Paul were returning to Bluffside together. After their arrival, Jeremy walked with Paul, bringing him up to date on the work.

Once they were out on Williams Bay, Paul glanced quizzically at the two, standing close together. "There is something we aren't hearing, Martha," he said.

"Well, I know Miz' Lora's got that same look she had as a little girl, when she'd stole some cookies. Whatever are you keepin' back, Miz' Lora?"

Lora looked to Jeremy, then shrugged as a blush crossed her face. "Only that in the first place, it's no longer Miss, it's *Mrs*. Father, I hope you won't be too upset at our surprise—Jeremy and I got married last Saturday. We wanted to wait until we got to the house to tell you, but I guess we couldn't keep our secret." Paul swept his daughter into his arms while Jeremy and Martha embraced.

"My little girl. You know, I've come to know this fellow you're married to...*married to?* I can see I'm going to have to get used to saying that. I think you've made the right decision, darlin'." He held his hand out to Jeremy.

At the house, they stepped into the living room. "Lord! I go away for a couple of weeks and look what happens," Martha cried. "You all sit right

282

down and wait while I put on a celebration dinner."

Maybe it's me, Jeremy thought, *but this house seems different, less formal.* Once again, he was grateful to Paul for his acceptance.

"I'm going to talk to Clarence," Lora told her father at dinner. "His firm's expanding and no one's filled *my* old job yet. I'm hopeful he can use Jeremy." At the end of the evening, Lora and Jeremy left for their own little cottage.

Word of the marriage spread fast. Frank and Charlotte insisted on a small gathering of their friends at Kaye's on Saturday evening, the park's last night of the season. Lora would be leaving for Chicago and the big Labor Day rally the following day.

They walked to Kaye's, taking the shore path from Black Point. At Villa Thekla, they picked up Victoria and Dan Cerny. Lora and Dan walked on ahead. Victoria slipped her arm into Jeremy's as they neared the brightly lit resort.

She stopped in front of the entrance pillars. "It seems only a few weeks ago that I met Lora at this very spot. It's hard to believe she's beaten Charlotte and me both to the altar. I remember asking her if she'd met her new mystery man-caretaker yet. Jeremy, please, always keep her as happy as I see her right now. And…no more black eyes, promise?"

"It's a promise. No more black eyes, Victoria."

Their group was down to six as they joined Frank and Charlotte at the bandstand. Like so many of the other summer residents, the Allertons and Strongs had already closed up and returned to the city. The sounds of waltzes and lively polkas filled the air as the final night went by all too quickly.

"Does it seem like yesterday that we were here, Lora?" Frank asked. They had rotated partners and he was guiding her across the dance floor. She nodded, suddenly steering them out of the way of another couple, an older man trying to keep up with his youthful dancing partner, inventing his own version of the polka as he moved.

"Jeremy's put a glow on your face that wasn't there on our last visit here. And I'm telling you that even though Todd's been my friend for years. The two of us aren't alike at all, but I'm going to miss his company." Frank glided her off the dance floor.

Their table was empty. The others were still out dancing. "You and

Todd wouldn't have been right at all," he continued. "You're too smart, and Todd is...well...Todd. There'll be a girl, or girls, for him."

Lora asked if Frank had heard from Todd since he'd gone to Seattle. "That's something I wanted to tell you. Don't worry yourself about him as you begin your new life. With that 'loan' he managed from Aunt Harriet, he's already started his new venture. I got a letter from him yesterday. By next summer he'll have three ferry boats going between Seattle and Vancouver Island, and if there's one thing he can do, it's handle anything that floats, provided he can stay sober enough."

"I'm glad to hear he's done so well, Frank, and in so short a time." Lora's heart was full and she wanted only happiness for Todd.

"That wasn't all. I know he left you a note, but he also told me to wish you well. He really was sorry about the party." She knew from his note that Todd had taken full blame for the fight. The others, flushed from dancing, were making their way toward the table.

"He said he'd always be in love with you...and to tell you as well that he was taking swimming lessons." Frank frowned. "I don't know what the devil he meant, not that he couldn't use the lessons."

"I do," Lora said. "It's private."

None of the dancers in the pavilion wanted to leave, as though they could postpone summer's end by drawing out the night. "Last number of our season, coming up, ladies and gentlemen," the band director said, as his musicians struck up "Sidewalks of New York."

"Happy Anniversary," Jeremy whispered as he held Lora close on the tightly packed dance floor. "One week."

During the night, he awoke and heard Lora in the bathroom. "I'll be all right," she said woozily as she tottered back to bed. "It was something from dinner." He wasn't sure, but he thought he heard her being sick again later on. She seemed better in the morning. "Just some nausea that went away. Nothing, darling," and she passed it off.

Sunday would be their last day together at Lake Geneva and also their first physical parting since the wedding. Lora was going back to Chicago to start her new job on Tuesday. Jeremy would stay out at Bluffside, finish up at the Observatory and return to Chicago on October 1st.

They were both quiet in the morning, feeling the coming separation. At the main house, Martha had made a huge breakfast. They sat down and, a moment later after looking at the food, Lora got up and stepped into the kitchen. She returned with a cup of milky tea and to pick at some toast.

Lora's trunk had already been sent ahead and she and Martha disappeared upstairs to finish packing. When they reappeared with her two grips, Jeremy placed them out on the veranda. The two walked across the lawn. "I never *did* get around to weeding these flower beds like I should have, and that's all your fault, distracting your caretaker so."

Lora and Jeremy stood together on the bluff, at the same spot where she had brought out their first breakfast on that dewy June morning, and from where they'd watched the *Dispatch* disappear beneath the waves. The large, temporary dome of the Observatory was now visible above the trees across the lake.

Jeremy carried her luggage down to the launch. Afterward, hand-in-hand, they followed along the shore path to the Black Point lagoon. They sat near the unattended drawbridge. The lagoon, filled all summer long with yachts and boats of every description, was nearly deserted. The *Lorely* had been stored. Only the *Rambler*, a squat, homemade little steamer and two or three rowboats remained. Lora picked up a small stone and tossed it out into the lagoon. It made a "ploop" sound as it hit the still, dark water. A dryness in the warm air marked the passing of summer.

It was just three months ago, he remembered, as he leaned back on the grass, that he and Paul had come through the storm's high waves, and had found a haven here in the lagoon. He reached for his mate's hand, the hand of the person he hadn't even known when he'd first come through that drawbridge.

"Happy?"

"Never happier," Lora answered. "A little sad at leaving you and Black Point. But aren't I being silly?" She glanced around, then leaned over, kissing him. "We're going to have a whole lifetime of summers here."

They talked quietly about their future while the sun began to draw lower in the sky. Finally, they stood and walked back to the house, saying goodbye to Paul and Martha and hurrying across the lake to Lora's train which was standing at the depot.

A large gathering was already on the platform. Summer residents with their servants and extra railroad porters busily loading trunks and assorted summer effects into baggage cars were milling about. Lora waved to a family she recognized. Last-minute tourists, out to make up for whatever had kept them in the city all summer also joined the throng. The newly-weds stood together, reluctant to part if only for a few weeks. At last, the baggage loaded, people began to stream aboard the coaches.

"I'll see Clarence tomorrow at the rally. I've got my fingers crossed he'll have a job for you, darling. I'll write the very minute I know. They held tightly to each other.

"All aboard, folks," the conductor called softly as a blast of steam escaped from the locomotive ahead. Lora kissed him, pressing herself close. He felt her tremble. "You promised me you'd avoid Stark. Don't break that promise because remember, you're the person I'm going to grow old with." She hurried onto the train.

Across from the depot and down the shore road, the constable, standing at the rear of a wagon, had been intently watching the parting. As Lora entered the coach, he turned and without any visible expression strode away, disappearing into the woods that bordered the railroad.

40

September 27th, 1895...

Paul had already bid his workmen goodbye and he and Martha had left the previous Thursday. Tommy Napper called Jeremy over to his window after their train had departed. With the summer season ended, Tommy was now doubling as postmaster. He handed over two letters. The first was from Lora. The other, a thin envelope, was marked "C. Darrow, 209 South LaSalle Street, Chicago," on the back. Jeremy sat down on the platform, tearing open the letter. He'd been recommended, it said, "to clerk in the offices of Collins, Goodrich, Vincent & Darrow, and the recommendation having been acted on, would he kindly present himself to start work on October 3, 1895. "Cordially," it was signed, "Clarence Darrow."

So I'm hired! She did it! And to start in a week with Clarence Darrow! He hitched a ride on one of the few wagons still going out to the Observatory and sat at the rear by himself, reading Lora's letter. It had been mailed a day earlier than Darrow's. She wrote she'd gone to see Clarence, telling him all about her new husband and his desire to clerk as a way to approach the bar exams.

"He listened," she went on, "seeming noncommittal, but sometimes that's his way. He said he had to take it up with his partners and so on. Darling," she'd correctly predicted, "I'm sure you'll be chosen." She described her own first week at the Art Institute—how she loved it. Setting up a new program was demanding but exciting and she was working in such a beautiful, brand-new building. She couldn't wait to show him around.

Rob Allerton had already dropped by and she had also run into an old friend and neighbor from Pullman, Jeanette Reilley, who was modeling for the life classes. *A model for the life classes? Lora had never mentioned this "old neighbor."*

On the last page of her letter, in her elaborate, back-handed script, she advised, "Tear up this part after you've read it," and she went on to write just how much he was loved and missed, and what was in store for him when they were reunited. At the very bottom she said she also might, she wasn't sure, have a little surprise for him. He did as she asked, tearing up the page after many re-readings.

On Saturday morning, he stopped over at the Lefens to say goodbye. Theis was standing on the porch. Jeremy learned that Mrs. Lefens and the children had already gone back, and Theis would be leaving by carriage that afternoon. Their conversation drifted back to the *Dispatch's* sinking. Little Marie had rebounded from the tragedy, Theis thought, though he was sure she'd carry the memory throughout her life.

"Marie's a sweet girl," Jeremy said, "And tell her I want her to study hard this year. Theis, I'll let you finish up your packing. I know you have a long trip, and I'll be glad to close up and leave myself, what with all these goodbyes." The two were walking slowly down the Lefens' mani- cured, formal driveway. With the exception of some stray leaves, it looked as it had all summer.

"Jeremy," Theis had stopped. "This is your first summer here. Take it from me; 'helloes' and 'goodbyes' are a part of owning a summer house and we're going to be bidding them to each other for years to come."

Jeremy went into the town of Lake Geneva on Sunday to say goodbye to Doctor Malcolm. He stood in the hall, waiting while Malcolm went in for a jacket. The door to the office was open and he entered. The examin- ing table he'd been on last May looked the same. The medicinal smell still came from the glass cabinet. On the wall was the calendar that had given him such a start.

"Isn't this about where you awakened after your accident?" the doctor asked as they walked along through the lakefront park.

"Over there." Jeremy pointed ahead. They stopped by the little forked tree.

"Has any more come back?" Malcolm watched his friend close his eyes tightly and then open them, looking intently up the hill where he had been coming from before his accident.

"It has," he said. They were turning back toward Malcolm's house. "It's quite a story. If you can wait until next spring, I'll be ready to tell you, though I'm not sure you'll believe me."

"Oh, I think I will," the doctor said as they parted.

On September 30th, his last day of work, Jeremy tied up the launch for the final time and strolled past the depot, enjoying the crisp, fall day. No one was in sight; Bill Wheeler had closed up his operation in the freight shed and gone. Finding no ride waiting, he shrugged and began walking up the hill. At first, he didn't see Lowery who'd stepped out from between two buildings and was standing in the middle of the road.

"God damn it to hell!" he muttered to himself. "My last day of work and I have to meet *this* guy."

"You'll be leaving I suppose, Slater?" Jeremy had tried being diffident to Lowery during the latter part of the summer, but today he had no desire to talk to him at all.

"As soon as I can," he answered, brushing by.

"Just a minute," Lowery growled. "You'd better know..." he drew close, so close his head was almost in Jeremy's face, so close that he could clearly see the scar running underneath. "I'll be here when you come back. So you think on that."

It's incredible, Jeremy thought, *here a whole summer has gone by, and yet he doesn't let up. Lowery's been hostile to all the Observatory workers, but he reserves some special venom, strangely, for me.*

Is it because I've stood up to him, or maybe something I've shown by my expression? I don't even care anymore. Thank God I'm leaving.

"And I bet you'll be back too, now that you've landed yourself the boss' daughter for a wife." Jeremy checked his temper even as he felt his face coloring.

"It surprised me, though," Lowery was taunting, standing out in the road, not moving, a sneer spreading across his face, "that Lockerby would let some drifter pluck that ripe little girl of his."

As soon as Jeremy had answered Lowery, he realized too late what a mistake he'd made—as well as having forgotten his promise to Lora to keep his mouth shut.

"My roots might be shallow, but I'll put them up against yours, *Mr.*

Stark."

When he saw the immediate effect that the name had on the constable, he knew Lora had the right person, which also meant he *was* the killer. Stark's eyes narrowed still further. His face was consumed with fury…but something else was there, too; a hint of fear? His lips twitched for a second or two and then formed a tight smile.

"I always knew you were too smart for your own good. And you sure aren't some drifter either, are you. But why did it take you so long to let on?"

Jeremy was in very deep trouble, he knew. And he cursed himself, knowing he'd been only hours from a getaway. Sweat was running down his back even on the cool day. He glanced up and down the street. Except for a single rider far in the distance, there wasn't a soul out. The entire town was deserted. The constable, exaggerating his movements, confident of himself again, slowly reached under his uniform coat. Jeremy was sure he kept a pistol in his belt.

This is crazy, he won't shoot me here in broad daylight. And then he remembered Lora's words. This would be the very same person who had fired into a crowd of spectators, hitting one and had then walked up and calmly shot two more bullets into the wounded, pleading man in front of that crowd. And he suddenly recalled Lowery's—Stark's—other words about putting a bullet into that prisoner's stomach and how he'd said that the man had to beg him for the second one.

"I'm going to give you a running start, Slater," he said, his hand out of sight but obviously on the handle of the gun. He was taking his time, enjoying the effect he was having on Jeremy. "I knew right away, the first time I laid eyes on you—you didn't fit in. I notice things like that. Debs put you up here, didn't he? I put that together when I found out Lockerby's daughter was one of his labor cohorts. And that surprised me, too. Well, your death is going to be a nice, fitting message for him and his band of troublemakers."

"I wouldn't do what you're about to do, Stark," he said, watching the hand inside the coat, hearing the shake in his voice. The adrenalin was pumping and a desperate idea was forming. He had no choice. If he ran, it would give Stark an explanation. He'd shot a fugitive, he'd say, and he'd likely slip a knife and some contraband into Jeremy's lifeless hand for the sake of appearance.

"I've left written, sealed instructions with three different people—Judge Seaver for one—that if anything happens to me they are to be opened. And in the letter I tell who you are, what you did, and *if* anything happens to me, 'who to see.' "

The last phrase really meant nothing, but he spit it out, hoping to add some mystery. A fraction of hesitation appeared on Stark's face. And then he heard the most welcome sound of his life. A wagon behind two wild horses was hurtling out of control down the hill, careening from side to side as it came into view.

The horses had gotten up a head of steam, and the driver, contrary to orders, must not have held them back on the hill. Both stared up at the team charging down on them. Jeremy saw that Jim Keane was atop the wagon, pulling on the reins with one hand, the other futilely on the brake. Jeremy and Stark dove in opposite directions as the wagon, its wheels locked, went by in a cloud of dust.

Jeremy rolled over into the gutter, tasting the dirt, trying desperately to scramble to his feet before Stark.

"Jim!" he called, then raced toward the wagon which had come to a stop down the road. As he reached it, he glanced back over his shoulder, ready to jump on and tell Jim to take off. But Stark was just getting up, slapping the dust off himself, his blue serge uniform now a dusty gray.

He yelled over to Keane, swearing at him to watch his driving or he'd be locked up. Then he regarded Jeremy fiercely for a long moment. He started off in the opposite way, his limp now prominent.

"I expected worse from him," Jim said.

"We just had some words," Jeremy gasped, his breath still coming in pants. "But let me tell you, I'm glad you came along, even if you almost killed me." He hoisted himself onto the seat. "He was going to shoot me," he said, drawing in a deep breath.

"Shoot you?" Keane exclaimed, turning quickly to watch the retreating constable. "And you run over to me? Thanks! Whatever did you say? I never saw that son-of-a-bitch walk away from *anything* before."

"I'll tell you in return for a ride out to the Observatory. I don't feel like bumping into him again." They drove down to the depot, where Jim delivered some motor parts for return to Cleveland.

"Your last day and you pull a wrangle with him," Jim shook his head. They had started up the hill, both warily looking for the constable. "All right, tell me your story and it better be good."

He did, or at least the outlines of what Lora had told him. Jeremy said *he'd* recognized the constable as the murderer, leaving Lora out of the narrative. "I know I won't win any prizes for brains getting into it with him, but I lost my temper."

They turned down the Observatory drive, still on guard even if Stark was nowhere to be seen. "I hear from Paul, you're staying out here over the winter to look after our machinery," Jeremy said as they jumped down from the wagon and headed toward the power station.

"I wanted to work on the Rockford lighting project, but we wouldn't trust any of these muddle-headed dolts to look after our stuff over the winter." Jeremy knew Paul and Jim had been discussing the problems. Both were dubious about letting anyone else have charge over the delicate electrical machinery.

"I won't mind staying out here as much now. Remember Tilly O'Neill? I've been courting her. But now I suppose I'll be looking over my shoulder for the constable."

"Just don't let him get your temper. Lowery never had it in for you like he did me." He fell silent as he glanced down at the dynamo, knowing he'd seen or checked in nearly every piece of it. He'd literally watched it grow over the summer, now realizing what a modern piece of machinery it was. A hundred years later there would be countless similar generators performing routinely.

Jeremy had witnessed a part of the passage of the bulky, awkward machines of the nineteenth century, some laughable and others, like the baler he and Lora had seen near Woodstock, ingenious. The use of such great amounts of manpower and horses, like this very Observatory project, would soon be history.

The two walked back out in front of the main building. Yerkes Observatory now had a very finished look—nothing like the site in the spring, which was little more than a hole and a foundation. But for its newness, it looked to Jeremy almost as it had when he'd brought his son Danny to visit.

"If you wait, I'll finish up my work at the power station and give you a ride back to town, though I'll put a tarpaulin over you to hide you." Jeremy was about to accept his offer, when he heard his name called out. The voice came from a covered delivery van from Williams's store. Earl,

Mrs. Ingall's son, was beaming down from the driver's seat.

"Look at the job ah' got. Made a delivery up the hill and thought ah'd see if you was still around."

"Your timing is perfect, Earl. If you're going back, I'd be obliged for a ride," Jeremy said, and as Earl waved him up, moving over to make room for him, Jeremy turned to Jim Keane. "The less seen with me the better off for you. I'll be back next spring to check up on you." He climbed up onto the seat, calling back to Jim as the big wagon clattered down the driveway. "Maybe by then you'll have joined the ranks of married men, though you probably still won't know how to control a team of horses."

As they turned out of the drive, he told Earl that this was his final day. "You were nice to me," Earl finally said, "never teased me or nothin' like the other boarders." he paused, forming his thoughts. "The constable was back after you moved out of the house. He asked after you."

"Can you remember what he asked?" Jeremy was scanning the road as they descended the hill into town.

"He wanted to know did ah find any cards or papers of yours. 'Your momma told me you sometimes find things and hide them, Earl. Did you?' Ah *said* ah didn'. You don't like him, do you, Jeremy?"

"No, I don't, Earl," Jeremy allowed himself a laugh, "and for sure he doesn't like me."

"There's somethin' else ah wanted to tell you." Jeremy nodded, listening. "One night, a long time ago, you left the house. Ah followed you out to the Observatory grounds, and kept back in the trees, so's you wouldn't see me. Ah can keep out o' sight better'n anyone. Ah saw you go into the shed. It was gettin' cold." Jeremy listened, remembering very well the raw spring night. "And ah was about to leave when you came out. Ah stayed back," his narrative slowed as he found difficulty remembering.

"Did you see me dig?"

"Oh, yeah," he beamed, "you dug way down. Ah thought to help you, but figgered you might get scairt o' me. Sometimes people do. You picked up the jar you carried out o' the shack and set it in the hole. Then you buried it real careful."

"Did you dig the jar up, Earl?"

"No, no sir! Ah never dug it up."

"Thank you. Can you keep it to yourself if I tell you what's in there?" Earl nodded solemnly, pulling the wagon up opposite the depot.

"When I learned about your mother finding my things," he spoke slowly, choosing the simplest words. "I decided to bury some things which meant a lot to me. These things aren't valuable like money or jewels. There were some papers I'd had and some photographs of my children."

"Where are your children?"

"They're a long way off. I don't believe I'll ever see them again, Earl. I buried those things because I didn't want the constable, or anyone, to take them from me."

"Do you miss your children?"

"Yes, very much." He was turned away, looking out across the bay.

"Ah hope you see 'em, and don't worry—ah'll never dig up what you put in the ground." Jeremy patted Earl's shoulder, stepping down to the roadside.

"Wait." Earl was struggling with a thought. "Ah didn't really tell the constable the truth. When he asked me if ah had anything o' yours..." and he fished deep into the pocket of his overalls. With difficulty he found what he was looking for and lifted it out.

"Here," he said. Earl thrust the missing "Visa" card at Jeremy. He gazed down at the blue and white card in his hand. He had been living in 1895 for more than four months, a time in which he'd made friends, dodged questions he couldn't have answered, witnessed a disaster; had even found love and marriage. He slowly turned the card over in his palm, rubbing the surface. The plastic card felt foreign. The name on the card said "Jeremy Sloan." His real name even looked strange. He handed the card back.

"Keep it Earl. You can remember me with it."

"Ah sure will," Earl shoved the card back into his pocket. "Goodbye Jeremy, and thank you," he called as he slapped the reins and drove off.

Jeremy started across the road. Tommy Napper saw him and came out of the depot. "Gotta talk to you," the station agent waved him over. "Do you know *what?* Your friend Lowery came through here before noon, no uniform on and carrying a suitcase and an old bulging box, looking like I never saw him look before. He bought a ticket for Chicago."

"Did he buy it through for anywhere else?"

"No, but that's strange," Tommy said, studying Jeremy, "because he asked a lot of questions about connections and how he could get out east.

He sent me looking through my train schedules to try to find information. And do you know? That man was *nervous*. He paced up and down while I was checking schedules. When I glanced up, I'd see him staring down at the yard. 'Why don't they get that damn train down here?' "
Tommy mocked the constable's growl.

" 'Gene,' " I said, " 'you know that engine just barely got in here. They've got to water and coal her and turn 'er around.' Anyway, he kept pacing up and down until the train eased in. I'll tell you that man was running from something," he suddenly paused in his narrative. "Jeremy Slater, you *know* something about all this, don't you?"

Jeremy allowed himself a broad grin. "I think Williams Bay has seen the last of its constable." That night, his final one at Bluffside, he slept soundly.

The next morning he closed up the house, covering the furniture, draining the pipes and disconnecting the little generator. He took a last quick look around. He'd had enough nostalgia, and was anxious to get to Chicago to rejoin his wife and start their new life.

During the trip across the lake, the *Lora L's* throttle stuck, causing the engine to race. Jeremy eased off and adjusted it. The same thing had happened a couple of times before, during the last two weeks, but he thought he'd corrected it. He made a mental note to tell Ben at the boat yard.

The Jewell boat works was the only busy place remaining on the lake on October 1st. Workmen and horses were hauling yachts up the greased timbers to their winter storage sheds. Smaller boats were lined up along shore in a row.

He spotted Ben and turned the *Lora L* over to him, then hurried along the shore path, the old grip swinging at his side. He bought a ticket, saying a quick goodbye to Tommy Napper and promising to see him next spring.

It wasn't until he'd settled back, relaxing with the train's motion, that he remembered he hadn't told Ben about the stuck throttle. *They'll probably notice it anyway,* he thought, and he'd drop a note later on. He turned his attention out the window to the passing red and gold autumn scenery.

41

Jeremy and Lora had gone downtown early and were finishing breakfast at the little restaurant on Adams.

"Now don't be so nervous," she said. She flicked a stray crumb from the corner of his mouth with her napkin. "Besides, I told you Clarence was very easy-going and natural. You'll get along fine." He paid the check, and they walked into the autumn morning.

"Are you sure you can spare the time?" he asked.

"Stop worrying. It's only eight-thirty and my first class isn't until eleven. And I'm only four blocks from the Art Institute." They turned the corner and stood looking up at the Rookery Building. Many of the windows were open on this morning, and clerks and secretaries were busily cranking out the awnings.

Jeremy had offices in this very same building for eight years, and had only given them up when all tenants were required to vacate in order that the building be restored to its original condition—just as it now looked. Lora mistook his silent studying of the familiar facade for apprehension, and she squeezed his hand as she led him inside.

The lobby too, looked much the same as he remembered it, only it was now more accentuated with the open skylight. He couldn't recall that. It must have gotten covered up in the intervening years. Jeremy took in the open stairways with their filigreed iron railings, the same stairs he'd dashed down when he was late for court, not waiting for the erratic elevators.

"Isn't it beautiful?" she asked, taking in the lobby. "I don't think I really appreciated it when I worked here. Now just tell me you have buildings in Indianapolis like this."

"Oh, dozens and dozens of them," he said softly, overcome with an emotion he couldn't quite pinpoint—regret, homesickness? Once inside the noisy elevator, he became uncomfortably aware yet again of the stiffness of his new suit. He'd been wearing denim work clothes for so long that he'd forgotten what suits felt like. And this turn-of-the-century one was tight-fitting with its starched collar. Lora gave him an affectionate little peck out of sight of the elevator operator, fussing one last time with his tie. When they got out on the fourth floor, he was greeted by a distinct and familiar odor, that vague mix of—what? Disinfectant, varnish, woodwork? The smell of the Rookery hadn't markedly changed over the years.

They stopped at a door with a smoked-glass window. On it was the firm name "Collins, Goodrich, Darrow and Vincent."

"Slater will go nicely right here." She pointed to a blank space underneath.

The waiting room was large but spartan by the standards to which he was accustomed. No piped-in music or hanging ferns here, he told himself. There were plain benches along the walls. The people seated on the benches wore the garb of workmen. They looked up only briefly as Jeremy and Lora entered. One of them, a husky Negro, had his shoulder and arm in a sling. There was an opening in the wall opposite them and a young woman could be seen typing. Lora walked over to her.

"Lora! I didn't see you come in. You look grand." Jeremy was introduced to Marilyn Price, a pretty, dark-haired girl, about Lora's age, with a wide, cheerful smile.

"I know Mr. Darrow is expecting you," she said, inviting Jeremy to take a chair. Lora chatted with Marilyn for a few minutes. Jeremy glanced over at the nearest workman, a middle-aged man with a weatherbeaten face. When he noticed Jeremy glancing at him, he turned away. Lora let Marilyn go back to her work, and sat down beside him.

"Are you *sure?*" he asked her again while they were waiting. It was the fourth or fifth time that morning he'd inquired.

She lowered her voice. "I told you I'm fairly sure, but I'm new at this pregnancy thing. I missed for the second time last week, and I *never* do that. I'll be seeing the doctor later this week. Aren't you even a little excited though?" she raised her eyebrows.

"You know I am." He reached for her hand. "It's...well, everything is happening so fast. It's going to take some getting used to."

At that moment the inner door opened and Jeremy was looking at Clarence Darrow. He felt like pinching himself as Lora introduced him. "Folks," Darrow said, calling over to the others on the benches in that smooth voice for which he was so famous. "This is one of our law clerks." Jeremy could feel a new interest on their part as they looked him over. 'Our law clerk,' Darrow had said, and suddenly he'd put Jeremy at ease as he held out his hand to him. "As soon as I show him around, I'll be with you." With that, he escorted the two through the door and back toward his office.

While he was immediately recognizable, Jeremy realized this was not the Clarence Darrow he had pictured in his mind's eye—that rumpled, aging sage he'd seen portrayed by Henry Fonda. This man leading them down the inner hall was a smooth-faced lawyer—well-dressed and only a year or two older than himself. The disheveled appearance would come in his later years.

He held the door for them as they entered his office. It was just as Jeremy would have pictured it, roomy with a large, cluttered desk in one corner, chairs facing the desk and a leather couch along one wall. Opposite were large, open double windows behind a false balcony.

On the wall above the couch were pictures. One was a portrait of Abraham Lincoln, the other was vaguely familiar but he couldn't place the person. He moved closer to read the inscription. "To Clarence, my great friend and counselor, Peter Altgeld." The governor, he remembered. The other walls were filled with glassed book cases.

Darrow faced Jeremy. "Your wife here has told me you want to become a lawyer. Why is it you don't want to go to law school?" Jeremy knew he'd better answer directly.

"I'm thirty-seven years old, Mr. Darrow. I'm sorry I waited so long to decide on this, that this is what I'd like to do. But at my age, and with a wife now," he looked to Lora , "and possibly a child on the way, well..."

Darrow studied him closely, then walked around the side of the desk, frowning slightly. *I swear to God,* Jeremy almost laughed, *he really does hook his thumbs in his suspenders!*

"You're right," he finally said simply, surprising Jeremy. "I earned *my* license by clerking. Oh, I went to law school, or at least I started. One year at Michigan, but I saw it wasn't for me...or maybe that was vice versa."

The mirth in his eyes showed through. "I found a job in Youngstown, clerking, and picked up my knowledge of the law there, or at least enough to present myself to a committee. I was with several other applicants. They were good fellows on the committee—wanting to help us—and passed us all.

"But," he continued, walking to the window. He was looking out across the false balcony and down onto LaSalle Street, "times have changed. These are modern times, now. You won't have a group like that. You'll be facing a stern Bar Association committee and a written test as well. And they probably won't like fellows who didn't go to law school. Can you take all that in your stride?"

"I can," he answered, liking Clarence already.

"Well, all that and you'll have to take me, too. And I doubt you'll be as good a clerk as your wife here. She all but ran my practice while the Debs case was going on."

Jeremy realized just how modest Lora had been about her work with Darrow—merely telling him she'd helped Clarence during the trial. It was Paul who'd first told him the details one recent afternoon at Bluffside, after Lora had returned to Chicago. He'd explained to Jeremy that he'd walked over one day to watch the Debs trial and had gone up to introduce himself at a recess. Darrow, upon hearing who he was, had led him across the street for lunch, asking him on the way about the Observatory project. "The man's astounding," he'd remembered Paul saying, questioning him on details of the proposed building and the telescope. And Darrow had gone on at length about Lora, describing how indispensable his daughter had been to him during the trial. But now, here was Darrow confirming it for Jeremy.

"So you may be expecting, eh?" Clarence walked over to Lora. "Well, let me congratulate you."

"Please," she said, a little flushed, "we don't really know yet." He asked about her new job. She perked up, filling him in on her duties and plans.

"I'll have to drop over and see how you're doing," he said easily. She asked him about some of the clients she'd known and their talk drifted into areas of shared experience. Now and then they'd laugh together over mishaps or near mishaps as their conversation flowed freely from Eugene Debs to some personal injury case.

299

Jeremy moved about the office while they reminisced, glancing at book titles and reading plaques. "This girl," Darrow raised his voice to include Jeremy again, "taught me much about the feminine mind." He was speaking now in that musical voice, the one Jeremy knew the juries loved. "Right away I liked her independence and her quick, intuitive grasp of things."

Jeremy was examining the books in one of the cases while Darrow was talking—more to Lora than to him. And he saw in the reflection on the glass cabinet that Darrow, noticing Jeremy's back was to him, had casually taken Lora's hand without missing a beat in his conversation. She shook her head and moved his hand. "Maybe it was because we were both a couple of teachers that we had that rapport," Darrow continued, not letting on his hand had been moved.

"I have to go," she said aloud, glancing at the desk clock and breaking in on Jeremy's thoughts. She said her goodbyes to Clarence and Marilyn, promising to stop by again soon. Jeremy, his mind and emotions tumbling, accompanied her to the elevator. He was starting to feel the same jealousy all over again that he'd felt about Todd early in the summer. It stunned him that another man might have known her.

"Why so quiet, darling?" she asked, giving his sleeve a tentative tug as they waited for the elevator. He tilted her chin and kissed her as the red "down" light blinked on. Wordlessly he watched her blow him a kiss as the cage descended out of view. Did she guess he'd seen Darrow reach for her?

The rest of the week was spent learning his new job. For a practicing lawyer of twelve years, the work of law clerk was simple. The *real* task was in convincing those he dealt with that he was seeing things anew. He knew it wouldn't be unheard-of for a disbarred shyster from another jurisdiction to pose as a law clerk and assume a new identity. He didn't want to stir up any such suspicions.

Despite his brilliance, Clarence Darrow was not a hard taskmaster. He was so inveterately considerate that it wasn't in his nature to be stern. Jeremy worked all the harder and soon found he was being entrusted to handle more of the work. Before long, he was asked to interview the countless people who sought Darrow's assistance

Just as his wife had said, Clarence Darrow was a man who couldn't say

300

no, and so Jeremy was given the job of screening his clients. Some, happily, he could help by merely writing a letter. He found himself consciously and unconsciously competing with Lora, wanting to gain the recognition she had won. It still hurt him to think of Lora and Darrow together, but he took consolation in the fact that *he* was the person she'd married.

And Darrow, despite whatever his relationship with Lora had been, was not someone to cling to the past, nor was he proprietary. When he brought up Lora's name, it was an honest inquiry about her health—she *was* expecting—or about her new job. After a few weeks, Jeremy had settled into a kind of routine, screening clients, handling some of the routine collection matters, and occasionally doing research for Darrow. Along with keeping his expertise concealed, his biggest challenges were to decipher the genius's illegible handwriting and to make sense of his atrocious spelling.

Lora's and Jeremy's domestic life gave him a happiness beyond his dreams, surpassing anything he'd ever known. His bride was even learning to cook under Martha's watchful eyes. There were many late nights at his new job, when Jeremy would find he'd have to interview some prospective client just as he was ready to leave for the day.

He was sympathetic to the stories he'd heard, far more than he'd ever been in his own practice, even to the point that one day in late October, Clarence took him to lunch. Darrow seldom stopped during the day but he began to give Jeremy a gentle critique after they'd taken a booth at Henrici's.

He was doing well—very well, he was told—and he had a natural flair for the law. "But..." Darrow paused, "you have to develop..." he started again, measuring his words, "you seem at least as good as your wife in a technical sense, yet she...beneath that pretty exterior, well, she was a little *grittier* than you."

Interspersed with the late nights were those shorter ones, when he'd wait for Lora on the steps of the Art Institute, standing between the lions until she came out to meet him. The newlyweds would then walk hand-in-hand down the steps and over to the crowded cable car, ready for the trip out to Kenwood—two lovers oblivious to the world.

42

"It's impressive and not so gloomy as I thought it might be from your description. But I know you're going to tell me appearances hide much."

It was Sunday, November 3rd. Lora and Jeremy were standing out on Florence Boulevard, at the entrance to Pullman. Since their marriage, he'd been badgering Lora to take him for a tour and finally she had agreed. Wednesday night they were lying in bed, and she was talking again about the town—about the school and the people. The day before she'd had lunch with Jeanette Reilley, triggering her memory about the town and strike.

"It's going to be getting cold soon, and you won't feel up to going out there, little mother," he patted her belly. She looked down at her growing stomach, thinking.

"You're right. I'll talk to Jeanette tomorrow. We'll go out there Sunday—and don't you tell me you have to study Sunday, either," she said.

Now they'd arrived, and Jeremy was holding a bag of toys for the Reilley children. Lora had made up an excuse that they had been invited to dinner elsewhere, knowing it would strain the Reilley's close budget to put out any plates for them.

Directly across from them was the huge, red brick Administration Building—quiet now on Sunday. In front was Lake Vista with its fountains throwing spray high into the air. The little decorative lake was surrounded by flower beds, with hardy marigolds still blooming in November.

"I suppose that's the Florence Hotel I've heard so much about?"

"That's it."

They crossed the street and stopped in front of the veranda. A few guests lounged in chairs, taking advantage of the weather. "Let's go in." He started toward toward the steps. She began to follow but pulled back.

"No. Wait. I don't want to—I can't."

"Oh, come on. The strike's long over, and you don't work here anymore. You aren't betraying anything."

She shook her head. Jeremy could tell she wanted to go in. "You never *were* inside, were you?"

"No," she answered, "never. You know we weren't welcome inside. First, the prices were too high, and second, Pullman didn't want his workers mixing with his customers and the important politicians he had as guests." She led Jeremy to the bandstand in the adjacent park where they sat on the steps.

The sense of paternalism was beginning to envelope him, more so since he was actually *at* Pullman.

"Lora? Lora Lockerby!" They both turned in the direction of the voice.

Lora stood, her hand over her eyes, squinting into the sun. Then she recognized the approaching figure. "Harriet!" she called and the two met, hugging. "What are *you* doing here?"

The woman was dressed in a plain but very expensive outfit. She was heavyset, in her mid–forties. "And I was just about to ask you the same."

"Harriet Pullman, this is my husband, Jeremy." He took her offered hand, sure he'd not heard the name right. Noticing his look of surprise, Harriet laughed.

"You didn't expect to see your wife talking to a Pullman, did you? Well, I'm apparently one in name only. It happens that I don't often agree with my father. I lived out here for a time and met Lora at the school, where we became friends."

"And a better friend the students and the workers never had," Lora interjected.

"Well, I'm so sorry about everything," Harriet waved a plump arm toward the main building. "Actually Lora, it's quite a coincidence running into you. You know, I haven't been back here in almost two years. I was just showing these folks around the grounds." She beckoned to a young couple to come over and introduced them to Jeremy and Lora. They were Dutch, and seemed to understand very little of what was being said.

"They came back from New York with me. I live there now. Well, I'll try to see father before I leave, but," and she put up her palms, "I don't think he recognizes that I exist. And Jeremy, that wife of yours! Make her tell you about the World's Fair Dedication Ball. Why, if it weren't for her resourcefulness and her extra pins, my poor dress wouldn't have made it."

"Oh, stop it, Harriet. But I do remember the pins."

The two women exchanged small talk, Lora telling her about the Art Institute, as Jeremy tried talking to the friends. Harriet was telling Lora about New York and he noticed she lowered her voice as they spoke, taking Lora's arm and mentioning something about seeing a Karl as they both scribbled their addresses and exchanged them, promising to write.

"We'd better be off," Harriet said, "before someone recognizes me and escorts us all from town." They parted company.

Lora and Jeremy left the little park, walking toward Market Square. Lora glanced up at the big clock. "It's eleven–thirty," she said. "Let's go. I don't want to keep Jeanette and Tim and the children waiting." Jeremy followed at her heels, turning to look back at the huge Market Hall, now deserted on Sunday.

"Aren't you going to tell me about Harriet?" he asked. They were walking up Langley past rows of nearly identical houses.

"She's just as she appears, sincere and unpretentious. I met her at school functions. She filled a vacancy on the School Board. When the school transferred under the Chicago Board, she resigned, but we stayed friendly. She even appeared at some of the early labor meetings, though she stopped coming when a few of the workers became nasty. They were distrustful of her, thinking that she was a spy for her father. It's really unfortunate, but I think she and her brothers have been disowned by their father. It's as though he only has one child, Florence," and she jerked her thumb toward the hotel.

At that moment a very pretty young woman came down the steps of her house toward them She and Lora threw their arms around each other and they laughed together as they hugged. The children waited quietly behind their mother, smiling but shy. Jeanette was a beauty, no question, he decided, and with a bewitching smile to boot. Unlike most people of the 1890s, he noticed, her teeth were perfect. Her bright red hair was close–cropped, almost boyishly, and the freckles on her cheeks made her look even younger. All the children seemed to have her flaming hair and fair skin. Lora introduced Jeremy to Jeanette, and she held out her hand.

She bent down and picked up the baby she introduced to Jeremy as Matthew.

"And hasn't he grown some?" she asked Lora, the brogue evident in her voice. "Sorry mother isn't here. She's off visiting neighbors," she explained as they started toward the house. Lora had reached down and taken the hand of little Bridgett, while the oldest fell into step alongside Jeremy. Jeanette was walking just ahead, holding the baby across her slim hip as she turned to talk to her company.

Tim Reilley was standing at the door. He was red-haired as well, with a wiry build and probably in his late twenties. Like so many workingmen Jeremy had met, Tim seemed shy at first meeting. The group moved inside, with the children leading the way. Lora took the parcels from Jeremy, and gave each of the children a gift. For Jack, she'd picked a little wooden dray wagon, and for four year old Bridgett, a lacy doll. Jeanette protested about such fancy gifts, but there was a smile on her face as she saw Bridgett hug the doll, the child's thanks on her face. For the baby, Lora had picked out a wooden seal which balanced a moveable red ball on its nose.

The living room had been divided to give the impression of two small rooms. As they moved away from the divided front area on a tour of the Reilley's small dwelling, it was immediately noticeable just how dark the house was with its windowless walls. Glancing again at Jeanette, Jeremy could hardly believe that this slender, child-like woman could be the mother of these three children. She had sent Tim off to pour some whiskey for the guests. Lora had been taken in tow by the children, who wanted to show off their room to her.

He and Jeanette had moved back to the divided front room where he'd seen some framed photos of the Columbian Exposition. He noticed the white buildings perched above the waterways. Then he saw the drawing. Actually it was the rich, gilded frame which first caught his attention. The subject was a shapely nude, lying on a divan with her weight resting on her right arm, her left arm on her hip. She was looking directly ahead, meeting the eyes of the viewer. The sketch wasn't immodest, but it wasn't one of the bland, stylized nudes of the nineteenth century, either. And the model was indisputably Jeanette.

She caught his eyes moving from the picture to her and back. "One of our artists—Karl," she said,"gave it to me. I modeled some for him that

305

summer, and he wanted to give me a present." Jeremy listened, fascinated by her musical brogue as he looked up again at the picture. "It was really generous, him givin' me this. He could probably have sold it for a good price. I suppose Lora's told you I model for the classes at the Art Institute. Do you like it?" She pointed to the drawing with a disarming directness.

"How could anyone not?" he met her question. Jeanette had a strong, female magnetism that Jeremy wasn't sure she appreciated.

"He did this," she continued, looking up at the frame, "one afternoon near the end of the summer. To tell the truth, I didn't know how Tim would react when he saw it," her hands were on her hips as she looked from Jeremy to the drawing. "I thought it would go up in the attic or under our bed. But he insisted we hang it right here. My mother, though, she'll never get used to her daughter..." she shrugged.

He noticed the drawing had been hung out of a casual visitor's sight. The front room had been divided, he guessed, with the picture in mind. Turn–of–the–century Pullman was still a place for a tenant's discretion.

"You have such a beautiful, smart wife, Jeremy, and she's pretty lucky herself if I do say so," Jeanette said, as Tim returned with the glasses and an ice bucket.

"Here's to your baby," she continued, lifting her glass. "I know he, or she, will make you proud. Next to him," she put her hand on Tim's, "no one's made me happier than my little ones." It was the first toast to his infant–in–making, and it brought home the reality of the baby's arrival in May.

Jeremy asked Tim about his job, trying to bring out the shy man. He worked in the repair shops. He'd had to go back, he said, hat in hand after the strike, turning in his A.R.U. card like the rest of the men. "There'll be a time yet for a union, though," he said firmly. Times were still clearly tough, but there had been a bit more work, and wages were up some. With Jeanette's earnings, they were managing.

"You can be real proud of your children," Jeremy offered, listening to their happy voices mingling with Lora's down the hallway.

"They're after growin' up so fast. It seems like yesterday when Lora and I were working together at the Fair." Jeanette seemed to realize she'd said too much.

"Were you a guide too?" he asked.

"Noooo," she drew out the word slowly, "but we," she paused, apparently at a momentary loss for words, "we worked together. Let me get Lora. This whiskey's going to waste, and her teaching around kids all week." With that, she stood up and went to fetch the others.

Lora returned, making noises about the time, and saying they'd have to leave, or they'd be late They said their goodbyes, promising to get together again soon.

The two strolled down 113th Street until Lora stopped him. "This is it?" he asked.

"Union School," she said, "for four years I taught here." He looked up. It was a red brick school, like so many of that era, and not unlike many of the older schools still serving late twentieth century Chicago. They were standing, silently lost in their own thoughts, when a train whistle caused them both to jump.

"I'd forgotten how close those trains were, not to mention the constant worry that one of them would leave the track. The noise and vibration were enough to drive a person crazy," she said, her voice raised above the clattering freight train.

They walked a few short blocks along the Illinois Central tracks. Jeremy saw the "Kensington Avenue" sign ahead. "I have one more thing to show you, darling, and then we'll catch the train back," Lora said.

"I think I already know where you're taking me."

She pointed, "That was the Relief Committee headquarters where Reverend Carwardine and I were the night Bill Anslyn was shot. Do you want to go over there?"

"Why not? Lowery—or Stark—is part of our past now. I'd like to see where the shooting took place."

"Miss Lockerby! Miss Lockerby!" A young boy was calling to Lora. Jeremy put his age at about ten or eleven years old. His hair was shaggy and he pushed it back as he approached. "I didn't know when I'd see you again. Are you coming back to Union School?" She paused for a few moments. Jeremy figured she'd have to remember the face from among hundreds she'd have known.

Eliot?" she asked. "Is that you? You're so tall! Let me see you." And she inspected him, turning him this way and that, and commenting on how he'd grown. "No, Eliot, I won't be back. I work downtown at the Art Institute now, and I'm not even Miss Lockerby anymore. I'm Mrs. Slater now. This is my husband. Jeremy," she said, "this is one of my brightest and best students, Eliot Ness. Eliot's father has a bakery right over there. Peter Ness is one of the most generous persons I've ever known. During the strike he tried to see to it that everyone had bread." Young Eliot joined them and the three walked down the street to the depot where the shooting took place. It was not the main I–C line, but a single–track branch. Lora pointed out the spots where she, Bill Anslyn, the Reverend and Stark had been standing.

As she started to describe the murder, her two companions grew quiet. Her account was so vivid Jeremy could almost hear the shots fired. He felt his palms sweating as he remembered his own experience with Stark.

Eliot was quietly watching, but he noticed the story's effect on Jeremy. "Did you know him, Mr. Slater?"

"I did, and I had a close call with him myself. Were you in the crowd that night?"

"Oh, no sir. I heard the commotion, but father wouldn't let me out. But I remember hearing the gunshots."

Lora scanned the depot clock. "We'd better start back, darling. If we miss a Sunday train, well..."

Eliot walked along down Pullman Avenue toward the station with them. The dusk was settling fast. It had turned cool, and from some-where in Kensington there came the smell of burning leaves. Lora tousled the boy's hair as their local approached from the south. "Keep up the good studies, Eliot."

Jeremy took his hand. "Nice to meet you, son. Say, did you ever con-sider going into police work?" Eliot's eyes widened with surprise.

"Why, yes sir. I have thought of it. Yes, I have. But I think, sir, that I'll be helping my father in taking over his bakery, more than likely." They said their goodbyes, and Lora and Jeremy climbed aboard the coach.

"How did you like your tour of Pullman?" Lora asked, shifting her weight, trying to get comfortable as she sat back.

"Oh, some surprises, darling. You didn't tell me what a beauty your friend Jeanette was, and I still have to get used to my wife being friends with a Pullman." He kept to himself what he had learned from Jeanette's telling him about her working with Lora.

"But going to the site of the shooting reminded me of our mutual friend. Let's hope we never meet him again!"

"Agreed." She nuzzled against him, noticing they were almost alone in the commuter coach. "But will you tell me one thing? How in the *world* did you know little Eliot Ness, of all people, would want to go into police work?"

"Just a random guess, sweetheart," he said, putting his arm around her.

43

Martha had cleared the last of the dishes and the diners sat back from the table, comfortable with the food and drink. Paul had lit a second cigar despite Lora's glare. It was late February, and their dinner guest was a colleague of Paul's. The talk over coffee and brandy had shifted to the Observatory and the coming year's construction. Paul was laying out for Fred Holloway just how the main and auxiliary telescopes, the floor, and the shutters would all be worked from a single set of control buttons.

Jeremy listened. He had become immersed in briefs, legal research, interviewing prospective clients and, on occasion, getting to watch the Master perform in court—all the things that went into becoming a lawyer. But sitting at the table and listening to Paul talk about the Observatory made him nostalgic. Next summer the big forty inch tube would be installed. If all went well, the dedication would take place on schedule and operations would begin by the fall.

Paul seemed to be feeling better, but his breathing was still short, and as Jeremy glanced over at him, he saw his face glowing red, probably from the brandy as much as anything. Fred was also an electrical engineer, from Eubanks and Brown, and he was speaking—lecturing really—about further applications of electrical energy. The conversation was getting over Jeremy's head. Fred, perhaps noticing he was losing his listeners, directed his one-way conversation to Lora.

He told her about some friends he knew who had just bought a house at Lake Geneva. "I know you folks have a place there, and I hope to get up and visit you." Jeremy suppressed a smile; he doubted Fred had been invited. "But you must meet this Jenkins, he's quite a character. He wants to just let his grounds get overrun, and erect a ruins on the property. He's made several trips over to England in the last couple of years, and would you believe that that's the style in England now for the wealthy—they let the rear of their estates just go wild and they actually build replicas of ruins back there."

"Well, if your friend Jenkins really wants an authentic touch, I think I have just the caretaker for him." Jeremy felt his wife's hand under the table as Lora continued to speak earnestly with Fred.

"And with that, if you gentlemen don't mind, I believe," she pushed back her chair, "that I'd better retire." The men stood as she got up from the table. Her pregnant condition was now very evident, affording her a perfect excuse to leave.

"I'll help you upstairs," Jeremy offered, as she bid goodnight and bent over to kiss her father.

"Fred, I'm leaving you in charge. No more cigars for him, and only *this* much brandy," she held two fingers.

"I'm going to have to start pushing you up the stairs from behind," Jeremy said, as they ascended the winding staircase. Lora had blossomed in the last month and Martha had had to let out all her dresses again. The next step would be the bulky maternity gowns in which women of the 1890s were not seen outside, and Lora was prolonging that switch as long as she could.

He took off her shoes as she sat on the side of the big bed. "Your son or daughter has really taken to kicking, and it's hard enough listening to Fred Holloway at *any* time without having someone turning somersaults inside you." She'd taken a leave of absence from the Art Institute, but had talked them into keeping the position open for her. She hoped to return at least part-time after the baby's arrival and a summer at the lake.

Lora had gotten up slowly from the bed and was undressing as she spoke. She'd selected the biggest nightgown from her dresser. "Just look," she wailed, standing and studying her naked image in the mirror. She turned to see her silhouette. "I look like a kangaroo."

Jeremy reached for her before she could put on the nightgown, pulling her over and down onto the bed. "I just happen to love kangaroos. How did you know?" He leaned down, giving her a long passionate kiss.

"Mmmmh," she murmured, turning on her side and facing him. "If I never told you before what a sweet liar you are, let me do it now."

He rubbed his hand over the mound of her stomach. "Let me try to feel one of the somersaults."

"I think our little dickens has finally fallen asleep." Lora's hand covered Jeremy's and she moved it downward. She grew silent except for her breathing.

She pressed on his hand. "There. Oh Jeremy! Right there," and she began to move against him, slowly and then faster as he kissed her lightly, her forehead glistening. For a few minutes, the only sounds were the soft rustling of the sheets and Lora's breathing, until finally she arched herself against him, her body stiffening, a small cry escaping from her lips. He held her close until at last she lay back spent, her breath returning.

"Your wife is utterly shameless, but you'd know that, wouldn't you," she purred drowsily.

"She's exactly the way I want her," he said, leaning down to kiss her.

"And she's more in love with you than ever. I do suppose you ought to get down to Fred and father though," she murmured at last. "Fred is probably already wondering what I'm doing to you. Also, darling, I do have a surprise for you." She sat up. Jeremy started to protest "No, you haven't taken a day off from your studies since New Year's. Besides, I won't be able to go out much anymore." She slipped her nightgown on. "Now it's all settled. Tomorrow belongs to me, so you be a good listener downstairs until Fred leaves." She lay back, pulling the covers over her.

The next morning the other side of the bed was vacant when Jeremy awakened. It was Martha's day off, and when he arrived downstairs, Lora had already prepared a big breakfast. Her days of being sick in the morning had long since passed, and she'd taken a liking to big breakfasts of bacon, eggs, and toast.

"Look at that beautiful day outside!" she exclaimed. The windows had become sealed shut during the long and brutal winter of '96 and Jeremy now strained to open them. A soft breeze blew into the dining room. If he hadn't been raised in Chicago, he would have found it hard to believe that two days before the temperature had hovered around zero.

"And where are we going today, my kangaroo?"

"You have to guess," she answered.

"Back to Pullman?" She shook her head. "The Auditorium?"

"No. Give up? I'm taking you on a tour of the World's Fair, or at least what's still left of the World's Columbian Exposition. How does that sound?" She caught his glance. "Never mind my condition. I'm fine. Now you finish up while I check on Father."

Their driver, a middle–aged Negro in a formal frock coat, called back, "You folks mind to watch out when you're over there. There's still tramps and scalawags around those ruins." The cab clattered down Cornell Street and past the Windermere, where she and Karl had spent the summer of 1892 together.

"Familiar?" Jeremy asked, as she studied the hotel.

"It was a meeting place during the Fair." Lora squeezed his hand, changing the subject. "I can't wait to give you one of my official guided tours."

They moved down Sixtieth Street, paralleling the old Midway. There was a new round of construction underway for the University. Lora pointed over to where different attractions had been or where she *thought* they'd been. The Ferris Wheel was long since dismantled and shipped elsewhere. Without the familiar landmarks she was vaguely disoriented. Their driver eased the cab under the rubble–strewn viaduct beneath the Illinois Central tracks, and across Stony Island Avenue. He had gone as far as he wanted to go. There was another carriage ahead discharging a family who, like themselves, wanted to enjoy the fine weather and to visit "where the Fair had been."

Jeremy paid him and helped Lora down. "My wife used to work here as a guide."

"Then she'll most likely be disappointed, sir. And mind you folks, don't go too far down that way." He looked down toward the south end of the desolate grounds. "And be sure to be out of here before dark."

"Be back by three–thirty," Jeremy said, handing him an extra fifty cent piece.

"Got you, sir," he said, tipping his hat, and turning the carriage, horse and driver picked their way around the debris.

Jeremy caught up with Lora. She was looking around at the heaps of rubble and stone, and the twisted shards of metal that reached skyward. "It's incredible," she said at last. "I knew the Fairgrounds as well, or better, than anyone. I watched it being built, and took people to every single building over the course of the summer. Dearest, I walked every foot of these grounds, and yet I hardly know where I am."

She did point toward a series of naked, metal trusses in the distance.

"Manufactures," she said. "At the dedication ceremonies that building held 70,000 people, 30,000 of us seated." Even in a skeletal shape, the building was awesome. "Do you realize it was over 1,600 feet long and 800 feet wide and from the floor to the ceiling it was 250 feet high?" And she told Jeremy how she and Enid Yandel had almost been done in by a drill that had fallen near them during the construction.

In the distance, behind the skeletal remains of the enormous building was a hugh statue, or what was left of it. "Big Mary. I stood down there in front of the Ad Building. When the President pulled the veil, the people next to us all asked, 'What is it? God? A woman? A man?' " She chuckled at the recollection.

"Let's follow them," Jeremy suggested, as a small group of people moved along a path of sorts toward a bridge. The day had stayed as bright as its morning promise, the temperature climbing to mid–fifties. Jeremy unbuttoned his coat, and Lora began to recover from the shock of seeing her Fair in such a run–down state.

"You know, Frank Millet told me last fall, 'Don't return, Lora. You won't like it. Just remember the grounds as they were.' " They passed a small, round building which had been gutted by fire and vandalized, and now bore a sort of nineteenth–century graffiti.

"White Star Pavilion," she said. "It's starting to come back, darling," and she took his hand as they followed the others across a still–intact footbridge. The lagoon they crossed was frozen, but they could see blue water and an occasional bubble beneath the thin ice on the surface.

"We're on the Wooded Island," she told him. "This was at the center of the Fair, but when you were over here, you seemed to be away from all the bustle. You could sit and just enjoy the trees and the flowers. You know, most of the people I escorted just wanted to stay here. It was all I could do to get them to move across the Island or over to the little boat dock."

Nearby, he saw that, indeed there was a crumbled wooden pier where launches, no doubt the *Lora L* and her sisters, had stopped to land, picking up and discharging visitors.

"What's that, a Japanese building?" he asked as they turned north.

"Ho–o–den," she answered, pronouncing the three syllables easily, as though she'd said them every day. "Originally, Olmstead wanted no buildings on the Island, but eventually this was allowed. I suppose it was

Burnham's idea. At any rate, it was a gift of the Japanese government, and I can remember stopping here for lunch in the summer of '92 and watching the Japanese workmen put it up. It was something to listen to their speech. Do you really want my spiel?"

"Sure."

She paused, setting her recollections straight, and then launched into her best tour guide recitation, right down to telling him that the inspiration for the pavilion was 'based on the Phoenix Hall of the Byodoin Monastery at Uji, built in 1053.'

"Is all that true, Lora?" he asked, awed by her memory.

"How would I know?" she laughed. "I was a guide, not a historian. They just told us what to say." Jeremy watched her step up along the side of the pagoda, afraid for a moment she might topple with her altered center of gravity, but she maintained her balance. The pagoda reminded him of something Frank Lloyd Wright would have built. He searched his memory, but couldn't recall if Wright would ever have been to the Fair.

Lora pointed across the lagoon toward a high steepled building, or at least the remains of one. "The Marine Cafe. That became a kind of favorite place for the tourists. In fact, as the summer wore on, that's where we started and ended our tours. It's where," she said, staring over, "I met the Hogans." He remembered her story, and how she had told it as they were crossing Lake Geneva on their way to see the Observatory, and now the memories of the Hogans—and the *Dispatch*—all came back.

They found a bench, still more or less intact, and sat down, watching a handful of children at play. "That looks like us a few years from now," she said, reaching for his hand as she saw the children scurrying in and about their parents' legs. The warm weather had brought out a large number of people. He had heard that visiting the old fair grounds had become a popular Chicago pastime. It was reported in the papers that the South Park Board was going to clear the area of the rubbish and the skeletal buildings and fashion a municipal park. Many of the visitors probably wanted a chance to see the grounds one more time and reminisce, visualizing where they walked when it had been the "White City."

A city policeman, night stick in hand, came around the bend. "Sure and it's a lovely day folks," he greeted the strollers in a brogue. "But don't be drifting down there." He pointed his night stick toward the southern end of the fair. "There's too many of the other type of folks down there.

315

And make sure ye're out o' here before dark." He stepped over to a lad lacing blades over his shoes. "And none of that, sonny. Can't you see the ice is too thin? I don't want to go swimming down there to fish you out." The boy made a face but unlaced his skates as the officer moved off.

Lora described the buildings as they sat on the bench, what each one looked like; and as she talked, it was almost as though they were still standing. She told how the search lights played on them at night and then about watching the great fire on July 4, 1894, during the strike. Someone, probably part of the rabble or even one of the soldiers sent to Chicago by President Cleveland, had likely touched off the blaze.

"I stood with Martha in front of our house and watched the pillars of flame shoot up. All night it burned. Whether no one cared to put out the fires or there were just too many for the fire department, I don't know, but it wound up..." and she swept her arms, "...like this! What that fire didn't accomplish, the vagrants and tramps have pretty much finished—at least down over that way," and she looked south where the Court of Honor and the major buildings had been.

"Could you've escorted any people I'd have known?"

"Important names, you mean?" she kidded, as they got up and crossed the other bridge, walking east and leaving the Wooded Island.

"I escorted so many, Jeremy. Mr. Millet originally placed me as a guide for the *distinguished* guests," she exaggerated the term for him, "But we all were pressed into service for the crowds in general. I escorted my share of farm folks and common workers. They were mostly all so nice."

They'd stopped in front of the Marine Cafe. "Important people though, let me think. Well, there was John Dewey, the philosopher. He was a very nice man but quiet. He hardly said ten words during the tour and I really don't believe he cared much for the Fair. He was here to participate in the Philosophy Congress.

"I also escorted a group of 'Vikings.' They were Norwegian seamen who'd come across the ocean in a frail bark replica of a medieval Viking ship. They were retracing the journeys of Leif Erickson who, they wanted to remind people, had preceded Columbus in the discovery of America. I don't have to remind you that at the Columbian Exposition they were given a polite but not overwhelming welcome."

Lora gingerly tested a railing in front of what used to be the Marine Cafe. Satisfied, she leaned upon it and continued. "The Roosevelts were a curious, graceful family. I remember them because the father was much older and in poor health. In fact, when I first met them I thought he was the grandfather. He had difficulty getting on the launch. After our first stop, we got him one of those rolling chairs and we, or, I should say, his son Franklin, wheeled him about the grounds. Franklin was a little gem of a boy. Just eleven or so but so grown up! You could tell he was conscious of his father's age and health, but he took personal charge of him. I remember he glared at some boys his own age who were staring at his father.

"Mr. and Mrs. Roosevelt stopped right here at the Marine Cafe for something to eat. While they ate, I took Franklin down there," she pointed to where the Manufacturers and the Electricity buildings had been. "What an inquisitive mind he had! I'm afraid I couldn't answer half his questions.

"On the way back, do you know what he said?" She provided the answer herself. " 'Miss Lockerby, in all the time we've been here, I've only counted three colored people. Isn't it too bad more haven't come to see this or do you think they feel uncomfortable?' Wasn't that the strangest remark for such a young man?" Jeremy nodded, listening.

"Mr. Roosevelt thanked me as we rolled him over to the railroad terminal where their private car was kept. When we reached it, he had me wheel him aside and then he produced a gratuity for me—too generous really to accept, but he insisted. Mrs. Roosevelt and Franklin rejoined us. Franklin took my hand like a little duke. Such presence and not at all a show-off. They got my name and address and do you know what?" Jeremy shook his head. "That fall, he wrote me from some preparatory school he was attending. It was the nicest letter—all about his studies and sports and it contained some pictures he'd taken on that day at the Fair."

"I hope you've kept that letter," Jeremy said, as they moved around the northern edge of the site. They could see the beach and the still-frozen shoreline of Lake Michigan.

"Over there," Lora said as she pointed, "stood a building you'd have recognized. The Ceylon Court," she smiled impishly.

"You bet I'd recognize it, my adventuress."

They rounded the corner of some rotting timbers and there, suddenly in front of him, was a building he *did* know.

"The Museum of Science and Industry." He said it in a low voice but out loud.

"No, dearest," she said, "that's the Fine Arts Building, the only real exhibition hall that survived. The science buildings were all destroyed."

He stood on the edge of the pond, brooding as he watched the lone survivor of the Fair, looking just as it had when he'd last visited it. He kicked a piece of ice down onto the frozen surface, where it spun to a stop. Their tour was leading back towards the bridge where they'd started. A chilling wind had come in off the lake, and he reached up and buttoned his jacket. An idea was surfacing, and he spoke.

"Tell me about the Dedication Ball, the one that Harriet Pullman said she was with you at."

"It was the most elegant Ball I'll likely ever attend. Everything was in red and gold for Spain, and many of the women wore gowns in that color." She cocked her head to one side as though trying to remember. "Although mine was green. And the next day, do you know how many people came to hear the dedication ceremonies?"

He sensed that she had glossed over the Ball. "Who did you go with?"

"To the Ball?"

He nodded.

"I went with Karl Bitter. He was—is, a sculptor from New York. He'd done the decoration work at the Administration Building. I'd met him the previous summer."

Jeremy asked another question, "Did you work for him?"

She paused. "Yes, I was his assistant."

"Is that where you met Jeanette?"

"That ninny Jeanette! What did she tell you? Yes, that's where I met her. She was a model, and," she hesitated, not knowing how much the garrulous Jeanette had told him. "I sometimes modeled, also, for the figures on the Ad Building. She had slipped again into the slang the Fair workers used and which peppered her narrative. "Karl and I began keeping company that summer," she said, using that most elusive of Victorian terms as she blushed slightly.

"He returned again only for the Dedication Ball, and I didn't see him again," she concluded with the small fiction.

"Could I see any of the works?"

"They were all destroyed in the fire. But," she shrugged, "they were really very temporary, never meant to survive the Fair, just made of staff," remembering as she spoke that Karl had kept the original clay figures in his studio loft.

His questions persisted until he'd succeeded in drawing from her a description of her work for Bitter. Finally she aimed a light slap at him. "You damn lawyer! Even if it's all past, I've told you all my deepest and darkest secrets," she said, telling substantially the truth. "And you've still told me next to nothing about yourself. Jeremy darling, after our baby arrives, can we *at least* take a trip down to Indianapolis? I want to see where you lived."

Jeremy looked up as she spoke and saw that their driver had returned, and was waiting for them in the growing dusk. *Well,* he thought, *I've brought this on by probing her.* He realized his real purpose in asking her the questions was to bring things to a head. He gestured to the waiting driver that they'd be along soon.

He put his hands on Lora's arms and looked directly at her. "We aren't going there, because the truth is," he took a deep breath, aware he had a slight catch in his voice which she would have noticed, "that apart from a landing at the airport, I've only been there twice in my life and that was to see cars, excuse me, horseless carriages, race." He looked down into the face of his beloved bride, her big brown eyes looking back at him uncomprehendingly.

"Darling, I waited for too long to tell you about myself, though God knows I've wanted to." He guided her over to the carriage. "This will take a little while. What do you say we treat ourselves to dinner? I'll tell you my story, or at least start to, over dinner."

The sun was nearly down and the air chilly as they left the grounds. He took Lora's hand in his, and she returned the pressure, but he could see she was nervous. She was chewing on her lip and the knot had returned to her brow. Jeremy gave directions, and when they pulled in front of the Chicago Beach Hotel, he helped her down. She gazed ahead, oblivious to the familiar surroundings from the summer of 1892 as he led her across the veranda, through the lobby and into the dining room.

When they were seated, he ordered a bottle of wine and told the waiter to hold the dinner order for a time. "I hardly know where to start," he fumbled, aware that having started he would have to convince her of his unbelievable story.

"Try at the beginning," she said, a hint of stiffness in her voice.

"It's nothing really bad, it's just hard to start." But he did.

They sipped the wine, ordering and eating dinner as he talked. She seldom interrupted, listening intently. He held back nothing other than his children. He didn't know why he withheld that one item except that it would complicate their relations, and he felt it was his last private link.

"And so that explains the *Dispatch*," she said, in a voice that was curiously flat. Aware that she might turn on him for not saving the Hogans, he told her he knew the boat would sink but only guessed it was on the day in question. "So you can see the future—like some clairvoyant?" she asked quietly, sipping her coffee.

"No, I can't see the future. I can only recollect the past. This was all past to me."

She shook her head as though to clear it. "So that was it. That was the reason you didn't know how to hitch Magnolia?" He nodded. "And so you really never had been on a horse before?"

"Right."

She continued to question, hoping perhaps to trick him into realizing that what he was saying was all untrue—all a fantasy. She asked about Debs. "What happened to him?" He tried to answer, feeling a growing discomfort at talking about the future.

"Darrow? What about him?" He gave her some answers, aware of their relationship. "And the Roosevelts? Is that why you plied me about them?"

"Please."

"What about Franklin?" her voice rising.

"Please, Lora," he glanced around at the few other remaining diners who were turning to look at them. He told her about Franklin. She listened, occasionally turning away with a frown. Her questions went on.

"Would that have been why you asked little Eliot Ness about becoming a policeman?" Her voice had risen again.

"It would have been," he answered simply. "I can't explain everything now." The evening wasn't going as he would have best liked. The waiter hovered nearby.

"Sir, it's Sunday evening. I'm afraid we're closing."

Jeremy looked around. They were the only ones left. He paid and they started to leave. His legs were stiff. He had been sitting almost rigid for over two hours. He held onto Lora, as she had trouble walking as well.

"Let me just stand here for a minute," she said as they reached the veranda. She took some deep breaths of the air now flowing across the chilled lake surface. The cold had returned with the darkness.

Lora realized that she had come up against a wall of clues, all of which pointed to the conclusion that what Jeremy had said was true—he had come to her from the future. There was no room for her questions to poke holes in that wall and suddenly she felt more defenseless, more insecure than she had ever felt with any man.

And now, the one man she had chosen to love and to trust could not be depended on. No, she thought, that was wrong. This time it was something else beyond them that ruled her life—their lives. What to say to him? What to think?

"Darling," he started.

Lora reached for him, "It's just that the husband I thought I'd come to know so well...I just..." she hesitated, uncertain as to how to go on and feeling her cold fear rising. "I don't know what to think, what to believe."

"Believe I love you!" he said, "And believe I'll never leave."

"I don't know," she said, shaking her head slowly. "If this is true, you might find some way back, or be taken back or—I don't even know what I'm saying. It's all so crazy!" Her lips trembled.

He reached over for her, no longer able to circle her waist. "But I don't *want* to go back or ahead or anywhere. I'm not trying to find any way out. I'm going to stay just where I am, right here with you forever."

She faced him. "You had no choice about arriving in 1895, did you? Well, you'll have no control over leaving."

44

May 3rd, 1896

The two of them were sitting on the front steps of the Woodlawn house. "I *know* it's only two days, Jeremy, and I'm not trying to be a baby—but it's going to seem like an eternity. And you can't stop me from missing you. I already do and you haven't even left." He was on the step beneath her. Lora was sitting sideways and having trouble getting comfortable with the baby now due in three weeks. Her arm was around his shoulder, her head resting on his. "Look at me," she was saying, rubbing her stomach, "I'll never be able to fit into the dress I picked out for Frank and Charlotte's wedding."

"You'll be down to size in no time after the baby arrives," he comforted.

They had been sitting out there in the bright spring morning for the past half hour. His same old grip next to him was packed and he had let cab after cab go by, but soon he'd have to hail one. Paul had asked him if he'd get the *Lora L* out of storage and check on the construction of their new stable at Bluffside.

"Do you know this is the first time we've been separated since October?" she spoke. Jeremy had finally stood up and waved over a cab. The driver had pulled the carriage to the curb and was waiting.

"Help me," she said, as he reached for her. "Look. I can hardly stand up anymore. Now don't forget to order the crib when you're in Lake Geneva." She looked away.

"Is that a tear? Do I rate tears for a two-day trip?"

"Stop it!" she said, trying to smile as she brushed her hand across her

322

cheek.

"Is it my leaving?" he asked, getting concerned. "Lora, have you felt a pain or anything? I mean this trip isn't something that can't be put off for a week. I can go..."

"No. Nothing like that. The doctor said I likely won't deliver early. It's not any pain. I just felt a sort of dread. Do you know what today's date is?"

"May 3rd." Then he realized what she meant.

"You told me it was a year ago today you tumbled back to this time. I just noticed the date this morning, that's all. You go ahead, I'm just being silly."

"Are you *sure?*"

"Of course. *Go.*"

"You look after our little stranger," he said, patting her stomach. They kissed good–bye, and he could feel her wet cheeks against his. Their arms stretched out before he let go of her hand and walked to the cab, looking back.

He arrived at the Chicago & North Western Station with no time to buy a ticket. He searched out the right track and started down the platform. The smell of the sulfurous coal from the engines was strong under the shed, making his eyes water. He was about to board when he heard his name.

Jeremy turned. The caller was a young lawyer, Edgar Lee Masters, hurrying down the platform. He shook his hand and they found seats just as the train began moving. Jeremy told him he was going out to Lake Geneva to check on a summer home for his father–in–law.

"You're lucky. I'd like to be going out there too," he said. Masters told him he was getting off at Des Plaines, where he was meeting a client.

"How's your boss—Clarence? I hear he's thinking about politics. I hope he doesn't succumb to that bug. He's too good a lawyer to lose to politics," Edgar had put aside his newspaper to talk.

"I know he's thinking about it, Mr. Masters. I suppose it will depend on what Governor Altgeld does."

"Say, Jeremy, I hate last names. Please call me Edgar. Just because you're a clerk and I'm admitted, we don't have to be so formal. By the way, you *are* going to try and become a lawyer, aren't you?" Jeremy said he was.

"Splendid. That's how I became one. I went to school for only one year. Knox College. I left and clerked with my dad until I got admitted. It's the way to do it. But one of these days all the lawyers will be from law schools." He turned up his wide nose, giving a laugh at that.

The conductor came by, frowning, having to fumble in his pocket to make change for Jeremy who bought his ticket on the train. Edgar was younger than Jeremy, who guessed him to be in his late 20's. He was pleasant looking, square–jawed and with hair that had begun receding, giving a preview of what he would look like in middle age. The wire glasses he'd been wearing were taken off and tucked away and as Edgar saw the conductor move out of their car, he propped his feet up on the seat opposite.

"And how is that wife of yours doing?" He chuckled at the circumstances of his meeting Jeremy.

Jeremy had been working at his little desk the previous winter. One of the partners, Mr. Vincent, had walked by, escorting two lawyers. They had been negotiating a pending case, and Jeremy had been introduced to them on their way in. Edgar was with his partner Scanlan. Jeremy was still at his desk writing as they were leaving. Scanlan and Vincent were talking. They passed by into the outer office. Masters stopped and Jeremy felt him tap his shoulder.

"I don't care *how* hard you work," he'd said, "you'll never be as attractive as the clerk you replaced. Do you know whatever became of her?"

Jeremy slid back his chair and smiled up. "Yes, I do—I married her."

Edgar looked out the train window, then brushed at a speck on his trousers, "Do you know, I used to stop by your offices on the same case *last* year. I hope you won't take offense, but her looks were so striking. I was sure I'd seen her before. When I returned to your office, I worked up my courage to ask her if she'd ever worked at the Fair. When she replied that she had, I knew she was one and the same person, that adorable guide this rural boy had fallen in love with at first sight."

"I'll tell her that. We're expecting a baby and Lora feels so huge these days, she'll be happy to hear your compliment."

Edgar said good–bye, hurrying out of his seat as the train halted at Des Plaines. "There's got to be an easier way to make a living, and I'm gonna' find it one of these days," he called back, hurrying down the aisle.

Jeremy settled back in his seat. Meeting Edgar and hearing his story had brought him back to Darrow and Lora. He didn't mistrust her—or Clarence at all. It was just the old envy that someone else had known Lora, and that someone also happened to be his boss; but he was determined to put it behind him just as they had.

Edgar was right, though. Darrow had gotten the taste for politics. Lately, it was all Jeremy could do to stop him long enough to get an answer from him or to discuss some files. The Democratic Convention would be in Chicago in two months. It was going to be an interesting time and he was looking forward to it.

At Williams Bay, he stepped off, looking around at the familiar platform. Tommy Napper had left a sign in the window that "the agent will be back at 2:00 p.m." There had been some changes. A new siding had been added and even the much put-off landscaping around the depot had been started. He crossed the roadway and began walking along the docks, only giving a glance up the hill toward where he'd thrown the chain on his bicycle exactly a year before. He picked the shore path to walk down to the boat yard.

"Halt in the name of the law!" Jeremy froze at the words. Then he recognized the voice and turned.

"Well for God's sake! Paul told me but I had to see it with my own eyes to believe it." He reached out and took Jim Keane's hand. In truth, he looked the part in his new constable's uniform, bright buttons and all—much more so than Stark had.

Jim filled him in. He'd stayed on at the Observatory last fall. After Stark's sudden departure, no one filled the constable's job and when it was still open, after the first of the year, he'd applied. They walked together down the shore path.

"I hope you'll arrest all those wild wagon drivers from the Observatory," he kidded, picturing Jim's fateful intervention last fall. "How is the former Miss O'Neill?" He was glad he'd remembered her name. She had become Mrs. Keane in March.

Jim had heard that his friend was about to become a father. They congratulated each other, promising to get together during the coming summer.

At the Jewell yard, he found the *Lora L* waiting. She'd already been launched and was bobbing at a slip. One of the younger men had come out to meet him.

325

"Ben's out delivering a yacht," he said, walking over to the boat with Jeremy. He told the young man that he'd be back on Sunday. The Lora L would stay docked there at the yard until Paul arrived in two weeks. He'd have to see Ben tomorrow when he returned with the launch. The youth gave Jeremy a hand with putting a dingy on the stern. With no pier put in at Bluffside as yet, he'd need it.

"Beautiful day, sir."

"Sure enough," Jeremy reached down into the water, testing. It was frigid.

The launch started up right away and he headed across toward Bluffside. It was good to get behind the wheel. When he reached the middle of the lake he looked over. The Seipp's house was visible, rising above the trees at Black Point, just as it had last year when he and Paul had crossed through the storm. As he got closer he looked but saw no activity on the point. There were still no boats that he could notice in the lagoon and no one was manning the drawbridge. The lake had a barren look without the private piers in place.

He dropped a pair of anchors off Black Point, put over the dingy and rowed to shore. Climbing the log steps of Bluffside, he walked to the main house, crossing the veranda. His footsteps on the boards echoed in the stillness. He let himself in. The furniture was still covered—just as he'd left it. Jeremy could hardly believe that over six months had passed since he'd closed up. Theis was right—the rapid cycles of opening and closing a summer house would become a part of his life.

The stable looked nearly complete; the workmen gone for the weekend. He walked around inside and breathed in the aroma of new timber. It seemed to be waiting only for a horse and buggy. He walked out in front and then down the path to the little cabin. Rather than open the main house, he'd stay here overnight. The same neighboring woodpecker from last summer was hammering away on a tree somewhere above.

Jeremy climbed the stairs and turned around, remembering how he had nervously invited Lora in for the first time. The cabin was musty, having that same closed–up smell as the main house. He stepped into the bedroom and looked in the corner, picturing where the crib would go. The baby would stay right in here with them this summer.

Back at the shore, he decided to go in and see Malcolm—tell him what he'd waited so long to tell. Then he'd order the baby's crib. That done, tomorrow he'd be able to go back on the early train, he thought, as he rowed out to the launch.

Once out on the water, he headed for the town of Lake Geneva. He began going over in his mind just what he'd tell Malcolm. He and Lora had discussed it late into the night the week before.

"Please, once more," Lora had said, sitting up and propping another pillow behind her. "Tell me what you're going to say to him. And remember *just* how he looks when you do tell him. I'll want to know his reaction." Since Jeremy had told her his story that evening in February, she'd come around to accepting it. She couldn't help him to account for the why or how it happened, but their happiness with each other helped her to overcome his odd origins. His background had, in fact just become another hump, a major one, but a problem two in—love newlyweds could solve. He only wished he'd confided in her sooner.

Lora even seemed to enjoy her status, being the only person who knew her husband's strange tale. And she'd taken to picking his brain now for information. Her resourceful mind had begun figuring how they might put such phenomenal powers to their advantage. At first Jeremy had to talk her into his telling Malcolm. Lora, after thinking about it, decided he might not be all that surprised. "I'm sure he'll be able to offer you—I don't know—some theory. But I'm telling you, dearest, you *have* to make Malcolm agree to show me that astounding watch you gave him. I can't wait to see it."

He throttled back as he drew opposite the country club. A few golfers were already out. He noticed two were playing a hole along the shore. He wondered as he watched if he'd have to shoot like they did. Was it only the equipment or some technique of hitting that would revolutionize golf? The golfers looked clumsy as one after the other they made scooping lunges, swinging at balls which traveled only short distances.

He felt satisfied, looking over at the Country Club and the fairways that stretched up from the water. After he'd become a lawyer, why they could apply for membership here. As summer residents it shouldn't be difficult. Rob Allerton could be his sponsor. Their son or daughter, or sons and daughters, could grow up out here. It would be a great life. He looked around at the wooded shoreline, feeling very much at peace.

But don't become one of those pretentious, self-centered idiots that semed to so abound in the nineties, he told himself. Which reminded him of still another great thing about Darrow—and about working for him. It was impossible to imagine anyone he'd befriended or turned out as a lawyer being pompous or vain. The price one would pay would be too high—the loss of Clarence's friendship and respect.

He squinted up at the bright blue sky as he entered Geneva Bay. It was a beautiful day. To his right he saw "Ceylon Court." He smiled, remembering their adventure in the tunnel last summer. The wind had picked up at the entrance to the bay, stirring up a chop on the surface.

The *Lora L* bucked at a wave that broke against her bow and sent spray flying over the deck. The wave also dislodged the front mooring line so that it hung off the bow and dragged, hitting the side of the boat. He thought about leaving it; he'd be at the pier shortly. Then he heard the metal buckle slap against the side. The launch was newly painted and that buckle's bumping would knock the paint off for sure.

Jeremy reached over, closed the throttle and climbed out of the hold to retrieve it. But while he closed the throttle, he left the boat in "forward." He moved carefully out on the short forward deck, made slippery from the spray.

He reached down and grabbed the mooring line, pulling it up and getting ready to return. Just then, the *Lora L* hit a cross wave caused by the wind at the mouth of the bay. He felt the bow dip down into the water and as the stern came clear he heard the engine race. The launch, left in forward gear, suddenly drove ahead, knocking him off his feet.

He landed squarely on the navigation light, blacking out for a second. The pain in his chest was intense. He blinked his eyes open, listening to the engine roaring under full throttle. He held onto the line trying to catch his breath. He could feel from the searing pain that he'd probably broken his ankle in the fall.

The launch was skimming along at top speed, the bow dangerously low from his weight. The park and the seawall ahead were growing larger every second. He tried to pull himself back to the hold, but he could barely breathe. He couldn't get back in time to turn the wild boat before it hit.

He'd have one chance, he realized. He'd have to wait until the very last moment and then slip overboard. If he went in too soon—into the icy waters in his condition—he'd be too far out to survive. And if he didn't get off in time, he'd impact against the seawall.

He watched for a moment as the onrushing park drew closer. He listened, hoping faintly that he might hear the throttle unstick itself. He held onto the line, waiting, about to roll himself off the boat. The area ahead was deserted, the lumber for the park pier was still stacked on shore, waiting to be set in place. What Jeremy couldn't have seen, only a few feet ahead and just beneath the surface, was the heavy wooden crib for the pier. The dry spring had drawn the lake level down a foot.

With the extra weight on the bow, the *Lora L* was riding just low enough that it struck the crib squarely, at full speed. Jeremy was hurled forward into the air by the impact. The launch, behind him, had veered off.

The pain in his chest was intense but he felt a kind of detachment. He saw he was going to land in the spot near the road where he'd hit last spring. His last recollection was the sickening impact as he slammed into the ground. He felt the same sensation as before—of searing, unbearable pain, along with the feeling that he was spinning out into a void, unable to stop still another trip through the frightening tunnel before the merciful blackness descended over him.

45

"Easy does it, fella'. Easy. You're gonna' be all right. Can you hear me? Okay, just nod. Fine. I'm a paramedic."

Jeremy blinked his eyes. He tried to take a breath but felt an excruciating pain and tightness in his chest. He could get no air.

A radio crackled with static. "Please, folks, move back." It was a police officer. Jeremy blinked again, trying to focus. He was on his back staring up at the man who was bending over him. The branches of a tree were overhead. A young woman in a uniform came over and replaced the man.

"Does it hurt here?" she asked. His grimace told her. "Rib fractures, lower right side," she said to her partner. "You just breathe easy. You're gonna' be okay." Her hand was on his forehead. "What's your name? No, don't start breathing so fast again. Relax."

He told her his name in a weak voice.

"Ah, how about a last name, Jeremy."

"Slater," he answered.

"Do you know where you are?" she asked, as he felt his pulse being taken.

"Lake Geneva," he said weakly.

"Good."

Her husky voice had a comforting sound to it. She asked him a couple more questions, as he felt the blood pressure cuff being applied.

She turned aside to speak to her partner who had returned. "Jeremy, we're going to put you on a stretcher. Easy." He groaned as they placed him onto the stretcher and secured him by running the straps across his body. He was being carried—no, he realized, he was being rolled on wheels.

The stretcher stopped. He was in the street. The pain in his head was starting to compete with his chest. The blinking red and white lights on the back of the ambulance were in his eyes.

"I know," she said, her hand on his shoulder. "These lights are awfully bright, but we'll have you going in a minute."

Suddenly there was an explosion of sound near by. He lurched on the stretcher, his eyes wide with fright.

"There," she said. It's all right. You look so surprised! Just somebody starting up a lawn mower, that's all. But they sure picked a bad time for it," and she glared at the teenager across the street. Oblivious to the ambulance, he'd started to mow his front lawn.

The other paramedic returned. He had been conferring with the policeman who was now trying to get statements from people in the crowd.

"Do you know how you got here?" she asked him as she reached over and wiped some matted blood from his face.

"I was thrown off a boat."

"A boat. My! Well, you're pretty close." She repeated his response to her partner as they rolled him into the ambulance.

Once inside, her partner closed the doors and went to the front. "Can you hold my fingers, close your fist on them? Very good." She made him repeat the action with his other fist and then she tested his reactions on the soles of his feet and his toes.

He felt the ambulance start up and heard the siren, muffled from the inside. She had started an I.V. "We're taking you to the hospital."

"Which one?" he asked weakly.

"Lakeland. It's only fifteen minutes away." The vehicle swayed to one side and then another, and he heard the siren's brraack! brraack! brraack! sounds. She reached to steady a sliding tray. Looking up at the front compartment, she shook her head. "That is, if we ever make it. That's *NASCAR Neil* driving us. Well! You smiled." He tried to smile again, but winced as he took a breath. He had begun hyper–ventilating.

"There, I'm going to give you some oxygen. It'll make it easier to breath. But," she shook her finger at him, "don't take those little panicky breaths. You'll get enough air. Just slow down."

"Tell Lora," he started to say as she placed the mask over his mouth. He heard her talk on the radio and a minute or so later he felt the prick of a needle as she gave him an injection. She held his hand with her own.

"We're already out on the expressway. It won't be very long now. Who's Lora?" she asked. "Your wife?" He nodded. "That's a nice name. Do you live around here?" He shook his head. He was aware of more talking back and forth on the radio. Then he felt the ambulance making a series of quick turns. It abruptly stopped and then backed up a few feet.

The doors opened and he was rolled inside the hospital, he closed his eyes tightly to shield the bright lights as he was wheeled down a hallway.

He was moved into a little bay where a nurse began poking at him and attaching things to him. He remembered someone taking off his shirt, and he thought he heard someone say that his pants would have to be cut off. From outside in the hallway he could hear the two paramedics talking. It seemed to him they had a wrong version of the accident. He wanted to correct them, but he didn't have the energy.

The blue–eyed paramedic stepped back inside and leaned over him. "Congratulations. I think we're both part of a new land speed record from Lake Geneva up to Lakeland. We're going to leave you now. How do you feel?" Her warm hand was on his forehead.

"Bad," he managed to say.

"Well, they're going to take good care of you." He may have drifted off for a moment or two. When he opened his eyes, he was still in the same room.

A young man in his mid–twenties, an intern, he guessed, was gazing down at him. His thick glasses magnified his eyes. "The x–rays on your skull were negative. But you have two cracked ribs and a displaced left talus. In plain words, you broke your ankle. We'll be setting it later."

He was talking to Lora. Was it an argument? He was telling her he was coming back and that was that. She seemed sad, he remembered, but adamant. "You can't, my dearest." He was agitated and tried to reach for her hand.

"There, there, Mr. Slater. You had a nightmare, that's all." He woke up and looked around. He was in a hospital room and noticed he was wearing a white hospital gown. The bright light above made him squint. The light fixture was modern and recessed into the ceiling. "Is that bothering you? I turned it on when I came in. There." The nurse switched it off, leaving a small light on behind his head. He lapsed off once again into a troubled sleep.

When he awoke, it was bright daylight. There was a tube to his nose. It was held on by a strap around his head. He found he could take it off and did. It led over to a green wall fixture marked "oxygen." He felt the terrible ache in his ribs again and put the mask back on. An I.V. solution above him slowly dripped through a line to his wrist.

He buzzed for the nurse. A different one came in and took his temperature, blood pressure and pulse. "That's fine. Dr. Miller will be in to see you shortly, Mr. Slater."

"Sloan," he said, the thermometer still in his mouth.

"What?"

He took the thermometer out. "I said my *name* is Sloan."

She wrinkled her brow, looked again at the chart, making a note. She replaced the thermometer in his mouth. "Well," she started, "the doctor should be here in a few minutes." Just then the doctor entered along with a young woman in a green jacket trailing him. She'd be an intern, he guessed.

The nurse spoke to them for a moment and then left. He studied the chart, showing it to his companion. "How do you feel?"

"Better," he said. In fact his head *was* aching less. His ribs felt just as bad, but he was learning how not to move.

"I'd like to take a brief history, not to tire you out. So it's Mr. Sloan, S–l–o–a–n? I'm terribly sorry about the name mix–up. You had no papers, and well, you know how those paramedic people can goof up names." He shook his head, making a correction with his pen.

Jeremy was getting more alarmed and troubled. He decided to be very cautious with his answers. The doctor took a history. For his residence, he didn't know why, he gave the Kenwood address. He answered he was a lawyer and gave his office address at 180 North LaSalle, his last one. The questions went on. He didn't know if Dr. Miller sensed his wariness. He did notice that the young intern after a few minutes looked distracted and began checking her watch.

When he finished the history, he checked his ribs. "Still very sore, ah? Well, I'm afraid you'll be that way for awhile. How's your ankle?"

He shrugged. It was in a cast but there was no pain. "You probably don't remember, do you? It was set last night. I'm told it was routine, closed reduction, and you should be out of the cast in fairly short order.

"We'll be getting you a cane later so you can get up and around. The

333

inhalation therapist will also be down to work with you; we want to keep those lungs clear. You had a bad spill, my friend but I think you're going to be all right. Only the next time that you go bike–riding, wear a helmet, please?

"Do you have any questions?"

Jeremy felt tired. His headache had returned. "Yes," he said, "how did it happen?"

Dr. Miller's eyes narrowed momentarily. Actually, Jeremy remembered the boat trip and all the events clearly, but he wanted to hear it from the doctor.

"We don't have all the facts yet, I'm afraid. The police are working on it, but you were the victim of a hit–and–run. Some sort of a delivery truck hit you while you were bike–riding, throwing you off. You hit the ground, maybe a tree. Fortunately you don't seem to have any spinal injuries. You *do* remember bicycling, don't you?" he asked. Jeremy nodded.

"Well, you suffered a concussion. The ribs I'm sure you know about and you also had a broken ankle. It is strange, though. The orthopedic doctor can't figure out how you managed to fracture the ankle and ribs in a fall. It's my guess you'd have fractured the ankle on the bike frame."

He pulled the covers around Jeremy. "We don't want to tire you. You rest. But, Mr. Sloan, I must tell you. Because of the length of time you were unconscious, I've consulted with Dr. Lambert, one of our neurologists. He'd like to see you. It's just a precaution to be sure of your recovery. He'll probably be in this afternoon. By the way, do you remember how you got to Lake Geneva? I forgot to ask you before."

"I drove."

"There were no keys nor any form of identification on your person."

Jeremy had a sudden thought, "Do you know where my clothes are?"

"I believe they were taken off in the emergency room, but I'll certainly check on that for you."

After they left, he lay in bed, his mind trying to fix on just what had happened to him. He would close his eyes occasionally, half expecting to hear Malcolm's voice or to see his beloved Lora. *Oh, Lora,* he cried to himself *where are you? We can't have lost each other! No, please, not after all we went through!*

Dr. Lambert stopped by in the afternoon. He was about Jeremy's own age. He had on a tweed sport coat and open shirt. He took the vital signs himself, scanning the chart as he did. "You know, what happened to you, kinda' scares me. I ride a bike a lot myself, and I shudder to think with all those idiots on the road, how close I've come to your same situation." His voice was friendly, without the professional edge of Dr. Miller's.

"Have you ever been bitten by a dog?" He had pulled up a chair. Jeremy shook his head. He pressed the button, raising his back so he could look at the doctor. Dr. Lambert saw him wince from the rib pain and he came over and helped him to get comfortable. "I think I know how you feel. I was out riding on a country road a while ago. I even carry one of those dog sprays. Like mace, you know?" Jeremy nodded.

"Anyway, I never saw him until he was on me. A feisty little cocker, but he took a bite on my ankle. I lost control and fell in a heap. He didn't keep after me. If he did, I'd like to have shot him. But, I'll tell you, I cracked a couple of ribs in that mishap and I kept the memory of that little cocker spaniel for a long time. I was able to have him found and get him impounded. You ever have to go through rabies shots—ugh!" *This guy sure enough knows how to get through to patients,* thought Jeremy.

He took another history, far more detailed than before, interspersing it with anecdotes, causing Jeremy to be careful with his answers. "It seems you told the paramedic you'd fallen from a boat. Do you own one?" Jeremy shook his head.

"Ride on one often?" Again, he shook his head. Dr. Lambert checked him over, testing his reactions and then he sat back down, regarding his patient. "Is there anything you'd like to tell me—or ask me, Jeremy?"

He was tempted to ask him—or to tell him—everything, but held back. For one thing, he didn't feel he had the stamina. And once he opened up...well, what *had* really happened to him? He would have to play for time.

46

The next day saw him up on his feet. The oxygen had been removed and his I.V. trolley followed him about, rolling on its rubber wheels. It was his first experience with a cast and cane.

A Lake Geneva policeman came in as he was practicing moving about the room. He looked very young, particularly when he took off his cap and set it on a chair. He was sympathetic, watching as Jeremy winced from the rib pain. It seemed he had also fractured some ribs playing high school football. Having broken ribs was another health hazard Jeremy had been spared. It seemed now as though every person who entered his room had his or her own cracked-rib story: the maid, Dr. Lambert and now the policeman.

"It makes you sick," the officer said, folding up his notebook. "Here a person like yourself is knocked off a bicycle by some hit and run motorist (they were close to finding him, he said) and might have been killed, and what does someone do—goes through your pocket and takes your wallet and keys. Hell, they even took your bike too, though from the impact I doubt if that bike was worth anything.

"Here, sir if you sign this authorization we'll tow your car and keep it for you. For now, though, we'll keep it under observation right where it is for another couple of days, but I doubt if anyone will try to take it. He said good bye, giving him the information about where he could pick up his car.

His phone rang for the first time. At first, he couldn't identify the soft beeping tone. When he picked up the phone it was Mary Kay, his ex-wife, on the other end. She talked to him for a few minutes, asking him about the accident before putting the kids on the phone.

At the sound of Amy's voice, he began crying. "Are you all right, Dad?" With an effort, he managed to stop his sobs long enough to answer that he was. "Are you crying?" she asked, "Are you?"

"I'm all right, Princess. I'm just glad to hear from you, that's all." He could hear Danny fighting with his sister to get on, and at one point the receiver at the other end hit the floor. Danny must have pulled the phone away. He heard Amy calling for her mother. "Dad," he said, sounding very man–of–the–world. "Sounds like you had a close call." Jeremy talked to him, struggling to keep control of his voice.

When Mary Kay got on she said, "We'll drive up to see you tomorrow. You take it easy." There was real concern in her voice. He lay back in the bed, dabbing at his eyes, thinking about his ex-wife and his children. His phone beeped again.

It was Ronnie Sanders, his close, old friend and another lawyer. "You gave me a start, buddy." After kidding him about the pretty nurses, he said he'd be up the next day.

"Do me a favor, Ronnie. Can you come up in the late afternoon? Mary Kay will be up earlier with the kids. And," he added, "there's something I'd like to talk to you about."

"You've got it. I'll be up there about 3:00."

Dr. Miller stopped by the next day. He seemed pleased, noting his progress was excellent. Jeremy was glad that the I.V. had been taken out. Seeing it would have scared the kids. "I checked for your clothes, Mr. Sloan. Apparently they were so torn and bloody that the people in the E.R. felt they couldn't be saved. I also learned your pants had to be cut off, I'm sorry but they were thrown away."

Jeremy was indeed sorry. It might have put some answers in place if he could have seen which clothes he had been wearing when taken into the hospital. After the doctor left, he walked up and down the hallway, finding he could get around quite well with cast and cane. His headache was all but gone. The only problem he had, except for the cast, were the ribs. It almost seemed they were getting worse. Shortness of breath was to be expected, he was told.

Jeremy heard Amy and Danny's voices as they rounded the corner of his wing. They were counting off room numbers as they got closer. When they arrived, Amy ran to him, throwing her arms around him. He winced as she squeezed him, but he held her tightly. Danny followed her. He reached his hand out to take his father's until Jeremy pulled him over, hugging him, the tears running down his cheeks in spite of himself. How often he'd despaired of ever seeing his children again.

From the doorway, Mary Kay watched the greeting their father had given the kids and their response to him. "Hey, you guys! It's only been ten days since you've seen each other." She took Jeremy's hand, reaching over to kiss him. If her kiss was cool, the concern in her eyes was real. "How is it no one in Elkhorn knows where their hospital is? Is everyone that healthy? We've been forever trying to find this place." They sat and talked, Jeremy cautiously describing the "accident".

"I always worried about you out in traffic on that bike," Mary Kay said at last. "And my heavens, riding all the way around Lake Geneva, and at your age!"

"Mom! Leave him alone!" Amy was sitting up on the bed. She moved closer and put an arm around her father.

When it was time for them to leave, Jeremy took his crutches and walked with them down the hall, even sneaking on the elevator for a trip to the main floor. As the door closed, Mary Kay, ever watchful, saw him staring around the little cubicle. "It's so modern," he said, looking back at the elevator as they got off.

"I'll be fine." They had reached the front door. He bent over and kissed the children, telling them he'd see them in Chicago in a few days. "Thanks for bringing them."

"You take care of yourself," she said, starting after the children. "No kidding, you look like you could use some rest. And don't let too many of those girlfriends visit you."

"They'll be releasing me on Friday," he said to Ronnie. They were sitting in the patient's lounge, drinking cokes. Jeremy had put his left leg up on a magazine table. His leg propped up in a cast seemed to accentuate his friend's own short stature. He opened Ronnie's gift, a cervical collar which he had put on and was now wearing around his neck.

"And I don't want to see you without it for a year, at least in public. The Lake Geneva police have the driver and that company has more insurance than they know what to do with." He swigged on the coke. "So you've given me my career case. In return I may even give you two–thirds of what I get."

"You're all heart, buddy. By the way, how's everything been back home?"

"Well, it's not like you've been gone all that long. But let's see...in the last three or four days..." Ronnie filled his friend in.

There was a gap in the conversation. "Listen, Jeremy, I've known you for more years than I'd like to admit. What's up? What's bothering you?"

He told him. Not everything. In fact he really just gave him a quick outline of his experiences. Ronnie listened, not interrupting, not saying a word.

The nurse stuck her head around the corner, telling him his dinner tray was in the room. They started down the hall. Jeremy saw Ronnie stop next to the orderly who was wheeling the dinner cart. Something might have come from his pocket and been transferred to the orderly but it was too fast to see. The man reached in, sliding over a tray and Ronnie took it, following Jeremy to the room.

"If I'm going to have to put up with an old 'Twilight Zone' rerun, it might as well be with a T.V. dinner," he said, pulling up a chair and setting his tray on the bed. Ronnie was wearing the cervical collar which Jeremy had taken off.

"Good God," he sniffed, uncovering the dinner tray. "Look at the tray I got! The guy who's supposed to be getting this must be coming out of a diabetic coma. Let me see what you have," and he reached over, spearing a hunk of his friend's meat loaf. Jeremy had climbed back under the covers.

He finished the story he'd started. "So you want to know what I think, right?" Ronnie asked, "Well, I think you're as nutty as I always said you were." He looked at Jeremy, balled up his napkin and aimed it at the waste basket, missing it.

"Really," he said, with mock seriousness, "What you've done is a simple practice of the occult. You just bi–directed into the nineteenth century for a time while the rest of you enjoyed a snooze under a tree in a Lake Geneva park. Nothing more than that." Jeremy reached for his cane to slam him, but it fell to the floor.

"So tell me anyway, what sort of a partner was Clarence Darrow?"

"I only worked for him as a clerk," Jeremy replied evenly.

"Good God!" Ronnie looked at the ceiling. "He can't even be grandiose in his delusions! That *is* insane!" They talked on in a light vein for a couple of minutes, sparring around a touchy issue.

"So you're being discharged in three days or so? How are you getting home?"

"I'm driving. Mary Kay brought me an extra set of keys." Ronnie patted his cast.

"It's the left leg. I'll have the seat all the way back. Doc says I can drive. The ribs will take awhile, but my head is okay," he said, realizing he was feeding Ronnie a great straight line.

"Oh, sure. His head is just fine, folks," He glanced in the corner at some unseen audience. "And he just got married and Eugene Debs was his best man. Did I get that right? Oh, no. Eugene was still in jail, sort of, except that he was out hunting with the sheriff. Sure, folks, as a matter of fact, his head is better than it ever was.

"Seriously, buddy. I think you're gonna' be fine. You got a nasty bump on the head." He was talking earnestly now. He'd taken off the comical collar and it had slipped unnoticed to the floor.

"Come home. Get back to work. If things still bother you in a few weeks, I know a good psychiatrist. I mean, he must be a good psychiatrist, his golf game is so terrible. I don't even know if I believe in psychiatry, but if you—if you're still worried—well, give him a ring."

He stood up. "Gotta' go." He leaned over the bed. "You be careful, you hear? I'll watch your court calls for you and I'll endorse all your checks." He started to leave, "Oh, one other thing. Does Lora happen to have a sister?" Jeremy shook his head. "It figures," he sighed, walking out the door.

At the elevator, Ronnie pushed the button and waited. Then he stepped over to the nurse's station. "Mr. Sloan. I just left him. When's he leaving—being discharged?" he asked.

"Hmm," she said, checking her records. "I really couldn't say for sure, but it looks like he should be discharged in a couple of days."

"Then his condition is good, right?" He said it casually as the elevator opened.

"Oh, Mr. Sloan seems to have made a fine recovery." She smiled, putting the folder back into the spindle.

"Thanks," he said, stepping onto the elevator just as the door closed.

47

Getting back into the groove of working turned out to be surprisingly easy. The cracked ribs had nearly mended and he'd gotten used to the walking cast for the ankle. Ronnie joined him for lunch a couple of weeks after he'd returned. Jeremy arrived first at City Tavern, going up to the bar. At 11:30 Ronnie came in, still ahead of the noon rush. "You're looking a lot better than on the day you came home from the hospital," he greeted his friend.

Ronnie motioned to the hostess for a table. It was another hot day in late May. Their talk centered around the Cubs—their injuries and recent losses. As they ordered lunch, Ronnie filled him in on all he'd missed around the Courthouse. He'd stepped in for him and had done a yeoman's job. And Jeremy could only nod agreement when Ronnie said, "You know, you really have to do something about Mrs. Cleary. She's got to be losing you thousands every year." He went on to give Jeremy a litany of the secretary's inadequacies. This talk carried them through lunch.

"Say, I mean you *look* all right," Ronnie said. They were finishing their coffee. "You tell me everything is healing up, but you have a kind of look about you—that says you've misplaced your propeller beanie. Are you still—you know—back there at the World's Fair or something?"

Jeremy decided to be honest. He'd been denying to everyone, the doctors and nurses at Lakeland, to the orthopod he'd seen in Chicago—and even to himself—his feelings. "Things *are* better," he started. "I can finally take a deep breath. In two more weeks this cast comes off the ankle, and he tapped his head. I guess up here—well it will take a little longer—but no more headaches."

"You mean you still have the, the visions?" Ronnie wailed, hitting his forehead. "Oh, God!"

Jeremy shook his head. "No. I don't still get visions—as though they were something new or on–going. It's just that what I remember seems real, totally like it happened. Although," he conceded, paying the check, "some of it is getting a little foggy. For instance, Ron, can you remember the details of what happened to *you* a year ago?" They both stood up from the table.

"Listen," Ronnie said, "we got here early. Come on up to the bar. We'll have a quick one for the road. And I want to give you something."

Ronnie ordered the beers. "Now don't go getting testy," he said, showing him the doctor's card. He gave his guarded endorsement of the psychiatrist.

"Look, you had a real good swat on the head. Maybe he'll tell you it's going to take awhile. Hell," he said, standing up, "maybe he'll even be able to sell you a time machine so you can go back. You didn't make it sound all that bad." He shoved the psychiatrist's card at his friend and turned, hurrying away to his own afternoon court call.

Which is how, three weeks later, he came to be in the Loop waiting room of Doctor L. Daniels, M.D., Doctor of Psychiatry. He was sitting alone in the outer room, flipping through a *Field and Stream*.

"Mr. Sloan," the receptionist's honeyed voice repeated his name. "The doctor will see you now."

Doctor Daniels looked little enough like a psychiatrist. He was tall and thin with unstylish, "Buddy Holly" glasses. His blue blazer, he noticed, looked worn and had a food stain. Jeremy studied the eyes. They were neither intense nor piercing as he had imagined. Together, they walked into his small, sofa–less office.

The first twenty minutes or so were taken up with a more or less standard history. And the psychiatrist had *his* own broken rib story as well. He'd fallen on icy steps three or four years before, cracking his ribs. Jeremy smiled slightly, empathizing as the doctor told him he felt he'd never again be able to take a deep breath.

The interview moved into a personal history. At the hour's conclusion, Doctor Daniels led him toward the door. He handed him a release form for his medical records at Lakeland.

"I'd like to see you in ten days. I want an opportunity to read over your records."

The next appointment came on too fast. He was preparing to obtain a temporary restraining order and was buried in research and dictation. As he had told Ronnie, he was slipping back comfortably into his life, and his existence in 1895 and 1896 was beginning to recede in his mind. He'd have forgotten the appointment if the receptionist hadn't called to remind him. He was even on the verge of giving some reason for cancelling when she purred, "Now don't you be late," and disconnected.

He sat down opposite Doctor Daniels, and this time the questions were more along expected lines. The doctor scribbled on a yellow legal pad as Jeremy answered. He asked about his personal history, his habits, any illnesses. Had he ever had delusions, hallucinations, or preoccupations? Was there any history of mental illness, of epilepsy in his family? Abruptly, the hour was up.

On the following Monday, Doctor Daniels went over his accident with him. He made him describe in detail his bike ride of May 3rd; he brought him down the hill, had him recall being hit by the truck, of almost gaining control, of hitting the curb and flying over the handlebars. He made him relive the events—to recall his thoughts—even the pain and the blackout as he hit the ground.

Then, abruptly, he opened a folder containing Jeremy's records from Lakeland. He inquired about his regaining consciousness, what *exactly* he remembered; how he felt. At last he began to question his patient about his "visitation," as he phrased it, into the past. Jeremy had begun to wonder when the doctor was going to get around to it.

Doctor Daniels was a skillful questioner, he gave him credit for that. What was more, he decided not to hold back any of his memories. Through the next three sessions, Jeremy spilled out his recollections of the events, from waking up in the park and noticing the changed appearance of things to meeting Malcolm. When he discussed being afraid of being thought crazy by Malcolm or any of the people he first met, he saw Doctor Daniels raise an eyebrow, continuing to make his short notes. By the end of the next session, he'd about finished his narrative.

He told about confiding his story to Lora, her reaction, and concluded with his ill fated boat trip and crash. The doctor made him go over in detail the events leading up to the second accident, his thoughts and feelings.

"What do you think?" Jeremy asked as he looked across at Daniels who had set down his pad.

"Frankly, I'm not completely sure. It's really quite a story. I'll have some suggestions next session, but I'd first like to review my notes as well as your medical records. You know, Jeremy, sometimes we're forced to pigeon-hole our evaluations, to over–categorize, and I don't want to. Psychiatry doesn't lend itself to that". He extended his hand, standing up. "Next Monday at 1:00, all right?"

After his patient had left, Doctor Daniels slumped down in his chair. He looked worn. The ordeal of listening to this bizarre story, be it delusion, projection or whatever had taken a toll on him—more than he would have wanted his very perceptive patient to have seen. He picked up his microphone and began dictating.

"The patient shows marked physical improvement from his accident. He reports virtually no physical after–effects. The medical records reflect his rapid recovery. While he had some initial reluctance to talk about what we have come to call his 'adventure,' he seems now to display a desire to tell everything. His memory for details is striking. His use of colors and sounds in his narrative, his recollections even of temperatures and wind directions make it difficult not to fall into putting myself back there with him.

"I'm not prepared to diagnose at this point, but some observations are called for. His thinking remains ordered, not obsessional. I could find no evidence of any underlying psychiatric problems that may have existed prior to the accident, and he has apparently made at least a superficial though still painful adjustment to living back in the 'present.' He is as intelligent and keenly aware of surroundings as I first judged. His 'adventure' lacks delusional characteristics. The patient is devoid of any overtones of paranoia. In his adventure, his character lacks grandiosity. In fact, he occupied a status in that society significantly below his own, something that may itself be worth exploring.

"Considerably more evaluation is needed, but at this point, I would suspect the patient suffered a far more severe trauma—more massive subdural hematoma than was originally thought. His chest injury and pulmonary problems at the scene and on his admission likely distracted from his neurological condition.

"The length of time he was unconscious indicates a possibly serious head trauma, despite the negative findings. Finally, his strong attachment to the past and his commitment to writing about this period in the Lake Geneva area, combined with the trauma he suffered while visiting there, have, in some way as yet unknown to me, combined to cause this flight or return to the past during the period of time he was unconscious."

He finished, snapped off the mike and sat back, but his expression indicated he was far from satisfied.

Doctor Daniels cleared his throat. Jeremy had seated himself. He opened the session by questioning the doctor. It was clear he had no more details to provide today, but wanted answers.

"I don't have a hard and fast diagnosis for you, but let me make some observations," Daniels started. "If you should feel like interrupting; if you feel I'm going far afield, tell me. First, I noticed in reconstructing events prior to your accident that you were tired, mentally fatigued. You wanted to get away from your routine. And, while it's getting distant in time, you still harbor some feelings of remorse and guilt about your divorce.

"Secondly, you had, and still have, a lively interest in the Lake Geneva area. You spent your summers there as a child and you frequently returned. You spoke of your interest in doing a kind of historical survey of the area and its people at the turn–of–the–century, the very time period in which you found yourself.

"You've exhibited a strong interest and knowledge of history. I'm going to guess you're attuned to social issues relating to the Pullman strike and the time of the Columbian Exposition."

Jeremy raised his hand, "I have to interrupt, Doctor. Thanks for the praise about my historical talent and all, but it's pretty limited," he shrugged, shifting in his chair and searching for the right words. "It's more a matter of interest than of any deep knowledge. I do know about the Lake Geneva area and the houses and people though, true. But really, my knowledge of the Pullman Village and strike is probably no greater than yours—or I should say *was* no greater than yours. And as far as the Columbian Exposition? Beyond knowing that the Science and Industry Museum was one of the buildings and that Pabst Beer won a blue ribbon, I couldn't have told you a thing about it. So *how* could I have known all those details?"

"Well, the subconscious is a broad and mostly uncharted sea," the doctor continued, retreating. "I was going to say that I also believe you suffered a more severe head trauma than was originally thought, or that you were told." He saw the startled expression on Jeremy's face.

"Oh, don't worry. Your recovery would seem to indicate you need not expect further trouble, although I would like to arrange a follow–up neurological examination just as a precaution."

He sat back in his chair and smiled shyly. "You must know that your case is very interesting, very unusual. You caused me to do a little snooping in the public library myself, not a place, I'm afraid, that I frequent much these days. Quite by accident, I discovered while reading about Darrow that both you and he had offices in the same building."

"And even on the same floor," Jeremy added. He simply had forgotten to mention this fact to the psychiatrist. He still didn't see its importance, and was getting restless with Daniels' explanation.

"What I'm saying is all these factors add up to a kind of syndrome. The trauma served as a vehicle by which you projected yourself backward and into a very, may I say, frightenly realistic experience. What I *don't* understand is how you compressed so much detail into that relatively short period of unconsciousness. And from what you've told me of your past and present sexual experience, I don't see your need to have generated such a character as Lora. But notwithstanding, I think it's significant that you projected yourself for the most part into known events and places—places and events you may subconsciously know much more about than you give yourself credit for."

He leaned over, studying his notes. Jeremy noticed the time was up. "I feel we're making real progress. In psychiatry, there are loose ends. Perhaps you'll never know all. Maybe what we need here is to find some sort of time capsule. But we *are* making progress," he repeated. "Next week. Same time, all right?"

Jeremy stood up, nodding. "Right. Next week."

As he left Doctor Daniel's building and walked out onto Michigan Avenue, something the doctor said hit him. "Maybe what we need is a time capsule." But he *did* have one! He had forgotten to tell the doctor about burying the wallet in the glass jar. It was a detail he'd simply overlooked in his narrative. As he walked he made up his mind. Back at his office, he went through his appointment book, calling and cancelling his engagements for the rest of the week.

"Listen," he was saying over the phone, "Ronnie, I've got to do something. No, no. Nothing strange. Don't worry. I'll tell you when I get back, but I just need a couple of days away," and he went on to give him the two court calls he'd have to cover for him. That done, he called in Mrs. Cleary and dictated a few of the more pressing letters. "You read them over carefully, Mrs. Cleary, and then sign my name. I'll call in Thursday or Friday."

With that he left his office. It was 3:00 when he got to his apartment. He put on a pair of Levis and a shirt and threw some extra clothes into a carry–on bag, went downstairs to the garage and drove onto the expressway, battling early rush hour traffic as he headed toward Lake Geneva. He felt better and more determined than he had in months.

48

Jeremy parked in the circular driveway in front of Yerkes Observatory and looked around. Most of the staff had gone home. He opened the trunk and took out the garden spade and bucket he'd bought on the way up. If anyone saw him, he would simply say he was digging night crawlers for tomorrow's fishing. He walked around the main dome. The days were noticeably shorter, and at 7:00 it would soon be dusk. There were a few twilight golfers still out on the adjacent course.

He walked over to the spruce tree. This couldn't be the tree where he'd dug. That tree would be long gone. He'd have to step off the distance from the south door of the building. Setting down the bucket and shovel, he stopped at the front steps. The exact direction that he'd paced before would have to be guessed. He was about to begin stepping off the distance when a door opened behind him. One of the staff, perhaps an astronomer, stepped out and closed the door, coming down the steps. "Nice night," Jeremy offered. The man acknowledged it was and started off.

The interruption over, he paced the 60 steps, trying to walk exactly as he had that spring night. He marked the spot with the bucket, then turned and squinted back toward the north door of the Observatory. The words "Erected 1895" were etched above the door, the numerals badly weathered. His line was fairly accurate, but to be sure, he repaced it again. This time his 60 paces left him about a yard short and slightly to the left of the bucket. With a last look around, and satisfied he was ignored by the few distant golfers, he broke the ground with the spade. Before he had dug down about two and a half feet; to be safe, he went down three. He found nothing buried.

Jeremy made a trench over to his second spotting. Nothing. It was now dark and he was soaked with sweat. He slapped at a mosquito and filled the trench with the dirt he'd piled up. Moving the line over, he repeated the trenching. Again, nothing. He dug and refilled two more trenches. *This might as well be a needle in a haystack,* he told himself, studying the ground. He'd covered over 20 square feet, but still, if his calculations were off, if the line of direction he remembered varied even slightly, he might be eight or ten feet away.

Well, he thought, putting the spade in for one last trenching effort, *I'm here and I'll be back tomorrow and the next day if I have to.* He dug the last trench out and was about to quit for the night when the blade struck something. His heart began to pound as he probed with the spade. Maybe it was just a rock or a piece of buried tile.

Whatever it was moved, and he knelt down and reached into the trench. He pulled out the glass jar. There was no moonlight, but even as he held it up, he knew he'd found it. Cradling the jar, forgetting the spade and bucket, he walked toward the car.

There was a light fixture above the Observatory door, and by its light he could see the top of the jar had corroded. The stuffing had deteriorated and was like powder to his touch. He reached in further and felt something, then pulled it out and scraped the dirt off. It was his American Express card—still intact with the soldier, or whatever he was, on the green background. The raised letters and numbers were perfect, except for the ink being worn off.

He hurried back to the car. Once inside, he fished through the jar. He felt down and pulled out the Shell and Texaco cards. They were in the same good shape, but nothing else had survived the ravages of moisture, insects and decay.

Back at his motel room, too excited at his discovery to sleep, he went down to the bar. The cocktail lounge had only a few customers. He sat thinking at the long bar, swiveling in his padded chair as he looked out the picture window over Como, a small lake that adjoined Geneva.

"What'll it be?" the bartender said, giving his new customer a less than hospitable look. In fact, Jeremy hadn't stopped at the room long enough to notice his appearance. His shirt was still stained by sweat and he'd rubbed dirt across his face.

"A draft beer," he replied. When the bartender returned, Jeremy handed him the American Express card he had been holding. "Notice anything different about this?" The bartender picked it up, examined it, squinting.

"Yeah," he said, "I do. Your card's expired." Jeremy picked it up. It *had* expired a month ago. "You going to pay cash? It's $2.50." Jeremy fished in his wallet and paid him.

He took a swig of beer, feeling euphoric. He couldn't resist. "You know what's really different about this card? It's been buried in the ground for nearly a hundred years."

The bartender gave him the same dour look. "How about that? No wonder its expired." He turned away and moved down the bar, drying a glass. Jeremy finished the beer and walked through the lobby toward the stairs to his room. For the first time, he looked down and saw the dirt on his pants and shoes. No matter. He was on his way toward finding answers.

The next morning saw him down at the Lake Geneva library, where he *should* have started his quest, he reasoned. He was sitting in front of the library door. "You must have been waiting outside all night," the cute blonde librarian said as she let him in the front door. "Our 'Know Your Library' program must be more effective than we thought," she laughed. He asked about the old newspapers back in the 1890s. "All our papers are on microfilm, but I know we go way, way back into the 1880s." She led him to the back room where she unlocked a metal cabinet.

"Take your pick," she invited, as she uncovered the reader and set it up. There were two papers, the *Herald* and the *Lake Geneva News*. He chose the *Herald* and the librarian showed him how to thread the film through the reader. "You make copies like this," and she punched a practice copy. "This old machine is temperamental, so you only have to pay for the ones that turn out. Good luck," she said, as she left him alone. After he'd sat down in front of the reader, he began to slowly crank its handle. The *Herald* appeared each Friday, as he remembered. The paper was delivered by boat, and dropped on the piers. He felt like he was resurrecting an old friendship as he wound the reader forward from January 1 of 1896.

He'd already forgotten the curiously formal character of the writing. His excitement rose as he reached May 1. The next edition of May 8 would be the one he was looking for.

He reached it and scanned the top of the front page. Nothing. The reader only showed half the page. He lowered the viewer and slowly cranked. There was a story of hidden treasure in Central America entitled, "The Golden Hand." He feathered the crank. In the next column he saw it...

No Body Found

> *A summer resident is feared to have perished in a boating mishap. Searchers continued to seek the body of Jeremy Slater, who was swept from the launch "Lora L." He was apparently thrown off the launch when he encountered rough water upon entering Geneva Bay. One Julia Bannerman, a servant in the employ of the Fairbanks family, who was assisting them in opening their estate for the season, was at the lake front. "Mr. Slater," she said, "was at the front of the launch and it was pitchin' something fearful. He seemed to fall, and I saw him hanging onto a line. After that, the boat disappeared around the point and I ran to get Mrs. Fairbanks."*

Jeremy read on.

> *The launch struck the seawall at the park where it caught fire and burned to the water line. No witnesses saw the boat strike the shore, and as no body was found upon or near the craft, it is theorized Mr. Slater was thrown or fell off the boat somewhere in the bay. He had just taken the boat from winter storage at the Jewell Boat Yard that morning.*

> *Mr. Slater is the husband of the former Lora lockerby, the daughter of Paul Lockerby, one of the prime contractors on the*

*Observatory. The Lockerbys just last year
completed their Bluffside home in the Black
Point area.*

He looked further, but there was nothing else in that paper. Jeremy spun the dial to the next edition, May 15. It was tedious to scan the paper, having to work up and down, backward and forward. At last, on page three, there was just a short item.

"Searchers abandon efforts to find body."

The piece explained that because of the chilly temperatures of the water, a body probably would not rise to the surface for some time. Inasmuch as the location where the victim met his doom could not be pinpointed, further search was called off.

He quickly replaced the reel with the *Lake Geneva News.* It was published, he noticed, on May 7. He'd seen the paper at the Observatory, but Paul didn't subscribe, and it was rather foreign to him. But sure enough, there was a piece.

"Boating Disaster Claims Black Point Summer Resident"

The article was much the same, giving the sketchy details of the unwitnessed accident, as well as some brief biographical material. Jeremy was referred to as a "legal associate" of Mr. Clarence Darrow, the eminent attorney. *A nice inaccuracy, to describe me as an associate,* he thought.

The article finished by describing the *Lora L* as another of the World Fair's launches, slightly smaller, but similar to the ill–fated *Dispatch.* "While, there were no witnesses, we could theorize (and they *were* 100% correct, he noted) the low–riding launch nosed down into the choppy waters, much like the *Dispatch.* This is a characteristic of these unsafe craft designed not for our lake, but the quiet waters of the Exposition lagoons upon which they operated. It is believed and hereby stated as our opinion (again, the curious, formal style) that the remaining World Fair's boats on the lake should be removed from service or redesigned to prevent any further tragedies."

Jeremy made copies of the articles and replaced the films. Looking at his watch, he saw it was only a little after ten. He thanked the helpful librarian, paying for the copies. He left the library, started his car, and headed toward Waterford.

49

Jeremy arrived in Waterford just after 11:00. Not quite knowing where to start his search, he drove around the small village, acquainting himself. The schools, both the elementary "Waterford Graded School" and the high school were much too new to have yielded anything, and both were still closed for the summer recess. After a tour of the community, he pulled into the library parking lot.

The library was small and mainly devoted to best sellers and encyclopedias. In the card catalog under "Waterford," there was a single entry, "Scenes of the Village, 1923."

Jeremy found the volume and sat down. He paged through the book, reading with a mounting nervousness. There were text and pictures of the ancient fire department and the downtown area. He turned the page to see a picture of a small school building, "Waterford Graded School." He hastened through the plodding text. The history of the school went back to a series of private schools in houses in the early 1800's. He read on. There it was.

"In 1902," it said, *"a large brick addition was erected. Ann Hovey, Miss Bradford, Ellen Wordsworth and Lora Slater were the teachers. Lora Slater returned in 1900, having been raised in Waterford, and having herself attended the Graded School as a youth.*

"In 1910, she was elevated to the post of principal, a position she occupies with distinction to this day (1923)."

Then, as though reminiscing, the author went on—*Her service to the youth of our community is particularly appreciated when it is noted the personal tragedy she has undergone. It will be remembered that the widow lost her only son on November 1, 1918. As a member of the American*

Expeditionary Force, young Lance Corporal Paul Slater died in battle during a heroic siege of the German defenses on the Meuse River."

"My son," Jeremy said softly as he felt the book shaking in his hands, the tears running down his cheeks. He read on. "Added to the death of her son, Mrs. Slater was given the further burden of raising her infant granddaughter when the child's mother succumbed to the European Influenza and passed away in 1919."

Jeremy sat numb for some minutes, then slowly reread the article. It concluded by saying that the granddaughter, Sarah, would herself be starting at the school in the fall as a first grader. He searched the book, but there was nothing further.

He dried his eyes, waited, and finally stepped up to the librarian's desk. Checking his voice, he inquired if there were any other books. The librarian apologized. There were no other books about Waterford, but perhaps...if he cared to go over to the Racine County Historical Society, maybe.

Did she know anyone, he asked, who might be able to help him with the history of the village, "oh say—about 1920." He was doing some research, he explained, on southern Wisconsin towns. A Sunday supplement article, perhaps, and he made sure to note her name.

Hearing about a possible article, the white–haired librarian sat pensive for some moments. It was obvious the town of Waterford, with its thin, single–volume "history" to 1923, was not overly inquisitive about its past.

"There is a fellow, let me think. Old Josh Wagner," she said. "He's an old timer. He has a memory for Waterford, all right. He might talk your ear off, but he's in his late 80's, and, you know," she looked at him and gave a shrug. His reliability for dates might not be the best.

"Where can I find him?"

"He might be down at the restaurant." And she pointed and named a small lunch counter restaurant a block away, "or the old devil might be down at J. D.'s Pub having a beer or two. You'll know him by his full head of white hair, and his red flannel shirt, even in August."

Jeremy found him at the pub. The bartender nodded down the bar in answer to his question. Josh was by himself. A good sign. Maybe he'd like some company. He noticed he had a bottle of Old Style beer in front of him and he ordered the same. "Hot enough?" he asked, filling his glass.

"Sonny, when you get to my age, it can't get too hot. It's the winters you worry about. But I remember hotter."

Jeremy asked him a few innocuous questions. He was right. The old-
ster did want someone to talk to—or rather someone who would listen to
him. Josh described a fire at the lumber yard for him. It occurred about
1930, he learned. As he went on, it was apparent he had more fondness
for older dates than for recent history. Fine.

"Did you go to school around here?"

"Sure did. Right down the street at the 'Graded,' " he called it, "and to
the high school next door. Not those buildings that are there now, you
understand, but the older ones. They ripped down the last of the old high
school.

"Charlie, when... when'd they tear down the old high school building?"

" '63 Josh," the bartender called back, "same year I graduated."

Jeremy let him talk about the old school. He calculated that he'd have
gotten out of the grade school about 1919 or '20. "Who was the principal, do you remember?" he asked easily, trying to hide his nervousness.

"Sure enough do. Old Mrs. Slater. She was all right too, but she could
show a temper," and he chuckled at some memory. "She taught all of the
grades art and, let's see now, history, too. Yes sir, I remember Mrs. Slater
all right."

He got lost in a digression about the dam for a few minutes. Jeremy
was fascinated hearing about Lora but was growing concerned. He
ordered them both a round of beers, knowing he would have to get the
story in just the way Josh wanted to tell it, but afraid he might become
too fatigued to continue. And sure enough. He came back to Paul Slater.
Josh hardly knew him, he said. Paul was about ten or twelve years older,
but he remembered him as good–looking and quick in studies.

"Of course, after he was shot up in the war, everyone made a hero out
of him. You know how that goes," he took a swallow of beer. "Married a
girl from Burlington, I think. She died right after him in the flu epidemic," he said, confirming the library article.

"Any kids?" Jeremy asked conversationally.

"Little Sarah," he answered right away. "She was younger than my
crowd, but cute as a button." His narrative was interrupted. The door
opened and the bright sunlight glared into the dark pub. Some men
about Jeremy's age, wearing "John Deere" hats entered, noisily calling to

Charlie to set them up.

They sat down on the stools next to Jeremy and began kidding Josh, asking him if his new girlfriend had moved out yet. Jeremy realized his story was going to be interrupted. He introduced himself and pushed his stool away from the bar. "Just passing through," he told them, as the conversation shifted to the latest losing streak of the Brewers.

After a time, he tried to get Josh to pick up the thread of his thoughts, but it was hard for the old man. Just when it seemed he had him back on track, one of the boys at the bar would rib him or get him started down some other avenue. Just as he despaired of getting any more information, Josh, likely sensing his companion and sponsor might be getting ready to leave, pulled on his sleeve.

"I remember you were asking me about the Slater girl, Sarah, weren't you?" Jeremy nodded, holding up two fingers for Charlie and turning his back to the other bar companions. "She went away to the college at Whitewater. Became a teacher like her mother—her grandmother," he corrected, starting to slur his words a bit.

"Did she come back here?"

"Nah, not to stay, leastwise. She brought back some fellow from the college that she'd married. Some kind of college farmer. In the '20's or was it the '30's? Anyways, I don't remember. Back then farmers didn't go to college much." He paused to think. "They both taught for a while and then he moved her over to some big farm near Lake Geneva."

"Lake Geneva?" Jeremy asked.

He repeated it. "Yeah," he said. "Lake Geneva. Don't you know where that's at? That's a big resort lake twenty-five miles or so down that road," and he waved his arm off. "You must be a stranger around here," he said.

Jeremy drew close to him. "Do you remember her married name?"

"Nah, I couldn't remember her name. You ask too many questions, anyways." He was getting tired and cranky. "If you want dates, go out to Oakwood." He motioned his hand in the opposite direction. "That's where everyone's buried. That's where you'll find your dates."

"Mrs. Slater, is she buried out there?" Josh half nodded, turning away. One of the other men had pulled his stool around and had started talking to him. It was clear Josh had done all the reminiscing he'd do for the day. At the first chance, Jeremy gave him a pat on his back, said good-bye and walked out.

He headed out of town in the direction Josh had indicated. He'd driven north on Route 83 for two or three miles, becoming convinced the old man had sent him off in a wrong direction. He came upon the cemetery so fast that he shot past it and had to turn around. There were two pillars, one saying "Oakwood," the other "Cemetery" on either side of the driveway. It was late in the afternoon as he drove in. The temperature and humidity were still high, even though the sun had dropped near to the tops of the trees.

He drove around the circular gravel drive of the small cemetery, parked the car and got out, finding himself alone. Being out here he should have felt more, of course, but the beer, the heat and the old man's ramblings had given him a headache.

He looked around at the rows of headstones and began searching the names: Wegner, Mearse, Kratz. They went on. After a few minutes, he realized he'd been wandering aimlessly. There were not that many graves. He started at the first rows and worked back.

At the base of a tall, old pine tree near the rear of the cemetery, he found them. There were three simple, granite markers. He saw Lora's grave first. At the top of the gray stone was the word 'Daughter.' Next were the stones of Paul Lockerby and Celia Lockerby. Celia's tombstone was more weathered than the others. Lora's looked comparatively new.

He knelt down and brushed the tall grass back from the stone. "Lora Slater 1868–1940, Beloved Wife (not widow, he noticed) of J. Slater, Mother of Paul, Grandmother of Sarah Angstrom."

It was probably the flowers that triggered him. He looked around. Many of the graves had small bunches of flowers, and some had been left in little ornamental vases.

He'd brought nothing with him. And suddenly all of the memories came tumbling back onto him. All the petty denials and all the wordy explanations of the last three months evaporated. He wept for his lost wife and for the son he had never known and for the father–in–law as well, who had shielded him. His sobs burst out of him as he cradled Lora's granite grave marker.

At length, he stood up, looking down at the three headstones. He walked over to the rear fence and reached over to pick up some scraggly black–eyed susans and a few stalks of chicory with their little blue flowers, the best he could do. He walked back and placed the wild flowers on the

357

graves.

With a final look down at Lora's grave, he stepped back to his car. Jeremy drove out toward Lake Geneva. Tomorrow, he said to himself, he'd try to look up Sarah Angstrom, the final piece in the puzzle.

50

He had little trouble locating Sarah Angstrom. She was listed in the directory and after five or six rings, picked up the phone. Her voice sounded slightly hoarse, as though she might have been napping.

Jeremy had a harder time using the cover story on Sarah than he had with the librarian. He adopted the same role as he had in Waterford—a free lance writer, working on a story about the area, its early schools and some of its residents. A Sunday supplement story, he told her.

"Well, why ever would you want to interview me? I'm an old, retired school teacher, hardly able to supply anything newsworthy, even for the most supplemental of Sunday inserts."

Jeremy liked the way she could turn a phrase. He told her he had been doing some research up in Waterford and the adjacent areas and her name had come up. At least he hoped he had the right person. She interrupted, "Well, I'm sorry, but I really believe you may not have the right person. You see, my married name is a fairly common one in these parts and I haven't been back to Waterford for ages. I've taught at the high school here in Lake Geneva and been living out on this dairy farm." She told him her husband had died several years before. A dog barked in the background.

"So you see," she paused, "I'm really sorry, but you couldn't want me. I've had virtually no connection with Waterford for, lord, nearly 40 years."

He *had* to say something. She seemed about to hang up. "Are you Lora Slater's grandchild?" There was a silence on the other end of the phone.

"Yes," she answered. "I am." Had her tone changed, or did he imagine it?

He went on. "Part of the article would be centered on the schools in and around the Waterford area, and on the early teachers and principals."

"Well, as I said, I've been away from there for so long."

He plunged ahead. He *couldn't* let her hang up, not now. "Would it be a terrible intrusion if I interviewed you about her...and about anyone else," he added, "you might know about. If you could give me 30 minutes or so. Perhaps I could meet you for lunch in town?"

She was thinking on the other end, he could tell, making up her mind. "I can't go into town. Could you..." she paused, "could you drive out here this morning?" He certainly could, he said. He looked at his watch. It was 9:30.

"10:30?" he asked, not wanting to sound pushy.

"That will be fine, Mr... I'm sorry, what did you say your name was?"

"Sloan." She gave him the directions.

Sarah's "Lake Geneva" address was one in name only. He followed her directions, turning east on Bloomfield Township road. He crossed the expressway and passed the little airport on his right. He was now out of the town and in the country.

He followed the turns in the road and slowed. Ahead were the farmhouse and surrounding buildings as she described. The neat buildings were painted white with green roof and shutters. As he pulled into the gravel driveway, he saw it was overgrown with weeds.

On the way out from town, he relected on Sarah's voice. When she'd first answered, he'd wondered if it might have some tone he'd have recognized, but he did not. It was simply the voice of an older woman.

He stepped from the car and out of the air conditioning. The hot wind blowing across the cornfield hit him in the face. The grass, he noticed as he walked toward the house, was dry and brittle, and it hadn't been mowed in some time.

Jeremy was usually wary of dogs, a habit he'd picked up bike riding, especially around farms. He liked to think he'd refined that wariness almost into an instinct, so he was startled when the dog appeared. It must have come from the side of the house. A big, gray German Shepard, with a muzzle as large as any he'd ever seen. What was worse, the dog was in a position to cut him off. He looked back at his Regal, parked so teasingly out of his reach. He remembered that while talking on the phone he'd heard a dog bark in the background.

The dog let out a low growl. He looked closely. It didn't seem so ferocious and he even saw the tail give a couple of tentative wags. He started talking to the dog when the door to the house opened.

"Easy, Heidi. Is that you, Mr. Sloan?" She was squinting into the sun as she came down the steps.

Jeremy stared at his last flesh–and–blood tie with the past. Sarah would be in her mid-seventies. She was a pleasant looking woman with white hair. She wore a light blue flowered dress, the pleats still freshly–pressed.

Heidi had moved over to inspect him, sniffing his hand he held out, but still not allowing him to pet her. He noticed Heidi dragged one of her legs. "Come in, Mr. Sloan," she said after she'd given him her hand. "It's much too hot out here to talk." She raised a hand to her forehead.

She led him up the front steps to the porch. It was a jalousied addition which gave a view down the driveway to the road. Sarah offered him a seat. "I'll be back in a minute." She held onto the wall, he noticed, as she went into the interior of the house. He listened to the little air conditioner in the corner laboring to cool the room.

The coffee table held a number of old photo albums. They looked as though they had recently been placed there. Sarah had no doubt retrieved them with a view toward his arrival.

She returned with a tray of iced tea glasses and a plate of cookies. Jeremy stood up and took it from her. He sat on the couch and she took a chair opposite him. Heidi moved in between, yawning and stretching herself out.

He tried a cookie and sipped on the ice tea while they made small talk. He asked her about some of the new houses being built up from town along the road.

"Do you still farm here?"

"Oh, heavens no." She had a whimsical tone to her voice. She went on to explain this was, or had been, a dairy farm. After Enoch's death, it had just gotten to be too much for her. "I was never a farmer, Mr. Sloan." She'd sold the livestock and leased out the land to others who farmed it.

She had him stand up and took him over to the back of the porch, cranking out the jalousie window. "See all the corn back there?" He did. "That used to be a big open pasture. Why you could see across the valley floor for a couple of miles. That's where our herd grazed. But the income from the rental helps, and besides, with these eyes lately, I couldn't appre-

361

ciate a view anyway. I was wishing you could have come when I could see better." She had developed cataracts, she explained, and her operation was not scheduled until the fall.

They both sat back down. "We should be getting around to your interview. Please call me Sarah. And what's *your* first name, Mr. Sloan? Last names sound so terribly formal."

"Jeremy," he said, watching her. She repeated it, more to herself than to him.

"That was my grandfather's name."

"Did you know him well?" he asked.

"No. Not at all. I guess you could say I come from a line of posthumous children, or almost so. I was only a year old when my father was killed, only a couple of months old when he left for service. And he was born after his father was killed in a boating accident."

He asked if she'd mind if he took some notes. If nothing else, he would look more official and it would let him write anything he wanted to remember.

Sarah sketched the family history for him, filling out what he had learned in Waterford. She described in simple words how her father had been killed in action. He listened intently, filling with pride again, and with that sudden sense of finding—and loss. Her mother had died during the epidemic of influenza.

"Then were you raised by your grandmother?" he asked. Jeremy had been listening silently as Sarah had given him the background. He had been fighting to control his emotions, listening to her talk about Lora and his son. When he spoke, he hoped she couldn't hear the small cracks in his voice.

Sarah had been raised by her grandmother. "She was always unbending," she said, "about my calling her grandma, though I think she often treated me more like a daughter than a granddaughter. When we went somewhere, people who didn't know us assumed that I was her daughter, perhaps just born to her late in life. She was a rather young grandmother. I think she was forty-eight when I was born. I'll show you some pictures later. Grandma stayed quite slender and kept her looks." Sarah chuckled, thinking. "Or maybe it was the contrast. Her looks never really fitted the prim, serious dresses she always chose."

And she never remarried?"

"No. Although she could have had any number of husbands. She never seemed to want to. I suppose she stayed busy enough. And she had her memories, she always said."

Then, furnishing what she must have supposed he was there for, she gave him a short rundown on the Waterford schools, what she could remember. She had gone through there, as had her father and grandmother. "I graduated with high marks, though with my grandmother the principal..." she laughed, letting the thought hang.

She opened some of the albums to look through. Many of the pictures were grainy and of a bad quality. "You'll have to excuse me Jeremy, the doctor tells me I'll be as good as new after the operations, but at the moment I can hardly see you, and reading is out." She reached over on the table and took out a magnifying glass as he opened the albums.

Heidi lifted her head, yawned, opened her enormous mouth and licked Jeremy's hand. Her friend now, he scratched her behind the ear as she settled back on the floor. The clock struck 12:00.

"Oh," she said. "Here I've been talking for over an hour. Let me get you something to eat."

"Please Sarah, I had a large breakfast," he protested.

"I didn't mean a *feast*. I'm gonna pop a cheese sandwich in the microwave for myself. I'll add one for you."

He followed her into the living room. He saw why she preferred to sit on the porch. Compared to its openness and view, the living room was dark, "farm–house formal," and vaguely musty.

"Over here," she spoke, her hand touching the furniture as she moved to the mantelpiece above the fireplace. On the mantel were some photographs in old–fashioned wooden frames, the kind that folded out like book covers. He saw a picture of young Paul wearing a dress–blue Marine uniform. On each side in the frame were other pictures. One was Sarah's own wedding picture and the other a picture of her parents together.

Jeremy carefully picked up the frame. He looked at the picture of Paul. He had taken some of his own looks sure enough, although he clearly favored his mother.

"Nice looking, wasn't he?" Sarah had noticed him holding the frame. "That picture was taken after he finished boot camp and just before he went overseas. I have another of him on that same leave holding me. I was just about a year old."

Jeremy wanted desperately just then to say something. He felt like reaching out and hugging Sarah, to try, somehow, in some way, to tell her everything. Instead, he just hoped she wouldn't notice his silence as she went on to describe her wedding picture. "I'll certainly be glad to be able to see these again," she said, putting back the frames she'd been holding up close.

"Now over here, she said, walking across to a corner table, is a picture of my grandparents together. Can you *imagine* anyone being so stiff and rigid in a picture? It's the only picture of my grandfather. Grandma said he had quite a sense of humor but you certainly couldn't tell it from *that* picture."

Jeremy stared down at the photo, still in its original frame. He picked it up, looking closer, straining to read in the darkness." J S. Medlar, Photographer, Woodstock, Illinois," the old strip beneath the photo read.

He smiled, holding the picture between both hands, remembering how they were both alternately laughing and trying hard to look as serious as possible while J. S. Medlar darted his head in and out of the camera's hood.

He held up the picture, looking for her hand. It was still out of sight behind his back. He'd like to have told Sarah that their strained looks had come from holding in their laughs and to tell her also where her very proper grandmother's hand had really been just as the flash powder had ignited.

They sat in the surprisingly modern kitchen while she made the sandwiches and brewed some fresh iced tea. Her conversation switched to her own life. She and her husband Enoch had met at Whitewater Normal School, both of them studying to be teachers. It was where her grandmother had also gone. *Do I, did I, really have a grandson-in-law named Enoch?* he thought, as Sarah went on.

On graduation they both found teaching jobs in Sheboygan. They'd married and moved there and had just finished their first year of teaching when his father suddenly took sick and died. They had to return. "Here," she said, indicating the farm.

"Enoch took to farming like he'd never left. I don't think he ever really was happy with all the books, though he was a fair student. You know, Jeremy," she said, getting up to take the sandwiches from the microwave and set them on the kitchen table, "I can't seem to even remember him reading a book again. His mother still lived on here. I could tell you that the adjustment was hard for me. Here I was, a young bride and just graduated from college. I was independent when all of a sudden I'm living back here with his mother. And it was *her* house, make no mistake. Do you know I could barely set a foot in this kitchen we're sitting in now.

"At any rate," she said, using her grandmother's expression. "I won't bore you with such talk. We never had children. I began teaching here in Lake Geneva and stayed until I retired in 1981. Did you happen to see the high school at the intersection where you turned?" He had.

They went back to the porch and Sarah opened some additional albums. "I'm afraid I've talked far too much about myself, my parents and grandparents and I've not told you enough about Waterford or its schools."

"Don't worry," he said. "The schools, the history, they *are* its people. I'd rather hear about the people than a description of some old buildings." He was looking through an album. There was a picture of Lora with Sarah at a beach, the two dressed in the comical swimming attire of the time.

"Is this Lake Geneva?" he asked. Sarah squinted at the picture, fumbling for the magnifying glass.

"It couldn't have been Lake Geneva. She never took me here. After Grandfather's death she wouldn't return. It seemed that she lost some good friends in a boating accident the year before and this together with his loss... She stayed in Chicago during summers after that, and when her father died, she put the place up for sale.

"It was years later, I think in the early fifties that I even ever saw her house or rather its remains up here. Enoch and I happened to take a trip on one of those lake excursion boats. I knew Grandmother had lived at Black Point, so when we rounded the point, I hushed up Enoch so I could listen. The 'Captain' or whatever his rank, was giving these announcements over the P.A.

" 'Over there you see the remains of *Bluffside*. This striking Italian Renaissance structure was built in 1894. It burned a year or so ago and the land is currently being subdivided.'

"We'd gone past and he was describing another house before I could even get a good look. And Enoch being raised on a farm outside town, he never had much use for the 'lake people,' he called them."

"No," she continued, squinting as she turned the page, "Oh. Now I remember." There was another picture of Sarah and Lora, this time surrounded by other people. "These pictures were taken at 'Eagle Lake Resort'. This was," she said, squinting at the picture, "the year Grandma saved a boy from drowning. We were on the beach. I was about seven or eight," she said, beginning to focus on the event. "I was digging tunnels in the sand."

"Grandma must have been looking out over the water and saw him fall off the float. I remember seeing her stand up. 'That boy's in trouble,' she said, to the people with us. They just laughed. They said it was horseplay. Then, next thing I knew, she was running across the sand to the water. Now mind you, she was then about fifty-five or fifty-six. She'd taken me out wading before but I didn't even know she could swim.

"As she got out in the water and it deepened she dove and began swimming. I've never seen anyone swim so fast before or since. And sure enough, she brought the boy up and towed him to shore. He'd fallen in and hadn't been missed by anyone.

"The lifeguard gave him artificial respiration right on the beach. And in a short time he was sitting up almost as good as new. I can tell you, Grandma was a heroine that day. But she tried her best to stop the article in the *Waterford News*. Something to the effect of it being undignified with the accompanying picture and all.

"Oh, turn the page Jeremy. That's her." He did, reading the newspaper account, complete with pictures. There was a picture of Lora, still so familiar to him, but definitely a middle–aged woman. He stared down at the picture for a long time, quiet and thinking. He was turned away from Sarah.

"She really was quite a woman, don't you think? Maybe I've given you something for your story."

"She was quite a woman, Sarah."

Sarah hesitated a moment, but continued filling him in as best she could on the details of the school.

Jeremy could see that Sarah was tiring. He glanced at his watch. It was almost 2:00. He apologized for over–staying. "Nonsense," she said. "I enjoy the company, and to tell the truth I feel as though I've known you. It's not as though we've just met."

He was at the door of his car. "Sarah, I really appreciate the time you gave..." he stopped, not knowing if she could have picked up the catch in his voice. He didn't trust himself to say another word, at least not right away. It had all caught up to him. His chest felt tightly knotted with the emotions he had been checking all day.

"Jeremy," she said, "give me a hand back to the house. There is something...there is something I have for you." Puzzled, he helped her back down the drive. He waited at the door with Heidi while Sarah went inside. He looked around. He could hear bees droning nearby as he waited with the dog. Heidi's tongue was hanging out in the heat and she lay back down at his feet.

In a few minutes, Sarah reappeared holding a manilla envelope. She leaned against him as they walked towards his car. She was silent and he was about to say something when she stopped. She looked out at the roadway where a pickup truck carrying some teenagers had loudly hurtled around a slow-moving car. It was quiet again when she spoke.

"And to think I might have hung up today," she started, as much to herself as to him. "It really *was* your call this morning that reminded me." She turned toward Jeremy.

"Grandmother gave me this." She held the envelope. A chill went down his back hearing the words.

"She told me probably I'd never have occasion to give it away. She was along in years at the time; she died only a year or so later. But she said it might come to pass that a man one day would come by, inquiring about the family, about me," she said, "about your grandfather and your father."

"As I said, she was fairly old at the time, probably as old as I am now," she smiled. "And her heart was bad. I was about twenty or so when she gave me this," and she tapped the envelope.

"I remember I didn't know what to think. Grandma had always been so bright, so alert and practical, but with her illness and age...she made me promise to keep it sealed—never to open it.

"How will I know who to look for?" I asked her.

"You'll know," she said, "mainly by the questions he'll ask. And Sarah, he'll probably be about in his late thirties, a nice looking chap and he'll be likely to come by in the mid-1990s, so you may have to keep this envelope a good long while, dear."

"How old *are* you Jeremy? In your late 30's?"

367

"I'm thirty–seven," he answered, "a month short of thirty–eight."

"Not a bad guess," she said. Her hand shook as she gave him the envelope.

"If whatever is in here doesn't apply to you, please seal it and mail it back, but I don't think you'll have to.

"Your questions. The catches in your voice. I know she meant this for you." (So she had noticed the catches.)

He took the envelope from Sarah and put his arm around her, drawing her to him in a warm hug. She would have felt him trembling as he held her. "This doesn't have to be goodbye," he said at last. "Can I see you again?"

"I'd like that," she answered, her own eyes glistening with tears.

He backed the car down the drive, turned and started down the road. He rounded a corner and pulled off the pavement onto the gravel. He tore the envelope open. Inside were folded sheets of yellowed paper. As he pulled them out and unfolded them, his eyes caught the familiar back–handed script at the top of the first page.

My Dearest Jeremy. . . the letter started.

51

Jeremy's hand shook. He knew he didn't want to start the letter there. He put the envelope on the seat next to him and drove back onto the road. He turned right, then left, following the meandering country lane, his mind blurred.

He could actually feel his heart beating as he glanced ahead down the road and saw that he was entering a town. "Twin Lakes," the sign said. Had he really gone this far?

The day was as hot as ever as he pulled down the single business street and parked. He put the pages back in the envelope and looked up and down the street. A sign ahead said, "Fairview Dining Room." He crossed the street and went in. The clock on the wall read ten minutes before three.

"We're not serving any dinner yet, sir," the waitress called out.

"Can I get a cup of coffee and maybe a piece of pie?"

"Sure," the waitress answered. "You've got the place to yourself." He moved to a table in the corner.

"You get a choice of peach and...peach," she laughed, looking at the pie tray. "It looks like everything else is gone."

"Peach will be fine." She served him the pie and coffee as he reopened the envelope. He read.

It's difficult to start a letter you feel will never be read. I've started this before and torn it up. I'll not tear this letter up, though. My last report from the doctor wasn't good. I may not be able to write this letter a year or even months from now.

Jeremy studied the paper. The script, with the same exaggerated loops he'd teased her about was still there, only it looked as though her hand had become shaky, and sometimes the writing trailed off, even to where a word was crossed off and rewritten.

If you're reading this then you will already know most of my story. I know you're tenacious, and certainly bright enough, my lawyer, to have traced me back to Waterford. I'm assuming you picked up the trail there. Sarah is a fine, beautiful girl. We can both be proud of her.

Jeremy dabbed at his eyes, aware that tears had been streaming down and falling onto the table. He looked around to see if the waitress had noticed. She'd gone back to the kitchen.

As I write this, Sarah is a Junior at Whitewater Normal, my old alma mater. Remember the photographs I made you look at? She intends to follow in my footsteps—be a teacher. She's been keeping company with a nice young man—Enoch Angstrom, and I believe they'll marry.

Perhaps as you read this, you'll have met one or more of their children. Darling, there is so much I wanted to say to you, how I missed you. How I still miss you—the man I said I wanted to grow old with. I couldn't go up to the lake when they dragged for your body. It was like going through the search for Kittie again, only this time I really believed you would not be found.

I couldn't explain it. I wouldn't explain it to anyone, but I believe you found some seam, perhaps the same one that brought you to me, and went back to your own time. It was too much of a coincidence that your accident happened at the same place and on the same day of the year as the one that brought you to me.

You might be surprised to know that I, of all people, grew religious after your disappearance, though as yet my religion hasn't provided me with any solid answers as to what happened.

I guess I believe God had some plan in mind in all of this. I've clung to the things you've told me. How everything has come to pass.

Jeremy smiled, reading on as she ticked off some events he'd recited to her in that spring of 1896.

I'm proud to say, I even got out to vote for Franklin—FDR they call him now, though when I see his pictures, I still see that serious little eleven year old who visited the World's Fair.

The only person I ever confided in was Malcolm. I wrote him some years later. He visited me in Waterford. He and little Pauly and I walked down to the park by the dam where he played with Pauly. Naturally, he swore he looked just like you. I told him everything that afternoon. Once I started, it all came out. I told him how we'd decided to tell him—in fact that you were on your way there to see him when your accident occurred.

He just listened, nodding, smoking his pipe. He told me he always believed there <u>was</u> something almost mystical about your appearance—and disappearance.

Just talking to Malcolm helped me. As he left that afternoon, he told me he wanted to give me something, something of yours. It was a pair of dark glasses. I've kept them to this day, Dearest. Of course, I know now they're sunglasses, though of a type I haven't yet seen. I even have them in front of me now as I write this letter.

The waitress came back and refilled his cup. "You haven't eaten much pie—is it really that bad?" she asked.

"Oh, no," he answered, looking down and scooping up a piece. She looked at the pages before him on the table, sensing he wanted to be alone and moved off.

You would know Father passed away a year after your accident. His heart, which I fear I have inherited, just seemed to give out. I eventually sold Bluffside. Martha stayed with me. She was such a dear. But I just couldn't stay in Chicago. Everyone was wonderful. The people at the Art Institute asked me to come back and for a while I even did while Martha looked after Pauly.

After a time though, I decided I'd go back to my roots. I wrote Waterford. They needed a teacher for the year. I made up my mind. I hated to leave Martha but Father had left her well cared for and, as a matter of fact, she found another position. She told me that she would be looking after a little boy—the son of a widowed negro doctor in the south side area. Can you imagine the irony of that? Her starting over again?

Pauly and I arrived here and we stayed on. Jeremy, dearest, you'd have been proud of your son. As he grew I told him you'd disappeared in a boat accident. When he was about five, he asked, 'Daddy come back?'

I had to tell him no, you wouldn't be. He didn't say anything, just nodded in that solemn way little boys have.

That night I went into his bedroom to check on him. I leaned over to kiss him and there, sticking out from under his pillow, was our picture. The one we had taken in Woodstock on that silly, wonderful day and, you know, our only picture of you.

You would know the story of Paul and that he was killed in the war. He's buried in the military cemetery at LeHavre, should you ever get a chance to

371

visit.

His wife Anne was a wonderful girl. I had really gotten to love her. Paul met her at a dance in Burlington. They fell in love right away. Paul was working in Waterford when they were married. Sarah was just born when the war came on.

Paul didn't want to wait to be drafted. Anne came over telling me he enlisted in the Marines. Do you know, I didn't even get to see him off when he went overseas. He called me from the depot in Racine." Jeremy turned a page. On the next one Lora had posted pictures of his son, one when he was about seven, riding on a tricycle. There was another unidentified tot in the park.

A second picture was of the Waterford High baseball team. She had (unnecessarily) circled Paul's picture. In the last picture, he and his wife and Lora were standing on the front porch. Lora was holding baby Sarah. Jeremy looked closely at the picture—Lora still looked very youthful—even as a grandmother.

I'm sure you've read the accounts of Paul's death and, he wiped his eyes again as he read a small letter from Paul to his mother which she had included. It was sent just two days before his death and in it he said he was looking forward to getting the war over once and for all and to coming home.

I've had to put the letter down for the night, Darling. It's now the next day, I reread it, but most of what I've said you'd already know and I wanted to write you to talk to you, to tell you how I've remembered the good times—however short—that we shared. How I laughed at the day you tried to hook up the wagon. My poor memory fails me on the horse's name but I still remember your expression.

And meeting you—I think it was the next morning on the bluff. You were so sweet—and, honestly, just a little jealous of that other boy? You know, it was that picnic breakfast on the bluff that June morning when I first knew I loved you.

Jeremy blinked back the tears. Had it been that early on?

The waitress had discreetly taken his cold cup and replaced it with a steaming one.

The rest of that whole magical summer has just kind of floated before me, down through the years. I sometimes feel my memory slipping. I pray to God these images will be the last to go.

He tried to picture the elderly lady writing this letter but he could only produce an image of the laughing young woman with the big brown eyes and the freckled nose, the one he'd known and loved. The one who had been joking about her pregnant condition and who, when he had last seen her, was heavy with their child.

She continued. *I still see us in that musty old tunnel under the Ceylon Court, hiding from those workmen and also the party at our house and you taking me off the* Dispatch, *your black eye and all. How I have thought of that day.*

I really believe I did *want to take you apple picking when Martha had left for Chicago and we were alone, do you remember that day?*

Jeremy found himself nodding, a little smile on his face as he recalled Lora with sundress and hat, the basket under her arm, stepping onto the porch on that hot August morning.

What I can't remember, is whether we actually did *any apple picking. I'm going on too long, Dearest, but I just wanted to share with you some memories, like that melancholy morning when we sat at the side of the Black Point lagoon, our first time apart.*

After your accident, the Seipps and the Lefenses were so wonderful. But you know, I could never bring myself to return to Black Point.

She sketched out other memories, telling him about the time years later she took a class on a trip to the Museum of Science and Industry, *Just as you had called it. It was in late February, almost the same time that we were there. When I looked out toward the Wooded Island, I could almost see us walking hand in hand.*

He turned to the last page.

I hope I haven't gone on for too long, though I know I have. I just wanted this letter to reach across to you—across the years to tell you of my love and to let it be the goodbye we never had. Goodbye my love. Your wife, Lora.

He'd been looking down at the last page for some time, and knew the waitress was near the table. He could see her shoes but he couldn't look up—not yet.

"Are you all right, sir? Could I get you anything?"

He shook his head. When he saw her move away, he put the pages of the letter back into the manila envelope. He fumbled for some money, left a couple of bills on the table and walked across the dining room, stepping out into the late afternoon.

373